A FAMILY CONCERN

by

Ken Gorman

 **New Generation Publishing**

Chapter One

"Stanley Matthews dribbles round the full back, he falls, gets up again, controls the ball and......shoots! Goal! Waargh...the crowd roars..."

"He missed!"

"Never! Matthews never misses!"

"You're kidding! Watch this."

"Who's this?"

"Tom Finney, Preston North End."

A second footballer takes the ball and moves off down the path. Feather-light feet push the ball a few inches at a time, left and then right and then left and then right. Suddenly there is an interception, the player in the brown jersey sidesteps quickly, pushes his sleeves back and races forward. Hearing that he is pursued, he stops, spins neatly and tries to bypass the tackler. This time, the side step is anticipated. Clumsily, the players collide and the ball teeters away from them. The two sprawl on the ground giggling helplessly.

"Alright, you stand further back and I'll be the goalie. I'll clear it then you can take a shot. Not too near mind! You've got to be ten yards out."

"Where's the goal?"

"The path. It's got to be inside the path. We'll take turns."

"O.K. Hoik it up!"

"Here she comes! The crowd is fifty thousand....the goalie lifts the......Oh, I'll take it again.....this time..er....this time!"

"Keep it straight!"

"It's up hill you know!"

"O.K. Now we'll see. Finney shows his control....he turns....he takes it out to the right....beats his man....beats another....and... shoots!

"Hi! That's too high! Keep it down! I can't reach that high!"

"Goal, a goal! Hurray! The crowd invade the pitch!"

The scorer does a celebratory forward roll.

"That's not a proper goal! It went over the top!"

"Never!"

"It did! Far too high!"

"Never!"

"Anyway, it's my turn now. It's easy for you, I've got to shoot uphill."

"I'm ready!"

"Right. This time it's Jackie Milburn racing through the centre. Dodges everybody and......and......wait for it......wait for it......wait.....shoots!"

"What a save! What a goalie! And the goalie clears the ball up the pitch..."

"Hi! You'll lose it, kicking it like that! It's gone into the bushes. We'll never find it!"

"Stop moaning, Hen, I'll help you look, come on!"

There were a number of bushes dotted about that side of the park. These particular bushes were the most massive.

"Urgh! It's wet in here.....and look at this rubbish!"

"You're always moaning, Hen. Ow! These twigs are sharp!"

"I can't get in. I'm going round the back. It went right over the top, remember?"

"No it didn't."

"I saw it."

"So did I. It fell in the middle."

"Well, I'm going round that way."

"Please yourself."

"Pete!" The voice had fallen to a whisper.

"Pete!" The whisper was urgent.

"Shut up, Hen! I think I'm stuck."

"There's a lad round there."

"What?"

"There's a lad lying round there, asleep."

"Now look what you've made me do. I've torn me sleeve!"

"Come on, Pete, never mind that, come and see."

"If you're kidding me I'll dot you one, after all this."

Pete had some difficulty in backing out the way he had come.

Together the boys approached the figure of a youth lying on his side to the left of the bushes where there was a break in the undergrowth.

"What's he doing sleeping here? Is he a tramp?"

"Course not, he's prop'ly dressed, isn't he?"

"It's a funny place to sleep, if you ask me."

"Maybe he's ill, maybe he's hurt himself."

"Shall we ask him?"

"Yeh. Go on, ask him!"

"No, you ask him!"

"Are you frightened? Henry's frightened! Henry's frightened!"

"No I'm not!"

"Well go on then, wake him up and ask him!"

"He might not like being woken up, he's bigger than us."

"Oh, get out of the way, I'll do it!"

"Hen! Hen! Run! Get away! His face is all swollen! Ugh, it's horrible! Quick, run! I'll fetch me Dad. Run, Henry, run!"

They reached Pete's back door almost together. It was locked. Pete hammered with both fists and kicked at the same time. Henry began to cry. It looked as though they were too late to catch anyone in. Suddenly there was an indignant shout from the side of the house. Pete's mother had emerged from the front door, dressed ready for shopping, prepared to do battle with whoever was creating mayhem at her back door.

"What are you two doing here? Trying to knock the door down were you? Why aren't you at school by now? Come in here, the pair of you!"

"Mam! Mam!..."

"I'll give you Mam, Mam...."

"Mam, will you listen! There's a body in the park..."

It took a while to impress their story on Pete's mother and it was Henry's tears that convinced her rather than her son's excitement. She had long suffered from over-dramatic stories of one kind or another. Her husband had departed for work a long time before and she certainly didn't want to see for herself so she decided she must get to a phone and tell the police.

"And if you are having me on, I'll tan your hide, that I will!"

The senior detective officer attached to the Clayton police force was Detective Chief Inspector Douglas Hart, a tall, weighty man, unmistakably a policeman. He had missed all the excitement of that day. He had enjoyed an extended free weekend with his wife on the south coast during which they had taken the opportunity to visit their daughter who was a student at Southampton University. He didn't return home until the early hours of Wednesday morning and was unaware of the discovery of the body until he received an early morning call from his assistant, Detective Sergeant Bailey, alerting him to the emergency and urging him to come into the office as soon as possible.

Douglas Hart wasn't entirely happy about his

weekend. It had started well enough - perfect weather, easy motoring, a change of air and a relief from work. However, when they reached Southampton, his daughter, Louise, had introduced him to her new boyfriend and he had taken an instant dislike to the young man. His wife, Sheila, had been more favourably impressed and had teased him about it, but he had found himself more disturbed than he cared to admit and he returned home with a lingering sense of unease. Consequently, he was rather pleased to be diverted by Bailey's voice on the phone, recalling him to duty. He needed a new challenge, something to get his teeth into.

When he arrived at Welbeck Road police station, Hart was refreshed and eager to get down to work. He was pleased to find that all the routine procedures had been carried out most efficiently and that an operations room had been set up and was already busy. John Bailey was waiting at one of the tables. Hart helped himself to a bundle of reports and beckoned him, together they went into the D.C.I.'s office.

"Well now, fill me in, what have you got so far?"

"Sir," Bailey read from his notes, "we know that the victim was Thomas Watson, 14 years old, 5 feet 4 inches tall, slightly built, dark haired, brown eyed, wearing a sports jacket, dark green pullover.....etc. etc.... He was killed by being strangled with a very fine cord of some kind..."

"It's sickening, a strangling, not very common."

"....He was found by two small children, Henry Wallace and Peter Jeffries who had been playing football and had kicked their ball into the bushes. The body was lying on its side, with its knees drawn up so that the children had, at first, thought that the boy was asleep. When they saw the bloated face, the children ran home and raised the alarm. The mother of Peter Jeffries phoned the police..."

"What was the time of the discovery?"

"About 8:30. The boys were on their way to school, they always left early to have a game in the park on their way..."

"Or they were dodging school. There is no school anywhere near the park."

"The first on the scene was Inspector Jordan who had the area cordoned off, sent for the doctor and the photographer, and initiated a search. You were sent for as soon as the Superintendent was notified, but you weren't available...."

"I don't need an account of police procedure, I need to go over what was found! Do we have the photographs yet?"

"Yes sir, they were on my desk this morning, I put them in your tray."

"Was there anything special about them?"

"No, I don't think so, sir. The face is certainly not a pretty sight."

Hart opened the packet and studied the photographs for a few moments.

"Very gruesome, it's always the same with a strangling. It's a heartless thing, sickening because it has to be deliberate...and it takes time. Of all murders, I think I dislike stranglings most of all. It is particularly heartless in the case of a young boy like this."

Bailey grimaced and continued.

"After the body was moved, the search of the pockets revealed a used handkerchief, a pair of bicycle clips, a box containing four cigarettes and an cigarette lighter.....quite an old fashioned lighter for a young boy to be carrying..."

"Was he given it or did he pinch it, do you think?"

"...The pocket of the shirt contained a pocket watch with the boy's name inscribed on the back."

"A pocket watch? That's a funny thing for a boy of

8

his age to want to carry about."

"But it was his, sir. The inscription was 'Thomas Watson. Born June. 17th. 1947.' There was some staining from grass on the back and shoulder of the jersey, the plimsolls were scuffed at the toes, otherwise hardly worn. They had soil in ..."

"Hang on, had there been any rain during the night?"

"No sir! I was out late that night, the sky was clear..."

"Was it now?"

"I got up early to take the dog out and the pavement was dry at 7."

"Was it now? Where's Jordan's report, ah, here, here...'there were no signs of a struggle, the ground was firm though the surface was damp due to a recent shower. The ground beneath the body was dry and revealed nothing...' You know what that means, don't you?"

Bailey was often irritated by his chief's thinking aloud, which could seem childish, but he would rather be included in the process than left out.

"Let's look at the doctor's report. Where is it? Here..... the doctor suggests that death had occurred more than 24 hours before. Those grass stains....if the body had fallen on the spot, which parts would have hit the grass first? The body was on its side, wasn't it? Surely there should be stains elsewhere not just at the back. There again, would the grass stains be pronounced just from a fall if the ground had been dry? Now, what do we know about Thomas Watson's background?"

"The boy lived with his aunt and uncle at 22 Selborne Street, their name is Grant, all we have so far is that his father is not known and his mother abandoned him to be looked after by his aunt and uncle.

9

Victor Grant, the uncle, worked at Clarkson's as a welder until a few months ago when he was involved in an accident and damaged his right arm. No other known relatives. School: Firby High. Not a great scholar, according to the Head. Head recommends that we see his tutor or other teachers for a fuller report..."

"What were his movements for the 24 hours prior to his death?"

"Not known, Sir"

"Not known?"

"According to his aunt and uncle, he went out on Sunday afternoon and didn't come back. When he didn't return the next day, they reported him missing..."

"That's a long delay, why did they wait so long?"

"They aren't the sort of people to make a fuss....they waited to see if he turned up"

Hart stared at his sergeant. Over the few months they had worked together he had formed the opinion that he was both sharp and tough. For a moment he thought he may have misjudged him.

"Have the possessions gone down to the lab?"

"Not yet, sir, I thought ...."

"Right, come on, then, let's take a look at them."

They hurried down to the operations room. A table towards the back was littered with shiny plastic bags. One by one, Hart took up the bags and drew out the contents with great care, starting with the clothes. He studied each item intently.

Green pullover - hand knitted, not very old. The green stains on the back were most certainly from grass or other such plants, they were not from paint. There was also soil among them. The back was generally rather dirty whereas the front was remarkably clean. There were no tears or scuffs except, he looked closer, on the lower inside part of each sleeve the wool was scraped or dragged and there was dust of some kind bedded in it. Was that recent? Climbing, he thought. Most boys climbed, it didn't have to have sinister significance.

Shirt - fairly clean, no obvious marks or tears.

Trousers - fairly well worn. Seat dirty, some damp patches still remained. Hart peered at them and sniffed. They were not oil stains nor, he felt sure, were they permanent. Perhaps the plastic bag had prevented them drying out. The smell was vaguely familiar, definitely musty...was it mould or decaying matter of some sort? The front was cleaner, no marks.

Just to be thorough, he turned out the empty pockets. There were no marks, no scratches. The button of the back pocket was broken and one half was missing, he couldn't have guessed whether that was recent.

The underpants, socks and handkerchief could tell him nothing.

Plimsolls - looked well worn, some mud splashes over the top, dry mud or soil in the grooves of the soles. Scuff marks at the tips with white pigment or chalky substance bedded in the scuff marks. There were darker marks on the base of the heels. The lab would have a field day with these, he thought.

He turned to the possessions.

The lighter and the cigarettes - Bailey was right, the lighter was rather heavy and old fashioned and the cigarette packet was not as crumpled as might be expected if it was in daily use by grubby schoolboy hands.

Cycle clips - straightforward, not new, clean and unmarked.

Pocket watch - large, old fashioned fob watch. A strange thing for a boy to own in 1962. He looked at the lettering, it gleamed at him. He looked closely, there was no dirt or discolouration in the grooves. The watch had been engraved only recently.

Carefully he returned all the items to their plastic bags and urged that they be taken immediately to the lab.

He turned to his Sergeant who had been studying his every movement.

"We haven't got very far, Sergeant! It will get cold on us if we don't hurry. I'm going to see the Grants. They must be where it all begins. You get along to the school, interview the whole staff if necessary and find out who his friends were and who saw him last."

Hart reached for the phone again.

"Inspector Jordan?...... door to door enquiries are in hand? Splendid! I'll be off to Selborne Street myself then. What? Reporters? No, I'm not nearly ready for reporters, keep them at bay, there's a good man. I'll slip out the back."

Chapter Two

Hart had been attached to the Clayton force for over a year now and prided himself in having a good knowledge of most of his patch. Having turned off the Headlaw Road he found himself in unfamiliar territory. This was, recognisably, a "respectable" district. Even on a weekday there were few people about. It was very quiet. Selborne Street was a double row of sturdy red brick terrace houses built about the turn of the century. Most of them were well maintained with good paint work and neat, tiny gardens standing out only three or four feet from the front wall. Each house had a shallow bay to the downstairs front window and two bedroom windows above.

No. 22 was second from the end. The curtains in the bay window were drawn against reporters' prying eyes. Three or four reporters were still lounging about the pavement and, as he approached, leapt to question him. He excused himself stiffly and knocked on the door. There was a long silence during which he appreciated the neat front garden, the scrupulously clean front step, the highly polished doorknob and letter box. He thought that here was pride in cleanliness. He knocked again. He glanced at the house on his left and saw that it was almost the same, perhaps not quite so bright in appearance. The house on his right, No.20, had an unoccupied look about it in spite of the curtains at the window and a glimpse of furniture. He was about to step over the low railing to look closer at it when a movement at the window at his left made him turn. A face glared at him through the parted curtains and a hand waved him away. Hart pulled out his warrant card and held it up to the window. The curtains were closed abruptly and, a minute later, Edie Grant opened her front door. The reporters immediately shouted for her

13

attention, there were two flashes as cameras took chance shots but she studiously ignored them, allowed Hart to squeeze through then shut the door with bold determination.

Edie Grant was short and thin, grey haired and sallow skinned. She held herself erect and her movements were quick, almost abrupt. Her face was lined but her eyes were bright and wary. She looked angry and tired. Clearly, she had been very upset and being harassed by insensitive reporters had not helped. She led him into the living room without speaking.

The living room was rather gloomy and Hart's first reaction was to look for a light switch but he controlled himself in time to see Victor Grant struggling to rise from a fire side chair, using one hand to push himself up. Hart motioned him back and sat down opposite him.

"Don't trouble yourself, Mr. Grant, I'm D.C.I. Hart, in charge of the enquiry. I'm sorry but there are a few more questions I must ask you. There is so much we need to know."

"There is no peace now!" chimed in Edie Grant.

Hart looked hard at her.

"This is a very serious matter, Mrs. Grant. I'm afraid that we will need to trouble you a good deal further if we are to get to the bottom of it."

"Edie and I will give you all the help you need."

Victor Grant's voice was steady and carried weight. He was not unlike his wife in appearance, being short and wiry with the same sallow complexion and grey hair, but he was stooped and his joints seemed stiff as he moved. His damaged right arm hung awkwardly and his hands were gnarled so that the overall impression was of a man much older than one still in his fifties. His eyes, like his manner, were gentle.

"I'll make some tea." Edie stumped out.

14

"Now, Mr. Grant, how old was Tommy when you adopted him?"

"Nay, we've never adopted him. We're his only relations, he's always lived with us."

"Since he was born?"

"Aye, he were Edie's sister's child. Never knew his father."

"So he's always lived here? Everyone local must have known him?"

"Aye, though he always kept himself to himself."

"You mean he didn't play with other children?"

"Oh aye, but not much. Everyone keeps to themselves around here. Tommy was a good lad. Kept his own counsel. He were never a chatterer. Even as a baby he were quiet. Took notice of everything but said little. He hadn't many friends but he was loyal. When he was younger, he would come down to the allotment and sit watching while I worked. He liked to help but he wouldn't disturb me. Sometimes I would turn and see a far-away look in his eye and wonder where his mind had drifted off to.

"He particularly liked to join me in the attic when I was working with my models. I had a model railway then. I used to turn some of the parts on my little bench lathe and he would watch then try his hand at it. Good he was too, but his Aunt Edie would worry him if he spent too much time. She wanted him to spend all his time on his homework, to better himself you see. I had to sell the railway.

"We went on holiday once or twice when he was little, just for his sake you know, we don't bother much with holidays ourselves, too much fuss and expense. He loved the seaside but he didn't bother much with other bairns. He seemed too serious for them. They wouldn't linger long and he didn't seem to care. Since he went to senior school he's been even more of a loner. He still comes to me for a chat, sometimes, but he's been a bit distant with Edie. She hasn't much patience with him now he's growing up. I think that he's a deep'un. I think he'll be alright....except....except, he won't now will he?"

Hart had made no attempt to stem Victor Grant's flow. Victor had needed to talk. There was great sincerity and simplicity in this man but Hart had to keep a distance. He was wondering how he was going to push on without causing too much distress when Victor himself helped him.

"Who would want to do him harm?"

"That's what we must try to find out." Hart was very gentle. After a pause, he went on.

"What did Tommy find to do ?"

"To do? Oh, he had a paper round. He liked getting around on his bike and he washed folks' cars at weekends. Nobody has a garage round here and most of them liked him to wash their cars, he were in demand. We didn't have much to give him and since I've been laid off with this arm, he's had to earn all his own pocket money. He was doing well. Very independent he was."

"What other interests did he have? Did he go out much?"

"No, not a lot. He went to the pictures about once a week and he would go round to friends sometimes but he was always back early. His friends never bothered us much."

"What did he find to do at home, apart from when he was helping you?"

"Well, when he were young, he had toys...and he had pets. He kept rabbits."

"In the yard?" Hart stood and glanced through the window into the yard. It was shadowy but empty and

16

spotlessly clean. Not a speck of dust nor a weed lingered anywhere, every inch looked thoroughly scrubbed.

"Well, they were, at first, but Edie didn't like the smell or the mess. We moved them down to the allotment."

"So he spent most of his time there?"

"Aye, he'd often help me down there. He kept them in the shed and he bred them there. Real good'uns, pedigrees!"

"Does he still have them?"

"Only a couple. Just about six months ago someone broke in and killed them. Sickening it was. Wanton vandalism. The lad was broken hearted. They were everything to him and he'd made quite a lot of money out of them as well. We bought him two more to help him over the shock, but he lost interest. Now it takes him all his time to go down to feed and water them."

"So he hasn't bothered much with the allotment recently?"

"Well, he has and he hasn't like. He's been mooching round keeping watch. He wanted to catch whoever had killed his rabbits. I think he thought they might strike again. If he saw anyone walking down there he'd jump up to see who they were."

"Can you see from here?" Hart interrupted.

"No, he kept watch from his bedroom. If he was outside, he'd climb onto next door's shed." Victor pointed to the wall between the two houses.

"Didn't they mind?"

Victor was taken aback.

"Mind? Oh no, there's no one next door, it's been empty for months.The Skinners only rented, you know, and he got a move to Manchester so they had to leave. It's still empty. There are about three houses still owned by the original builders, they let them furnished. This one must still be to rent. Every now and then, a man from the estate agent comes to inspect it"

At this point Edie stormed in with a tray of tea things. Hart suspected that she always stormed.

Chapter Three

Hart looked round the room as he sipped his tea. It was very tidy. There wasn't much furniture, two small fireside chairs, a drop leaf table with straight chairs at either side and a plain sideboard, but every piece gleamed with polish. The fireplace was small for a living room and there was a low fire burning in the grate. Its tiles were of a mushroom colour with strong light-brown mottling. They too shone, in spite of the poor light. The walls were covered in a textured paper of a colour resembling oatmeal and there was a border of a darker colour where once there had been a picture rail. The floor was covered with a patterned carpet of an uncertain and faint design, a mixture of fawns and light browns. Between the carpet and the walls glowed stretches of highly polished brown linoleum.

The whole affect should have been cosy, especially with the coal fire burning, thought Hart, but somehow there was a chill, not a chill exactly so much as a lack of warmth. He recalled a tag from his schoolboy Shakespeare, "cribbed, cabined and confined," though why, he wasn't certain.

On the mantelpiece was a small pot plant and a clock. On the sideboard opposite was a brightly coloured biscuit tin, an ornamental jug, a small ceramic tray and a photograph in a modest frame.

Victor had followed his glance.

"Now that tray was Tommy's. Made it in pottery at school. He were good, his teacher said so, but his interest didn't last."

18

Hart rose and went over to the photograph. Edie frowned disapproval but Victor was encouraging.

"That's an old one. It's Tommy, Edie and me on holiday five years ago. They were happy days."

The photo showed a boy about nine or ten, gawky and uncertain, smiling yet somehow serious. Edie was standing stiffly to one side, and Victor, with his arm round the boy's shoulder, was standing at the other. The bond between the boy and his uncle was happy enough. The aunt did not look happy.

"Do you have any other photographs?"

He thought that Edie and Victor exchanged glances.

"No," said Edie, "we lost the camera, and anyway it's all very expensive"

"You don't have a family album?"

"No!" she cried out crossly.

"Well," Victor spoke slowly, "we did have, of course, but it was destroyed in an accident."

"Oh, how was that?" Hart tried to keep his voice light.

Edie pushed in, pinching at her elbows nervously.

"It was my fault. I cleared out a lot of rubbish and somehow the album got mixed up with it."

"She was very upset over it, you know," Victor smoothed, "but it hardly matters now, there's no one to hand it on to..."

"You had no children of your own?"

There was a long silence.

Edie was the first to speak.

"Yes. We had a son. Went off to sea. An engineer he was..."

She seemed to be struggling with herself.

"Went off to sea and we've never seen or heard from him since."

Victor shook his head and Hart looked at him, but Edie went on.

19

"He suddenly made up his mind. He was 21. Old enough, I suppose."

Her voice was harsh with bitterness.

"Served his time at Pomfret's."

There was a silence.

"He came in, went upstairs and brought his things down, said he was going. He had a ship to go on. That was it!"

Victor took up the story.

"It were a shock. I didn't know anything about it. He'd applied properly, got Pomfrets to recommend him. I knew nothing of it. Never said a word. No letters came here. He just got the job and went."

"And you've never heard from him since?"

They shook their heads. Hart sensed a certain relief that they had got the story off their chests.

"Why, I shall never know!" cried Edie, after a pause.

"Boys will be men. I'm sure he's alright, wherever he is."

Comforting words from Victor but little, if any, contact, Hart noted.

"But why....never to have written... and now the lad..."

There was a great internal struggle going on but Edie's gaunt face remained rigid.

"You never enquired of the shipping company?"

"No, never! Why should we? Why should we seek him out, he left a perfectly decent home without quarrel or warning. It was his wish to go. He'd turned his back on us. It was for him to do the proper thing, to come home or write. We've stayed the same....why.....?"

She broke off, trembling with anger and hurt, fighting to keep her control.

Hart waited a few moments then asked if he could see the boy's bedroom. Edie turned to lead him but Hart met her eye and firmly said that he wished to see it for himself.

Tommy Watson's bedroom was bare and not very cosy. It was at the back of the house overlooking the yard. The walls were painted a dull blue. There was a single bed to the left of the door with old-fashioned boards of mahogany at the head and the foot. Beside it was a low table with a shelf which served as a locker. There was an upright chair in one corner and a dark single wardrobe between it and the door. By the window stood a box seat made of plain unvarnished wood, possibly homemade.

There were no posters or pictures on the walls, no possessions lying about, no clues as to the personality of the occupant. On the table by the bed was a simple reading lamp, on the shelf below were two books arranged neatly one above the other. They were both public library books, one on Inventions and the other on War at Sea. Hart picked them up and shook them gently. Nothing fell out nor did they fall open at any particular place. He returned them most carefully to their position.

Next he opened the wardrobe and peered in. There were not many clothes in it. On hangers were a grey suit, a pair of flannels, and two or three shirts. A small, neat pile of vests and two pullovers lay on one of the side shelves and similarly neat piles of handkerchiefs and underpants occupied the shelf below it. One further shelf was occupied by bundled socks. Hart let his hand run through all the shelves but there was nothing hiding there. At the bottom of the wardrobe there was a well-worn pair of black shoes, some old sandals and a pair of gym shoes.

Hart sighed. Everything was shipshape, too shipshape. Did the boy keep his room tidy or was it his aunt? Did he have any private possessions, if so where did he keep them? Hart's eye moved to the box seat, it looked very like a low piano stool with raised sides with holes in them for handgrips. He reached down and felt for the front edge. With a tug he raised the hinged top and looked inside. Here was the nearest the room came to acknowledging disorder. A small portable radio with an ear piece lay on top of a pile of scraps of paper, pencils, pens, pencil-sharpener, elastic bands, broken set squares, one or two small cardboard boxes and odd pieces of string. All schoolboy junk but junk linked to a classroom not personal junk. Hart looked into the little boxes, they were empty, then he pushed his hand in among the scraps of paper. Amazingly, the pieces of paper were all blank, waiting to be used. No amount of shuffling turned up any writing but he continued for a while until, near the bottom of the pile, he disturbed two small photographs. He studied them and put them carefully in his wallet.

The D.C.I. was nothing if not thorough. He examined the lining of the curtains, turned up the mattress, looked carefully at the top of the wardrobe and, finally, studied the carpet under the bed. Edie Grant's daily cleaning was thorough. Not a speck of dust or loose fluff lay anywhere.

He strode to the window and looked out. There was a clear view over the back yard and part of the yard of next door. The view extended over the allotments. Hart wondered which allotment belonged to Victor Grant and whether it was clearly visible from this window. He could just detect the path through the allotments, it wasn't easy but he was helped at that moment by the movement of two heads, presumably two people walking side by side. If that was all that could be seen from the window, how could the boy know whether a moving head belonged to a genuine gardener or a potential villain? Perhaps he knew all the owners by sight?

He looked at the window frame. The window was open at the top, Edie Grant would certainly have insisted on plenty of air to the room. He tried the window, it moved easily and silently. The house may be old but everything worked. The drop to the ground was at least ten feet but to the left was a strong drain pipe, the six inch feed from the toilet.

He looked at his watch and turned to go. He took a last look round. Somehow, he found it very difficult to imagine the occupant of this room, it was so impersonal. He sighed. His daughters' bedrooms had been cheerful and very, very untidy.

Chapter Four

Downstairs, Victor and Edie Grant had composed themselves. Hart was deliberately blunt.

"You don't smoke, do you, Mr. Grant?"

There was a snort from Edie. Victor shook his head and said that he had given up a long time ago.

"Do you know that Tommy smoked?"

Victor looked astonished.

"I never thought that he would. He had strong ideas about keeping healthy. I can hardly believe it.... are you sure?"

Edie broke in, "I wouldn't have smoke in the house! His clothes never had a hint of smoke about them, I can assure you of that!"

"Nevertheless, he had a packet with some cigarettes and a lighter in his pocket when he was found. Oh, and another thing, do you recognise these photographs?"

He drew from his wallet the photographs he had taken from the box upstairs and placed them on the table. There was a gasp from Edie and a cry of astonishment from Victor.

"That's our son, young Victor," he whispered, pointing to one, "and that's me when I were young."

"How did he get hold of them and what was he doing with them?" cried Edie. They looked at each other, genuinely astonished.

"I thought you said you had thrown away your family album, Mrs. Grant?"

Edie swallowed and grew sullen. "I did!"

"Then how did the boy come by these?"

"I don't know, he must have found them in a drawer. He must have been rummaging, though I've never known him do such a thing. Anyway, I keep my drawers tidy, I would have seen any photos."

Hart could tell that though she was blustering, she

was pointing out the truth. He turned to Victor.

"When was this taken?"

"That was taken before Tommy was born. He never knew our Victor."

"Did you talk to Tommy about your son?"

Edie pushed in again. "Didn't need to! When he was a baby there were other things to think about. When he was older, we didn't want him getting ideas, did we?"

Hart turned to Victor.

"So you never spoke of him?"

"Well, I may have mentioned him once or twice." He looked at his wife and shook his head sadly.

"Then what was he doing with your son's photo?"

"And why mine?" Victor was genuinely bewildered.

The two figures undoubtedly shared a family likeness. The father looked lean and strong jawed, the son was softer in outline, less well braced and Hart thought that there was a slight caginess in his expression. Give a dog a bad name, he thought.

"You say that Tommy never saw or met your son?"

"We're certain of that." They both answered.

"Now, Mr. Grant, will you go over when you last saw Tommy. I know that you have already made a statement, but I want as full a picture as I can get."

Victor cleared his throat.

"I last saw him Sunday dinner time. He'd been out delivering Sunday papers, then he washed a car, the Drysdale's, I think. He came in at about half past 11, went to his room, came down sharp when Edie called him to eat. That would be half past 12. He were gone in half an hour, never did take long to eat his meals. We never asked him where he went because he was free on Sunday afternoons and if he went anywhere special he used to tell us. He usually came in for tea and if he was going out at night he'd always tell us where he was going.

"Tea were at half past four but he didn't arrive. Edie were proper cross because she'd made hot sausage rolls and his favourite cake. She went on and on. When he didn't come in at bedtime I sat up. Edie went to bed. I looked down the allotment and up and down the street. Last thing, I went round to the lad he does the papers with, Jim Hibbert's, but they hadn't seen him. I fell asleep in front of the fire and didn't wake up while three. I thought he'd come in because a coat had fallen off the back door, so I locked up and went upstairs.

"The next morning, Edie said his bed had not been slept in. We were both upset, he'd not been out all night before. I went down to the allotment again to see if he were there. He might have been in trouble and slept rough in the shed, I did that once, when I were just a lad myself, but there was no sign of him.

"We talked it over and decided we'd better tell the police. There wasn't anything else we could do, we were that worried. We haven't got a phone so I walked down to Welbeck Road station and reported him missing. Yesterday afternoon they came and asked me to go and identify him....I, we haven't got over the shock yet. It was terrible seeing him lying there..."

Victor Grant covered his eyes with one hand and shook his head.

Hart had experience of such difficult occasions. He waited a suitable interval then thanked him gently and turned to his wife. At first, it seemed that she was unwilling to say anything but Hart put on his gentlest expression and assured her that everything she said would be important in building up a complete account of events. She sat for so long that the D.C.I. thought that he would have to leave without hearing from her.

"I can't think straight, I'm so upset. He was a good

lad, I suppose, but he had grown so big and awkward and he would never talk to me. He got on alright with Victor but I couldn't get much sense out of him. He was alright as a little bairn, cheerful enough, but he'd grown so private, a bit like our Jane, his mother. Of course, we never knew who his father was and Jane would never have told us.

"I suppose he was good natured, he went messages and did jobs about the house, but he wouldn't let on what he did at school or outside the house. This last year or so he wasn't much of a help, but he took on washing cars as well as his paper round. He was good with money, careful what he did with it.

"Very regular he was, never late for school or his paper job, never missed. He was never ill, he was a strong boy, very healthy. Liked the gym at school, but he didn't play football, I don't know why.

"He was tidy enough, a bit clumsy, he was growing and he took some clothing, I can tell you, but he never asked for much, not like some, I dare say. He had to be reminded of things but he was alright really. I had to have words about his radio. Far too loud. He got himself an earplug thing and after that we never heard him. He would sit in his room for hours and we never heard a thing. I suppose he was good that way. We were no company for him."

She came to an abrupt halt.

Hart was surprised that this thin, sharp and bitter woman would soften in this way. He was loath to intrude but he sensed that she would need prodding.

"What about his friends....?"

"Friends, yes, he had friends but they didn't trouble us much here. He didn't invite them and he didn't talk about them much. He used to like Victor's company best when he was little. In the last couple of years he seems to have grown away from us. Spent more time out than in. I'm worried that he doesn't do enough homework, if he doesn't get his O levels he won't get a decent job and we can't be looking after him all his life."

She had unconsciously slipped into the present tense.

"Did he show any signs of worry recently? Had anything been disturbing him, do you think?"

"No, I haven't seen any signs of worry. The same silent Tommy, the more I talked to him, the less he spoke. He went out on his bike, came back for his tea then spent the rest of the night in his room listening to his radio. Sunday, he went off on his paper round, came back, put his bike away and went off to wash the Drysdale's car, came back about half past 11, went up to his room, came down for his dinner at half past 12 then slipped out again. He didn't say where he was going. He can't have taken his bike because it is still in the yard. I expected him back for tea, he knows what time it is. I expect him to have his hands washed, sitting at the table at half past four prompt. I did something special, well, it was Sunday. He didn't come back. I was that vexed! All Sunday night he didn't arrive. Victor said, "Edie, you go up, I'll wait for him." Next morning, his bed had not been slept in. I was right upset. He'd never been away from home before. Victor looked for him down at the allotment but he wasn't there. He said to wait, the lad might have stayed with friends then gone on to school, though he'd never done that before.

"I thought that he had been in an accident, but Victor said we would have had the ambulance men round. We haven't a phone you see, we've never needed one. We talked it over, we didn't want to make a fuss but there was nothing else we could do so Victor went down to the police station and reported it."

"Thank you Mrs. Grant. You said that Tommy's bike is still in the yard, could I see it please?"

They led Hart out into the back yard. Immediately, Hart remembered staying with a cousin before the war in exactly the same sort of house. They had played together in just such a back yard with the outhouses down one side. There had been the same coalhouse, wash-house, outside toilet and roofed space for dustbins and firewood. He remembered the lingering smell of washing, there was no such smell here. A faint smell of burning, perhaps, but no other. The yard was spotlessly clean. Although the back of the house was in shadow, the paintwork glowed. The bike was under an open roof next to the bin which was tucked well back with its lid firmly in place.

"It's a fine looking bike, nearly new?"

"He's only had it a couple of months. Paid for it himself out of his own pocket, the money he got from the paper round and from washing cars. He's very proud of his bike, kept it spick and span, wouldn't let anyone else touch it."

Hart inspected it closely. It was in pristine condition. There were no signs of any damage. He could see the merest film of oil on the brake cables. There was no excess grease on the chain or the pedals, no drips on the wheel cylinders, the frame was clean, the chrome gleamed, down to the last spoke, however, there was heavy mud clinging to the tyres and it had spread onto the wheel rims in places and a few pieces of grass and gravel were bedded in it.

He looked again at his watch. He had been longer than he had anticipated. He decided to go. He said goodbye to the Grants, thanked them for their co-operation but warned them that their ordeal wasn't yet over, and left by the front door.

Chapter Five

Firby High School was not large, but, like many city schools, it looked forbidding. It was a double storied building of dark red brick and black stone - black because no one had ever got round to cleaning the stonework. Its windows were tall and narrow with a hint of the ecclesiastical about them, their frames painted an institutional dark green. It stood foursquare in a sea of concrete. There were no bushes or trees to relieve its outlines, no flowerbeds to lend a hint of colour to its stern front. There was no grass, its playing fields belonged to the local rugby club a mile or so away. The low brick buildings at the outside edges of the concrete yards were outdoor toilets, caretaker's stores and the school kitchens. Green painted railings, six feet high, marked the perimeter at the front and the back.

Bailey shared a grimace with his companions as they entered the school yard. He had been lucky enough to have attended a bright new school, surrounded by playing fields and woodland, in a county far away.

They entered by the nearest door up a few steps and found themselves in a gloomy cloakroom with walls of dark brown tiles and a pervasive smell of damp clothes and milk. Immediately, three small boys rushed out from behind a rack of assorted raincoats and fled through the door opposite.

"What have they been up to, I wonder?"

"Don't!" said Bailey, grinning, "We haven't got time."

Beyond the second door, they found themselves in a small hall, marked out as though for basketball, but there were no posts, just a stack of tressle tables at one end. A figure in a brown overall coat, carrying a mop and bucket entered through the swing doors opposite.

"Oi! You've come in the wrong door. If you want the Head, you'll have to go along this corridor and turn left at the end."

The caretaker, or whoever it was, didn't ask any questions or wait for any explanations but hurried past them. They crossed the hall and pushed through the swing doors into a corridor. A mixture of sounds assailed their ears. There were four classrooms on their right and a blank wall, much scratched and battered, on their left. It would not have been easy to guess what teaching went on in any of the classrooms. It seemed that most of the teachers in this school shouted and shouted almost continually. The first two classes were particularly noisy, the third was quiet yet the teacher in it was still raising his voice. The fourth classroom had a different sound, a repetitious chanting by all the occupants. Bailey recognised a French verb being conjugated.

Turning left, as they had been instructed, they found themselves in a shorter corridor with a few pictures on the walls and a table with a vase of flowers upon it. The main entrance was on the right and on each side of it there was an office, one for the school secretary and one for the headmaster.

Sergeant Bailey, diplomatically, tapped on the secretary's door. A deep voice bade them enter. Behind a dense cloud of tobacco smoke lurked a large figure appropriate to the voice he had just heard. The room was small, piles of textbooks and exercise books occupied most of the floor, all of the windowsill and part of the table. Three or four wire trays full of papers jostled for space on the rest of the table next to a large, ungainly typewriter. Jammed among them was an outsized ashtray full of cigarette stubs.

"Oh! Ah! Can I help you?" The deep voice rose

from behind the table and the smoke and revealed its owner to be a middle aged lady of above average height and build. She was smartly dressed in a brown corduroy skirt and cashmere sweater. Her abundant hair, a light chestnut colour, was bound back into a large, casual-seeming but efficient bun. Apart from the cigarette dangling from her full lips, she didn't seem to identify with the chaos of the room.

Bailey didn't have time to speculate further. He introduced himself and his companions and asked to see the headmaster.

"Oh, yes. Tommy Watson. Such a dreadful thing! I do hope that you will find whoever was involved. I'll see if the Headmaster is free."

The school secretary was light on her feet, she slipped past the three men, crossed the hallway and knocked on the door opposite. A few seconds later, she beckoned them into the headmaster's study.

Alfred Higthorpe did not like any interruptions to his routine. He only felt efficient when his routine was smooth and undisturbed. He was in his late fifties, of medium build with a well-developed paunch, a bald head, a clipped moustache and nervous grey eyes. Unexpected visitors were a trial. He had suffered a number of trials in the last twenty four hours. Appalling pressmen in slovenly clothes had invited him to be indiscrete, they had not come together but had arrived in twos and threes at different times until he was forced to risk bad publicity by instructing his secretary to refuse them entry. His phone had not stopped ringing, first the police, notifying him of the death, then an investigating officer, then the local press, then the Chief Staffing Officer, then the Director of Education himself, cautioning him about discretion in dealing with all enquiries. Now it was a team asking to interview children. It was all becoming a nightmare. Where did he stand in the matter of allowing children to be taken out of lessons? His first instinct was to refuse and he was about to bluster when Detective Sergeant Bailey's smooth voice broke in.

"I'm sure you realise that this is a very serious matter, Mr. Higthorpe. It concerns us all. There must be no delay in our hunt for the murderer. I assure you that we will be as quick as we can and we will try to disrupt as little as possible."

"So long as you realise that I have a duty to look after my children, Sergeant."

"Did you know the boy well, yourself, sir?"

"Oh no! I only know a few of the older pupils, those in responsible positions. We have a very efficient system here. Each boy or girl is in a House for administrative purposes and is allotted a Tutor to oversee his or her progress. Classes aren't fixed, of course, because of setting, so there aren't class teachers as such. If you want to know about the boy, you must ask his Housemaster and Tutor."

Higthorpe buzzed his secretary.

"Mrs. Sanderson, the boy Watson, who were his housemaster and tutor? Ah! Yes. Mr. Dishforth and Mr. Vane, thank you. Well, sergeant, those are the gentlemen you should see, there will be a break at 11. They will be in the staffroom at the end of this corridor, unless they are on duty..."

He was about to ring his secretary again when Bailey interrupted him.

"Yes, we certainly would like to interview these gentlemen and perhaps one or two other members of staff who taught the boy. Is there a room we could use for the purpose?"

"Mmm. I'll ask my secretary, she knows the availability of rooms."

Higthorpe was beginning to regret his willingness to co-operate. It sounded as though this was turning into a major operation. Also, he didn't like being pushed.

"We'd like to start with the staff then talk to some of his friends and classmates. As it is 10 o'clock already, do you mind if we start straight away? We could go to the staffroom while you are making the arrangements. Someone there will be able to help us, I'm sure."

Bailey gave the headmaster his most engaging smile as if he had just agreed with the headmaster's own scheme, stood up, stretched out a long hand to grasp the headmaster's, and, before Higthorpe recovered from his astonishment, the three had left the room. Such was Bailey's charm that he had not given outright offence, but Higthorpe was smouldering at having been bowled over. He reached for the phone.

"I'll bet that secretary knows more about the school than he does, Sarge."

"I'm sure of it, Ridley, what's more I don't think he wants to know more than he does. Delegation's his game." Bailey's reply was sharp.

They knocked at the staffroom door and entered. It was small and overheated and crammed with furniture. There was hardly room to move between the tables and chairs. In spite of their number, all of the tables were occupied by books and papers. There were cupboards and bookshelves on the wall opposite the windows and a huge notice board above the fireplace, all were overflowing. There were two small armchairs on each side of the fire and one was occupied.

"Hullo, not looking for the headmaster are you, he's......"

"No, we're here to ask about Thomas Watson. I'm Detective Sergeant Bailey and these are Detective Constables Ridley and Philips."

"I'm Tom Hadley, the deputy head. Did the headmaster send you along?"

"We've just come from him. We need to talk to the boy's tutors and some of his friends."

"You'll need a room then, won't you? There's a small prep room next to the labs upstairs. That will do well. Come along, I'll show you. Would you like some tea, or coffee? I'll send some along during the break. You'll need a programme. Who do you want first, Dishforth, I suppose, then Vane. Right, I'll send them along and I'll have a word with the others at break time. Now the children are another matter. His friends won't all be in the same class."

"I dare say that we will soon know who his particular friends were."

As they talked they were climbing to the next floor. Hadley moved quickly. He was a tall loose-limbed viking of a man with an ease of manner and a command of the situation altogether in contrast with his headmaster.

"Ah! Here is Dishforth!"

Coming towards them was a thin figure in an academic gown. Hadley opened the prep room door, ushered the policemen in and beckoned Dishforth to follow.

"Robert, this is Detective Sergeant Bailey and his team, they would like to have a word with you about Thomas Watson. Are you taking a class?"

"Yes, I was just going to take 1B. in the main lab."

"Right, I'll look after them until you've finished."

Just then, a bell rang out in the corridor. Doors opened with a crash, footsteps thundered by, voices shrill with relief and delight.

"Right then, Sergeant, I'll leave you to it."

"You are Tommy Watson's housemaster, I believe.

What can you tell us about him?"

Mr. Dishforth frowned and arranged himself in his chair. He was lightly built with strong dark hair and a thin moustache which stood out against his very pale face. His lips were thin and red and seemed to Bailey to be set in a permanent expression of disapproval.

"I'm afraid I have a poor opinion of that boy. He was a frequent absentee and never gave a satisfactory excuse. He used to be a good worker but over the last twelve months he stopped working. I tried hard to find out why. He wouldn't speak, wouldn't listen. He was sullen and obstinate. I found him personally offensive - what in the forces they call dumb insolence. I sent a note round to his parents but they didn't bother to reply. I thought that he wasn't going to manage his O levels. I wanted to see his parents on parents' night but they didn't appear. I presume that they weren't interested...."

"I thought that he didn't have parents?"

"Of course, by parents I meant those responsible for him....."

"When you say he was an absentee, you mean that he was away from school for long periods?"

"Ah, that is where the cunning of the boy comes in. He attended school every morning and was marked present but every now and again he skipped out. He missed a lot of lessons."

"This was reported to the headmaster?"

"Oh yes! I'm afraid that our particular headmaster doesn't like to hear bad news. He felt that it was our responsibility to see that the boy was in school once he had been registered. It was a matter of internal concern and that we should keep an eye on him. Easier said than done. In any case, he missed the afternoon's registration on the occasions he skipped out. I was in favour of bringing in the Education Officer but the headmaster was bitterly against it...."

"What sort of number of missing days or lessons are we talking about?"

"I would have to refer to my records back in the staffroom...."

"At a rough guess?"

"There was no exact pattern..... two or three times a month."

The two listening detectives exchanged glances.

"Hardly a chronic absentee, sir, I would have thought that there were many others in the same boat."

"Ah, but he was in the O level class, that makes a difference."

"So, he was slacking off and he was insolent. Do you think that there was anything troubling him recently?"

Mr. Dishforth gave a snort and smoothed out his gown with a flicking motion of his left hand.

"I don't think anything troubled that boy! Cool as a cucumber. Didn't have a care for anyone. Not a thought about his future, he could have stayed on for A levels if he really worked, but he didn't want to, not he......."

"What subjects was he good at?"

"Not enough! His English was variable, when it was good it was very good. Vane speaks well of him. About the only one who does. Geography fair. History poor. R.E. bad, Physics poor, Chemistry poor, Maths down the drain. I can't remember them all. Oh yes, Art, he did well in Art, but who doesn't these days?"

"Well, that about says it all, thank you Mr. Dishforth. We won't keep you from your lesson any longer."

Bailey ushered Dishforth out, biting his lip as he did so. As soon as he was sure that Dishforth was out of sight he let out a low roar.

"Pompous little prick! A Housemaster at that! Pity the poor pupils who get on the wrong side of him. He wouldn't notice if one was suffering from bubonic plague and wouldn't care so long as he turned up for his O level classes."

Ridley and Phillips smiled in sympathy but said nothing.

Tom Hadley knocked and re-entered.

"Who do you want next? I'll see if I can get Hector Vane for you..."

"Oh, Mr. Hadley, would you take D.C. Phillips to meet the rest of the staff? He could be covering some ground while we work here."

"Certainly, there's usually someone in the staffroom every period. He can see them all a few at a time. I've been thinking about Watson's friends, I think that the one closest to him would be Stewart Potts. I'll look him out for you."

They were interrupted by the powerful figure of Mrs. Sanderson, the secretary.

"Oh! There you are! You are looking after them are you Mr. Hadley? The Headmaster thought you would be able to. I looked up the list of 'free' rooms and this was the only one. I'm glad that's all settled. Oh, would you like to stay for lunch? Lunches are quite good here, aren't they Mr. Hadley?"

"Well, we have a lot to get through, I'm not sure how long it will take...do you mind if we leave it open?"

Bailey didn't much relish the thought of school meals among the pupils.

"I'll warn the cook, just in case, I'm sure she won't mind."

Mrs. Sanderson's expression rather indicated the contrary but she was well versed in diplomacy. She smiled wryly and vanished as silently as she had appeared.

Chapter Six

There was silence in the Prep Room for several minutes. The two detectives listened to the sounds that echoed about them. It was quieter upstairs. The sounds were all more distant. There was a sharp rap at the door. Ridley went to the door and admitted a dark haired, skinny youth with a pronounced Adam's apple.

"I'm Stewey Potts, Mr. Hadley sent me."

The boy's speech was lively, as though he felt under obligation to be distinct. He, himself, looked tired. He stood awkwardly, his boney wrists dangled from his pullover sleeves and his ankles seemed to extend well below his trouser legs culminating in an enormous pair of feet. His hair was abundant and lank, his face was very pale and he had the whispy beginnings of a dark moustache, but his eyes were bright and restless.

"Come in Stewey and sit down. We've come to ask about Tommy Watson. Were you a good friend of his?"

Stewey Potts looked wary but he sat down and faced the Detective Sergeant squarely.

"Yeh, we were good mates."

"You were in the same class?"

"Yeh."

"When did you last see Tommy?"

"Saturday."

"Morning or afternoon?"

"Morning."

"What time was that?"

"'Bout 12o'clock."

Bailey waited.

"He came round to mine. We was going to the pictures. He said he couldn't go, there was something else he had to do."

"What did he mean, something else to do?"

"I dunno, do I? He never said. Said 'e'd see me

later."

"Did you always go to the pictures on Saturdays?"

"Sometimes we went to watch 'The Town'"

"When they were at home?"

"Yeh."

"They weren't at home on Saturday?"

"Nah, we don't always go when they're at home, though. Costs too much."

"The pictures are cheaper?"

"You don't need the bus."

"He could afford the pictures every week?"

"He always had enough."

"Had he a lot of money?"

"Well..... he always had money. We always shared, me and him, mostly me." The boy smiled briefly. "Me dad hardly gives me any money, skinflint! Says I should work for it."

"Did Tommy work for it?"

"Yeah. Tommy had a round."

"That's why he always had money?"

"Yeah, a big round. Good pay. He saved most of it."

"What was he saving for?"

"Said 'e was saving it for his uncle."

"For a present was it?"

"I don't know, do I?"

"You didn't have a round?"

"Nah, I didn't have a bike. I had a round once but I had foot trouble and had to pack it in." Bailey smiled to himself, trying hard not to look down at the boy's feet.

"Did he see you later?"

"Nah, he didn't come over on Sunday. I don't know what happened."

"Do you think he stayed out?"

"He never 'stayed out'." The boy looked puzzled.

"So you never saw him again?"

The boy looked down and shook his head.

There was a long pause.

"Did you know where Tommy went when he went missing from school?"

Stewey Potts gave the detective a sharp look.

"Nah, he just took off."

"Weren't you his best friend?"

"Tommy never said much any time. No use asking. If he wanted you to know, he told you."

"He wasn't thieving, was he?"

"Nah, never! Tommy was straight, very straight."

"Did he smoke?"

"Tommy! Never! He wouldn't touch one. Got at me because I used to fancy one."

"Had he ever been in trouble?"

"With the police? Nah, never!"

"At home?"

"His Aunt Edie was always on to 'im, he told me, but not his Uncle Victor. He would do anything for his uncle Victor. He was always home early......"

"At school?"

"He was always in trouble at school," the boy smiled, "If the teachers got on to him he would play up. He never cheeked them, he'd just shut up and be contrary like. He was a laugh."

"How did he get on with the rest of the class?"

"Some didn't like him because he didn't say much. In the second year they tried to bully him. He had to fight Billy Simms and he won, Billy was nearly twice his size, then. They left him alone after that. Tommy would never start a fight, mind."

"You've been friends a long time?"

"Since that fight with Billy Simms," Stewey smiled again," I held his coat."

"Was anything bothering him when you last saw him?"

"Nah, nothing bothered Tommy."

42

"You would know if he was upset about anything?"

"Yeh, sure. He was just the same Tommy."

Bailey felt that there nothing further he could ask at that moment.

The bell for break sounded just after Stewey Potts left. There was an immense surge of bodies out in the corridor accompanied by squeaks and squawks. These were younger classes making their way downstairs and out into the school playground. Moments later, a young woman came in with a tray in her hand. Bailey and Ridley were impressed by the service and were grateful for the refreshment. A knock heralded the entry of a middle aged man of medium height, fair hair and ruddy complexion.

"Hector Vane." He introduced himself. "Tommy Watson's tutor. This is a dreadful business! How can I help you?"

"Just tell us, as simply as you can, all you know about the lad, Mr. Vane."

"I'm his tutor but I also taught him English. He was a strange boy. A one off. Nobody quite like him. A dreamer. When he was interested in a topic and could let his imagination go, he wrote very well. Other times he was just average. I think that he was quite bright. Tests, when he started here at eleven, proved it. Sadly, he got on the wrong side of a number of my colleagues. He seemed to sense a dislike or a disapproval and he would react to it. Some colleagues thought him badly behaved, but he was not as badly behaved as many of our boys, it was just that he had started as a very obedient child and had grown and changed and colleagues didn't accept that he should change.

"As his tutor, I had to go over his reports with him. It was hard going. He would work if he liked a teacher or if the teacher had some sympathy, empathy is the word, I suppose. His reports were getting worse and he'd been sneaking off in the afternoons. I have to say that he took very little notice of the bad reports. We got on well enough but he wouldn't say much. I only know that, in spite of what anybody says, he was a very.... caring boy. There were only a few close friends and he was very loyal to them. If they got into trouble he always stood with them. It was his silence and his stubbornness that made people think him rude or surly."

"Was he always silent?"

"He was quiet from the beginning. It was only when he had reached the third year that his silences became deliberate, so to speak. For some, that was a lack of co-operation, for others it was insubordination or offensiveness. Some thought him untrustworthy but I would have trusted him far above most boys. There was something very sincere about him."

"Did you have contact with the aunt and uncle?"

"I met them once, when he first started the school. They were a diffident, self-effacing couple, very caring, anxious for him to do well. I got the impression that they were a very private family. They didn't talk about his parents, they simply said that they didn't know his father and that his mother had left him with them to bring up."

"You've never seen them since?"

"No. We sent a letter to them last term, reminding them of an important parents' meeting but they didn't turn up. I was sorry not to have the chance of talking with them."

"You've never been round to their house?"

"No. I've never felt that there was anything so urgent as to warrant disturbing them. I was so sure that he was going to grow out of his awkward stubbornness and that his natural intelligence would help him to recover."

"He never gave you a hint that there was anything disturbing him?"

"No."

"Did he confide in you?"

"Not really, though I think he trusted me. Once or twice, when he was in the third year, he talked to me about his difficulties with other teachers and their lessons, but, beyond that, no. He remained a very private boy and I respected his privacy."

"It's a pity you did, sir."

"What do you mean?"

"If you had probed a bit deeper, do you think that you might have unearthed something?"

"Not really. I had no idea that that there was anything seriously wrong and I doubt whether I could have got that close to him."

"Not even in hindsight?"

"Ah! In hindsight. Oh dear, Sergeant, what a terrible question! I shall be tormented for years by doubts. Would a visit to his home have made a difference? Was it anything to do with school? Could we have helped in any way?"

"We just don't know yet, Mr. Vane. Is there any particular thing that stands out in you memory over the last couple of weeks, anything at all that was unusual in his conduct, his appearance, his dress?"

Vane sat for several minutes, then shook his head.

"He was a boy who never showed his feelings. Whatever was going on inside didn't show, in any way. Could it have been a chance killing?"

"We have no idea, as yet. There doesn't appear to be a motive."

"It's just possible that he could have blundered into something, you think?"

"That, too, is a possibility. We only know that his

death was no accident."

"Well, if I can be a help in any way...." Hector Vane was genuinely upset.

"Thank you, Mr. Vane, if there is anything you remember let us know immediately." Bailey shook his hand and led him to the door.

Chapter Seven

The bell for the end of break had long gone. Another figure was waiting at the door as Hector Vane departed, a fair, freckled lad, blue eyed, big eared, tidily dressed. He was beckoned in.

"And you are?"

"Jim Hibbert." There was just a hint of a stammer.

"You knew Tommy Watson well?"

Bailey went through the same round of questions. Jim Hibbert lived not far from Tommy but had not really known him until he found himself working for the same newspaper shop. Since then they had been quite friendly. They were not in the same class, but were in the same set for certain subjects. He sometimes went with Tommy and Stewey Potts to the pictures. Not every week, he sometimes had to help his father at the weekends. His father had an invalid mother in Bardsley and Jim had to go and help from time to time. He had last seen Tommy at the paper shop on Saturday morning. They had chatted about their bikes. Jim had told him he would be with his Dad in the afternoon. Tommy had not said he was going anywhere. Jim did not know what his plans were for the weekend.

Tommy did not do well at school because he didn't bother. He knew a lot, though. They were seated for maths and Tommy had sometimes helped Jim during tests when Jim was stuck.

"Does that mean that Tommy did well in tests?"

"He always got good marks when he wanted to."

"Where did Tommy go during the week?"

Jim Hibbert looked at Bailey, puzzled.

"He always went home."

"He always went straight home after school?"

"Yes, I usually walked with him."

"Did he go out again at night?"

"Not that I know of."

"Isn't that a bit unusual?"

"Yes, I suppose it is really."

"You didn't see much of him then, except at school?"

"And at the weekends."

"He was pretty much on his own, you think?"

"Oh yes! That's why I didn't know him before the paper job."

"You mean he didn't have friends near his home?"

"I don't think there are many kids at all in Selborne Street. They're nearly all old folk."

"Did you know his aunt and uncle?"

"Just a bit. I was round at their house once. They were alright. His aunt was a bit fierce but his uncle was friendly."

"Did Tommy get along with his aunt and uncle?"

"Oh yes. He was proud of his uncle, he once punched big Jeff Sullivan for saying something about his uncle. I don't remember what it was. Sullivan was careful after that."

"Do you think that anything was worrying Tommy during that last week?"

"No. He was quite happy on Saturday morning."

Two more youths were sent along by Tom Hadley but they weren't really close to Tommy Watson. They had nothing to add and Bailey suspected that they were volunteers, escaping from their lesson to find out what was going on. They talked excitedly about the newspaper men who had been at school.

The next visitor was more illuminating.

Jane Mason could easily have been taken for eighteen. She was well developed and wore her school uniform as a fashion model might, swinging her hips gracefully. She had a trim figure and long, light hair,

48

not really blonde. She sat down, fluttering her eyelashes and crossing her legs self-consciously. She was very much aware of herself and of the handsome sergeant who was about to question her.

Bailey started on a different tack.

"How well did you know Tommy Watson?" he began and almost bit his tongue at the crudity of the question. Jane, however, thought it quite natural and launched into reasons why she had fancied Tommy.

"Did he fancy you then?"

"I don't think he did. He was very cool, but I was working on him." She gave Bailey a very knowing look and pulled at the hem of her pullover.

"Did you go out with him?"

"He was too shy, really. He was the strong and silent type."

"But you went about with him?"

"Sometimes we would sit beside him and Stewey Potts in the pictures."

"Did you know all his friends?"

"He didn't have many friends. I was a bit sorry for him."

"Did he have other girl friends?"

"No. I think he was a bit young for girlfriends really. You know what I mean." She grinned and again looked meaningfully at the sergeant, who avoided her glance.

"When did you last see him?"

"Saturday night."

"When and where, on Saturday night?"

"I was going to the pictures, the Roxy, and I saw him outside."

"You had arranged to go with him?"

"No.....I didn't know he was going until I saw him outside."

"Did he speak to you?"

"No. He was talking, so I walked across, ready to

follow him in."

"Did he go in?"

"No," she pouted, "He was standing in the light right outside the door one minute then he was gone the next. I thought he'd gone in, but there was no sign of him when we got inside."

"Who's we?"

"Angela Thurrock. I blame her. She came up to me and started talking so that I had to take my eyes off him. I was right vexed at the time. We went in together. We looked everywhere in the interval when the lights went up, but he wasn't there."

"Did you see who he was talking to?"

"Somebody in a cap."

"You didn't recognise him as anyone you knew?"

"A stranger, that's all. He only spoke for a minute, then waved his arm and walked off."

"You were too far off to hear what was said, I suppose?"

"He only spoke for a minute."

"You are sure it was Tommy Watson?"

"Sure I'm sure!" She crossed her legs the opposite way just to emphasise the infallibility of the feminine instinct.

"You couldn't describe this stranger, could you?"

"It was Tommy I was looking at! This man was tall, taller than Tommy. Wore a raincoat and a cap, that's all."

"What colour raincoat?"

"Oh, Fawn, I think. It wasn't dark, I know."

"What age do you think he was?"

"Thirties, not old, not young."

"Could they have walked off together?"

"The man was just going away when Angela stuck her nose in. I thought Tommy had gone in."

"Did Tommy Watson go to the pictures every

week?"

"I don't know, well, I think he did most weeks."

"Good picture or not?"

"I don't know, I've just recently taken an interest."

"In films or in Tommy?" He couldn't resist it.

She scowled, a little uncertain for a moment, but her smile returned.

"Tommy, of course."

"Did he ever go alone?"

"I don't know. Usually he went with Stewey or Hibbert or Robert Shaw."

"I haven't seen Shaw yet, is he outside?"

"No, he's in hospital, Robert. He was taken away with a bad attack of yellow jaundice."

"When was that?"

"The ambulance came on Sunday morning. He lives just opposite me. I saw them take him away."

"Do you think that Angela saw Tommy and the man he was talking to?"

"What, Angela? I doubt it. She wouldn't notice a horse if it sat on her!"

"Thank you, Jane, you have been very helpful...."

"Have I?"

Jane Mason stood up reluctantly, gave her skirt a shake and a twist, opened her eyes wide and asked, in her deepest voice,

"Will you want to see me again?"

"It is just possible..."

"Goody! Be seeing yer!"

"Now that's the reason why coppers should go about in twos, Ridley!"

"A real hot little cookie, Sarge. She looked nearly twice her age!"

"I think that we should have a word with Angela Thurrock, just to clinch things."

51

Jane Mason had been right. Angela Thurrock turned out to be a dizzy blond, plump, bespectacled and probably giggly. When she came to see them, she was far from giggly. She was overawed and frightened that policemen should want to speak to her. She confirmed that she went to the pictures with Jane Mason but said that she hadn't seen Tommy Watson at all. Jane had said that Tommy had gone into the cinema and they had looked everywhere for him in the interval but they hadn't seen him.

Chapter Eight

As he left No. 22, Hart noticed a team of D.C.s moving from door to door, further up the street. He smiled with satisfaction and hoped they would not take too long, he wanted to have the reports on his desk before the end of the day.

He thought about the Grants' back yard and regretted that he had not seen beyond the back door. He would do that now. He pushed past the reporters who tried to cling to his elbows and walked briskly to the end of the street, turned right along the side of No. 24, then right again into the back lane.

There were no surprises. The lane was narrow, just room for delivery vans or dustcarts. There was no pavement on either side. The higgledy-piggledy nature of the fences on the other side of the lane clearly spelt out allotments, but they were all too high to see over. All sorts of timber and scrap had been used to build these fences. He could identify floorboard planks, railway sleepers, pieces of old shed, occasional panels of corrugated iron, strips of plywood and patches of tea-chest. There were even old wooden doors with their paint peeling, jammed into place between posts. Absent-mindedly, he stretched out a hand to open one but there weren't any fittings and he knew that none of these allotments would open directly onto the lane.

Half way down the lane was the opening, a narrow earth track that led to the heart of this horticultural realm. He strode along it a little way and paused to take in the whole scene. From where he stood he had a good view, since the land stretched in a gradual slope for about half of a mile until it reached a railway embankment, its natural boundary. He was astonished how big these allotments were. He guessed that they were all the same size, roughly, but they looked very different from each other because of the variety of sheds that stood on most of them. He didn't think there were many allotments without a shed, some had two or three. He could make out the occasional pigeon loft, taller and more brightly painted than the sheds and there were henhouses too, the sound of hens was quite close.

Some allotments had small trees and bushes, others had fruit cages. Most, as far as he could see standing on tip-toe, were devoted to raising vegetables. There was a common pattern of rows of green and brown. He wondered which was Victor Grant's and was cross with himself for not asking to be shown his allotment. Perhaps he could come back later in the afternoon while it was still light. By then, maybe, Bailey would be free to go with him. He felt that there was a connection with the allotment, hadn't the boy been watching it?

He looked down and saw that the earth track was soft in places. Here and there, allotment holders had sought to make the path less bumpy by filling in the hollows with stones and the occasional half brick dug from their plots. There was plenty of long grass at the sides of the path and there was enough soft earth to make it possible for tracks to show. He was thinking of the bicycle.

He was also thinking of his own childhood, of a long walk with his grandfather to visit his Great Uncle Fred's allotment. He had been very small at that time and the narrow lane had presented many hazards, not least a profusion of stinging nettles. His grandfather had brushed past them but he had dragged behind, only too aware of the vulnerability of his bare knees. He recalled the feeling of being let down because Great Uncle Fred had not been in his allotment and that the visit had been in vain and the nettles had to be negotiated again all too soon. He had found a gap in the fencing and longed to look through to discover what lay beyond but his grandfather wouldn't wait, simply asking him if he was tired and urging him to keep up. The high wooden fences, many of them creosoted, dark and rich smelling, made him think of primitive castle walls. A dog behind one of the fences had barked fiercely as they passed, turning that allotment into a sinister lair. It was not really surprising that, for a long time after that walk, he had thought there was something mysterious and alluring about allotments.

This was not a time for daydreaming, he told himself firmly. He returned to the car and, negotiating a narrow three point turn, drove back to the office.

Hart went carefully through the statements the Grants had given to Bailey and checked them with what they had told him, making a few notes of his own. He went over them again in his mind then reached for the other reports on his desk. He studied the photographs of the body and sat back. Not much to go on, yet.

He reached for his phone and asked the station sergeant if there were any D.C.s available.

"What? All out? Someone's keeping them at it! I wonder who? I suppose I'll have to do my own dirty work. Would you get Pomfret's Engineering on the phone for me, yes, Blaney Road Works, I think."

"Detective Chief Inspector Hart, Clayton Police, here, I would like to speak to your Personnel Manager. Yes. Ah, I wonder if you could help us. I'm wanting to trace a Victor Grant, joined your firm about 1940 or thereabouts, left in 1946. Yes, it is a long time ago but your records will go back a lot further than that. He left to go to sea, your company gave him a reference. No, I don't know his date of birth, I only know his address, 22 Selborne Street......he was 21 when he left, presumably he had finished his apprenticeship. No, I don't suppose you can tell me immediately. When you find out, would you please phone me? Thank you very much. It is most urgent. Good-bye."

"Sergeant, get me Firby High School, please."

"Mrs. Sanderson, D.C.I. Hart, Clayton police, could I speak to the headmaster, Mr. Higthorpe, isn't it? Good morning, Mr. Higthorpe, sorry to trouble you, would the school have any recent photographs of classes or teams, we haven't been able to get a recent photograph of Thomas Watson? Yes. A sportsman? I couldn't say. Could you ask him to have a word with Sergeant Bailey, I'd be very grateful.....Oh dear, I'm sorry about that, he is very young and eager to get on with things, I'm sorry if you were offended, I'm sure he wouldn't have meant to be rude. I shall certainly have a word with him. Thank you, good-bye."

Hart went off to lunch feeling a small sense of achievement.

When he returned, he was rather surprised to find Bailey back at his desk.

"So soon? Did the headmaster give you the cane? Well, he should have done! He's been complaining about you pushing him about."

Bailey grinned.

"I only suggested he find us a room and let us get on with it. If I hadn't, he would have had us waiting for morning break and lunch-time."

"Yes, I think he probably would, but you can't go leaping in without making sure the management is happy. Whether you like the management or not you have to keep it happy if you want co-operation. Anyway, did you see everybody concerned?"

"Yes, Ridley and Phillips are typing up their reports now."

56

"Did you manage to get a photograph?"

"No, but the games teacher said that Tommy Watson was a good runner and should be on a team photograph from last summer's sports day. He promised to seek it out, if he still has one."

"You did tell him it was urgent? We must get some publicity out. We have nothing to go on. We depend on 'last sightings'. The Grants don't have a family album. They don't have any recent photographs of Tommy."

"Surely, everybody has photographs of their family?"

"Not the Grants. They're a strange pair. The house is spick and span ... and dead. They have a son, by the way, went off to sea before Tommy was born. I suspect his clearing off made them introverted, or made them more introverted, I don't think there was ever much natural joy in Edie Grant. She must have taken on the boy out of obligation, I suspect she brought him up without much affection and that is why the boy wasn't communicative."

"What happened to the sister, Tommy's mother?"

"I don't know and I'm not sure that it's important, except that it must have troubled the boy as he grew older. The atmosphere in that house couldn't have been good for him. No one talking. Things that couldn't be mentioned. An undercurrent of guilt and anger. I look forward to what the neighbours have to tell us."

"He must have wondered who his father was."

"It could have been anyone. It was after the end of the war, it just might have been a soldier on leave, someone she met casually."

"Sir, I found the Grants very uncommunicative. It could be that they were hiding something...."

Hart shook his head gently.

"They might be. There might be things they don't talk about but they are genuinely shocked at the death of the boy and I don't think they had anything to do with it."

Bailey's youthful enthusiasm was not dinted.

"I do have a sighting, a Jane Mason, provocative little piece, saw him outside the Roxy on the Saturday night. She saw him talking to a man in a cap and light raincoat, she thought he was going in, another girl distracted her so that she didn't actually see him go in. She looked for him in the interval but he wasn't there."

"Any corroboration?"

"The other girl confirms the search for him but she didn't see him or the person he was talking to outside."

"We need to get onto that as soon as we have a photograph. It's a forlorn hope but, perhaps the girl in the box office will remember. How about a photo-fit?"

"It was a Saturday night, sir, they're always busy."

"I might say that it doesn't fit in with Edie Grant's account. She says that the boy didn't go out again after his tea."

"What else did you get?"

"Nothing much. A depressing picture, I'm afraid. I'm glad I don't go to that school. It's an old secondary modern in the process of going comprehensive. It has some of the ideas of the new comprehensive but none of the new atmosphere. They have setting for many subjects instead of rigid classes and they have housemasters and tutors instead of class teachers. That's about it. Tommy Watson's housemaster was a self-important little..er..he hadn't a good word for him. What was most interesting, Tommy had the habit of absenting himself two or three times a month. He came to school then sneaked off, usually in the afternoons. Not even his closest mates knew where he went. He never talked much, annoyed just about everyone with his silence, staff and classmates, did well when he felt

58

like it, opted out when he felt like it..."

"Like most schoolboys."

"Played up with his silent obstinacy. Gave as good as he got, just about sums it up. They all said he was a good worker when he first went but he became awkward and unco-operative as he got older. No one noticed anything particular about him in the last week or so, not even his few friends."

"None of the staff had a good word for him?"

"His tutor, a man called Vane, had quite a lot of sympathy for him, he seemed an understanding sort of bloke. He hadn't noticed any change either."

"Was Tommy bright?"

"The general picture was that he was bright but underachieving. He did well in his first two years. He was in the 'O' level stream but wasn't bothered."

"Well, that's not an unusual story for a boy of his age and, given his background, it might be expected. How does it all tie in with his murder?"

The telephone rang at Hart's elbow.

"Hart. Oh, thank you for ringing, Yes. But I was given to understand that he had obtained a reference from you. This is what he told his parents. You don't know anything more, for instance, did he ever ask for a reference at a later date? Did he complete his apprenticeship? No record of enquiries? So that was the last of him as far as you are concerned. Well, thank you for your trouble, Oh, one last thing, was he ever in trouble with you, did he have a clean record? Right, I'm very much obliged."

"That was Pomfrets, the engineering firm down Blaney Road, the Grant's son, Victor, was apprenticed there. He left home fifteen years ago, telling them he was going to sea and that Pomfrets had given him the necessary reference. They knew nothing about it and were both shocked. They never saw him again, never tried to trace him. If, as that watch says, Tommy was born on June 17th. 1947, young Victor never knew about him. He left home before the birth. Tommy's mother left as soon after the birth as she could. It may not be important to the case but it keeps the picture clear. Incidentally, there is no record of misbehaviour while Victor was at work. The company's report simply said that his apprenticeship had been successful and that he had been punctual and his work had been of an acceptable standard, scarcely high praise, but not a stick to beat him with."

"Pomfrets aren't marine engineers, Sir."

"There are no marine engineers in this area but that doesn't mean a time-served fitter couldn't get a job on a ship."

"It still sounds odd to me, times aren't all that easy for getting jobs at sea. I would have been suspicious if I had been his father."

"Sergeant Bailey, you do sound old-fashioned! Don't forget we are talking about fifteen years ago."

"Why wasn't he traced?"

"His mother was bitter, she felt it was his obligation to keep in touch, not hers."

"That doesn't seem natural to me. Do you believe that, sir?"

"I believe that of Edie Grant. But I can't help thinking that there has to be a stronger reason for leaving home apart from reaching 21 and finishing an apprenticeship - and dodging a bossy mother. Records might help us."

"You think he might have a record? Wouldn't the parents have known, Sir?"

"Not necessarily. They might be hiding it, of course, but I don't think so. I'm sure they were straightforward. Check records anyway."

Hart was silent for a few moments.

"If something happened to persuade young Victor Grant to run away to sea it might well be something recorded in another place, the local paper. That's the place to find out what happened in 1946. Fetch Ridley in, he's just the man to check for us."

D.C. Ridley was despatched to the office of "The Gazette" to study every newspaper of that year.

"Isn't there a particular date or event you are looking for, Sir?" Ridley had been dismayed at the enormity of the task.

"No. I know that Master Victor Grant left Pomfrets on September 30th. 1946, but that date is simply important as the day he was clear of his apprenticeship contract. Whatever may have been instrumental in causing him to leave home might have occurred months before, even years."

Ridley had not been comforted by this thought and had left as quickly as possible.

"Now, while it is still light, let's go and have a look at Victor Grant's allotment."

Chapter Nine

There was no sign of the reporters when Hart and Bailey arrived at No. 22 Selborne Street. This time it was Victor Grant who opened the door. He explained that his wife was out shopping. Hart was not unhappy about this, he knew that he would have easier co-operation from Victor while Edie was out. They explained the reason for their visit and Victor fetched the keys, let them out of the back door and led the way down the path to his allotment.

He had kept his allotment well. The fence was in good condition all round. Like most of the others, it consisted partly of stakes, partly of panels and partly of planks. The gate was an old door with its original white paint weathering away interestingly. The fence wasn't one of the highest, they could see over it with a stretch. Inside, the vegetable patch showed signs of regular attention. There was a small compost heap in one corner and, nearby, a place where rubbish was burnt. A wheelbarrow stood at the ready next to it and beside it was an old box with empty plastic bags folded neatly inside it.. In the far corner at the right stood a small, gleaming greenhouse. Hart could see that the shelves were full of plant pots in orderly groups. Next to it stood several outsize plant pots and a number of trays of small ones. Immediately to their right was a large shed, recently creosoted. It had all the signs of care and attention that an amateur builder would bestow on a motley assortment of used timbers.

Victor unlocked the padlock and beckoned them in. It was dark and cold. There were some narrow shelves along the back wall with old tins of paint and turpentine, jars of screws and nails, stakes and string, oil cans, old door handles and all manner of small hardware items awaiting re-use. An old wooden form stood on the floor beneath them and at one end was a hutch partly covered by a tarpaulin. The smell was quite distinctive.

"This is where young Tommy kept his rabbits. Look! Here are the two new ones."

"You had to make a new hutch?"

"Yes, look, over here, I've got a bench and some tools."

"Why would the vandals wreck the hutch?"

"Oh, they did more than that. They almost wrecked the shed. Mind you, it wasn't in much of a condition. The floorboards had some rot and the window was broken. It gave me an excuse to rebuild the whole thing."

"You had vandals in here?" Bailey needed to be brought up to date.

"Yes, they broke the padlock and forced their way in. They destroyed Tommy's hutch and strangled some of the rabbits. We think the others got away."

"Why would vandals want to get in here?" Bailey persisted.

"Perhaps they were lads who knew the rabbits were here."

"But why smash up the shed after they had killed the rabbits?"

"Oh, I couldn't tell you that. People do such terrible things without reason."

"Did they steal anything?"

"No, there's nothing much worth stealing, the tools are fairly old."

"But you checked?"

"Yes, there was nothing missing."

"If they wanted to smash things, why didn't they smash up the greenhouse?"

The thought made Victor Grant wince. Hart interrupted.

"You never reported it to the police Mr. Grant?"

"No, there was nothing anyone could do. It was more important to get on with repairing the damage."

"Was any other allotment shed broken into at the time?" Bailey was following his line tenaciously.

"No, I don't think there was. From time to time there is some pilfering, that's why the fences are high and everyone has a lock. It isn't much, because it is too far for anyone to carry things away, all these paths. People wouldn't break in unless they knew there was something to steal. I reckon they broke in here because they'd heard of Tommy's prize rabbits and they were jealous. That's what I think."

"You may be right, Mr. Grant. Is the light from the window strong enough to see by?"

"If I'm working in here, I usually leave the door open for extra light. I don't often come down here after dark. No reason. There's a storm lamp to see by, if I do come down."

"Was the storm lamp used by whoever broke in?"

"I didn't think of it at the time, but much later, when I came to move it I found it was empty."

"You're sure about that?"

"Yes, it was a big surprise because I had filled it not long before and it should have lasted for hours when it was full. I only fill it once or twice a year at most."

Bailey peered round impatiently. He couldn't see much point in this visit. He well knew his Chief's insistence on getting to know the backgrounds of his cases but he saw little hope in linking a spot of vandalism here with a murder a mile away. Besides he was feeling cold. There was a chilly breeze from the east telling him that he was a little underdressed for the outdoors.

"What are these targets, here, Mr. Grant?"

Hart pointed to three cardboard targets pinned to the

wall below the shelves. They were faded and dirty but it was still possible to see groups of holes close to their centres.

"Someone has been a good shot, are they yours?"

"Oh them! I've had them for years. I took up shooting when I was in the Home Guard. I used to be a good shot in those days but I haven't done any since. Tommy found them one day and put them up here. Edie was going to throw them out but Tommy rescued them."

They took a walk round the allotment, talking rather aimlessly about the vegetables and the planning of the work concerned in growing them.

"You haven't thought of growing fruit here?"

"I have had some bushes, I were very fond of gooseberries at one time, but the birds tended to get most of them. I've still got a few raspberry canes and over there are some strawberries. That's all I can do with. I used to have some rhubarb. Four or five crowns, over there, but, a year or so before I started the shed I dug them out. Edie wasn't so keen on rhubarb, anyway that's where the shed had to go."

They hadn't taken long but the light was beginning to fade. At the gate, Hart paused, took out a penknife and prised away a fragment of paint. Without speaking to the others, he found an envelope inside his jacket and dropped the fragments of paint into it. Victor was too busy wrestling with the padlock to notice. Bailey was taking a last look over the fence.

"By the way, Mr. Grant, did Tommy have a key to the allotment?"

"Oh, no, he didn't need to. The key stays on a hook behind the kitchen door."

"Did your son, Victor, ever help you in the allotment?"

"Yes, sometimes. I thought I had him going on a

65

patch of his own, but he weren't keen enough."

"Nobody shared this allotment with you at any time, did they Mr. Grant?"

"No, it was always my private place. Just the boys when they felt like it. Not even Edie came all the way down here."

In the car on the way back, Hart explained to his sergeant that he had taken the paint fragments because there were traces of white paint on the tips of Tommy Watson's plimsolls.

"This boy Tommy Watson was careful with his clothes, for a fourteen year old. He had to be, hadn't he? Those marks with the white paint could well be the result of climbing or sliding down something like a wall or a door shortly before he died. There may be nothing to it, boys will be boys, but he was watching the allotment for intruders and may have followed someone down there and climbed up to see what they were up to."

"Could be, Sir."

Bailey felt tired. It had been a busy day and he had lost sleep recently. His wife was pregnant with their first child and was restless during the night. He had had to get up to fetch her water or tea, even food. He sometimes felt that his chief was relentless. Hart, unmindful of Bailey's new problems, thought his sergeant's concentration was slipping. Abruptly, he tested him.

"Were your eyes open? What did you see?"

"See, Sir? You mean the shed?"

"Shed? No, I don't think there was anything odd about the shed."

He looked sideways at his sergeant.

"You usually have sharp eyes. You aren't coming down with a cold, are you? It's the wrong time if you are!"

Bailey wondered whether he should talk about his domestic problems but thought better of it. With such a serious matter as a murder enquiry going on he thought it inappropriate, it would sound as if he was whinging.

"Well, it may not have meant anything to you, but Victor Grant doesn't smoke and doesn't believe his nephew smoked yet there were two cigarette ends near the shed and one near the wheelbarrow."

"That's why you asked him if anyone else came to the allotment...but they could have been left by whoever vandalised the shed or by Tommy Watson's friends, he had that packet on him, Sir."

"They may not mean anything. They could have been left by a casual visitor, but, from what you have seen of the Grants, do you think they had many casual visitors? Even at the allotment?"

Bailey was silent. It was a very small straw and he was a little niggled at being found wanting about such a small thing. He wasn't to know that the Grant family were non-smokers. They travelled for a while in silence but silence was much less preferable to Hart's banter. Bailey spoke up.

"Why was his body left in Chevely Park, sir?"

"I'm not sure. Chevely Park is nearly a mile from his home, it's way out on the edge of town, but it's sheltered by trees on two sides and the railway line on the other. It shouldn't have been too hard to move the body there without being seen. The nearest main road is over the embankment beyond the trees. The only open entrance is from the housing estate."

"Whoever they were, they wouldn't risk coming through the estate would they? Too many eyes, even at night."

"They could have come from the other side of the line but there are two live rails to negotiate in the dark.

67

And where would they be coming from, there's nothing on the other side."

"A vehicle could come right up to the gate but it might arouse suspicion late at night. It couldn't come into the park because it would be difficult to turn. We didn't find any tyre tracks. We are assuming he was brought there in a vehicle. What if he was killed on the estate somewhere? He could have been carried into the park."

"Well, we are clutching at straws at the moment. We don't know where he was killed or why. We only know that he was dumped in Chevely Park. My guess is that there wasn't time to bury the body or get rid of it in any other way. They left it in a quiet spot where it wouldn't be found immediately...."

"They didn't attempt to hide it, did they? It was at the side of the bushes, not behind them. Was that deliberate, Sir?"

"Probably they were worried that they may have been seen if they lingered. That suggests that it was at a time when people might still have been about."

"Do you think that by putting it in a public place like a park, they were hoping to suggest that the boy was killed by a vagrant or a stranger or someone casual?"

"Could be, but I think it was more simple than that. It was an available space, that's all. We will have to start a door to door at the estate....if ever we get a reasonable photograph of Tommy Watson."

They were lucky. The games master from Firby High School had left two photographs for them at the station. They were not official photographs they were snapshots, one of a group of contestants and one of three winners. They were runners in a variety of kit. There was no doubting Tommy Watson, partly because he was in the centre of the three winners, partly because he had unusually light coloured eyes. The two detectives studied the photographs carefully.

"Not too clear are they, sir?"

"They aren't, are they? I think the team photo is the better bet. It's slightly sharper and the boy looks more relaxed. Yes, that's the one, we'll have that blown up and see what it looks like on a poster. Now, I'm going home, I need a good feed. Then I'm going to tackle those statements. I suggest you do the same and meet me back here at 8."

Chapter Ten

At 8p.m. Hart began working on the results of the door to door enquiries of Selborne Street. Sergeant Bailey sat at another table checking through the statements that D.C.s Ridley and Phillips had brought back from the school. He was the first to break the silence.

"Sir, these statements from school are all pretty much the same. Nobody saw anything different about him right up until he went missing. Does it not suggest that this was a random killing?"

"You mean a happenchance crime, not a premeditated one?"

"Yes, the boy is out on his bicycle, gets involved in something unexpectedly and is killed...."

"He sees something he shouldn't and is murdered so as not to speak as a witness? Don't forget that his bike was left at home......well, you can do some different checking, local violent attacks. There is one thing we can be thankful for, this isn't a sex killing, according to the doctor, so you will be looking for violence rather than deviance."

"Anything interesting in the house to house of Selborne Street?"

"It's absolutely amazing how little the neighbours knew about either the Grants or their nephew. It seems that the people of Selborne Street kept themselves to themselves. Anyway, that's as far as I've got. Now, push off and do those checks, or you'll be here all night."

Hart shuffled his pile of statements and sighed. They were a very mixed bunch. He wasn't satisfied that they were equally thorough, he wondered what sort of training his men had that the statements should be so different in character, he would have to have a word with them. Nevertheless, he knew in his bones that, however the thinner statements might be expanded, they would reveal little more if anything at all.

The residents at the near end of the street knew least about the Grants, except for the Fosters at No.10 who knew Tommy well. The Fosters were friendly folk who took time to chat to their newsboy and who employed him regularly to wash their car. They were shocked by his death because they had taken an interest in him. They were in their early forties and were lively. They had a son of 20, away at University. He had played football in the lane with Tommy when they were both younger but, partly because of the age gap and partly because they went to different schools, they had grown apart. Sunday had been a normal day for them. Husband, a keen gardener, had spent most of the morning in his allotment. They had taken a run in their car over the Hempstead Hills in the afternoon and had tea out. T.V. in the evening and early bed. They could add nothing of interest. They hadn't seen Tommy that morning.

Now that was a good statement. Hart thought that he knew the Fosters after reading that statement. He particularly liked the comment about the Fosters being 'lively'. It helped to make the statement more meaningful. He paid closer attention to those concerning the nearer neighbours.

At No.18 lived the Nesbits, in their 80s, they had lived there for nearly 60 years. Knew the Grants by sight. Knew Tommy, he delivered their papers, he was very polite, a quiet boy. They liked him and were upset at the news of his death. They seldom left their house and had not seen him for several days. On Sunday they had had their nephew and his wife for the day. They hadn't gone out. They had not been troubled by noise or anything unusual. They rarely heard anything outside the house as they both suffered from increasing deafness.

At 19, the Drysdales were a couple in their 60s, had lived in Selborne Street for four years, had employed Tommy Watson to wash their car for nearly a year, ever since they had seen him washing a neighbour's car. He had washed their car last Sunday morning, he was as thorough as ever and had been as quiet and serious as ever. They had not noticed anything unusual about him.

At 23, lived the Harrisons, mid-fifties, both worked as librarians. Lived there since first married. Knew Tommy since he was little. Polite, well behaved, had to be, Mrs. Grant very strict. Hadn't seen him for some time. Out all day Sunday visiting relations, got back about midnight, didn't see or hear anything unusual.

At 24, next door to the Grants, lived Mr. and Mrs. Butterman, again in their fifties, unmarried son 32 living with them. Sidney Butterman was a draughtsman, his son was also a draughtsman but was currently free-lancing. Mr. and Mrs. Butterman went to church on the Sunday, Mr. Butterman was a sidesman. Late lunch. Quiet afternoon, reading newspapers and watching T.V. Had a visitor for tea, went to church again in the evening, as always. Son, John, had been out all weekend staying with friends at Northrop... Hart immediately checked on a map behind him. Northrop was a village about 10 miles to the north east...got back in the early hours of Monday. They knew the Grants reasonably well, thought Tommy well behaved, were shocked at his death. Had no idea what the boy 'got up to'. They didn't see very much of him.

Hart checked back through all the statements and flung them into a filing tray in disgust. Incredibly, there were four or five couples who had lived in Selborne Street for thirty years yet had no idea who the Grants were and who hardly knew their immediate neighbours

72

on either side. There were a number who had briefly glimpsed their paper boy yet had not known that he had lived in the same street. The average age of the inhabitants was over sixty, not surprisingly, since there were three couples of over 70 and two over 80. It appeared that there were three recent arrivals, they had lived in that street for less than five years. None of them was young. There were no young children. Hart calculated that within ten years, if there were no changes, every individual inhabitant could be retired.

Why did they not know more? Did they not see Edie Grant go shopping? Did they not talk to her in the butcher's or the baker's? Did they not walk in the same street? Surely some activity was shared and some exchange of conversation was made? Why didn't those who had their cars washed bother to talk to the boy? Seemingly it was a case of "Thank you, here's the money."

He looked at his street map. The majority of local shops were on Headlaw Road, four blocks away, or three by the crow flies. That wasn't too far, even for Edie Grant who was at the opposite end of Selborne Street. Alternatively, she could cut down the end of Selborne Street via the side lane to The Causeway where she could catch a bus into the city or to the nearest large shops. He sighed. That could be it. She would have avoided all contact with her neighbours in Selborne Street by shopping some distance away. But why should she do that? He couldn't leave it. He would send someone round to all the shops in the area and check.

There were things he needed to know himself, these statements were not telling him what he needed to know. He would go round to the Fosters and the Buttermans tomorrow. He would need to get a statement from the Butterman's son anyway. Meantime he had to wait to see what Ridley and Bailey could turn up. At this time of night, he was not the most patient of men. A whole day had gone by and he was no nearer understanding a possible motive for this killing. All the statements, so far, were the same - all unhelpful. He sat back in his chair and went over it all again in his mind.

His phone rang. It was Ridley from the offices of the Gazette. He had looked at every copy of the paper for 1946, nothing of significance, nothing exciting locally, a few road accidents, one or two burglaries, none of them involved anyone called Grant. Plenty of weddings, funerals and planning applications. Could he leave it until tomorrow? Hart growled his discontent into the mouthpiece.

"To be fair, sir, I don't really know what I'm looking for...and I haven't eaten since lunch."

"Oh alright, constable, leave it! Call in here tomorrow morning and I might have something more for you to go on. You may have to go through 1945."

D.C. Ridley stifled a groan and rushed off to fortify himself.

Bailey returned soon after this with a folder in his hand.

"Sir, there are three villains on our patch who could fit this job. All are violent and free at the moment."

He handed the folder to his chief who took it eagerly.

"Jefferson, Albert Edward, 43, Breaking and entering, Assaulting a constable, 3 years; brawling outside a public house, bound over; robbery with violence, 5 years. Married with three children, Penshaw Road. Employed as bricklayer at Fletcher's for last three years. Going straight! His last conviction was nine years ago. He doesn't sound right.

"Bates, George Arthur, 35, Single, Wilson Street, G.B.H. Oh, I remember that case. Fell out with his

74

brother in law. Lay in wait for him near the bridge at Welby and was lucky not to be charged with attempted murder. That wasn't so long ago, yes, four years ago, he'll hardly be out yet."

"He got four years for that, Sir, but with good behaviour he will almost certainly be out now."

"Fenton, James Antony, 30, married with four children, Ice cream vendor, Accessory to robbery, probation; G.B.H. 2 years; violent temper, served full term. That was over two years ago, Sergeant, I don't think that any of these three....a strangling...."

"But look at the address, Sir, Ogilvie Drive, it's part of the Chevely Park Estate and he's still got his ice cream van."

"Oh, come now, Sergeant, you are putting two and two together and making a clear dozen."

"I know it's just speculation, Sir, but we have to start somewhere. It is a vehicle, it is well known and wouldn't cause suspicion moving about at night."

The D.C.I. stared steadily at his Sergeant for a long time but he didn't shake the young man's conviction.

"All we have to do is ask a few questions and look over the van, Sir, all routine stuff."

"Right, Sergeant, he's yours, as far as the preliminaries go. Start first thing in the morning. I'm running a door to door of the Chevely Park Estate as soon as we have that photo printed. You could always use that as your excuse to interview him."

Chapter Eleven

The following day was exceptionally busy for the squad at Welbeck Road police station. Photographs had been printed on handbills and as many constables as possible had been mustered and briefed before departing to make the door to door enquiries at Chevely Park estate. A few had been detailed to enquire of the shops in Headlaw Road. D.C.Ridley had been sent back to the offices of the Gazette. Detective Sergeant Bailey had departed on his specific mission to interview James Antony Fenton. Superintendent Gresham had looked into Hart's office to enquire how things were going and had received a very simple answer.

As soon as possible, Hart himself slipped out. He needed to return to Selborne Street. He was happy to drive, feeling that he needed to be more familiar with the area, to know the streets Tommy Watson cycled along, to sense the daily life of these people. It was all too easy for him to become office bound. He drove down Headlaw Road, taking care to glimpse each street leading off to his left. He was looking for alternative shops, small confectioners or barbers. After some negotiations with the busy morning traffic he turned off and proceeded more slowly. At the end of this particular street was a small general dealer's, he pulled in.

The door to this shop gave a cheerful, loud clang as it opened and the multitude of cards and posters on it scattered and flapped an undoubted welcome. There was an immediate smell of warm bread with a hint of spice in the air. Hart's memory stirred. While it was scrupulously clean, the shop was old-fashioned enough to have a rough wooden floor, high counter and wooden shelves reaching right to the ceiling. There was a flypaper dangling incongruously above one end of the counter. The shelves were stacked very neatly and distinctly, labels were small but clearly written. Little daylight managed to pass through the tightly packed window display, but it didn't matter for there were two unadorned light bulbs dispensing a warm glow over the centre of the shop and counter. The counter itself was crowded with open boxes and trays of biscuits, cakes and sweets. There was abundance but no confusion. This was a shop to test the senses, a shop to linger in. As he walked further in, Hart's nose detected a magical mixture of aniseed, string, pine, lemon, candle wax and shoe polish.

The proprietor was a man in his fifties, tall and slightly stooped. His voice was friendly yet firm enough to be business-like and to discourage wafflers. Below a pair of shaggy eyebrows lay humorous still grey eyes. Hart thought that if he wasn't a happy man himself, he could envy this man, his temperament seemed so well adjusted to his work and his contentment in it was so manifest.

"Good morning, I'm glad that you are quiet for a moment, I need to ask you a few questions."

He produced his warrant card and introduced himself.

"I'm concerned with the death of this young lad Thomas Watson. Did you ever come across his relations, Victor and Edie Grant? Were they ever customers of yours?"

The man behind the counter looked hard at Hart and thought for a brief moment.

"I'm Bert Hardman, I knew Victor Grant years ago..."

The doorbell clanged and two women pushed in, talking loudly.

"Cissie! Can you come through?" Hardman shouted through the door into the room behind the shop.

A tiny woman with white hair combed back severely into a bun hurried in. She had a well-scrubbed face, a sharp pinched nose and bright, light brown eyes. Hart immediately thought of a mouse, where else would a mouse be more at home?

"Excuse me, I've got to have a word with this gentleman. Come on through will you?" Hardman beckoned Hart through into a small sitting room, comfortable with cushions.

"I read about it of course. A terrible thing!"

"You said you knew Victor Grant?"

"Yes, we were apprentices together at Clarksons. That was long before the war of course. Hard times but happy days. We used to go dancing together. He was light on his feet young Victor in those days, the girls all fell for him."

Bert Hardman smiled broadly at the memory.

"I was sometimes jealous of him. He seemed to have the pick and I was often left out, but we were always friends. Then I got married and we didn't see much of each other anymore."

"Did you know his wife, Edie?"

"Oh yes. Edie was quite a looker in those days. Her name was Watson then. She lived up the turnpike in one of the new houses. Her parents were well off, they had a draper's shop in Cuffley and they had a car. Those were the days when hardly anybody had a car. I remember that it was a little Austin 7."

"Did Edie go dancing too?"

"Yes. It was at the old Co-op Hall. That was where all the big dances were held in those days. It's not there now, it burned down ten or twelve years back. A shame, it was the heart of the place. Anyway, she turned up and became a regular dancing partner for Victor. She was a bright young thing. I thought she was a bit flashy, myself. She was never short of new clothes, her father being a draper, I suppose. She was very keen on Victor but I don't think he was so very keen on her at first. Then I started courting Cissie and dropped out of the dancing. We got married and moved away to Fallowfield. The next thing I heard, Victor and Edie had got married."

"You haven't seen them recently?"

"No, I didn't realise that they lived in this area until I read the paper."

"You never saw him after he married?"

"No, Edie was very possessive and took him away from most of his friends, I believe."

"How long have you lived here, Mr. Hardman?"

"Since September 3rd. 1939. The day war broke out! Impossible to forget. I never finished my apprenticeship. We wanted to get married as soon as possible. I needed money and took to labouring. Lang's the builder. I was lucky, I was never laid off. We saved like mad, Cissie had a job as a typist. We made up our minds to be independent, we knew that we could be out of jobs at any time, people were being laid off all over the place. We had our hearts set on a little shop. Somehow we managed it, the luck held. We had just enough for the deposit, the insurance and the stock. Had the business not been settled when it was, we would never have had a shop of our own, the war would have finished us. As it was, I was called up and Cissie had to manage for three years on her own, then I was invalided out and everything came right. She was a brick all through those hard times. Neither of us has ever regretted it."

"Victor Grant was called up was he?"

"No, he finished his apprenticeship and stayed on at Clarksons. It was a reserved occupation, war work, you see."

"If Victor Grant was in full employment all these

years, shouldn't he be fairly comfortably off now?"

"Oh, I should imagine so, the paper said they lived in Selborne Street. They were pricey houses at one time. Anyway, Edie's father would leave them a penny or two."

At that moment, Cissie Hardman returned to the sitting room. Her husband made a formal introduction, then the shop bell called him out again. Hart rose to go but Cissie Hardman motioned him to stay. He was surprised but sat down again.

"You remember Victor and Edie Grant, Mrs. Hardman?"

"Yes, very clearly. I don't think Bert knew what happened to them but I used to hear a lot of women's gossip. I never passed it on to him. We were working very hard in those days. We had to make our own way. If we had stayed in Chapeltown we might have kept in touch, but we had the chance of a house in Fallowfield and we took it. I say might.... Edie was a bit cantankerous, I had the idea that she thought she was a bit above us. Anyway, things didn't work out so well for the Grants after all, so I heard. We've lived such a busy life we've almost forgotten those days and it was only the report in the paper that brought it all back. You see, when you have a family of your own and a business of your own and none of them have to do with that bit of the past, you tend to forget, don't you?"

"In what way did things go wrong for them, Mrs. Hardman?"

"Well, when Fred Watson, Edie's father died, he left debts. It seems that in the hard times he had extended credit to a lot of folk who never paid up. And there was a much younger sister, Jane, who was a bit odd. She had always been spoiled, as had Edie, and she wasn't able to work. Some said she was simple. Victor Grant had to take on the debts and look after the sister, Jane, as well as his own wife and son. There was no money in Victor's family so he must have had a struggle to pay out of his own wages. I don't think Edie ever went back to work. She would have her hands full with her child and sister and the home to look after. The last I ever heard of them was that they were living in Fred Watson's house up on the turnpike while Mrs. Watson was still alive. The shop was sold, of course, but there were the debts to pay off and there was no money left over. The final straw was that Edie's mother took against her and left the house and most of her things to her brother, Jim Watson, who had a big family of his own. Anyway, until the newspaper report about the boy, we had heard nothing more."

"You wouldn't have known that Jane had had a child?"

"No!" she paused, completely taken aback. "I'm fairly sure that Jane was simple. I wouldn't have thought that she would .... in that case, what happened to her?"

"The Grants say that she left home?"

"Left home? If she was simple, how could she leave home on her own?"

"A good question, Mrs. Hardman. Perhaps she didn't leave on her own."

"You mean, with a man?"

"Well, that's a possibility, isn't it? Maybe she wasn't simple."

"It was her child, this boy Thomas Watson that was killed was it?"

"Yes."

"Oh, what a dreadful life Victor Grant must have had. When I think how light hearted he used to be at the dances in the Co-op Hall. He was everyone's favourite, you know. I used to fancy him a bit myself, before I started going out with Bert. Bert was the steadier one, I thought."

She had stood all the time they had spoken, now she was silent; she sat down slowly and closed her eyes. After a pause she spoke again.

"How very lucky we have been."

Chapter Twelve

Douglas Hart considered himself very lucky in having stumbled upon someone who had known the Grants at his first stop. He left the little shop and proceeded on foot. He didn't know where he would be calling next. In fact, the next shop was only a little distance away. It was a butcher's and, at that time of the morning, was very busy. Clearly it was a favourite shop among locals and Hart was impressed by the quality of both the meat and the service. At first, the senior assistant didn't understand what he wanted and became irritable. The customers became restless and there was an unpleasant atmosphere until a tall figure, almost as well built as Hart himself, burst through the door from the back. A volley of cries broke out, indicating that this must be the owner. Before the man had time to speak, Hart drew him to one side and quietly showed him his warrant card. The big man paled, glanced round the shop and beckoned Hart into the back room.

"What is it?" The big man was asthmatic. He wheezed and perspired.

"I'm looking into the death of the young lad, Thomas Watson..."

The butcher exhaled abruptly and beamed at the D.C.I.

"Oh, I thought you had brought a complaint. We don't normally have complaints. We've not had a policeman in here since the war. What can I do to help?"

It was to no avail. The Grants did not shop there and were not known. Hart had brought one of the posters. The butcher did not recognise Tommy but he agreed to display the poster in his window.

As Hart was leaving, a middle aged woman in a head scarf bustled up.

"'Ere! That's Tommy Watson isn't it?" Her voice was loud and abrasive.

"Our Robert's a friend of 'is. What 'appened to 'im, the poor young sod? 'E was alright was Tommy, never did no 'arm. Who did it? You're a policeman, aren't you...."

"You must be Mrs. Shaw."

Hart's interruption stopped the woman in mid-sentence. She was very impressed.

"'Ere..."

"Your Robert's in hospital isn't he? Do you know when he will be out, Mrs. Shaw?"

The woman's mouth threatened to stay open.

"I'll need to ask him about Tommy, with your permission. If he is going to be in for a while, I might have to visit him in hospital. Can you tell me where he is?"

"Eeh, er, the Cottage, ward six..."

Before she could recover, Hart thanked her politely and strode off across the street. He had no wish to bandy words at this stage with a raucous woman intent on abuse, however indirect.

The next shop was a fruiterer's and was of no help. It stood next to a thriving newsagent's. Here, Hart discovered, was the newsagent Tommy Watson had worked for. The proprietor took him to one side.

"I thought you would be round before long, the poor young bugger, anything I can do to help to put whoever it was inside?"

"Mr. Price, we need to know Tommy Watson's last movements, particularly what he was doing on Saturday and Sunday. When did you last see him?"

"Sunday morning, he came in early, as usual, he was always the sharpest for time. He was so dependable, never had a paper boy like him."

"Did he say anything about what he was going to do that day?"

"No, he never said much. He never did. He watched that he got the right numbers, he was good at that. You see, if there was a mistake he would lose money. He never lost a penny."

"He never talked about himself, then?"

"Not really, I used to hear him talking to the other lads. He was very friendly with them."

"How many other paper boys were there?"

"Four altogether, Jim Hibbert, Terry Phipps, Gil Spence and him."

"They were all friends together?"

"They got on very well, always joking and teasing each other but I don't know about being great friends."

"Did they all go to Firby High School?"

"No, I think Terry and Gil went to St. Saviour's."

"Did he hang about when he had finished his round?"

"How do you mean?"

"He didn't stay for a chat with you or the others. The shop wasn't a meeting place for them?"

"Oh, sometimes he would be about on a Saturday afternoon, he and Jim on their bikes, but not on a Sunday. There's hardly anybody about on a Sunday morning. Jim didn't have a round on Sundays, just the three of them."

"He earned good money, I believe?"

"Yes, he's been working for me for two years now and last year he took over another lad's round as well as his own, they were next to each other, you see, and Tommy being so reliable, I didn't hesitate to give him it."

"Do you think he gave all his money to his folks?"

"I don't know about that. He didn't spend much on himself, he never bought sweets. I heard him say that he was saving up, that's all."

"He didn't smoke did he?"

Price's eyebrows shot up.

"No, I'm sure of that. He never tried to buy any, if that's what you mean. I've seen Terry and Gil having a quiet one outside but I've never seen Tommy or Jim with a cigarette."

"You never saw him with any other friends, did you?"

"Well, there were one of two used to gather around. One was called Stewey, I think. Another was Robert Shaw. That's about the lot."

"Did the boy's uncle ever come in?"

"I wouldn't know, I wouldn't have recognised him if he had. I've never met him."

Hart thanked the man and, having asked him to place a poster in his window, withdrew.

At the end of the same street was a baker's shop but there was a poster already in the window so Hart was aware that he was trespassing on his team's territory. In fact, he had arrived back at Headlaw Road. He decided to rest content with what he had gained and returned to his car.

He drove a couple more blocks and turned left again. Ahead of him, at the end of the street, on the corner, was a smartly painted green and red pub, The Cavalier. He glanced at his watch. It was not yet 11 o'clock, too early for it to be open, he would pop in on the way back.

Selborne Street was the next street and a sign indicated quite clearly that it was a cul de sac. Hart considered this and realised that this would pose a problem for anyone wishing to arrive and depart in a hurry by car or any other vehicle. A three point turn was necessary. Even if someone knew about the side lane, he could hardly negotiate it at speed and unnoticed.

Remembering his own struggle to change direction only yesterday, he decided to turn at the road junction and park at the corner. He would walk down Selborne Street. As he got out and turned to lock the car he was surprised to see that he had parked outside a very modest shop window. It was so narrow that it looked more like a normal house window. It was a cobbler's shop. It didn't need a window for it didn't sell shoes. He went in.

A thin young man sat at a bench in a dark corner. It seemed that all the corners were dark. There was only a small lamp over what looked like a lathe on the workbench. The bench and the floor were littered with small scraps of leather. Baskets full of assorted shoes stood against one wall. Above them were nailed cards of rubber heels and shoe laces and 'protectors' or segs, as he remembered them.

"Can I help?" The words were faltering. The young man had stood up. He was painfully thin and as he spoke his adam's apple bobbed outrageously. His complexion was waxy and glowed a dull yellow, his face was dirty from his hands. When Hart brought out his warrant card, the young man held up a hand, turned and shouted loudly and unintelligibly. Hart saw a heavy hearing device over each ear.

"What's that?" There was the sound of footsteps on stairs and a lively figure hastened through the door at the back.

Hart dispensed with preliminaries.

"I wonder if you can help me? I'm enquiring about the death of Tommy Watson who lived in Selborne Street. By any chance, did you know the boy or his relations, Mr. and Mrs. Grant?"

"Are you from the press? There was a reporter in

here yesterday morning asking all sorts of things."

"No, I'm in charge of the investigation."

Hart was obliged to get out his warrant card again. This seemed to relax the cobbler. He was a small man in his forties with a round, cheerful face and thinning hair. He wiped his hands on his apron as if to demonstrate his preparation for serious questioning.

"Yes, I know Victor Grant. He comes in quite often and we always have a chat. He is always careful about their shoes. They aren't well off and he makes the shoes last as long as possible."

"Did you know the boy at all?"

"I knew Tommy very well. He was a good lad, if he came to the shop he always had time to talk to Eric." He nodded towards the youth at the bench. "Eric was born with serious hearing and speech problems and he's never been strong. He had to go to a special school. He's never had much of a life nor many friends. He was always pleased to see Tommy. He popped in almost every Saturday."

"Did he call in last Saturday?"

"Yes, he came in about two o'clock."

"Did you know if there was anything worrying the lad?"

"No, I can't say that there was. He seemed the same as ever."

"He didn't say what he was going to do over the weekend, did he?"

"No."

The cobbler turned to his son and articulated carefully,

"Did Tommy say what he was going to do last weekend?"

His son looked stricken and shook his head vigorously, glancing sideways at the D.C.I. He then mumbled out a long string of sentences, becoming agitated. The cobbler nodded and patted his son's arm.

"Eric gets very upset thinking about Tommy. He says that Tommy sometimes went off to Grammond but not at weekends."

"To Grammond? Could you ask your son when he went and what he went for?"

This time the cobbler brought his son over to the little counter. The youth was trembling and looking rapidly from Hart to his father and back again. Hart smiled encouragingly and spoke slowly and clearly.

"Eric, when did Tommy go to Grammond?"

There was a silence. Eric looked down and shook his head slightly. When he looked up again his eyes were wide and Hart sensed an appeal.

"Eric, we need to know everything we can about what Tommy did. We must all help to catch whoever killed him. If Tommy was missing school or doing anything he didn't want anyone to know about, it can't be a secret any more. If we are to help we must know everything. Tommy can't be hurt any more or punished in any way, not now. Please tell us everything you know."

There were tears of anger, frustration and grief in the youth's eyes. He dashed them away angrily with a blackened hand. With a struggle, he spoke as clearly as he had ever done.

"Tommy bought a watch. A pocket watch. It was for his uncle's birthday. He bought it at Grammond with his own money. He showed me. He was going to have his name put on it."

"When did he buy it?"

"Three weeks ago."

"Do you know where he was going to have the name put on?"

"Yes, he said he was going back to the same shop."

"In Grammond?"

"Yes."

"You never saw it after he had it done, did you?"

"No."

"Do you know why he bought it in Grammond?"

"He saw it in a window once when he went to watch the football."

"And he went back later, did he?"

"Yes, he slipped out of school and took a bus there and back."

"It's a long way to Grammond."

"He went instead of his dinner and got back before five o'clock. He had to be home before five o'clock."

"Did Tommy smoke?"

Eric stared at Hart in astonishment and shook his head sharply, finding it difficult to muster further words. The effort of so much talking had exhausted this frail figure, he staggered slightly and his father led him back to his seat by the bench.

"I don't think we should push him any further, the poor lad's worn out."

Hart agreed. He was about to take his leave when he thought of his car outside and tried another tack.

"Do you have trouble with cars parking hereabouts? The streets are narrow and people have to park in the road."

"Well, there aren't that many cars belonging to the people round here."

"You would notice if there were any strange cars, then, would you?"

"Yes, when we aren't busy. There's always a problem with Selborne Street because strangers think they can get out at the bottom, but it's only a footpath down there you know. They either have to reverse or do an awkward turn. Mind, you can come up the back lane and out here into our little street, or you could reverse here into the back lane to help turn."

"Do you get many strangers driving up here?"

"Not many. Just the odd van delivering. If there are callers for Selborne Street, they often park here at the corner so that they can get away again easily."

"Have there been any 'callers' for Selborne Street recently?"

"I can't think...."

"Has anyone parked near you overnight, or very late, in the last week or two?"

There was a commotion from the bench. Eric was making a great effort to speak. His father rushed over to him. It took a long time to get the message clear.

"Eric says that there has been a blue van late at night when he went to bed but it had always gone by the morning."

"He can't say whether it had any writing on it or anything to distinguish it by?"

"No."

Further efforts were proving most difficult and Hart began to feel guilty about going on, but he felt it necessary. This could be a breakthrough.

"How many times has he seen this van, and was it always late at night?"

Eric indicated that he had seen it on a number of occasions, recently, always at night. When he was asked if he had ever seen the driver, he launched into what sounded like a description then sank back silent. It seemed that his strength had left him. Hart moved round the counter and took one of the boney hands.

"Thank you, Eric, I'm most grateful."

"The name's Semper, by the way." The cobbler smiled at Hart's gesture.

"Tell me, Mr. Semper, why is it that so few people in the same street know so little about the Grants?"

Mr. Semper was silent for a moment.

"I think I understand. You only know people if you

do the same things at the same time, like going to football or going to the same church or playing bingo. Since television came, people stay indoors of a night. The Grants never went out. They didn't go to church nor play bingo. I don't know what they did except they kept themselves to themselves. Most folk down there are the same. They only come out to shop."

"Where did Edie Grant shop, do you know?"

"My missus sometimes sees her at the shops down at Keynes Road."

"Does she speak? Talk to your missus, I mean?"

"Yes, I think so but never for long. She's a very private sort of woman. She'll say good morning and that's about it."

Chapter Thirteen

Eleven thirty in the morning was not the time to find
either Mr. or Mrs Foster at home. Nor, to Hart's
surprise, were the Grants at home. However, next door,
at No.24, Mrs. Butterman was. She was not too
pleased to see the warrant card. She had already been
interviewed by a policeman and she had suffered the
indignity of being cross-questioned by a crowd of very
dubious newspaper reporters on her own doorstep. She
turned back from the door and bade Hart enter with a
short gesture of her podgy hand.

Although short and plump, she carried herself well,
there was almost an imperious air about her. She was
dressed in a well cut skirt and jacket of pale blue and a
cream coloured silk blouse. High heeled blue suede
shoes completed the outfit which Hart thought must
indicate that the lady of the house was either about to
leave or had just returned.

"Were you about to go out?" He asked
apologetically.

"Oh, no trouble, do sit down, I'm sure you wouldn't
have called if it hadn't been important." There was no
welcome in the tone of her voice, in spite of the words.

"Mrs. Butterman, I need to go over the statement
you gave yesterday..."

"Something wrong was there?"

"No, I don't think so, I need to ask a few more
questions, that's all..."

"Well, if you must, you must."

"Quite! How long have you lived at this address,
Mrs. Butterman?"

Mrs. Butterman gave a short gasp as though the
question was an impertinence. She had been standing as
though she wished the interview to be as brief as
possible, now she sat down with a sigh. Every fibre of

her closely knit being indicated that she was inconvenienced and wished the world to know.

"We came here in 1931 so we have been here just over thirty years now."

"Would that be around the same time as the Grants, your neighbours?"

"They were here before we arrived."

"So you have been friends for a long time?"

"Well, I would hardly say friends, but we have certainly known them for a long time."

"You would know Mrs Grant's sister, I believe she lived with them when they first came here?"

"Really, Chief Inspector, I hardly think that that poor woman can have anything to do with your murder enquiry!"

"Mrs. Butterman, I need to know everything I can about the Grant family if I am to make progress......"

"I can tell you very little about the Grants. We were quite friendly when we first came, our son John used to play with their son Victor in the lane but he was four years older than our John. We saw very little of the sister, she wasn't well and didn't get out much. Mrs. Grant preferred to keep herself to herself. She never admitted anyone to the house. She never joined anything. When her son left home she stopped talking to everyone. Now she barely acknowledges me in the street. Not that I see her very often."

"When you say she didn't join anything, do you mean a club or society of some kind?"

"Well, of course we belong to St. Mary's, there are all sorts of things going on there, the Grants were Methodists."

"Surely the Methodist Church must have social activities too?"

"I believe they do, I wouldn't know. I can only tell you that the Grants were keen for a few years then they simply let it go. I don't think they attend at all now."

"Would that be after their son left home?"

"Well, about that time, but it may have been earlier."

"What sort of boy was Tommy Watson?"

"Always polite. He was well brought up, I'll give the Grants that. Edie Grant was very firm with him. No noise, no nonsense."

"Was he happy do you think?"

"Happy?"

It was as if the concept of happiness had never entered the lady's head. She took a moment to think.

"Well, I suppose he was. He never said much. He was quiet..."

"Did you never hear him laugh?"

"Laugh?" Another pause. "No I don't think I did, but I never heard him cry either."

"It seems to me that it was a very quiet household, Mrs. Butterman."

"It wasn't so quiet when their son Victor was at home."

"Oh, was he particularly noisy?"

"When he was little, he and John were inclined to be noisy. We didn't like them spending too much time together. I never liked the young Victor Grant, he was too old for John. I thought he was sly and a bit of a bully. When John was eleven we sent him to private school. My husband Sidney thought that he wasn't mixing with the right sort of boy."

"So they stopped playing together after that?"

"Yes, naturally, they only met occasionally after that."

"Where is your son, Mrs. Butterman, I would like to have a word with him? He wasn't at home when our constable called, we will need a statement from him. He is not employed at the moment, I believe."

At that precise moment, Hart thought he heard a door closing somewhere out the back.

"I'm not sure whether he is in. He wasn't up when I went out this morning."

Mrs. Butterman made no move to call her son or to see if he was at home. This irked Hart. He wasn't sure whether she had heard that door close and was deliberately being obstructive or whether she was treating the matter with ignorant off-handedness.

"He was a draughtsman, I believe." His voice became sharp.

"Yes, he worked for the same company as my husband. It was a good job, well paid, regular hours, very respectable."

"Why did he leave it?"

Mrs. Butterman bridled.

"He was offered a better one. He is now working for himself."

She seemed unaware of any contradiction.

"He was persuaded to leave?"

"I hope that you are not implying that there was something wrong?"

"No," Hart was pugnaciously blunt, "I took it from what you said that the idea of leaving was not your son's own idea. Is he still working as some form of draughtsman?"

"He is now a consultant."

"In what line?"

"I really couldn't say, you will have to ask him." She rose with an air of triumph as if to conclude the interview. Hart sat still for a moment then stood to tower over her.

"Has your son always lived at home, Mrs. Butterman?"

"Certainly, there is no question of my son leaving home before he is ready."

"He has not contemplated matrimony then?"

"Really, Inspector! I cannot think that that can possibly be any business..." Hart hastened to interrupt in his most charming manner.

"A wise man, I'm sure, with such a comfortable home."

Indeed, the house was expensively furnished and decorated. There seemed no lack of money although everything was not to Hart's taste, the word that formed in his mind was 'excess'. It most certainly presented a huge contrast to the house next door.

"Nevertheless, you will appreciate, Mrs. Butterman, that we will need to speak to him. Please ask him to call to see me at Welbeck Police Station as soon as possible."

"At the police station? Is that entirely necessary?"

"This is a very serious matter and your son may just happen to be a material witness."

"Nonsense, the very idea!" Mrs. Butterman reddened. "I cannot imagine how that can be. My son has nothing to do with this business. He was away visiting friends over the weekend, he wasn't even here!"

"Was your son friendly with Thomas Watson?"

"John must have been fifteen or sixteen when that boy was born."

"I don't suppose he would play with him as an infant, but being neighbours, he must have spoken to him now and again."

"I don't think John spoke more than once or twice a year, they never had occasion to meet."

"Your husband drives a car, Mrs. Butterman?"

"Yes, he drives to work every day."

"Where does he keep it?"

"He keeps it round the side at nights. It's out of the way there on the side of the path."

"Does your son John drive?"

97

"Yes, he learned to drive as soon as he was eighteen."

"Was he driving at the weekend when he was away at Northrop?"

"I'm not sure. You'll have to ask his father." Mrs. Butterman was building up a resistance.

"You will appreciate that we must check on everyone who knew the Grants, including your son. Please pass my message on, won't you, Mrs. Butterman."

Hart thanked her briefly and left without further ceremony.

By this time he was feeling both hungry and thirsty. He felt he needed to wash away the disagreeable taste Mrs. Butterman had left in his mouth. Where better than at The Cavalier? He crossed the road then remembered the Drysdales at 19. Yes, he would need to see them, Tommy Watson had cleaned their car that Sunday morning.

Mrs. Drysdale was very nearly the opposite of Mrs. Butterman. She was thin and wispy. Her greying hair tended to fly free of its pins at either side of her head, her hands were busy, her movements quick. She was dressed in familiar woollens and a well-worn apron. It turned out that she was in the middle of baking but she welcomed the D.C.I. into her kitchen and offered him tea immediately. He relished the warmth of this kitchen and the kindly hospitality of his hostess but he had to get on with his business.

"Tommy Watson washed your car on Sunday morning?"

"Yes, he was a very reliable lad. John, my husband, trusted him completely. I think he took pride in his work. John had him wash it every fortnight, it wasn't absolutely necessary but John was pleased to employ him."

"Was he easy to talk to?"

"Well he wasn't a great talker but he was most polite and John always had a wee chat when he paid him."

"He never gave any hint that anything was wrong did he?"

"No. We were really shocked when we heard the news. We went over and over Sunday in our minds but couldn't say that there was anything different in the lad."

"Did you know his aunt and uncle very well?"

"No, I'm afraid we didn't. We've lived here four years and we hardly know a soul apart from our immediate neighbours. We have friends in the Choral Society and we visit each other but we don't know the people in this street all that well. I've seen Mrs. Grant from time to time but I don't think I would have recognised Mr. Grant if he hadn't come round on Sunday night to ask if we had seen Tommy.

"Did the boy talk about his family at all?"

"He often mentioned his uncle, he seemed very fond of him... not so much his aunt. He told us about his uncle's accident and that he was laid off work."

Mrs. Drysdale took a moment or two to see to her oven and Hart's eyes wandered round the room.

"How was he dressed that morning?"

"Sunday, you mean? Now, let's see. Grey trousers and a shirt and pullover, brown I think."

"Were those the clothes he always wore to wash your car?"

"Just about, as far as I remember. I don't suppose he had many clothes but he always looked clean and neat when we saw him cycling in the street."

"Did you often see him out and about? Most people seem to think he spent most of his time indoors."

"Oh, we've seen him a few times in the street,

always on his bike, mostly on his own and mostly on a Saturday. He seemed friendly enough to us."

"What shoes was he wearing when he washed the car?"

"Black shoes, ordinary school shoes, I think. They usually got very wet."

"Do you see much of his neighbours, the Buttermans?"

"Well, we know the Buttermans. He's a sidesman at the church, she's rather proud. My husband doesn't care for either of them, calls her a pouter-pigeon."

Hart grinned.

"What about the son? He lives at home doesn't he?"

"Oh, John Butterman? Yes, he does. He used to go to work with his father, he seemed to go everywhere with him, always together, now he is always on his own."

"I have yet to see him. What is he like?"

"A big fellow, same height as his father but broader, looks as though he's running to fat. He must be about thirty or late twenties, young face, a bit flabby."

"Have you ever spoken to him?"

"I was once introduced to him at a church fete just after we got here. His mother dotes on him. I'm sure he was spoiled as a boy. We've not seen him to speak to since then."

All the time she had spoken, Mrs. Drysdale had been busy flouring a board and rolling out pastry, cutting it into shape and turning it. It seemed to Hart that it was the most natural thing for her to do, she was endlessly busy and absorbed in her work.

"Do you have children of your own, Mrs. Drysdale?"

"Oh, yes, a son and a daughter and two grandchildren. They are all coming for tea today, that's why I must get on. I'm sorry to be so rude but there is a lot to do, they have good appetites, all of them."

"It is I who should apologise, for distracting you, but it is so important to find out as much as we can. The whole business is very baffling. Nobody knows where the boy went on Sunday afternoon. Were you in on Sunday, Mrs. Drysdale?"

"In the afternoon, you mean?"

"Yes."

"After lunch, John and I sat in the front room with our feet up. He dosed off and I read the paper. Later, we put the telly on and watched the film. That's about it."

"You would see any movement in the street, I suppose?"

"Yes, it was very quiet, hardly anybody about."

"No cars went by?"

"No, oh, yes a car parked across the road, visitors for the Buttermans. It came just after we switched the film on. It had gone by the time we finished tea. A couple visited the Nesbits, the very old couple opposite, relations of theirs, they come to see them regularly...."

"You didn't see Tommy Watson cycle past?"

"No, not on Sunday. We never saw him on Sunday afternoons, now I come to think of it. I have a feeling that his aunt thought that he might disturb people by cycling in the front street on a Sunday. She was pretty strict with him I believe."

"Was it a religious objection, do you think?"

"Perhaps it was. Anyway, he could use the back lane and come out at the top if he was going anywhere in particular, he wouldn't disturb anyone going that way."

"Well, thank you for your help and the tea, I mustn't interrupt you any longer. If you think of anything at all, remember anything about Sunday or the weekend that could possibly have anything to do with the Grants and their nephew, please don't hesitate to phone us.

However trivial, you won't be wasting our time, I assure you."

He let himself out.

He was feeling cheerful as he entered The Cavalier. Considering that it was surrounded by seemingly endless streets of dull red-brick houses, quite unrelieved by greenery or architectural variation, The Cavalier was an amazingly cheerful haven. It sparkled. Glass, brass, woodwork and leather all smiled a welcome. If that was an illusion, the man behind the bar, with his brisk manner and ready smile was not. It appeared that he was delighted to see strangers come through his door.

There were only a few customers, mostly elderly. They nodded towards Hart and carried on their discussions. The D.C.I. ordered a couple of beef sandwiches and a pint of best bitter. He decided to wait before he talked to the barman so he lifted a tabloid from the bar counter and took it and his beer over to a bench seat against the wall.

As he turned a page he took a good look round. The bar room was surprisingly big and a blunted L shape. In the toe of the L part there was a small snooker table and a little beyond it a rubber mat that plotted the dart area. A dark haired man in his twenties was leaning over the table practising potting, a pint glass at his elbow. The bar itself was solid, old-fashioned and highly polished but the other furnishings were relatively new. At that moment his sandwiches arrived and Hart tucked in with gusto. They were particularly good, the beef was generous and tasty and the bread fresh. The pint, too, was very good and Hart determined to visit The Cavalier again.

Having finished eating, he took his plate to the bar. The customers who had recently arrived had all moved over to the tables near the wall so he was able to have a discreet word with the barman. He leant towards him on one elbow.

"Excellent sandwiches. My compliments to the cook!"

"My missus, she'll be pleased you liked them."

Hart quietly passed him his warrant card and spoke in a low voice.

"I'm investigating the murder of that boy in Chevely Park, I wonder if you...."

There was a crash behind them, a shout and a door banging. Hart swung round. The snooker player was standing staring at the floor where his glass lay shattered amid the remains of his pint.

"What happened?" Hart asked the barman. The barman's jaw had dropped but he quickly resumed his cheerful manner and shrugged.

"Who was that, Dave?" he asked the man at the table.

"That was John B. He was just going to buy a round when he turned and rushed off like the devil was after him. I've been waiting to play him for best part of an hour!"

"One of your regulars?"

"Yes, I wonder what got into him?"

"John B. That wouldn't be for Butterman, would it?"

"Yes it would. How did you guess? Do you know him?"

"I called to see him earlier this morning but he was out. I'm sorry I missed him. Does he come in most days at the same time?"

"Not every day, but most, about the same time."

"At Weekends?"

"He was in on Saturday night but not on Sunday. He doesn't usually come in on Sundays." The barman was beginning to look curious, Hart was quick to reassure him.

"Being the next door neighbours, I have to talk to them. Does the father come in here?"

There was a pause as the barman rinsed a couple of glasses.

"John's old man? No he never comes in here. I don't know if he drinks but he doesn't drink in here."

"What about Tommy Watson's uncle, Victor Grant, does he drink here?"

"Ah, old Victor. Now he used to drink here, years ago when I first came, but he hasn't been in for a very long time. I think he hit hard times."

"Has young Butterman always been a regular?"

"No, he wasn't until about six months or so ago since when he's been   in almost every day, sometimes he stays all afternoon. He likes to play snooker."

"He doesn't work then?"

"I don't think he does but he seems to have enough of money to spend."

"What sort of time does he come in in the evening?"

"He's usually in around nine but he hasn't a fixed routine. Last Saturday he didn't come in until nearly closing time."

Chapter Fourteen

34 Ogilvie Drive was a yellow brick house with small windows and the main door round the side. There were gardens to three sides of the semi-detached house but they were trampled almost bare of vegetation. Set back a little stood a battered wooden garage with broken window panes. Its paint, like all the paint at windows and front door, was peeling and faded so that it was hard to ascertain what the original colour had been.

Before Detective Sergeant Bailey could raise his hand to knock, a black mongrel dog appeared from behind the house and began to bark. Immediately it was echoed from inside by screams from a baby then shouts of children's voices then a roar of rage from a man and answering yells from a woman. The door was jerked open and a thin figure, dressed only in grubby vest and trousers, stared at Bailey, wide eyed with rage.

"What the hell do you want? What do you mean by skulking round here? From the council are you?" The man stepped out and drew back his right arm menacingly. Bailey stuck out his jaw and stared back at the man without flinching. "Detective Sergeant Bailey, Clayton Police. I'd like a word, Mr. Fenton, if you don't mind."

"But I do bloody well mind!" Fenton had been jolted out of his rage but he was trying to save face by blustering. "I've done my stint, you've nothing on me. Leave me alone will you!"

"I advise you to calm down, Mr. Fenton, or you will let all your neighbours hear everything..."

"To hell with the neighbours!" Nevertheless his voice sank.

"What the hell do you want, disturbing the wife and kids?"

"Can we go inside, Mr. Fenton?"

"You think you can go anywhere, don't you, you are all alike, one mistake and you are onto a man's back....I've been ill all week and now that I'm better I have to put up with you pushing in."

"Mr. Fenton, we can talk here or we can talk down at the station, which is it to be."

The man subsided, turned and kicked the door fully open. His wife stood just inside holding a very young baby, looking very worried. He pushed her roughly to one side.

"The bloody law, never leave anybody in peace."

He led Bailey into a small sitting room which was crowded with a faded three piece suite, a pram, a pushchair and a variety of boxes. There was hardly room to turn. The furniture was covered in loose piles of clothes and all manner of battered toys. A small television set flickered soundlessly in one corner. Fenton roared in frustration and swept some of the objects from one of the chairs with a wild swing of one arm.

"That's alright, we can talk standing up, don't bother."

There was a noise from the doorway and two small boys began to push their way in.

"Out, out, go on!" Fenton rushed to the door, pushed the children out and shut the door firmly behind them.

"What's it all about?" He was much calmer but still truculent.

"This is a murder enquiry. A fourteen year old boy was found dead in Chevely Park on Tuesday morning...."

"Nothing to do with me, you can't pin that on me...."

"....We are conducting a house to house enquiry, we need to know if anyone has seen anything....."

"Oh, that's alright then. No, we've not seen anything."

"Can you tell me where you were on Sunday evening?"

"Me? On Sunday?"

There was a long pause. The man's eyes stared at Bailey and swung away again.

"What time would that be?"

"All of Sunday evening."

"Well, I'll have to think."

Fenton had become very quiet. There was a noise of scuffling beyond the door and crying broke out. Fenton seemed glad of the interruption, he strode over the settee leg and pulled at the door.

"Shuttup you lot! Shuttup, you hear? We're talking!"

"Sunday, Mr. Fenton, Where were you?"

"Oh yes, Sunday, well I was down at the Three Bells having a jar or two with my mates. The missus can't get out on account of the kids."

"Would that be the Three Bells on Firtree Road?"

"Yes, my mates will confirm that."

"What time did you leave?"

"Er...Er... well it would have been closing time, wouldn't it."

"You came straight back here?"

"Well," Fenton glanced at the door which was now ajar, "I stopped off at Charlie Beck's, he was having a little celebration..."

"What address was that?"

"16 Wansley Terrace." His eyes were on the door again.

"So you got back here, when?"

There was a long pause.

"About One."

"Your wife can confirm that?"

"No... No! She was asleep when I got back."

"No one saw or heard you return?"

"I don't suppose so. What are you getting at?"

Bailey took out one of the handbills and showed Fenton the picture of Tommy Watson.

"Have you ever seen this boy before?"

"Never!"

"You are sure?"

"You don't think I can remember all my customers do you?"

"You still sell Ice-cream do you?"

"It's my living isn't it?"

"Could I see your van?"

"You're not an inspector are you? There's nothing wrong with the van, I keep it spotless."

"Well, you won't mind me seeing it then, will you?"

Fenton glared at Bailey but he took him outside and opened the garage door. The contrast between the van and the garage which contained it was startling. The van gleamed. It was elderly by normal standards but it was, as its owner said, spotless. Its chrome work was highly polished, its windows sparkled, its paint looked fresh. Bailey reflected upon the untidy, crowded room they had just left. From what he could see from where he stood, the interior of the van was highly organised with boxes neatly stacked and surfaces scrupulously clean.

"Could I see inside?"

"I can't stop you, can I?"

Bailey reached for the door handle and opened the door into the back of the van. The floor inside was dirty, the mat was crumpled and there appeared to be pieces of grass and other debris scattered about.

"What is this then, Mr Fenton?"

Fenton came round to the back and looked down.

"What the hell?....."

He appeared to be genuinely astonished.

"When did you last use the van?"

"Sunday afternoon, I always go out on Sundays, it's

always a good day, whatever the weather. I wasn't feeling well on Monday so I stayed in."

"And you put the van away in the garage straight away, on Sunday?"

"No, I usually give it a clean out first, ready for Monday. That's what I did on Sunday, as soon as I got back."

"When was that?"

"Half past five, it was getting dark by then..."

"And you never took it out again?"

"No."

"Think, Mr. Fenton, if you cleaned it out and didn't take it out again, how could it get like this?"

Fenton stood frozen for a long time.

"What route did you take on Sunday?"

Bailey had to repeat the question.

"I do this estate first then I go round Welbeck and then cross over Headlaw Road."

"Did you go up to Selborne Street by any chance?"

Fenton was looking very pale and his voice had sunk to a whisper.

"Speak up, Mr. Fenton. I can't hear you."

"Yes."

"You go up Selborne Street regularly?"

"No. Just if... just if business is not good at the other places."

"But you did go up there on Sunday?"

"Yes."

"You are sure that you didn't see this boy on Sunday?"

Fenton shook his head wretchedly.

"Tell me about Monday, Mr. Fenton?

"I...er...didn't take the van out on Monday. I didn't feel well. I had a drink down at the club then I came back and went to bed."

"You were in bed all day, you didn't get up again?

Mrs. Fenton will confirm that?"

Fenton drew the tip of his tongue round his lips before replying.

"No. She took the kids round to her mother's. She didn't come back till three. I got up in the afternoon but I didn't go out."

"I'm afraid we will have to make a detailed inspection of your van, Mr. Fenton. We won't keep it long. It may not have anything to do with our enquiries, in which case you'll have nothing to worry about. For the time being, please hold yourself in readiness for further questioning."

Bailey expected a torrent of abuse at this but Fenton simply hung his head and stared at the ground.

Chapter Fifteen

Hart had only just got back to his office when Bailey burst in.

"Sir, I think there may be a lead. It's Fenton. There's soil in his ice-cream van and his story about the weekend is crooked.

"Fenton claims to have been ill since Monday. He put his van away on Sunday evening after clearing it out. I've looked at his van and there is a mess inside. It is just possible that it has been used to carry something unusual, for example a body. His reaction has been very odd. He started cocky and ended up silent. There's something wrong. I've had the van brought in for examination."

"Well now, you have been busy. Did you check with the immediate neighbours?"

"Yes, a neighbour opposite claims he heard the van being driven back in the early hours of Tuesday morning."

"Tuesday! That seems to fit. So far, so good. We'll have to wait for the results of the examination, though. The trouble is that there has to be a motive. Did you show him the picture of Tommy Watson?"

"Yes, there was no reaction to that, but he had taken the van up Selborne Street on the Sunday afternoon."

"That in itself doesn't mean much. What are we looking for here? A kidnapping? An accident with the body concealed? No, neither fits. It was daylight, probably too public for either. You say that he cleaned out the van that evening, where, at home? Wouldn't his family have seen him?"

"Actually, a neighbour witnessed him cleaning the van. He always cleaned it before he put it away. The same witness said that Fenton hasn't taken the van out on his rounds since."

"Did he always keep it clean?"

"Yes sir, He kept that van in very good condition, that's why it was such a surprise to find the mess on the floor inside."

"Was it a surprise to him?"

"Yes, it appeared to be, but if the van had been used in a hurry in the middle of the night, he may have overlooked the floor in his haste to put it away."

"True, but could anyone else have used the van without Fenton knowing?"

"The garage is a wreck, it wouldn't have taken much to get inside. If someone else used it with Fenton's knowledge, that would account for his surprise."

"Very good thinking Sergeant Bailey, You'll make a detective yet! When will all the Chevely Park results be in?"

"I think the door-to-door is finished now, it will only take an hour or two to complete the reports."

"Too long, it always takes too long. The Headlaw Road shops enquiry reports are not through yet. Shops! Ah, now there's something you can do while we are waiting for the van examination results. I want to know of a watchmaker or jeweller within walking distance of the Grammond City football ground, it may well be somewhere between the ground and the bus station. Get on the phone to Grammond, someone on the force there is bound to turn it up for you. I'd do it myself but I'm expecting a visit from a resident of Selborne Street."

Hart took pen and paper and jotted down everything he had gleaned that morning. He thought that it had been a productive morning in one sense, he felt he knew more about the inhabitants of Selborne Street, however, in the light of Bailey's discoveries, perhaps it would come to nothing.

He was interrupted by the station sergeant.

"Excuse me sir, there is a young woman to see you, says it is urgent. About the enquiry. Do you want to see her yourself?"

"A woman? I wasn't expecting one. Put her in the interview room. I'll send Sergeant Bailey when he is free."

He was curious but he was intent on getting through some of the reports awaiting him in his in-tray and he wanted to see John Butterman when he turned up.

The first one he picked up was the pathologists report. He went through it thoroughly but it told him little he didn't know already. The last meal Tommy Watson had eaten was his lunch on the Sunday. The time of death was not pinpointed accurately, the official opinion was that it had been more than twenty four hours prior to the body's discovery.

Hart quickly skipped the description of the effect of the ligature on the brain and other parts and picked out the paragraph that claimed that there were no bruises or abrasions to any other part of the body, but there were a few scratches to the fingers and palms of both hands and a tiny deposits of soil, brick dust, calcium carbonate and oil found in the finger nails and in the deeper creases of the hands.

Hart was interested in this last information. He was curious to know what kind of oil and in what order these deposits occurred. He reached for the phone immediately.

"Get me the Path Lab please, Sergeant. Could I speak to Dr. McBride please? This is D.C.I. Hart. Thanks. Ah, David, thanks for your report, could you enlarge upon it for me please, I need to know what kind of oil it was you found under the boy's fingernails. You can't say! Why, with the kind of detail you've given me in the past, I thought you would have been able to give me the name of the garage and even the oil well! It was light oil? So it could have been bicycle oil then? Ah, now, could you say in what layers, strata if you like, these deposits were found? You know what I'm after, time and place, the boy was on his bike earlier but not when he was killed, so the oil should have been first....O.K., O.K. so I'm assuming the boy had clean fingernails to begin with...alright, you win....yes, the soil probably first, then the oil then the brick dust, what put you on to that? Oh! Then you can't be sure of the order. Mm. Then this calcium carbonate, I presume you mean chalk of some kind... could it have been paint? Not really? Well I'm clutching at straws at the moment. Oh, I don't suppose you know if the lab has finished with the clothing yet? Oh, great! Top marks. O.K. I'll stand you a drink....Oh, sometime, trust me!"

Hart sat back to think but was interrupted by John Bailey returning from his last assignment.

"That didn't take you long. Did you have any success?"

"Yes sir, I was very lucky. There was an Inspector who had just been making a security check on city jewellers, he was just leaving when I phoned. He was happy to oblige. I've noted down the names, there happens to be three within walking distance and two of them lie on the main road back towards the bus station. It isn't the right part of town for most of the jewellery trade...."

"No matter." Hart looked at his watch, it was after three. "I might just make it before they close."

"You'll have to be mighty quick, sir!"

"Oh, there's a young woman waiting to see you in the interview room, Sergeant, says it's to do with the enquiry. I'll let you get on with it. By the way, if a Mr. Butterman calls to see me let him kick his heels until I get back and don't let him go until I've seen him."

"Right, will you be coming straight back, sir?"

"As soon as I can, now off you go!"

Chapter Seventeen

It took nearly an hour for Hart to find his way to Howland Road. He felt that the shop in question had to be on the way to the bus station simply because he believed that Tommy Watson's purchase of the watch had been spontaneous. The boy must have been drawn to something in the window and he had decided that there was the present he wanted to give to his uncle. He would have collected his money and gone back to buy it later. What was exceedingly puzzling was that the boy had had his own name engraved on it and not his uncle's.

The first shop was brightly lit with a wide range of stock. Hart studied the window. Watches of all shapes and sizes, with prices reaching four figures, were well displayed. There were, also, carriage clocks in brass and silver and a number of different kinds of table clocks, wall clocks and alarm clocks in many sizes. He failed to see any pocket watches. There were trays of rings and displays of costume jewellery in the side window. Everything was new and up to date. It was inevitable that the man behind the counter should shake his head at Hart's enquiry, nevertheless, the D.C.I. brought out the handbill and quizzed the salesman about Tommy Watson. No, there was no recollection of such a boy entering the shop.

The second shop was not so glittery and it did have a more old-fashioned window display. Its trade seemed to be concerned with tankards and trophies as well as watches and clocks and small pieces of jewellery. Sure enough, there were a number of pocket watches at one side of the window and their prices ranged widely. With or without chains, they would have been within the reach of a thrifty schoolboy. Hart entered the shop. It was not well lit but it was warm and welcoming.

116

There were two short counters at right angles to each other and a single upright chair with a cane seat stood against one of the counters. Leading off the back wall of the shop was a wide doorway, with a strip of curtain at one side of it, it was clear from the cluttered table visible inside that this was where the engraving took place. From time to time a young woman passed by this doorway and a murmur of conversation could be heard from somewhere behind the curtain.

A middle aged man with dark hair and thick eyebrows came from this back room with a ready-made smile for a customer. The smile faltered when the man saw Hart.

"Can I help you, sir?"

"Yes, I believe that you sold a pocket watch to a young boy a few weeks ago. I think it was this shop. The boy came back later and had it engraved."

"Nothing wrong, sir, I hope?"

"No, I don't think so. How long does it take to have engraving done?"

"Well, sir, it depends on how many words and what style. It usually takes only a few days. It also depends on how busy we are."

"You don't do it on the spot then?"

"Oh, no, sir. We usually have work on hand. We could only do on-the -spot work in a few special cases, then the customer has to come back a few hours later."

"Quite. Then you have a record of all the engraving work?"

The man behind the counter looked sharply at Hart.

"Certainly." He spoke loudly and inclined his head to the left.

"You would be able to tell me whether this boy bought his watch here then? The engraving instructions will be in your records."

"Jenny!" The man called out unnecessarily loudly.

117

There was total silence from the back room, then a tall, thin, good-looking girl came out. She was dark haired and above a long white overall coat showed a smart black polo necked sweater. She had dark, shaped eyebrows, a strong narrow nose and arresting lips. Later, Hart realised that the striking thing about the lips wasn't so much the shape so much as the subtle colour of the lipstick and pondered so long over the description that his wife was convulsed with laughter.

"Jenny, would you please fetch the engraving book. It should be in if we did it but sometimes we just write it down on a piece of paper if it isn't a big job." The man's eyes didn't stray from Hart's face.

"What date did he have it done?"

Hart didn't answer immediately but took the book from the counter where the girl had placed it and turned the pages for himself. The man behind the counter made to protest but changed his mind.

"Ah, there it is: ' Thomas Watson, born June 17th. 1947.' Not a lot of work really. The address...." Hart broke off amazed, "14 Hendry Street, Clayton."

"Nothing wrong is there?" The man's voice remained rather loud and its slightly aggressive tone irritated the D.C.I.

"Not that I know of. I think that this is the boy we have been talking about." Hart took out one of the handbills and thrust it under the man's nose. "Do you recognise him?"

The man stared at the likeness, startled by the sudden gesture, then he shook his head, but the girl took the paper and looked hard at it.

"I remember him, it was me who served him. I remember, now, he took a while to make up his mind about what he wanted to inscribe. The other thing was that it seemed such an old-fashioned thing for a boy to want, a pocket watch. Obviously it wasn't meant for someone else."

"But it was!" Hart said it over and over to himself on the way back. Why did he change his mind? Was it something to do with Victor? Everybody had said how proud and fond he was of his uncle. What could have happened to change his mind? Victor Grant couldn't have been involved in the murder, Hart felt sure. Something had happened, the boy had found out something or seen something. What on earth could it be to make him change his mind about a present for his uncle? He sighed. There were too many mysteries concerning the Grant family.

Chapter Seventeen

John Bailey would not have described the woman waiting in the interview room as 'young' but she had a natural vigour that may well have given that impression to many. She was of medium height and build and was smartly dressed. She wore a light raincoat over a suit and a small felt cap barely controlling a mass of light brown hair. A pair of sharp brown eyes met his immediately he entered. She spoke as soon as he had shut the door.

"I'm Evelyn Foster, I live at 10 Selborne Street. One of your officers came round yesterday and took down statements about Tommy Watson. I'm sorry to say that there was one thing we got wrong."

"Oh, pleased to meet you, Mrs. Foster, I'm Detective Sergeant Bailey. I'm sorry but the Chief Inspector is not available at the moment. What was it you say you got wrong?"

"Well, it was my husband, at lunch time today, he suddenly said that he had seen Tommy on Sunday afternoon. He hadn't been in when your officer called. I just gave him my own memories of Sunday. I said that we hadn't seen Tommy that day. Of course, I meant that I hadn't. It turns out that my husband had seen him when he was checking the car just before we went out for the afternoon."

"Where would that have been, Mrs. Foster?"

"It was in the street just in front of the house. Jim likes to have a check before we travel any distance. He said that he saw Tommy come out from the lane at the end of the street. There was an ice-cream van further up in Stoker Street not far from The Cavalier, just before the street turns out of sight, and Jim saw Tommy stop at the van."

"Are you absolutely sure of this?"

"Yes, when Jim mentioned it, we had just been talking about Tommy, saying that he never seemed to have very much. We never saw him eating sweets, for example. Just an occasional ice-cream, Jim said. I said that I had never seen Tommy with an ice-cream. Jim replied that he had seen him with one only last Sunday. Later it dawned on me that I had told your man that we hadn't seen Tommy on Sunday. I was quite worried, it seemed nothing but I thought I should come down here straight away and tell you."

"You did right, Mrs. Foster, quite right. It's that kind of detail that helps us get everything clear."

"Will it help you find the murderer?"

"I wouldn't say that exactly. We haven't got that far yet. At this stage, every little detail is important. What time was it that your husband saw Tommy?"

"It would be about quarter to two."

"Right, thanks very much."

They stood up simultaneously.

"Thank you very much for coming in, Mrs. Foster. Will your husband be in this evening?"

"Yes, after five o'clock." She looked anxious.

"Don't worry, Mrs. Foster, it's just that this may be our last sighting of Tommy Watson and I'd like to have a signed statement from your husband."

"Anything we can do, Sergeant. We liked Tommy. Anything to help catch his killer."

Bailey escorted Mrs. Foster to the front door, waited until she was out of sight then ran round to the back of the building. There were a number of outbuildings, mostly garages, attached to the main building via a covered space affectionately known as 'the shed'. It was in the shed that a careful examination of the ice-cream van was taking place.

"We are just finishing, Young John!"

The grizzled sergeant in charge of the operation had always called Bailey 'Young John', ever since Bailey had arrived at Clayton. It was a friendly, good natured greeting and Bailey had never taken exception to it.

"Anything promising, Jock?"

"Well, I think you might consider it promising."

"What? What? This is a helluva time to keep me in suspense."

Jock grinned.

"Not so fast, everything will have to be confirmed by the lab, as you know."

Bailey clenched his fists and glared at his tormentor. The sergeant grinned again but drew Bailey over to the piece of carpet that had once covered the floor of the van.

"Three small stains, could be blood. I've got sufficient samples for testing. There are at least two distinct kinds of soil, some grit, some wood fragments, fibres of string, one or two man-made fibres, vegetable remains...."

"Vegetable remains?"

"Yes, tiny pieces of grass, a leaf or two from a brussel sprout, fibres that look like plant roots...."

"From an allotment, maybe?"

"Yes, quite possibly."

"No identifiable footprints, I suppose?"

"No, there are marks from feet, probably wellingtons, but they are far too messed about."

"What about fingerprints?"

"Now there are plenty of those round the front of the counters. You'll have the results before very long."

"Excellent, Jock! You are worth your weight in gold. Did anyone tell you that?"

"Oh aye. My mother told me every other day."

It seemed obvious to Detective Sergeant Bailey that

122

Fenton must be brought in.. As the Chief wasn't in he must take the necessary action. He lifted the phone and made the necessary arrangements. Once Fenton was on his way he would send a D.C. to interview Fenton's wife. Meantime he would study the reports on the Chevely Estate door-to-door.

This took some time. No one at the town end of the estate had anything to contribute. Further up, one or two residents complained about traffic in the night but were too vague to take into account. One, several doors away from Fenton, claimed to have seen the ice-cream van return around one o' clock on Monday morning. This made Bailey sit up. He had made a point of questioning the men who interviewed the occupants near No. 34, he hadn't expected that someone as far away as this would have had anything so important to say. He shook his head impatiently, he must never jump to conclusions, he must read on and keep his mind open.

He was particularly careful to study the observations of the residents near the park end of the estate. Most had seen and heard nothing in spite of staying up to all hours, two thought they had heard a car, taxi they thought, arriving and departing around midnight. Another thought that he had heard a heavy vehicle turn round at the very end of the road. It had not stopped except to engage gears very noisily.

When he had finished, Bailey was very aware that the male inhabitants of Chevely Park estate, Ogilvie Drive in particular, were exceptionally mobile. They seemed to spend little time indoors but wandered from home to club and pub and other houses and returned at astonishing hours. He guessed that it was the freedom that belonged to a Sunday, every minute had to be action packed before the tedium of Monday's work set in again. It certainly wasn't like that for the women, or if it was, they weren't telling.

Surely, someone walking through the estate at the times given in the reports must have seen something.

One thing was for certain: there were more cars and fewer people about on the Monday night. The pattern was earlier to bed for most of the inhabitants and a sounder sleep. No one seems to have heard anything in the small hours of Tuesday. There were cars about but 'nothing unusual'. Were there no courting couples? No, they wouldn't have noticed anything either, or would they? Bailey stuck doggedly to his task. He went steadily through all the papers on his desk noting down the names and addresses of all the sons or daughters who had claimed to be out with girl or boy friends. He reached for the phone and asked for two D.C.s. When they came, he handed them the list and sent them to make further enquiries. On their way back they were to call at 10 Selborne Street and take a statement from a Mr. Foster.

Chapter Eighteen

"Your man Fenton's here, Sergeant Bailey, Interview Room 3." The desk sergeant was brisk.

"I'll be right there!"

Bailey leapt to his feet, adrenaline pumping. Now for the challenge! He rushed to the door to find his exit blocked. The obstacle was the substantial frame of D.C.I. Hart, just returned from a good meal at his own table.

"What's the rush, Sergeant? What's been happening in my absence?"

"I've brought Fenton in, sir. There were spots of blood on the mat in the ice-cream van...."

"Were there? Human blood, I take it?"

"We won't be sure of that until the lab has checked, sir, but...."

"It fits your idea, I suppose?"

Bailey was rather taken aback by his Chief's cool response.

"There are one or two other things, Sir. The neighbour who heard and saw the van being returned to its garage in the early hours of Tuesday morning, another who claims to have seen the van in the early hours of Monday morning and the fact that Fenton lied about it and the fact that he lied about visiting Selborne Street on the Sunday. He has to account for all that."

"Yes, he does. What's that about Selborne Street?"

"I asked him about his movements in the van on Sunday, he claims that he visited Selborne Street. Someone saw him at 1.45.p.m. He sold an ice-cream to Tommy Watson."

"The devil he did! He didn't recognise him, of course? Who was your witness by the way?"

"Mr. Foster of No.10. His wife came in this afternoon to say that her husband had seen Tommy

Watson on the Sunday but she hadn't known this when our man asked her yesterday."

"Very good of her. Selborne Street was one of Fenton's regular patches, was it?"

"No, according to him, he only went up there if trade wasn't so good elsewhere."

"You've been through all the Chevely Park Estate statements?"

"I've gone through them thoroughly, sir. As I said, someone from further down Ogilvie Drive says he saw the van return in the early hours of Tuesday morning, nothing else."

"Well, do your best with Fenton, Sergeant, I wish you luck!"

"Do you not wish to see him?"

"No, I'll leave him in your tender care for the moment. Oh, has Mr. Butterman not turned up yet?"

"Not that I know of, sir. The desk would have told me, I'm sure."

"Right, Sergeant Bailey, go to it!"

D.C.I. Hart settled down to work at his desk, he had enjoyed his excursions and was now reconciled to paperwork. On top of his in-tray was another file labelled Laboratory Report. He studied the contents carefully.

Pullover: Stains on back essentially chlorophyll, perhaps from grass, more likely algae. Ingrained dirt contained coal dust, ash and soil together with decayed vegetable matter. Sleeves of both lower arms had similar dirt plus calcium carbonate, brick dust and very small pieces of lichen.

Shirt: Faint tracings of the same dust.

Trousers: Stains on seat due to oleaginous vegetable matter. Faint smell characteristic of decaying kitchen waste. Faint staining in small patches near ankles of similar composition. Similar composition of dirt on the seat of the jeans as on the jacket. Crust of same material on the broken button of back right hand pocket.

Plimsolls: Splashes of common soil on both front uppers. Indents of both soles contained deposits of common soil, as above, plus traces of calcium carbonate and brick dust. Toes had strong deposits of calcium carbonate in scuff marks.

Hart took a deep breath and exhaled.

"Oleaginous vegetable matter!" He also wondered what the difference was between plimsolls and sandshoes. Plimsolls seemed such a pernickety word.

Another report stated that there were clear palm and thumb prints on the pocket watch belonging to Tommy Watson. There were no clear prints on the lighter. There was one clear print of a thumb on the side of the cigarette packet. Along with the report was a card with photostats of the fingerprints.

Hart sat back with his hands behind his head and thought. Tommy Watson did not smoke, therefore he had picked up this lighter and the cigarette packet. There had been the same brand of cigarette on the ground near the shed. Had the smoker dropped the lighter and packet there also? Why had Tommy Watson carried them with him? Had he found them only recently? Clearly, there had not been indiscriminate handling of the cigarette packet as in offering the cigarettes round. Had Tommy been playing detective? His uncle had said he had kept a look out for the people who had wrecked the shed. Perhaps he thought that he had found them.

Hart picked up the fingerprint card and walked down to the front desk.

"Get one of the team to check these with records,

will you, sergeant. I'll just slip in to see how Sergeant Bailey is doing."

There was a sudden movement from the bench behind him and two local reporters clamoured at his elbow.

"Sorry lads. I've nothing to give you yet."

"Chief Inspector, is it true that you have brought a suspect in for questioning? Can't you tell us more about him?"

"It's Tony Fenton, isn't it Chief?"

"His ice-cream van was brought in for examination wasn't it? Come on. Chief, give us a break!"

"Well, I didn't bring it in. Now clear off! I'll tell you when I have something positive, not before!"

It took a little while to shake the local terriers off but Hart remained placid, left the desk sergeant to quieten them and went down the corridor to interview room No.3.

Tony Fenton sat at the table, his head sunk on his chest. Even with a few-days' stubble, he looked pale. His hair and his clothing were dishevelled as though he had just risen from his bed. His eyes moved to Hart as he entered but they didn't seem to register anything. Perspiration caught the light as he moved his head. He raised cupped hands to the table then lowered them again to his knees, he didn't seem to be in control of them.

"You must have some explanation." Bailey was saying. He stood up and walked over to his chief.

"I can't get anything out of him, sir. He's not responding to anything. Would you like to try?"

Hart nodded and sat down opposite Fenton. He spoke briskly as though he knew nothing of what had gone before.

"Mr. Fenton isn't it? I'm sure you want to get home.

Don't we all! There are some things we have to get clear. You possess an ice-cream van, don't you?" He looked sharply at Fenton and raised his chin in a short movement which demanded a reply. Fenton stopped thinking for a moment, licked his lips briefly and said "Yes."

"You returned from your round on Sunday, late in the afternoon and cleaned it as usual?" Again the gesture. Again the automatic reply.

"I washed and cleaned it thoroughly. I don't know what time it was but it was almost dark when I finished."

"Did you take it out again?"

This time there was a hesitation.

"You didn't go out on the Monday? I believe you said you felt ill.?"

"Yes. I didn't go on the round. I went for a drink in the morning, didn't feel better and went to bed in the afternoon. The missus sent for the doctor...."

"And he came.....?"

"He didn't come till five." The eyes began to glaze over. Hart raised his voice a little.

"What did the doctor say?"

"What do they always say? There wasn't much wrong. He gave me a prescription and said I would be alright in a couple of days."

"And were you?"

"Yes." The man licked his lips suspiciously.

"Did you feel well on Tuesday - the next day?"

"No, I stayed in bed."

"You stayed in bed all day, you didn't go out?"

"No, I didn't get up till Wednesday."

"You didn't have any visitors?"

"Visitors? What visitors, no I didn't have any visitors!" An inspiration occurred to him. "Until he came this morning."

Hart rearranged himself on his chair and spoke with an air of confidentiality. "Mr. Fenton, could anyone take your van out of the garage and drive it away without you knowing?"

The idea created a stir in Fenton's mind. His eyes wandered rapidly from Hart to Bailey to the constable near the door. They rested briefly on the table then moved to the wall on his right. He seemed to have gained the time he required and had ordered his thoughts when he spoke again.

"Well, the key's loose, they might get it started." His voice had grown a little stronger. "Yes, it's possible."

"Even without a key?"

"Well, they might have got another key to work."

"Wouldn't you have heard it drive off?"

"With the kids and the telly, you don't hear nothing in our house."

Hart paused again.

"You have a houseful, Mr. Fenton. Four children, isn't it?"

"Yes, four, all young 'uns."

"You have a dog as well, don't you?"

"Yes...." He hesitated.

"Wouldn't the dog have told you if someone tried to drive your van away."

"Ah, well, when we have him in the house, he doesn't hear either."

Hart leaned forward and stared at Fenton fixedly.

"Your van was driven away and returned in the early hours on Monday and on Tuesday. Why would anyone want to take it away twice?"

Fenton shrugged.

"More than that, why would anyone bother to return it?"

Another shrug.

"It wouldn't be anyone doing a round at that time of

130

night, presumably it wouldn't be a thief, would it? There was nothing missing was there?"

"No...no."

"But you haven't checked, have you?"

The eyes wandered again and perspiration began to flow faster.

"Well, I..."

"You can't have checked or you would have noticed that mess, wouldn't you?"

There was a long pause. Hart went on in the same quiet voice.

"Mr. Fenton, I have to tell you that we are enquiring about a murder. The men examining your van have found bloodstains on the mat. Think! Think about yourself! It is possible that your van was used to carry the body? Now, it is clearly your van. What are we left to think?"

"I have nothing to do with any murder! You can't pin that on me!"

"I'm afraid that is exactly what we can do if we don't get any more answers."

"I've told you...."

"A pack of lies!" Hart raised his voice for the first time. "You don't realise what sort of trouble you are in. What have you got to hide?"

Fenton slumped back in his chair and refused say anything further.

"That is what he was like just after I got started. He just clammed up. Shall I book him?"

"What with? We'll leave him here until we've checked with his missus. Get her account, then we'll decide." They had drawn to one side, Hart turned back to Fenton.

"We'll leave you to think about it, don't take too long!"

131

"We'll need something more substantial before we can charge him. All you are basing your suspicions on is a previous record of violence..."

"But, sir, he was one of the last to see Tommy Watson..."

"Come off it, Sergeant Bailey! Unless he knocked him over, and I would point out that the medical evidence is against that possibility, there is nothing to connect Fenton with Watson. He failed to recognise the picture, didn't he? He wasn't faking that was he?"

"No, I don't think so."

"Well then..."

"Sir, if it was simply a matter of using the van to help someone else move the body, there would be the connection."

"I agree with you there, but if you were only the chauffeur and you stood a good chance of having to stand the rap for the murder, would you hold back? No, you would spill the beans, I'm sure. In the case of someone like Fenton, it would be sooner rather than later."

"Unless he has something to gain by holding out for a while."

"Well, we'll give him a little while longer."

They had walked along the corridor, this time away from the desk, thus avoiding any further skirmish with reporters. By turning right, again, they were able to return to the D.C.I.'s office.

"I sent Phillips out to check on Fenton's wife, sir, he should be back soon."

"Good, now what do we know about Fenton, apart from his record? He has a wife and four kids, he sells ice-cream, what else? Where does he drink? Who are his pals? Where does he go, with or without his wife?"

"He said that he had been drinking in the Three

132

Bells on Firtree Road on the Sunday night."

"That's a fair distance from Chevely Park. It's a lively place and fairly big, if my memory serves me right. We must find out who he met there and whether it is his usual haunt."

"He also uses the club at Maudsley Terrace, sir, that's just at the bottom of Ogilvie Drive."

"The Working Men's Club, you mean, just where the estate begins?"

"Yes sir, but he also said that he had called at a friend's at Wansley Terrace on the Sunday night after he left the Three Bells. Wansley Terrace is just one away from Maudsley Terrace."

"It's time all this was checked, it should have been done straight away. Who've we got left?"

"Phillips and Ridley are both out and I sent two other constables out to check on courting couples. I thought that one or other of the sons and daughters who claimed to be out with their partners on Sunday night or Monday night might have been in or around the park and might have seen something."

Hart couldn't help smiling.

"That just shows how important it is to have a young man on the team. Well done!"

The phone rang.

"D.C.I. Hart....yes, that's quick! Thank you, that's rather general, isn't it? Not very conclusive. Can't be helped. Thank you anyway. Good-bye."

"The lab, thought I should know immediately that it is human blood on that mat. Group O, rhesus plus."

"The same as Tommy Watson's?"

"Yes and the same as a few million others. We have to be careful, I'm not at all happy about Fenton."

They sat silent for a few minutes.

"Sir! You were going to send someone out..."

"What time is it?"

133

"Ten past eight, sir, and I haven't eaten since lunch."

"Right then, we'll both go and I'll stand you a bar meal at the Three Bells."

Chapter Nineteen

The Three Bells was a big pub set back from the main road with a concrete forecourt and a very large car park at the back. There was a restaurant at one side with a cocktail bar next to it, a generous bar-lounge and a long ordinary bar. For their purposes, Hart and Bailey chose the long bar. It was warm, cheerful and well patronised, most of the customers clung to the bar though there were tables against the wall opposite.

They pushed themselves through and Bailey ordered a steak and kidney pie. Hart declined to eat, contenting himself with a pint, and they found their way to a table. As Bailey ate, Hart had a good look round, pondering where his move should be aimed. A quieter time would have been best. There were two people serving behind the bar, a man in his forties with thinning hair and a bottle blonde in her twenties. The man was a typically loud voiced barman who was proud of his wit and laughed a lot. The brassy looking young woman was relatively quiet but smiled at her customers and seemed to be very pleasant.

Between mouthfuls, Bailey grinned at his Chief.

"I'm wondering if Fenton was a lady's man? Shall I speak to the barmaid, sir? If he was one for the ladies, I reckon she would know."

"I reckon you should leave the barmaid to me, Sergeant, you've only been married a couple of years, I don't want your missus complaining." Hart smiled, "Hurry up, I want you alongside to listen."

They took the plate and their empty glasses to one end of the bar and were soon attended by the lady in question.

"Excuse me, do you happen to know a man called Tony Fenton?"

"Oh yes, I know Tony Fenton." Her voice was low

pitched and she answered with only casual interest.

"Is he not one of the regulars, then? I was hoping to see him tonight."

"Well," she turned to fill a glass, "I haven't seen him tonight but he's not usually here during the week, he's more weekends really."

She wandered away in response to a call and didn't return for a while. The barman came to their end in search of a particular bottle. While he was stooping to reach the shelves below counter level, Bailey took a turn.

"Tony Fenton been in tonight, mate?"

"Tony Fenton, nah, haven't seen him." His head came up and he looked briefly at Bailey. "Ask Charlie over there, there by the far door! I'll fetch him, Charlie!"

Hart shrank as best he could onto a bar stool. It was very difficult for him to avoid looking like a policeman. Bailey had no trouble because of his light, wiry build.

Charlie was a small, watery-eyed man of indeterminate age and a pronounced limp. He had a grubby trilby pulled well down and a grubbier mackintosh pulled tight in the middle. In spite of their grubbiness, these items retained a certain air of their former smartness. Hart guessed that they had been expensive when bought many years ago. The man's shoes were strong brogues, horribly scuffed. A cigarette, with an extraordinary length of ash still clinging to the little between the lips, and a deeply lined and weather-beaten face completed the picture. This had to be a man of the turf. Hart quickly took the lead.

"What'll you have Charlie?"

"Mine's a gin, guv, what can I do for you? Cecil says you wanted a word. I warn you, I ain't got nothing for tomorrer. Saturday now, that's different, but it'll cost yer."

"That's good of you, Charlie, but we don't want a tip just now. We wanted to have a word with Tony Fenton, have you seen him?"

"Strewth, guv, haven't you heard, I suppose you haven't," he dashed off his gin in case his news was too much of a disappointment, "He's been taken in by the law, just now, just today."

The little man wagged his head from side to side as he spoke, not unlike an inquisitive bantam.

"Damn, we needed to talk to him! Business. What they got him for?"

Charlie licked his lips and looked exceedingly thirsty, a natural actor, he never needed to rehearse. He was presented with another gin.

"I thought it was because of the bother with Charlie Beck but someone told me it was about this murder, you know, the young boy."

Charlie gave a knowing twitch and raised his arm almost to shoulder height to down his gin with professional vigour.

"Murder? Tony? Never! Charlie Beck, that's different, what's Tony been up to this time?"

Charlie's hand wandered almost to his face in a vague gesture Hart easily recognised.

"What are you smoking, Charlie? Try one of these."

Bailey was astonished to see his Chief take out a cigarette case and offer the contents to Charlie. That indefatigable man of the world took one with an easy grace and lit up. His right hand fell with a thump just next to his glass which was again empty. The fingers twitched once or twice before he allowed his watery eyes to glance down at the glass.

"Get him another one, will you, John?"

"Thanks guv, it's been a long day. Well, you know young Tony, always had an eye for the women. He was chatting up this bird in the lounge on Sunday, her man

137

came in from next door and didn't like it. Tony legged it until the coast was clear then went off to Charlie Beck's. Charlie was having a bit of a party. I should know, it was me who tipped him, wasn't it? "Frazzle" 20 to 1 in the three o'clock. Charlie had a fiver on it then he put the lot on "Toby Sunshine" on the last race. Didn't it win by six lengths!"

Charlie got so excited that he gripped Hart's elbow and shook it. Hart looked down at him and smiled broadly, genuinely sharing in the little man's pleasure.

"3 to 1 guv! Pockets stuffed with fivers! Charlie had a real night of it. When he finished here he took a couple of crates back home with him. I think it lasted all night."

"Lucky name, Charlie!" Hart gave the little man a pat on the shoulder.

"You're right there guv!" The tipster laughed so loudly that he fell into a long coughing fit. As soon as he had recovered Hart pressed on quickly.

"Young Tony ended up there, did he?"

"Yes, he turned up all right. Like everybody else he was well away. Started the same lark, this time with one of Charlie's women No sooner was he in trouble there, mate, when this other bloke he'd upset down here turned up. What a caper! What a punch up there was! Best of it was, though," the little man clung to Hart's sleeve in a paroxysm of hilarity, "young Tony escaped, hopped it, without a scratch!"

He exploded into wheezy laughter, punctuated with spluttering coughs. He had great difficulty in recovering his breath and for a moment or two it looked as though he might collapse. Hart pushed his unfinished drink towards him.

"Watch it, Charlie, you'll do yourself a mischief!"

By this time, most people at the bar were joining in, the laughter was amazingly infectious. Hart frowned inwardly, he wanted to push on, there was no time for unnecessary diversions.

"Mind you, his luck ran out, didn't it?"

"Oi, that's Tony Fenton you're on about, isn't it." Someone standing nearby interrupted.

"Silly bugger!"

"Nasty piece of work!"

"Nah, he's just a bit thick."

"He'd have to be, mixing with Chopper's girl friend."

"You'll not see him round here again in a hurry."

"Not likely, not if he knows what's good for him."

"Chopper'll make sure he gets what's coming to him, it might not be today or tomorrow, but he'll catch him just when he thinks he's forgotten. I know Chopper!"

"Who's this Chopper?"

"Who's asking?" The last voice came from a tall, thin man who had been watching Hart for some time.

"Friend of mine." Charlie chirped up, by now well warmed by double gins and fully expecting further refreshment. His hat had slipped round to a silly angle but it only served to make him more endearing.

"A copper, more like."

This remark was drowned by a general cheer as Charlie tried to straighten his hat and missed. The barman sidled up to Hart, who had another gin waiting, and whispered, "Old Charlie's had a few already, he's still celebrating Charlie Beck's winnings."

Bailey had had no part in the conversation, but he had remained alert. He stepped back from the crowd and stood alongside the thin man who had spoken and thereby threatened to end Charlie's tale.

"Do you know who they are talking about?" He smiled disinterestedly at the man. "This Chopper?"

The man looked carefully at Bailey and grunted.

"It seems it gets lively in here." Bailey walked back

to one of the tables as if he didn't expect an answer.

A movement at the bar and the arrival of more customers left the thin man temporarily isolated. He was only a step away from Bailey's table. He decided to sit down. Bailey nodded to him and sipped his pint.

"You with that fellow in the corner?"

"Yes, I'm in the same business."

"He's a copper, isn't he?"

"He's certainly big enough, I'll tell him you thought so, he'll be tickled pink."

Bailey coolly picked up a newspaper from the next table and opened it up. The thin man was most disconcerted, he looked back at Hart then at Bailey, he could have sworn he was right. There was another burst of laughter from the bar. Bailey looked across and intercepted a signal from his Chief. He finished his drink and stood up.

"Excuse me, business calls, goodnight!"

Hart joined him after a difficult leave-taking from little Charlie who thought he had made a friend for life.

Outside, they both took deep breaths.

"Sir! I'm not sure that I am ever going to believe you again, after that performance."

"I once belonged to an amateur dramatic society, do you believe? I gave it up because the only parts they wanted me to play were policemen."

"And I didn't know you smoked."

"I don't, but a few cigarettes come in useful once in a while."

They laughed briefly then Hart's manner changed completely.

"The name of the 'sinister' Chopper is Morton, a wholesaler from the other side of town. That's as far as I got. We had better have a quick word with Charlie

140

Beck."

They climbed into their car and were just driving off when the car radio called for them. D.C. Phillips had returned and was asking for them, so had D.C. Ridley. Hart asked for them to stay where they were, he would return as quickly as possible.

"Everything happens at once! Whatever Phillips has for us can wait until we know what happened at Beck's."

It took no time at all to find Wansley Terrace but there was no answer at No.16. They enquired of a next door neighbour, this time producing their warrant cards. The response was instant. This neighbour was aggrieved. She and Charlie Beck did not get on well together. There had been such a row on the Sunday night that, had she possessed a phone, she would have contacted the police. It had started about midnight, wild laughter and shouts, not to mention music. Later there had been a real row with screams and thuds. The fight, or whatever it was, had spilled out into the street. There had been shouts and the sound of running feet, then it quietened down a bit, but the noise of music and laughter went on until four in the morning. It wasn't right.

Asked if there had been any cars moving about, the neighbour said that there had been at least two taxi loads arriving and departing at various times. Why there had to be shouting and slamming of doors she knew not. Total lack of consideration. She hadn't been one to complain in the past, but there had to be a limit. She had even heard a private bus coming and going. Asked how she knew it was a bus, the neighbour said that she had taken a quick look out of the window and had seen its back door standing open. Of course it could have been an ambulance, but there had been no lights flashing. No, it had been too dark to see any letters or such and she wasn't one to go standing at the window for all to see in the early hours of the morning. Never mind the time, she'd been kept awake for so long it could have been any hour. It just wasn't right to be deprived of sleep by brawling neighbours. It wouldn't have happened if her husband had still been alive....."

The two men exchanged looks, asked the neighbour her name and address, said that if anything serious arose from their enquiry they would be in touch again, and set off back to the station as quickly as possible.

Chapter Twenty

The two D.C.s were chatting in an outer office. Hart signalled Ridley to wait and beckoned Phillips into his office.

"It must have been urgent for you to have had a call sent out. What have you got for us?"

"Sir, Mrs. Fenton said that her husband went out again in the early hours of Monday morning, I thought you should know that straight away."

"Well now, start at the beginning and tell us the whole story."

"Sir, she was upset at her husband being taken away, she didn't know why, he hadn't said anything to her. I said that there was a murder enquiry going on and that we needed to know about his movements on Monday and Tuesday. She was very defensive. She wasn't going to tell us anything. There were tears and temper but Policewoman Fraser calmed her down.

"Fenton went out as usual on the Sunday with the van, came back about five and cleaned it and put it away. He had gone out in the evening to the Three Bells, as he usually did on Sunday evenings. He was very late back, she heard him because she was feeding the baby. Instead of staying in, he had gone out again, she heard him drive the van out. She didn't hear him return because she must have been asleep. He must have had a skin full because he didn't get up in the morning and said he wasn't well. She took the children to her mother's, leaving him in bed and didn't get back until three. He told her that he had gone down to the club about midday but didn't feel too good when he got back so went to bed. She had to go to the clinic with the baby so she asked the doctor to call. The doctor was not pleased when he came, gave her a prescription for him and said he would be alright in a couple of days. They

143

had all stayed in and watched T.V. on that Monday night. About 10 o'clock somebody came to the door, her husband answered and she could hear sharp words. She was just going out to see who it was when her husband passed something out and shut the door quickly. When she asked who it was, her husband went mad and hit her. She was upset because he had been lolling round the house all day while she had had to look after the kids."

"She didn't hear the van being driven away?"

"No sir, I asked her that. She said that they'd had a blazing row when he hit her and the kids all started yelling."

"And what about hearing it come back?"

"She said that they had made it up and had watched T.V. then gone to bed about midnight, she'd seen to the baby then they had slept right through till seven. Not even the baby woke her."

"Thanks, you've done a good job there, Phillips."

The D.C. had barely gone when Bailey burst out.

"Sir, it rather looks as though he did lend his van out."

"Yes, it looks that way, but whether it has anything to do with our murder is another matter. I wouldn't mind betting that Chopper Morton and Charlie Beck are involved and that their business, however shady, has no connection with the death of Tommy Watson."

"We don't know though, do we sir? It could be that Tommy Watson stumbled on something to do with this Morton or Beck."

Hart shook his head.

"Morton's business is in the other end of town, I cannot think he can have anything to do with Watson. But you can find out, can't you, sergeant?"

Bailey grinned, he liked the idea of doing some enquiries of his own.

"Does that mean that we will have to let Fenton go, sir?"

"Yes, it does, but we will hang on to him for a little while longer."

D.C. Ridley knocked on the door. He looked thoroughly fed up.

"Ah, Ridley, have you had a productive day?"

"Sir! I've been at it solidly. I've noted down the main events of the year according to the Gazette and I have to say that nothing looks as though it had any connection with the murder."

"Now that was 1946, wasn't it? If there is nothing for us there, I might have to get you to look at 1945 as well."

Ridley was unable to stifle a groan.

"Cheer up! At least you were warm and under cover. All splendid experience for you. What time is it, by the way?"

"It's 10.30, sir."

"Is it? Well, tomorrow, I want you and Phillips to go round to 16 Walmsley Terrace and find out what a Mr. Charlie Beck was doing last Monday evening and Tuesday morning. Get there at 7 in the morning and catch him before he has a chance to leave the house. If there is a problem, bring him in."

Ridley was quick to make his escape.

"It has been a long day, Sergeant. You'd better arrange for Fenton to stay overnight, then you can get back to your long suffering wife."

Bailey grinned and departed.

Hart was feeling a little jaded himself. It certainly had been a busy day. He hadn't expected to be finishing quite so late. Anyhow, he felt that some sort of progress had been made but whether it was really leading anywhere he could not be sure. He was just pausing at the door to put the light out when his phone rang.

"Hart."

"Sir, it's the desk sergeant, I have a gentleman to see you. Very worried he is, the name's Butterman."

"Is it bedamned! Right, sergeant, shunt him along."

He was far from pleased. He had been ready to leave, he was tired and irritable, not the best mood for clear headed interviewing. He had the feeling that he was not going to like this gentleman and that meant trying to compensate the whole time. He sat down at his desk, switched on the lamp and picked up some papers to give himself a show, at least, of being busy.

"Mr. Butterman, sir!"

Hart was completely taken aback. Before him stood a tallish, stout man in his late fifties. He was bespectacled and bald with a fleshy face and a high colour. Apart from his height, Hart thought he had many of the characteristics of Mrs. Butterman.

"Detective Chief Inspector Hart," he introduced himself and indicated a chair, "I wasn't expecting to see you, Mr. Butterman, it was your son I wanted to talk to."

"Sidney Butterman. Well now, Chief Inspector, I am most unhappy about that, I cannot see why you should wish to talk to my son, John. He can have nothing to do with this matter, he hardly saw the boy....."

Hart saw red. He had endured the same pompous denials from Mrs. Butterman that morning, now, here, at this time of night he was being subjected to another round of obstruction.

"Mr. Butterman, it is late, where is your son?"

The sharp brevity of Hart's question shook his visitor.

"Er, well, that's just it."

Sidney Butterman's fleshy jowl dropped, his chin

146

lost some of its resolution. Hart judged this man to be a petty bully with the same in-built sense of superiority as his wife. He was well dressed in a smart blue suit and expensive looking shoes. The same question formed itself in Hart's mind as had occurred to him earlier that morning - why were the Buttermans content to live in a street of ordinary terrace houses?

"That's why I have come to see you."

There was a long pause.

"We haven't seen him all day."

Hart sighed. He felt that he owed this man nothing.

"Mr. Butterman, it is only half past ten at night. Is there not a chance that your son may yet return home?"

"He usually comes home in the evening for a meal. He went out this morning and hasn't been back for any meals."

"What time did he leave this morning?" Hart's question was mischievous but was lost on his visitor.

"My wife says he left in the early part of the morning."

"Mr. Butterman, are you here to excuse your son's failure to report to me or are you here to report him as a missing person?"

Butterman coloured. Hart had seen the same ugly red-purple on his wife's face some hours ago. The man was a natural blusterer but he was at a disadvantage in his present situation. Hart continued in the same measured tone.

"I have no intention of waiting any longer for your son, tonight. When he does return home, please tell him to report first thing in the morning."

"But...but...we are quite worried. He would have said if he had intended to stay out all day."

"Why are you worried now? I believe your son does not work regular hours and that he is, occasionally, late in at nights. I suggest that you go home and wait to see if he turns up. If he does not, call again tomorrow and we will do something about it. It is much too early to consider him a missing person."

Hart stood up and his visitor was obliged to do so too. Sidney Butterman looked a little helpless but Hart did not soften. He felt that this family was not particularly deserving of sympathy. There were many questions he could have put to Butterman Senior but they would wait until after he had spoken to his son.

Chapter Twenty-One

Hart was always a better man immediately after breakfast. He might rise in something of a fog, his motions might be entirely automatic until his last piece of toast had gone down but, once his gastric juices were in full use, he felt ready for the world with all his senses alert. It was no use saying anything important to him until after breakfast. His children had long ago come to terms with that. After breakfast they could ask him for the world, they wouldn't get it but he would be very sympathetic about it.

On entering the Station his manner was always cheerful and brisk. Those who had got to know him realised that however gruff and grim he had been the previous night he was always pleasant and amenable first thing in the morning, much against the rule for most senior officers. It wasn't a trait that always worked in his favour, he was often bothered with trivia before he could get down to his serious work. Over the years his ear had become a little less sympathetic and newcomers had to be wary.

This morning, he was stopped by Inspector Jordan before he had reached his office. Jordan was 'neat and crisp', one of Hart's wife Sheila's expressions. Tall and thin, glossy black hair neatly trimmed, long face, keen dark eyes, immaculate uniform, he was in his early thirties and ready for promotion. He would get it, he was remarkably efficient, recalled Hart. His present duties included being in charge if the 'pool', a term used both for the group of officers allotted to the enquiry and for the information gathered by them.

"There was nothing from the Headlaw Road enquiry. One or two thought they knew the boy but none of the Grant family were regular shoppers in the Headlaw Road area. The general request for sightings produced 36 possibles on Saturday and only two for Sunday, one of which was that late one from somebody called Foster..."

"Who was the other, can you look it out for me please? That could be very important."

"The Chevely Park Estate enquiry produced a number of people who knew the boy, all of them because children in the families went to the same school, he sometimes cycled round that estate looking for friends. He never stayed long at anyone's."

"Probably didn't want to lose his bike."

Jordan permitted himself a brief smile.

"There was one report I thought important. A courting couple saw two figures running in the park at about one in the morning of Tuesday."

"Running? What did they mean, running?"

"The words they used were 'crouching low and running'. The couple were worried because they thought that they might have been looking for them. This couple were among the bushes..."

"Look, can you bring me the report itself. I agree with you, it sounds very promising." Hart was anxious to get his coat off and he had seen the same two reporters who had troubled him the previous day hurrying in from the street. Jordan nodded and disappeared into a back room.

In his own office, Hart sat down at his desk aware that there were hours of report reading and mental work ahead. Bailey knocked to say that he would be off on the track of Chopper Morton, his chief envied him but gave him his blessing and he departed. Jordan reappeared with the reports he thought Hart wished to see. The D.C.I. smiled, Jordan moved like a well-oiled castor, always smooth and precise, so efficient that he almost anticipated demands. He would be sorely missed, if his promotion took him away from this division, as it almost certainly would. For a brief moment, Hart pondered the promotion prospects of Sergeant Bailey. He couldn't quite see him fulfilling Jordan's role but that was simply because they were such different characters, valuable in such different ways. He would like to see John Bailey get on, he was so lively and so keen to succeed.

"What about Fenton, Sir?"

"We'll keep him until this evening, the full 24 hours. I'll have another go at questioning him later this morning. It may be that a couple of my men will be able to add something when they return, they shouldn't be long. I told them that if they had any bother with the man they are going to see they were to bring him in. I expect that they will be back within the hour. Someone called Charlie Beck, have you heard of him?"

"Charlie Beck, he doesn't come to mind, Sir."

"There was one thing in particular you could do, Inspector. I want a few posters put up round the entrances to the Town ground before tomorrow's match. They should ask if anyone saw Watson on Sunday. I know the lad went to Grammond to watch the football now and again."

"Right, Sir. Oh, have you thought about a television appeal, sir?"

"A great idea! That would mean going to the studio in Grammond, or would it have to be Rockborough?"

"We could try both, sir, to make sure we catch the early news tonight. Someone will have to take the photographs, but I was thinking of a personal appeal."

"You mean, appear in person. Who would that be?"

"You, sir. You are the officer in charge, it would have to be you."

"You know what that would mean? They would want to interview me and I would have to tell them that very little progress has been made. No, Inspector, photographs will have to do. Their own announcers can make the appeal. Anyway, there is far too much to do here. Can I leave that with you?"

"Certainly, Sir."

"And the posters at the ground?"

"Right, Sir." Jordan withdrew.

Hart shook his head, he would not like to appear on television, at least not until the crime had been solved. So far, he had never been required to do so and he wasn't in a hurry to have that experience. He had always felt sorry for Chief Constables or Inspectors or whatever who appeared on television news at inopportune moments. The television people enjoyed having them at their mercy, lingering over their predicament, yet when things had gone well for the police, television interviews had always been short and snappy. That was his opinion, anyway. He would get on with his work and await results. It was typical of Jordan to have thought that up, he would certainly know how to handle television reporters, Hart smiled again.

He read the report on the couple who had seen two men in the park on Sunday. Ernest James Bell, aged 18 of 23 Ogilvie Drive and Theresa Potts, aged 17 of Ventnor Way had been out late on Monday night. They had been to the cinema and after they returned to the Chevely Estate decided to stroll in the park. They were kissing and cuddling by some bushes when they heard someone coming. They hid and saw two men crouching and running. It was too dark to see what they looked like. One was tall and the other medium sized. They were looking back as they were running so they thought they were being chased. No one else came and the men didn't come back so they waited for quarter of an hour and then they went home. The officer who had written this down had added in brackets: 1.00 a.m.

Potts, the name was familiar. Hart read it all again then sat back and reached for his phone.

"Inspector Jordan please. Ah, Jordan, I want to see Bell and Potts, the two in this report you gave me just now. Can you get someone to bring them in? You have the addresses? Right."

Potts, Hart puzzled, fidgeting with his notes. Potts. Then he remembered. Stewey Potts, Tommy Watson's school friend, this could be his sister. Hart suddenly felt that he should give more attention to what the school friends and acquaintances had to say. He dug out the reports that Bailey had left in his tray. There was very little real information but he made a note to have further words with Jane Mason. There was one person who hadn't yet been seen, Robert Shaw. How long would he stay in hospital? He wondered how serious the yellow jaundice was. He remembered the mother and thought that a hospital visit would be much preferable to a home visit. He decided to act at once. He telephoned the hospital and made enquiries of Master Robert Shaw in Ward 6. He gleaned that his liver problem had given cause for concern and that the boy would be in hospital for a week or more until further tests were made. He thanked the staff and rang off. That gave him a little more time.

His mind had swung away from Fenton and Chevely Park and had returned to Selborne Street. He wondered why he had got no answer from the Grants when he had last called. It was strange because he had formed the impression from everyone he had spoken to that the Grants very rarely went out and certainly not together. If he had the chance, he would call again today. He would also call on the Buttermans if their son had not reported in before then. He pondered the business of the dark coloured van that Eric Semper had seen. Was it coincidence or was it important? He would call in

153

again to see that youth too.

The arrival of Ridley and Phillips quickly returned his attention to Chevely Park. They said that they had caught Charlie Beck before he was up. He had been very stroppy but they had persuaded him that co-operation then and there was preferable to going with them to the station. He denied that there had been a fracas on Sunday night, just a few friends helping him to celebrate his winnings on the horses. He worked as a senior storeman and driver for Trevor Morton. He had known Tony Fenton a long time. Fenton was foolish, didn't think what he was doing and was too fond of the ladies. Yes, he had had words with him but that was all. Fenton had fancied a lady friend of his. He didn't know anything about Fenton crossing Morton. The party didn't really break up, people just drifted away. The last went about 3.30. No, he had not noticed when Tony Fenton left. He, himself, had only three hours sleep as he had to go to work that morning. There were twenty or thirty at the party. He couldn't or wouldn't give a list. Said he couldn't remember everyone, some were friends of friends and he didn't know them all. Yes, Trevor Morton was there. No, he didn't have a fight with Fenton.

"Pretty thin, don't you think? Was he being cagey?"

"Probably, sir, he had time to think what he was saying. It didn't all come out in a rush."

"Well, it will serve for the moment. Thanks. Oh, Ridley, I haven't had time to look at your findings from the Gazette. Don't go too far, I might want you to go back."

Ridley kept a straight face until he was in the corridor. Inspector Jordan bumped into him as he was wrestling with a particularly ugly facial contortion.

"Not nice, constable! Looks as if you need to go sick. But not yet, you'll be needed."

Ridley's apology was abject and for days he had to endure Phillips' banter.

"Bell and Potts are here, sir. I've kept them separate. Rooms One and Two. They don't know that they are both here."

"Excellent, Jordan! That was quick."

"They were both unemployed, sir, they were able to come straight away. I sent two cars so that we could have separate stories."

"Would you like to join me? I'll take the young man first."

"Right, sir."

Ernest James Bell was a sandy haired youth, still wrestling with the problems of adolescence. His face was pale and spotty with one or two moles from which tufts of sandy hair sprouted. There were outcrops of blackheads in the furrows of his nostrils and at the edges of his eyebrows. His eyes were light brown and clear but moved quickly and nervously. His lips were large, the upper fringed by a light yet pronounced moustache, but when they parted, they revealed remarkably good white teeth. He was thin and boney and moved his limbs awkwardly.

He was sitting uncomfortably when the two police officers entered, not knowing what was expected of him. Hart spoke firmly and clearly.

"I'm glad you were able to come in, Mr. Bell. We need to get your story clear. You say that you were in Chevely Park on Monday night and that you saw two figures hurrying past, running I think you said? Is that right?"

"Yes," the boy's neck gave a little forward movement, "We were er, er, necking in the park.."

"Perhaps you had better start at the beginning. Your

girlfriend is Theresa Potts, I believe, and you had taken her to the pictures?"

"Yes, we went to the second house to see "Days of Wine and Roses" with Jack Lemon. I didn't like it much. We came out before the end and went to her house. Her brother was watching the telly so we went for a walk instead."

"Would her brother be Stewart Potts?"

"Yeh, Stewey," the neck made two forward movements, "How did you know that?"

"What time was it when you went into the park?"

The youth wriggled and his arms made a short flailing movement.

"I'm not sure. It must have been about eleven."

"You were in the park a long time, then?"

"I don't know." The wriggling continued and a blush rose slowly up the youth's face.

"We must get the times right, if we can. Did you have a favourite spot?"

"Er, yes, we liked to go up the mound round the back of the long bushes."

Perspiration was beginning to run down the sides of his face.

"You were still there when you heard someone coming?"

"Well it was Tess that heard them at first, I didn't. We just lay still and let them go by."

"You didn't want to be seen, so you lay low?"

"Yeh, Tess was dead worried, it could have been anyone."

"You mean, it could have been someone who knew her and she didn't want to be found..."

"Yeh, yeh," the youth was very agitated, "it was late and she might have been in trouble..."

"So you lay low until whoever it was went by?"

"Yeh."

156

"When you told your story to the officer who called, you said that they were crouched and running and you also said that one was tall and the other was medium size."

"Yes, they was."

"But how could you tell if you were lying low trying not to be seen?"

"That was the second time."

"The second time? You didn't mention a second time."

"Well, there was a second time. It was the same blokes coming back."

"How do you know that?"

"By the sound. It was the same sound of feet only they were faster the second time, lighter like."

Hart and Jordan exchanged glances. Jordan took over for a short while.

"Do you think you were the only ones in the park that night?"

"I don't know, really. I think we probably were."

"I thought that park was popular with courting couples?"

"Yeh, you're right, but it was late and a bit cold like."

"It didn't put you off. Were there no other people walking through the park, then?"

"Too late by then. It's only people walking their dogs, anyway. The park doesn't go anywhere. By midnight there isn't anyone about."

"You had it all worked out?"

Bell grinned and shuffled awkwardly, Jordan had given him no clue as to whether he approved or disapproved. Hart resumed.

"How was it you managed to see these figures when they came back?"

There was a pause. The youth was wrestling to find

words and his embarrassment was extreme.

"Well, we was taking a bit of a breather. I was sitting up when they came back and I saw them."

"Did Theresa Potts see them?"

"I don't thi...she might have done, I don't know."

"Think hard, Mr. Bell, can you remember anything particular about these figures, anything at all?"

"Well, they were men and both wore caps, one was smaller than the other, he was in front, the other was taller because he was more crouched down like."

"What sort of build were they?"

"They had coats on so it was hard to tell. I couldn't see their faces because they were looking back when they passed me."

"There wasn't anybody following them though, was there?"

"No, we waited for a long while in case anybody else came and there wasn't anybody. So we went home."

"You never saw anyone on the way home?"

"No, nobody."

"Mr. Bell, I would like you to make a complete statement and sign it, so that we have something positive. You have been a great help but I want you to do one more thing for me. I want you to go with one of my officers and point out the place where you saw these men. Would you do that?"

Ernie Bell beamed with relief that it was all over. He nodded his willingness and said he would certainly do so.

Out in the corridor, Hart smiled at Jordan.

"There isn't much doubt as to what they were up to. I believe him, do you?"

"Yes, sir, it sounded convincing enough. I don't suppose the girl will be quite so willing to tell us what

158

they were up to."

"No I don't suppose so, but I don't think that they have invented this story, I really believe that they did see these figures and they were the men who dumped the body. It doesn't get us very far though, does it?"

Inspector Jordan was right, Theresa Potts proved to be a problem. She wept copiously for most of the interview and the policewoman in attendance was hard put to calm her. After a long struggle she vouchsafed only that she had gone to the park with her boyfriend and that they had kissed and cuddled behind the bushes and that she had heard men passing and Ernie had caught a glimpse of them. She had not seen them.

Hart and Jordan were embarrassed by the continuous flow of tears and by their failure to cope with them. They felt that Theresa's statement was almost a waste of time.

Chapter Twenty-Two

The Superintendent popped his head round Hart's door soon after he had returned to his office and the D.C.I. was obliged to give him a run down on the case up to date. It was very brief. Hart was not one to dispense optimism where he felt none.

"What about the press, Douglas? Have we nothing to give them?"

"Just that we are following a number of leads but we are heavily dependent upon the public coming forward with news of the boy's movements that weekend."

"An appeal rather than a bulletin, you mean?"

"Yes, there is to be an appeal on local TV tonight. I thought it worth trying." A stab of conscience made him add, "It was Jordan's idea."

"Ah, Inspector Jordan, a good man there!"

In Hart's eyes, Superintendent Gresham's prime virtue was that he never lingered long. As soon as the door closed behind him Hart took out the file of Chevely Park reports again. There was nothing tangible about traffic at the entry to the park that night. Surely the people living at the end of Ogilvie Drive just by the entrance would have heard or seen something. He studied every report and found nothing worthwhile. Even young nursing mothers had heard nothing when they had fed their babies in the middle of the night. He felt certain that had the ice-cream van been used it would have been heard or seen at the end where it had turned. In any case, to his detective mind it seemed to be too conspicuous to be considered for such a purpose. Passers-by might overlook a car or a small van at night but they would certainly notice an ice-cream van. He simply couldn't believe that all of the inhabitants of Ogilvie Drive, or of the whole estate, come to that, would cover up for whoever was involved. Whatever

Fenton, Beck and Morton had been up to, he didn't believe that it had anything to do with the murder of Tommy Watson. He flung the file back into the tray.

He strode into the 'operations room' and planted himself in front of the huge map pinned to a blackboard at one end of the room. Inspector Jordan hurried up.

"I need to know the layout rather better, Inspector. When will our man be back. Oh, here he is, D.C. Phillips, now tell us where Bell and Potts were up to their tricks."

D.C. Phillips pinpointed the spot and Jordan ringed it with a coloured pen. There was another ring round the spot where the body was found, it was a mere twenty yards from where the couple had lain.

"Phillips, what was the cover like where Bell said he was?"

"Sir, it wasn't as good as the cover where the body was found. Their bushes were the last from the estate. The bushes where the body was found were the biggest."

"But they were a good cover for them?"

"Oh yes, sir, they had a cosy hideaway alright. There was a good space behind the bushes just below the railing. It was well chosen."

"We're stupid, that's what we are, stupid!" Hart made everyone jump with his cry. He smote his head with one of his large hands.

"Look, Inspector, they heard the figures pass and return. Pass and return, but they were further away from the entrance than the place where the body was found. That means one of two things, either the murderers didn't come from the estate or these men were not the murderers."

He shook his head and continued to stare at the map. The park was, in fact a cul-de-sac. It had a tarmac path from the proper entrance at the end of Ogilvie Drive that wound down into the centre, climbed up a bank at the opposite end to the entrance and turned left to peter out at a small football pitch. The railway embankment rose on the right and it was in front of the embankment that the bushes grew which provided shelter for the couple that night. At right angles to the embankment, a good deal further on, was a row of young trees planted closely as a barrier between the park and the area of allotments which belonged to the older part of town. The allotment fence could be seen behind these trees. At the end of the row of trees was the football pitch. It was much used but officially neglected. It was on top of a rise and lay alongside much of the park on that side. Except at the park side, the pitch was contained by a tall, strong timber fence. The fence was fronted by a row of trees planted close together, exactly as the trees in front of the allotments. The left flank of the estate was its remaining boundary. It was, indeed, a small park and it formed a basin, since there was a rise of one steepness or another all round. Its main virtue was that it was sheltered, its main drawback was that it was occasionally used as a dumping ground for rubbish. Seats had once been provided but they had long since disappeared. Small boys loved it for their games of miniature football. Older boys would organise more serious games on the pitch itself. There was no obvious access except by the official main gate.

Perhaps the running figures were totally irrelevant. Young Bell had almost certainly seen them but they had nothing to do with the murder. In which case, what was the purpose of their brief visit? There was the possibility that the men had come over the railway but there was nothing across the railway but an irregular field then a disused goods yard then the road from Clayton to Forberry. He thought it a very hard task for

162

anyone to carry a body all the way across from that road and then negotiate the live rails in the dark. There were trees on the other side of the embankment but there was no cover when crossing that yard or the field, besides, where would they be coming from, and what a way to come to get to the park. Why the park, anyway, if someone had come by that road? Surely there were other places to leave a body? He tried to shake off some of his irritability and studied the map further away from the park. Roads from Forberry led northwards to Grammond, eventually, and southwards towards Bardsley, but neither routes were direct, they were, at best, B roads.

Jordan, seeing the direction in which his eyes travelled, assured him that the area on the other side of the embankment right up to that road had been searched by his men. Nothing had been found. Nothing had been found on the railway nor on the football pitch.

Hart groaned and glanced at his watch. Coffee time, when given the opportunity, he always enjoyed a coffee break.

"Are you going to see Fenton again, Sir? He's asking for a lawyer."

"Is he? Well, I'll see him now, I won't wait for Bailey, he might be all day. Let's have him back."

Fenton had had time to think but he had no clear plan of defence. He remembered that he had seen films where people on murder charges had been given the services of a lawyer so he had asked for one. He decided to make this matter part of his defence tactics. He brushed aside Hart's polite greeting and demanded to know where his 'lawyer' was.

"You mean a solicitor, I think. Well, Mr. Fenton, I don't think you need one yet and if you will just tell the truth, I don't think you will be needing one."

"And what about my business while I am in here?"

"I thought you were too ill to go out on your rounds?"

"Well, I'm better now, aren't I. You are costing me money keeping me in here."

"It is entirely up to you. Just co-operate and you will be out in no time."

"What about my van, then?"

"You can have that too, when you have told us the truth."

Fenton lapsed into sullen silence.

"Now then, who was the visitor who called at your house on Monday evening?"

Fenton almost leapt from his chair in astonishment.

"Come along, Mr. Fenton, we know more than you think we do. Was it Charlie Beck?"

"Don't take chances, don't waste time. If you don't speak up now you will end up on a murder charge then you really will need a solicitor."

There was a long pause.

"I don't believe you are involved with this murder. I believe there is someone you are protecting and, whatever the reason, you are in trouble. Just take time to think. Nothing is more serious than a murder charge. Whatever you or your friends have been up to is nothing compared with a murder charge. What sort of trouble are you in?"

Another long pause. Fenton's eyes roved ceaselessly, his hands, folded inside each other, twitched. Once again, perspiration gathered on his brow.

The phone rang.

"Oh, he has, has he? Brief him, will you, Inspector, then bring him along."

"That was your 'lawyer', just arrived. I don't know who he is but I know that he will advise you to co-operate. You may be lucky and come out of this without a scratch, it depends on what you've been up to. Meantime I'll leave you to do some thinking."

Hart returned to his room and ordered coffee. He reached for his personal notebook and turned the pages. As he did so he pondered a few gaps in his understanding. When did Tommy Watson normally clean his bike? When and why did he first begin taking afternoons off school? Why did he walk about with that cigarette lighter and packet in his jacket? Why did he change his mind about the words on his watch? Why did he give a false address to the engravers? That last he could act upon. He drew the phone towards him and phoned the poolroom. He wasn't too surprised to learn that Tommy had given the jeweller the address of Jim Hibbert. There was no point in checking, it was almost certain that it had been chosen on the spur of the moment. But why did he not give his own address? Was it because he didn't want the watch to be traced to his own address? But why? The watch hadn't been stolen. The gap in time between the purchase and the engraving was only a matter of raising the extra money. No, the mystery must lie with the shop itself. Again, he had recourse to the phone.

"Grammond? I wonder if I could speak to your senior Detective Officer? Rawston? Yes please, if he is in. This is D.C.I. Hart from Clayton. I wonder if you could help me? You may or may not know that I'm involved in a murder enquiry concerning the death of a boy, Tommy Watson. I happen to know that this boy had some engraving done at a jeweller's called "Garrett and Morrison" on Howland Road about a week or so before he was killed. I'm wondering if they're entirely straight? Would you be able to help? I'd be grateful for any information you can give me. Thanks."

Jordan phoned again to say that he had briefed the solicitor appointed to Fenton and that he was seeing his client now. The report of the sighting on the Sunday had come from an old gardener who had seen Tommy Watson in the allotments about three o'clock in the afternoon. Hart took the name and address of this witness, he intended to visit Selborne Street that afternoon, it would be useful to interview this man, himself.

Now, before he was summoned to hear what the solicitor and Fenton had worked out between them, he could catch up on statements. The first on the pile was Ridley's jottings culled from The Gazette. Hart sighed, obviously he couldn't have read all the newspapers himself but he wondered how thorough D.C. Ridley had been. No stamina there, he thought, looking down the list. It included a major fire at a Co-operative Hall at Chapeltown, he immediately recalled what Bert Hardman had told him; an insurance swindle involving a local councillor where the case had dragged on with big local headlines for several weeks; a major pile up in fog on the A1; a major robbery involving £100,000, an exceedingly large sum in those days; a murder case involving a stepson and a personal secretary; an attempted arson on a furniture warehouse; a case of gross child neglect; an attempted murder of a publican by his wife's lover; a theft of jewellery from a big shop in Grammond. There wasn't much there, nine events from a whole year. He sent for Ridley, who came very quickly, wondering whether Inspector Jordan had mentioned his face-pulling.

"What is this?! Detective Constable Ridley, do you mean to tell me that all you have got out of a whole day's work and a whole year's papers is this miserable list?" Hart waxed wrath. Ridley swallowed but stood his ground.

"Sir, these are the major stories. I didn't know what you were looking for so I left out all the smaller events. These were in, several days running."

"We are dealing with the murder of a schoolboy, what had he or his family got to do with the murder of a publican "by his wife's lover", for example? And what can be the connection with a pile up on the A1?"

"I don't know, Sir, Someone connected with the case might have been involved. You didn't say. I couldn't have checked every..."

"Don't you know the names of the family in this case?"

"Yes, Sir, Watson and Grant. I kept my eye out for those names, even in the Births Marriages and Deaths columns but there was nothing that could connect with this family as far as I could possibly tell."

Hart softened, momentarily impressed by the way that Ridley had stood up to him.

"Alright, let us see what sort of detective you really are. Did you check the names of those killed or injured in the A1 pile up?"

"Yes, Sir,! Ridley took out a small note book, "there were five killed and thirteen injured. No one of the name of Grant and no one by the name of Watson. None of the victims came from this area. I included this in my list because there may have been a relation with a different surname."

"Good," Hart was genuinely impressed, "let us try the £100,000 robbery."

Ridley read from his notes again.

"Took place on December 11th, 1945 at the Clayton Branch of Chester Securities. Two masked figures, dressed identically in blue overalls, held the staff up with revolvers just as boxes of bank notes were about to be loaded onto vans for distribution to various big stores. One of the staff was directed to load the boxes onto an unmarked van immediately outside the side door. Just after he had finished loading, he swung the door back, knocking the gunman's arm. The gun fired, a bullet struck another member of staff who died of the wound later. On hearing the noise, the driver of the getaway van drove off immediately, leaving his rear door open. The two masked men rushed into the street to try to escape. One managed to jump into a taxi and forced the driver to take him well outside town, he then tied up the taxi driver and left him in a ditch. The taxi was found abandoned twenty miles away. The other ran into a cul-de-sac by mistake and was trapped by two police patrol men giving chase. He fired at the policemen then ran at speed with his head down back into the main street, hoping to avoid being tackled. He ran straight into the path of a bus and died later in hospital.

"The escaped thief was arrested three days later. The taxi driver had identified him from police records. He had served a sentence for armed robbery. The judge at the trial had emphasised the need for a stiff sentence and had given the man 20 years. At the time of the report, the driver of the van had not been found and none of the money had been recovered."

Hart had listened patiently.

"Have you got any names?"

"Yes, Sir, the dead man was a John Thresher and the one who was caught was a Clifford Morton."

"What? Repeat that?"

"John Thresher and Clifford Morton."

Hart leaped for the phone.

"Jordan, would you check on a Clifford Morton, sentenced to 20 years in 1946 for armed robbery, at Grammond County Court I should imagine, I'm particularly anxious to know if he has a brother called Trevor."

He turned back to Ridley.

"Well, I don't know whether you have turned up trumps exactly but I   think you have given us something to work on. Let's see what else you've raked up. What about the Grammond Jeweller's?"

"22nd. October 1946. Foxstead's, Maple Street. Two men held up the assistants just before closing time. Fifteen trays of rings and brooches, various clocks and watches to the value of £20,000. Charles Firbank and Trevor Watts caught trying to sell individual items. Sentenced to eight years each."

Hart shook his head, that didn't have loose ends, there had to be some kind of thread to connect with the present.

The phone rang, Jordan said that the solicitor was ready.

"Right, Ridley, get all of these details typed up, will you, I can't stay. You've done better than I had thought. Next time, just don't present me with a useless list, I need a digest not a list. You know what a digest is, I hope?"

"Yes, Sir."

"Right, push off!"

Chapter Twenty-Three

Hart decided to have lunch at his new discovery, The Cavalier. He needed cheering up. He had not enjoyed his meeting with Fenton and his solicitor. He hadn't intended charging Fenton with anything, not until Bailey turned up something, if indeed he did, nevertheless both he and the solicitor knew that Fenton was involved in something shady. The solicitor's job was to see that Fenton was not charged with murder or as an accessory to murder, he wasn't concerned with anything else and he had cautioned Fenton to say nothing. Even with his considerable experience of such matters, Hart was irritated. He had found himself being stubborn and awkward, almost against his will and, after Fenton was released, he was annoyed at himself. It would never do to allow any case to irritate him. It had rarely happened before, why should it happen today?

Suddenly he realised what it was. There had been something about the solicitor that had reminded him of his daughter's new boyfriend. What was his name? Francis. Even the name was an irritant. He couldn't explain to Sheila why he was so set against him. Sheila, like Louise, seemed to have fallen for the charm, the smiling good manners. Hart had thought that overdone, he thought the young man insincere. There was too much self-consciousness about him, dammit, he was almost an actor. He could forget the man, he was worried about Louise. She was vulnerable.

She had taken after her father in many ways. She was big and rather plain. She was an achiever without being overly bookish. She had been a formidable hockey full-back. She was sociable and popular but she was basically shy and, he believed, she had had little emotional experience. He dreaded that she should be hurt. She had had occasional boy-friends at school, but no real involvement. Why couldn't her first real boyfriend have been a straightforward character?

Beckie, her older sister, had been different. She had been a loud, cheerful extrovert who had seen her way clear in almost every situation. She had been positive and self-assured without being selfish or insensitive. They had had no doubts about her boyfriends because Beckie herself had had no doubts or illusions about them. As soon as she had finished her education and had settled into a job she enjoyed, she had looked for a husband and had found one. Hart smiled at the thought that her husband may not have had too much of a hand in the matter. Beckie was happy and had every prospect of a happiness for the rest of her life. He very much wanted it to be the same for Louise.

Sipping his pint at the bar, he relaxed. The same barman had extended the same cheerful welcome. He enjoyed being treated as an ordinary customer, because at that moment, that was what he was. He had ordered a chicken and mushroom pie and he found it remarkably good. When he had finished he took his plate to the bar and expressed his satisfaction.

"Did you find him, yesterday?"

"Find who?"

"You were looking for Johnny Butterman, weren't you?"

"Yes, I was. Was he in today?"

"No, he hasn't been in since. Does he know you are looking for him?"

"I left word with his parents, that's all."

"Funny, isn't it. The lads he usually plays with haven't seen him either. There was a tournament last night and he didn't turn up." A thought clouded the barman's brow. "Nothing to do with the murder is it?"

"Give him a chance, it's only been 24 hours. He could be anywhere. I just want to speak to him about his neighbour."

Everybody seemed quick to assume that John Butterman had 'gone missing'. Hart was curious but unwilling to jump to any conclusion. Lots of people were nervous of policemen for many different reasons. All the same, the sooner he could speak to Butterman Junior the better.

George Hepworth, the gardener he had come to see, lived on the opposite side, further down from The Cavalier, just next door to the little cobbler's shop. As he approached the shop, Hart thought he would pop his head in and exchange a few words with the deaf boy. Eric was delighted to see him, immediately becoming excited. He beckoned Hart to listen. Speaking carefully and slowly, he said that he had seen the van again, only last night. He had woken up, with a sore throat and had got up for a drink of water. He was just about to get back into bed when he saw the light from a car's headlights moving on the wall. It was after midnight. He went to the window and saw a van being parked just below his window. A man got out and walked down Selborne Street, on the same side.

"Now we have to be sure, Eric. Was it the same van and was it the same driver?"

Eric thought so but couldn't be absolutely certain. This time the van had driven off at ten past four. He had lain awake with his sore throat and had seen a light again, he had leaped out of bed and had seen the van drive away again.

"Could you describe the man, Eric?"

Eric shook his head. The man wore a cap and a big coat and he was just below the window so he couldn't see much of him. He thought he must be tall, having seen him standing beside the van as he got out the driver's side. It didn't look as though there was anybody else inside.

Hart was impressed that Eric had thought and spoken so clearly. But for his handicap, he would make an excellent witness, unfortunately there was nothing to go on, nothing concrete. In spite of the clandestine hour, it could have been anyone, there wasn't necessarily a connection with this case.

Hart thanked Eric once again and said that he would be grateful if he continued to keep a watch. If he could get the number of the van it would be great. Better still, if the van came back, perhaps he could phone the station, whatever the hour.

George Hepworth was a very lively octogenarian. He welcomed the D.C.I. into his tiny house and introduced him to his wife. They could have been twins except that George was clearly more weather-beaten. They were the same height and build and possessed the same broad cheeks, lightly hooded eyes and short pointed noses. Even their hair looked the same, his being long and hers being short. They were both very alert and full of natural curiosity, so much so that they asked more questions than they answered. Finally, Hart asked the old man to go with him and show him where he had seen the boy. This appealed to the stalwart gardener, who clearly enjoyed being outdoors as much as possible.

They trudged off down the narrow lane between the allotments. George's allotment lay beyond Victor Grant's, closer to the railway embankment. He opened the gate to reveal a well maintained plot rather different from the last allotment Hart had visited. In the first place there wasn't a proper shed nor was there a greenhouse, there was only a shelter with a bench inside and hooks from which hung a hoe, a fork and a spade. In the second place, this was a vegetable plot first and last. It gave the impression of having been planned and organised to the nth degree. There was nothing casual about it. There was a manure heap in one corner and a compost heap in the other. There were no crates or plant pots, no plastic bags, just a few cloches lined up at the side ready for use.

Hart had no time to express his admiration, George Hepworth led him briskly to the shelter and pushed him down onto the bench.

"This is where I sit when I want a rest. I light a pipe from time to time. This is where I caught sight of that boy. Look, yonder."

Hart was surprised to see his arm pointing up and beyond the allotments.

"You mean he was on the embankment?"

"Yes, he was sitting there, all alone, at the very top, staring back over the allotments."

"You saw him clearly?"

"I may be getting on, but my eyesight is still good. It was that boy alright. I've seen him often about the place, I would recognise him easily enough."

"What was he doing, do you suppose?"

"Just sitting, it seemed to me that he was looking for someone back here."

"I don't suppose you saw whether he had his bike with him?"

"Ah, now there it is," the old man smiled at the memory, "it may surprise you to know that he had taken it part of the way with him. It was lying there just below where he was sitting. It was the gleam on it from the sun that first caught my eye."

Did he often go up there?"

"That's the first time I've seen anyone up there and I spend a lot of time here."

"Yes, I'm sure you do. Tell me, Mr. Hepworth, what is the busiest time at the allotments?"

174

"Saturday afternoons and Sunday mornings, after that, I suppose it's Sunday afternoons."

"So there would be quite a number of people busy in their allotments that afternoon?"

"Well, a few."

"So, if the boy was looking for someone in particular he would need to climb up there to pick him out."

"Yes, I imagine so, it would be a good look out post."

"Did you know the boy's uncle, Victor Grant? He has an allotment back there."

"Yes, I know Victor, we always have a word. I haven't seen him for a bit, he hasn't been able to do much recently, he hurt his arm at work."

"So there was no one looking after his plot on Sunday?"

"Not that I know of."

"Do you get many strangers about the allotments?"

"Well, these allotments change hands from time to time. I wouldn't know any of the new holders."

"There is no through road here, is there? I mean you can't get through to the park from here, can you?"

"No, the path ends in an allotment not at the fence. When you reach the end of the path you have only a gate to another allotment so you have to turn back. Anyway the path wanders a bit and it would put most people off trying to come through."

"But the boy got to the embankment, presumably from the path or one of the paths?"

"Yes, for some unknown reason or other, there is a gap between two allotments there, not a proper path. He must have squeezed through there."

"Do other children play on the railway?"

"I've never seen them and I've been here fifty years."

Hart excused himself to take a look for himself.

There was indeed a narrow gap between two high fences. It was overgrown but the various weeds and grasses had been battered down. He was able to squeeze through without too much trouble. It was a perpetually damp place and a few partial footprints were discernible through the tangle, but there was no sign of tyre tracks. Perhaps the boy had carried his bike through the gap. The embankment was quite steep and well grassed but there were miniature screes of gravel and cinders at intervals. As he climbed awkwardly he noticed that there were plenty of scuff marks where the boy had climbed then slid down, perhaps he had had a struggle to lift his bike up the slope, perhaps he had seen something and rushed off in a hurry. There were marks where the bike had rested too. He turned where he thought the boy must have been sitting and squatted down. From where he crouched he could see into almost half of the allotments and he would have been able to see enough of the others to be able to tell whether they were being worked or not. Hart's glance took in the whole of the rear of Selborne Street from the side lane at the west end where the Buttermans lived to the proper lane or road at the east end which divided Selborne Street from Stoker Street. Someone came out of one of the back doors and unwittingly gave Hart a welcome sense of scale. Yes, the boy had a marvellous vantage point here, but what or who was he looking for?

Hart returned to George Hepworth who was just locking his gate.

"How long did the boy stay up there, do you know?"

"I've no idea. He was still there when I locked up. He must have been there for well over an hour."

"Did he often come down this far, I mean his uncle's allotment is further back, isn't it?"

"I think he liked to exercise his bike. Once in a

while I saw his head bobbing along as he rode past, when his bike was riding over the bumps. He was just a boy, you know."

Chapter Twenty-Four

"Just a boy." Yes, a silent, secretive boy, self-contained, independent and vulnerable. He belonged to a family equally silent, secretive, independent and vulnerable, or so Hart had thought. He would now take a more determined line, hurtful though it may be. Hart knocked loudly on the door of No.22. It was opened by Victor Grant who looked more shrunken and depressed than he had at Hart's last visit.

"Oh, it's you Chief Inspector!" He hesitated as though Hart had caught him off guard. He stepped back involuntarily and Hart entered. There was a shout from the top of the stairs.

"Who is it?" Edie's unmistakable voice had an extra edge of irritation to it. Hart was astonished to hear another voice, subdued and querulous, in the background.

"It's the Chief Inspector again."

"I'm too busy, I'll come down in a few minutes."

"Come through, Inspector, what can we do for you?"

"Mr. Grant, have you a birthday coming up?"

"Why yes. It's next week."

"Did you always celebrate it?"

"Not really, just a bit of extra cake at tea, that's about it."

"Tommy always remembered it?"

"Yes, he was very good that way. From first going to the Junior School, he always remembered our birthdays."

"You didn't know that he already had a present for you?"

"No, I didn't, but he had asked me from time to time what I would like."

"Was one of the things a watch?"

178

"No, I never did tell him anything. I left it up to him. Why do you ask?"

"You haven't got a watch?"

"No, I used to have a pocket watch but it wasn't much good. I had it repaired once then when it went wrong a second time I threw it away. It wasn't worth spending any more money on."

"Now I have to ask you what became of the boy's mother...?"

"I thought you would be asking, sooner or later."

It was Edie who had entered the room quietly. Hart turned and saw her eyes blazing with resentment, her body rigid, her elbows in her hands.

"You'd better see for yourself, then." She turned and led the way upstairs. Hart followed, not knowing what to expect.

In one of the front bedrooms, propped up in an awkward position amid at least three pillows and a mountain of covers, lay a pale figure. Her hair was thin, almost colourless, her features were flaccid, her mouth slack, her eyes closed. It was hard to tell what age this woman was. One arm lay outside the covers with the sleeve drawn back. The flesh was flabby but the skin at the wrists and the back of the hand was raw from scratching. Edie Grant gently folded the arm back under the covers whereupon the woman opened her eyes and started up with a low moan, saliva trickling from her open mouth.

"Never mind dear, go back to sleep, we'll not bother you."

This woman was a helpless, mindless invalid who would need constant nursing. Hart had just time to notice the eyes, dull, unfocused, moving aimlessly. Nevertheless, that glimpse of the eyes with their unusual pale grey colour and something about the nose made Hart recall the photographs he had seen of the boy. It was not easy to reconcile the images of the boy with the figure before him, but the eyes were distinctive, this had to be his mother.

"And now, if you don't mind!"

Edie Grant ushered Hart out of the bedroom and downstairs again.

"That is my sister, Jane Watson. We brought her back from the nursing home yesterday. Now you shall know it all. She was simple from the day she was born. When she had the baby she had a complete breakdown. She was unable to cope with it and had to go into care. We couldn't let her be neglected so we put her in a private nursing home. We never told the boy. Now it doesn't matter, the boy is no longer with us and we can no longer afford to pay for her so we've brought her home."

There was a long, nervous pause. Hart braced himself and asked the all-important question.

"If your sister was simple and seldom left the house... who was the boy's father?"

"Who said she never left the house? She went for walks, sometimes by herself. She even went to one or two dances. She wasn't ill then, she was just...not very bright."

Edie Grant's whole body shook with hurt and defiance. Victor stretched a hand to take hers but she snatched it away with a sharp movement, she denied herself any comfort.

"Before the family album was destroyed, did the boy see any photographs of his mother?"

Victor tried to answer the question.

"He did ask when he was very young and we had one or two photographs of Jane. He asked about his father too but we put him off, saying his father had gone away, like his uncle Victor. After he started school he stopped asking questions. I think he guessed.

Perhaps other children asked him questions he couldn't answer and he was upset but he didn't grumble to us, he just stopped asking questions."

"It has been one long struggle..." Edie, again, fighting self-pity but unable to contain it.

Hart hastened onto a different tack, turning to Victor.

"When he was younger, did your son Victor have much to do with John Butterman, your neighbour?"

"When he was very young, yes, he played with him out in the back lane. Victor mostly played with friends from school of his own age."

"Did he see John Butterman much after he started work?"

"A few times, I dare say. By the time John Butterman had started work, Victor had gone."

"When did Tommy clean his bike, as a rule?"

"He gave it a rub down every time he brought it in. He was most particular. If it was after dark he would borrow the torch to clean it by."

"You remember that the bike had mud on the rims when we looked at it. Surely he wouldn't have left it like that if he had finished with it for the day?"

"No, he wouldn't."

"So either he went out again in a hurry after he brought it home or he was interrupted, somehow."

"We thought that he had gone out in the afternoon without his bike."

"George Hepworth saw Tommy sitting on the embankment with his bike beside him on Sunday afternoon. He was still there when George left to go home."

"But we didn't see or hear him come back in."

"Would it not be possible for him to come and go without you knowing?"

"Well, I suppose so, we were sitting in the front

room on Sunday afternoon, but Edie has sharp ears, she doesn't usually miss much."

"He hadn't been in trouble with you, had he?"

"No, we hadn't a cross word with him for ever so long. He was a good lad."

"He hadn't fallen foul of any of your neighbours?"

"No."

"Not even the Buttermans?"

"Why do you ask that? We haven't had anything to do with the Buttermans for a very long time. Tommy sometimes washes their car but there hasn't been any trouble about that. They pay him promptly."

Hart sighed inwardly. Apart from being a little nearer to establishing the time of death, he felt that he wasn't making any progress.

As Victor was letting him out of the front door, Hart asked him if he possessed a television.

"No, that's a bit out of our reach, what with the Nursing Home and me being off work. We make do with the radio."

"I was just going to say that we are having an appeal on local television tonight. Maybe that will bring in a few 'last sightings'. At the moment we haven't got very far. It will be put out on radio, too, so beware, don't let it upset you."

He was just turning back to say goodnight when his glance took in No.20, next door and on a whim he asked, "Who is the agent handling this house next door?"

"Mackavel's, the estate agent on the High Street."

"Goodnight, Mr. Grant, please thank your wife."

Chapter Twenty-Five

John Bailey was both energetic and enterprising. Long before he attempted to speak directly to his quarry he had made exhaustive enquiries about him. He knew when Morton had begun to trade as a fruit and vegetable wholesaler, he had a good idea of his turnover, he knew the rates he had to pay for his premises, he knew that his payments to his men were often very generous, he knew that he was renowned for obtaining almost any goods for special customers, he knew how many people worked for him and he knew that at least three had criminal records. He knew that Morton owned two lorries and two lightweight vans and that he kept his wholesale premises in good condition. He knew that Morton enjoyed gambling, particularly on the horses, and liked cars. He was happily married with a wife and two small children. He also knew that Morton had a nasty temper and was not to be crossed. There were rumours of pressure on customers and all manner of shady deals.

It was the middle of the afternoon before he was ready to speak to the man himself. He and D.C. Phillips walked casually into the open warehouse and were able to take a good look round before anyone became aware of their presence. It seemed that there was a discussion going on behind one of the vans which was backed up against a door into a large store above which was the general office. The discussion had become an argument and the raised voices had prevented anyone hearing the approach of the two detectives. A secretary emerging from the office onto the railed balcony above saw them strolling between rows of vegetable crates and raised a shout. A big man with a battered boxer's face swung round from behind the van and shouted, "Oi! What do you want?"

Bailey raised his warrant card and introduced himself and Phillips.

"The Law?" The man had shouted and there was the sound of scurrying feet behind the van, the door to the shed was slid into position and the van doors slammed to. Phillip's immediate reaction was to rush forward to see what was so clumsily being concealed. Bailey restrained him with a gesture.

"We're here to see your boss, is he in?"

"Someone looking for me?"

The voice came from the top of the stairs. Trevor Morton was a tall, thin figure with black oily hair, heavy eyebrows, a long nose, and prominent red lips, all the more pronounced on account of his very pale face. He wore an expensive looking grey suit and a bright red tie.

"Yes, Sir, I'm Detective Sergeant Bailey, could I have a word in private?"

There was a brief hesitation.

"Certainly, Sergeant, come up, will you? What are you lot hanging about for?"

There was a scattering of feet, three burly characters moved off in different directions and began busying themselves. Suddenly there was a furious knocking. It came from the van. Phillips, half way up the wooden stairs turned to watch. It turned out that in their haste to close the van doors, the men had shut one of their mates inside. The sound of feet moving off had caused the trapped workman to panic, he was obviously claustrophobic and needed to be released immediately. When he was released, this figure sprang from the van like a jack rabbit, flinging one door open wide and hurling a string of grotesque obscenities at his unthinking mates. A burst of laughter from everyone broke the tension. Phillips resumed his climb.

"We're investigating the murder of a youth found in

Chevely Park on Tuesday. We have reason to believe that his body was taken there after he was killed. During our investigation we have found that an ice-cream van belonging to Antony Fenton of Ogilvie Drive was taken away and returned in the early hours of Tuesday morning. I believe you knew this Antony Fenton through your foreman Charlie Beck?"

"Fenton?"

"Yes, I was told that you were at a party given by Charlie Beck on Sunday night."

"Was I?" Morton stared at Bailey unable to gauge the situation.

"Yes, Charlie Beck told us this morning."

Morton pulled a face.

"I didn't see Charlie this morning, he went off on a long run, Spalding, wont be back till late. Obviously, he didn't mention it."

"Did you have a word with Fenton on Sunday?"

"Now you remind me, I was at Charlie's, me and the missus. I remember Fenton, a cocky little runt. I didn't like him."

"A neighbour says that there was a big row that night, can you tell us about that?"

"Row, no, there was a lot of noise, Charlie was celebrating, high spirits and all that."

"What time did you leave Charlie Beck's house, Mr. Morton?"

"I don't remember exactly. We got home just after three."

"Do you remember the ice-cream van outside the house?"

Morton's eyes widened. The question startled him and he wasn't sure of his position. There was a long pause.

"Remember that this is a murder enquiry, Mr. Morton, it's a very serious matter..."

"I don't know what any of us have got to do with this murder. Anyway, I don't remember no ice-cream van."

Bailey took a chance.

"Fenton left the party, went home, got his van out and returned to the party with it. Why did he do that, Mr. Morton?"

"How the hell should I know!" Morton's face had turned a muddy colour.

"You weren't in on the plan?"

"Plan! Plan! What plan? I don't know what you are talking about!"

Phillips chimed in and left his sergeant mystified.

"Would you mind us taking a look at your store below, Sir?"

"What? I bloody well would mind! What has my store to do with your murder?"

"That's all right, Sir, we can get a warrant."

Morton stood up, he was angry and upset.

"I think you had better go. I've nothing to do with Fenton, whatever he's done. You can't pin anything on me, when Charlie comes back you can ask him. Now I've got work to do. Sandra, show these gentlemen out."

When they got downstairs, Phillips explained. When the van door had been flung open, he had seen boxes not of vegetables but of what he thought must be electrical goods of one sort or other. His hunch was that they were stolen goods being loaded or unloaded. The store must be where they were kept.

"You may well be right, Phillips, we must try for that warrant before they have time to switch the goods."

The van, of course, had already been driven away.

When Hart returned to the Station it was nearly seven o'clock.

He met Bailey talking to Jordan in the foyer. Bailey was bursting with excitement. Hart couldn't help teasing him.

"One of the first rules for a detective is, stay cool whatever happens."

Jordan interceded.

"A smart bit of work and very quick off the mark, too, I think you will agree, Chief."

"Come along in and tell me, then."

Bailey and Phillips had returned from their visit to Trevor Morton's warehouse and had discovered from the files that a burglary had taken place in Bardsley about midnight on Monday. An electrical wholesaler's had been broken into and a range of goods had been stolen. An eyewitness said that he had seen a light coloured van being driven away, it was like a small ambulance. On that basis, Bailey had got a search warrant almost straight away and, taking a team with him, he had found Morton's store piled high with stolen goods and had caught Morton and his men red-handed trying to load all their loot onto lorries.

"Almost too good to be true, Sergeant. I wish all our work could be as simple as that."

"I was lucky in the timing, Sir. If there had been a delay with the warrant they could have got it all away."

"Well, you can train all your guns on Fenton now."

"Ah, Sir, I'm afraid my theories about Fenton and the murder are all wrong now."

"This burglary business has changed your mind has it?"

"One of Morton's men had a bandage on his hand. He cut it when he was loading Fenton's van with the loot. It is likely that the bloodstains on the mat will turn out to be his. The soil and the fragments of veg. came from the floor of the warehouse when the boxes were unloaded."

"But why was Fenton's van used instead of Morton's own?"

"To avoid Morton's vans being recognised, they have lettering plastered all over them."

"So Morton persuaded Fenton to let him use his van?"

"More like blackmailed him, Sir. I reckon that he brought the van to Charlie Beck's to let Morton see if it was going to be any use to him. He decided it was and Fenton had to let him have it. It fits in with Fenton's wife's story."

"At least you can get Fenton as an accessory. You can keep the Tommy Watson murder hanging over them, just in case they get stubborn. I'll let you get on with it, it's your case. Well done! And congratulations to Phillips, it is good to think our detectives can use their eyes."

A little while later, Inspector Jordan came in to announce that he had been successful in digging into the £100,000 robbery at Chester Securities. Clifford Morton was Trevor Morton's cousin. Trevor Morton had been questioned at the time on account of the missing money but had a confirmed alibi and no real connection with his cousin. He had been watched for a long period after the robbery just in case any of the money should filter through his hands. As a result, he, himself, had been prosecuted on three different occasions for burglary. He had never benefited from the Chester Securities job as far as could be ascertained. His lifestyle was flashy but not suddenly so. It was thought that he couldn't have resisted spending the money had he come into possession of it.

"What about Clifford Morton? Is he still inside?"

"No, you'll be amazed to know that he was released

only last year, seven months ago, in fact. The Bardsley police continued to keep an eye on him but he never made a suspicious move, although he slipped his tail once or twice, never for long. Two months later he was knocked down by a car outside a pub. He was very drunk, the driver was blameless. He lingered in hospital for another two months then died. A careful search was made of his digs and nothing came to light. The money is still missing."

"£100,000 was a huge sum then and still is today. Do you think that he knew where it was?"

"The Bardsley police had a theory that he did know. He was a very violent character and they think that whoever drove the van would be too scared of him to dispose of the money. They think that Morton kept in touch with the driver and had some plan to skip off when he thought the time was ripe."

"It's a very long time to keep money hidden. Fingers must have been itchy."

"My contact in Bardsley told me that someone visited him in hospital regularly. He gave the staff to believe that he was from the police, but he wasn't. He sat by the bed for a spell most days, but Morton didn't emerge from his coma. The hospital only discovered that he wasn't from the police after Morton died. "

"Was Morton visited regularly in prison?"

"I asked about that. His only visitors were old lags who had known him in prison and who came back from time to time to see him. It seems that none of these characters visited him regularly. There were no relations among his visitors."

"Inspector, I wouldn't mind betting that Clifford Morton had a relay of these old lags checking on his investment, or should I say his banker."

"Sixteen years is a very long time, Sir, I would have thought it had been spent long before now. Whoever the driver was could easily have skipped the country and dodged Morton. He could have covered his tracks if he had any nouse."

"Yes, I think you are right, Inspector. If I was a villain, I think I would have done that. The trouble is that if you are a villain, you can't do much without other villains knowing. They would come flocking for a share out, then they would shop the driver to Morton for another share out. If you were an amateur it wouldn't be so hard to skip."

"Would Morton have worked with an amateur?"

"Possibly, we mustn't forget that there was another villain, a John Thresher, perhaps he had a hand in choosing the driver."

Jordan smiled dryly.

"You would like me to look up this Thresher?"

"Good man, yes, it might help, though what help it is to me I don't know. I'm supposed to be enquiring into the death of Thomas Watson!"

Chapter Twenty-Six

Hart had not been sitting for long when the Desk Sergeant phoned.

"Mr. Butterman to see you again, Sir." Hart groaned, he didn't feel like facing Sidney Butterman at that precise moment.

"Right, show him along."

"Chief Inspector, I've waited almost twenty four hours. My son John has not been home. I know there must be something wrong. He has never been away from home like this without letting us know."

"Sit down, Mr. Butterman. How can we help? Have you checked with his employer?"

Sidney Butterman looked bewildered.

"We don't know his present employer. I've had a look in his room and there is no correspondence or letter or anything to do with any employment."

"He told you he had another job when he left the firm you work for, is that correct?"

"Yes."

"And you believed him?"

"But of course..." The former bluster reappeared.

"He has been at home most of the time since he gave up working for the same firm?"

"Well, yes..."

"And he has spent most of the time that he wasn't at home in The Cavalier"

"What.... how dare you....?"

"Mr. Butterman, I have made a few enquiries. Had you, yourself, gone to the trouble of asking just a couple of questions you would know what I do, that your son did not go out to work, at least not during normal working hours, and that he had plenty of money to spend. Can you account for that?"

Butterman was astounded. His mouth dropped open

then his face grew purple, he spluttered with incoherent rage.

"How dare you? How dare you...suggest...cast doubt...I came here to ask you to find my son and you sit there and... this is monstrous!"

Hart leaned forward and fixed his visitor with a firm eye.

"I'll tell you how I dare, Mr. Butterman. I'm conducting an enquiry into the death of a neighbour of yours, a next door neighbour. I simply called to get a statement from your son and to ask a few more questions. I believe that your son left the house while I was there. Later, he arrived at The Cavalier while I was there, saw me and fled. There are witnesses. Why did he do that, Mr. Butterman? Why has he gone missing? Has he anything to hide?"

Sidney Butterman screamed and jumped to his feet.

"I shall protest to the Chief Constable. I will not have you cast doubts on my son in this way. This is monstrous! Absolutely insupportable! My son has lived a blameless life, I....I will not have it! You have chosen to hound him for no reason, none at all. I will not have it!"

"Mr. Butterman, you may leave if you so wish and submit a complaint. Nevertheless, I will conduct my enquiry as I think fit. I have more questions to put to you as well as your son. You may answer them while you are here or tomorrow at your home when you have recovered, as you wish."

Hart's tone continued to be very calm and very firm. There was an insistence that penetrated the defensive anger of the raging figure on the other side of his desk. Butterman hesitated, the spluttering died, albeit unwillingly and slowly.

"Don't try to fob me off, Inspector!"

"Sit down, Mr. Butterman."

"I prefer to stand!"

"As you wish. Did you employ Tommy Watson to wash your car?"

Butterman glared, perspiration gathering on his upper lip as well as on his brow. He was outraged that this policeman was continuing as though oblivious of his terrible threat. Was the man without thought or.... Hart repeated his question. Butterman answered, very unsure of himself.

"Yes, from time to time."

"When did he last clean it?"

"Two weekends ago."

"Did you 'hire him' or was it your son?"

"There you go again....!"

"It is a simple question. If your son asked him to clean it, your son must have spoken to the boy. I want to establish what was in the boy's mind as near to the murder as possible. I want to know if your son had any conversation with the boy."

"Ah!" There were deflationary noises and a few moments of mental and physical readjustment. Butterman sat down again.

"Yes, I believe he did ask him. The car needed cleaning and John knew we needed to go out that weekend so he asked him to clean it. I don't know whether he actually had a conversation with him."

"Did the boy usually do a good job of cleaning your car?"

"I believe he did, we had no complaints."

"Did he do a good job the last time he cleaned it?"

"I don't know, I suppose so or John wouldn't have paid him."

"Was it usually John who paid him?"

"No, it was whoever asked the boy to do the job. John wasn't always in."

"You didn't have it washed every week?"

"Oh, no, it was never more than once a fortnight and even then it was only if the car needed washing."

"Did John use your car last weekend?"

"Yes, he asked whether I needed it and I said no, he could use it."

"So he drove to Northrop, did he?"

"Yes."

"What time did he leave?"

"There you go again, what has this...."

"Just answer my question, please."

"He left just before lunch on Saturday. He said that he would eat out."

"What time did he arrive back?"

"Oh, it was in the early hours of Monday. We were asleep, we didn't hear him come in."

"Were you all at home on Monday night?"

"Yes. We were watching television."

"Was John with you all evening?"

"Yes...er...he went out later on to see friends, he said there might be an important contact."

"An important contact?"

"Yes, to do with his business."

Hart was hard put to stifle his scorn.

"What time did he get back?"

"We didn't hear him come back. Both Mrs. Butterman and myself are very sound sleepers."

The way he expressed it made it seem that heavy sleep was a virtue of high moral order.

"Well, Mr. Butterman, I share your concern for your son John's absence. I will put an alarm out as soon as possible. Do you think that you could provide us with a recent photograph of your son?"

"Oh certainly, we have one or two good ones from..."

"Fine. What I would like to do is send one of my men round immediately, if you could let him have a photo, we could get it duplicated ready for circulation tomorrow. There is no time to be lost."

Hart stood up. Butterman stood too, quite bewildered by what he took to be Hart's change of heart. He adopted a superior grin as if to say that he had won the contest they had just indulged in. He adjusted his coat fussily, thinking of returning to his earlier threat, but Hart had the last word.

"Remember, Mr. Butterman, it is in the interest of both of you that I have news of your son as soon as he turns up. I, for my part, will certainly let you know if I hear from him. Goodnight."

Chapter Twenty-Seven

The broadcast requests for news of Tommy Watson brought in a flood of telephone calls to Welbeck Road Station. The enquiry team were hard at work, sifting and logging them when Wellbeck arrived the next morning. Inspector Jordan was at his post, smart and efficient as always. They exchanged nods and smiles, that was all they had time for. There were reporters at the front desk.

"Chief, Chief, what's happening?"

"Chief, what happened to Tony Fenton?"

"Chief, was Fenton in on the murder?"

"Chief, I hear you brought in Trevor Morton?"

"Chief, Chief......"

Hart clapped his hands to his ears. There would be no peace if he didn't offer them some crumb or other. It had been four days since the body was discovered. He would speak to the Superintendent and they would reach an agreement as to what was to be said.

"I haven't got time now, come back at 12 o'clock and I'll tell you if there have been any new developments. Frankly, I don't hold out much hope."

The clamour increased, they wanted to know what leads he was following up, were there any leads, what had come of the Chevely Park door to door...Hart strode off in the direction of his office. He ought to know better by now.

His in-tray bore D.C. Ridley's typed reports from his Gazette enquiry. Hart studied them with care. He had almost finished when Bailey knocked and entered.

"Sir, we've wrapped up the Bardsley burglary business. We got statements, eventually, from all of them, Morton, Fenton and Beck. There won't be any problems when it comes to trial."

Hart smiled at his sergeant's enthusiasm.

"Splendid, Sergeant Bailey, but never be sure until the sentence is passed. What time did you finish last night?"

"After midnight, sir, they were an awkward set of villains. They tried every trick, every wriggle until they were exhausted. Morton finally admitted to four burglaries, all midnight jobs, all of them in stolen vehicles. His use of the ice-cream van was just to save going to the trouble of stealing someone else's."

"Right, then, do you think you are ready to assist me once more?"

"I think so, sir."

"I mean, you are not just in it for the promotion are you?"

"You can promote me any time, sir." Bailey beamed.

"Work, work is what you are here for, Sergeant, you can fetch me a coffee for a start and on the way back you can ask Inspector Jordan if he has any news for me on Thresher."

There had not been time for Jordan to check on Thresher, the switchboard and the team had been occupied continuously from the end of the television appeal until now but had Hart looked at the Garrett and Morrison report? Hart blinked at the messenger and scrabbled deeper into his in-tray.

His contact in the Grammond police had telephoned after Hart had left last night. There had been problems with Garrett and Morrison years ago. From time to time items of stolen jewellery had turned up in their window. They were prosecuted in 1954 for receiving, had pleaded not guilty and had been acquitted. In 1955 there was a change of ownership, someone who worked there and a partner bought the original Garrett out. Since then the business had prospered. The police were not entirely happy as it was known that thieves visited the shop. The shop was searched after one city robbery in 1956 but nothing incriminating had been found.

Hart thought back on his visit to that shop. He was quite convinced that the man behind the counter had raised his voice to warn someone of his presence. He was sure that his size had signified that he was a policeman. He didn't think that the girl was the person who had been warned, there had been a conversation going on before she came through. There had been someone else, had that person been a thief or was he the partner handling something he should not have done? Had Tommy Watson seen something in the shop which, inadvertently, had led to his death? It had caused him to change the name to be engraved on the watch. Why had he not wanted the shopkeeper or the engraver to know his address? The name...there was only one possible explanation.

"Sergeant Bailey, you and I are going to Grammond, but first we are going to see a person we've missed out so far, young Master Shaw."

Bailey was completely at a loss but he followed his Chief out via a back door. They walked round to the side and got into Hart's car.

"Keep your eye out, I'm not ready for those reporters yet. I'll see them later, when I'm ready."

They drove cautiously round the front of the building but the reporters were still inside.

"But there's someone I've seen before."

Bailey pointed but they were picking up speed and turning into the main road, Hart could not have seen who he was pointing at.

"Who was that?"

"You probably didn't see him that night, but there was a tall, thin bloke wanting to stir up a bit of trouble. He insisted that you were a policeman..."

"But I was."

"Yes, but he was going to spoil it all, I had to try and persuade him that you weren't. That was him, standing by a car, waiting for someone."

"He is allowed to wait for someone, isn't he? He wasn't on a yellow line was he?"

"No, sir, but it seems odd. Who was he waiting for?"

"Trevor Morton perhaps?"

"No, sir, they were all released on bail last night."

"You're convinced he's a villain?"

"Yes, I could swear to it."

"Well, keep him in mind. There is nothing you can do about him at the moment."

A short while later they parked in front of the main entrance to the Cottage Hospital.

"'Ere, 'ere. Can't you read?" An indignant attendant rushed up to them. "You can't park 'ere, there's a park right round the back, go on 'oppit! Sling yer 'uck!"

Hart left Bailey to explain, it was useful having your sergeant with you for moments like that. He enquired at the main desk and was directed to Ward 6. He was just getting into the lift when Bailey joined him.

"An officious little noddy, that! Mind you, Sir, it would have helped if you had avoided the bit that said Ambulances Only."

"There was plenty of room, anyway we are on official business."

"If there happens to be a major accident in the next few minutes, you will have caused unnecessary delay, Sir!"

"Oh, Sergeant Bailey, you do go on! Alright, you can drive the rest of the way, then you can have the responsibility of parking in Grammond."

Ward 6 was quiet. It was large and old-fashioned with

elderly metal beds of a kind Hart associated with the army. There was an office just by the entrance and as they hesitated in the doorway a young nurse rushed to them and signalled them to be quiet.

"The doctor's just making his round. What do you want?"

They explained who they were and said that they needed to talk to Robert Shaw.

"Oh, he's in the end bed on the left. He's just being looked at now, you'll have to wait."

They could see that curtains had been drawn round the end bed.

"Something wrong?" Bailey looked anxious.

The young nurse laughed. "Oh no, it's just for privacy."

"He's alright then, is he?"

"Robert? He's been quite ill but he's almost over it. His tests have proved satisfactory and it looks as if he will be out in a few days."

As she spoke, the curtains were drawn back and the doctor moved on, making notes on a little board as he did so. The patient they had just dealt with eased himself in position and put his hands behind his head. By the time Hart had explained his mission to the doctor and had reached the bed, its occupant had almost drifted back into sleep. His smile indicated very clearly that he found hospital life very much to his liking. He was no longer poorly. At the mention of his name he opened his eyes with a start.

"We've come to ask you a few questions about Tommy Watson, Robert. We've asked most of his mates but we hadn't got round to you because you were ill. Are you strong enough to be able to talk to us?"

"Yeh, why not. I'll be out soon, the doctor said I was nearly ready to go home."

"You knew what happened to him?"

"Yeh." He looked troubled, the death of a friend wasn't something he could think of easily.

"When did you last see Tommy?"

"On Saturday afternoon. He came round to mine, we went off on our bikes."

"Where did you go?"

"Just round and about."

"Nowhere in particular?"

"No, we ended up in the park."

"Chevely Park?"

"Yeh, We sometimes had a game of footie there."

"I thought that you were going to the pictures?"

"We were, Stewey and Tommy and me, but Tommy changed his mind, he said he had something to tell me. Just me."

"So you went up to the Park so you could have a secret talk?"

"Yeh."

"What did Tommy tell you?"

"He said he couldn't tell me everything straight away, not yet, but he said he knew who had wrecked his shed and killed his rabbits. He said I was to meet him on Sunday afternoon at the allotment. He needed me to help him."

"But you couldn't go?"

"Nah, I wasn't well on Saturday when I got home, I went to bed and got worse. They sent for the doctor and he sent me to hospital in the morning."

"Tommy didn't give you a hint at what he'd found out?"

"He showed me a lighter and a cigarette packet. He said they were the clues."

"Was he very upset while he was telling you?"

"Nah, Tommy was always cool. He looked a bit fierce, that's all, a bit like when he fought Billy Simms."

"Why didn't he ask the others to help him as well?"

"Stewey's not very fit and Jim was going to be away. He said there should only be the two of us."

Rather unexpectedly, tears began to flow. There had been no warning. Hart stooped and patted the boy's shoulder for a moment.

"He didn't mention any names?"

Robert shook his head and turned away.

"I have had a feeling about that allotment all along. Chevely Park has misled us just as the murderers wanted it to do. Tommy Watson was killed somewhere nearer home and his body was carried along the railway line and dumped in Chevely Park. I've been a fool! Now we've got to get the team out and have a thorough search of the allotment and 22 Selborne Street."

"You can't mean that he was killed at home. You said that Victor and Edie Grant were straight."

"I'm sure of it, but there's something...."

They were hurrying back to the car. Bailey had never seen his Chief looking so angry and determined. He could hardly keep up with him. The two men shot out of the main entrance without a glance at the receptionist who was trying to attract their attention.

"What the.....!" Hart positively exploded with rage.

An ambulance was parked at right angles to their car making it impossible for them to move. Bailey stared at it and had a sudden urge to laugh but he managed to control himself. He opened the driver's door and pressed the horn, keeping it down hard. The noise was unbearable.

"For God's sake, Sergeant, it is a hospital!"

"It's the only way, sir."

"No it's not!" Hart's rage had given way to a practical urgency. He brushed Bailey aside and leaned over to release the hand brake.

"Now push!"

Together they managed to push this very heavy vehicle a matter of six feet further on. By this time, a number of people had arrived on the scene, including the attendant who had first spoken to them.

"What you doing? What you doing? I don't care who you are!" He screamed at them, waving his arms in horror. "You can't move ambulances like that! I shall report you! I shall report you!"

"Stand back please." Hart and Bailey got into their car and drove off at a shocking pace.

The need to organise a search back in the area of Selborne Street put the visit to Grammond out of their minds. They arrived back at Welbeck Road Station in a very short time. This time there was no thought of dodging the reporters, they simply pushed their way through them. Hart signed for Jordan to follow him into his office.

"Get every available man and get a search under way of 22 Selborne Street and the allotment belonging to the Grants. We'd better include the houses on each side. We'll need a warrant for the Buttermans, probably. The keys to No.20 will be at Mackavel's the estate agents in the High Street. I'll send Ridley, he can bring somebody back with him. He'll need a car."

"Right, sir. Has something happened?"

"Yes, Jordan, a sudden conversion! I'm following an early hunch. The boy was murdered on home territory and carried to Chevely Park via the railway line."

"Right, sir."

Chapter Twenty-Eight

Hart decided that he would tell the Grants what his men had to do. He felt that it was his responsibility and it would give him an opportunity to make it easier for the sister by directing his men away from that bedroom. Edie Grant was fiercely indignant, as he anticipated. Victor accepted that a search was inevitable. While the squad busied themselves out in the yard, Hart drew Victor aside.

"You said that you had never seen your son, Victor, since he left home."

"No, he's never been back."

"You don't think he might have been back in this area since then?"

"No, he wouldn't have been back without coming to see us."

"Who was he particularly friendly with when he lived at home?"

"Well, there wasn't anybody....there was Arthur Goodson and Gordon Bentley, lads he went to work with, I don't think there was anybody else. He was friendly with everybody but there wasn't anybody close."

"Could Victor drive a car?"

"Yes, when he was eighteen, he took lessons with Gordon Bentley's dad, passed first time. We never had a car, but I thought that learning to drive might come in handy." He smiled at Hart. "Not if he was on board ship, though, would it?"

It was a brave attempt at humour and rather unexpected.

"Where did Victor spend his time, he wasn't at home all the time, was he?"

"No, he wasn't like Tommy. He liked to get about. There was a youth club at the chapel, then. He liked the pictures, he watched football, he liked the girls, and dancing... he was never in."

"He was never in trouble?"

"No! Why do you ask? It's fifteen years ago."

One of the men invited the Chief into the yard.

"Sir, there's been some recent burning in the dustbin and there are scratches on the wall here and marks on that down pipe."

The officer pointed to a few small marks on the wall between the two yards, then up to the pipe where rubber burn marks were just visible. Hart recalled the freely moving widow and the drop to the ground. He had guessed then, that Tommy Watson had made his way in and out of the house by that route more than once. He also recalled that Victor Grant had said that the boy made use of the next door shed to look out onto the allotments. He lifted the lid of the bin, yes, that was what he had smelled last time he had been in the yard. He picked out a plastic bag full of rubbish and peered at the ash in the bottom of the bin.

"Take this out, will you, I want to be sure what it is." But he had a good idea. The photograph album had been burnt very recently.

There was nothing else to find in the yard. He had hardly expected anything, the yard had been kept so scrupulously clean. Samples of mud were taken from the bicycle, they would only confirm that the boy had been up to the embankment.

Noises from the yard of No.24 told him that a search was taking place there. He was surprised, he believed that there would have been a tremendous fuss by the Buttermans and he half expected to be called to bring pressure to bear. Sergeant Bailey triumphs again, he smiled. He was not sure whether his Sergeant possessed charm or gall, perhaps it was a mixture of the two, whatever it was, it had proved successful. Nevertheless, he didn't think that No.24 would yield anything.

There was nothing to be found in the back lane either, in spite of a thorough examination of the rough grass in front of the allotments. It looked as though all the nearest allotments would need to be searched. That would require the co-operation of the council. All of them would be locked and the owners would need to be traced. He strode round to the front and phoned back to the station.

"Inspector, can you expedite the list of allotment holders please. If you can send the list on here it would save a lot of time and trouble."

A car drew up in front of No.20. It was D.C. Ridley and a tall, languid figure with thin straggling hair and a large pointed nose. Ridley introduced him as Mr. Crimpton from Mackavel's the Estate Agents. Mr. Crimpton affected an air of vagueness, cultivated deliberately to give clients the idea that he was a disinterested party. His eyes, however, were sharp enough to suggest that he could sum up age, occupation, income, status and social ambition rapidly and accurately.

"D.C. Ridley has told you what this is about, Mr. Crimpton? I'm sorry to trouble you but we need to carry out a search."

"That's alright, Chief Inspector, it makes a bit of a change from office routine. I've never been involved in anything like this before, it will be a new experience."

He produced a bunch of keys and made to open the door.

"Has this property been empty a long time?"

"About six months or so."

"Nobody wanted to rent it or buy it?"

"Oh yes, it is rented, technically...."

The door opened easily and they moved inside. All

three paused. There was something wrong. Beyond the inner door there was a sensation of heat. The door to their right gave into the sitting room. There was nothing there to excite interest. The next room was different. There was a gas fire going full blast in the fireplace. On the floor close to it was a body. It had been there a while, it was smelling strongly.

"Right, Ridley, get onto the station, we want the doctor, the photographer, the whole works."

Hart knelt down and examined the face. It was horribly swollen and discoloured but he had seen that face on a photograph in his in-tray only that morning. It was John Butterman. He had been strangled by a fine cord from behind. He was just in time to prevent Mr. Crimpton from turning the gas down.

"Don't! Don't touch anything, sir! Fingerprints! We don't want yours on everything."

Crimpton was feeling faint. The heat was overpowering and the body was only too near the fire. He asked to be excused and rushed out into the fresh air. Hart followed him but pushed past and summoned some of his squad from next door.

"Now, carefully! I don't want anything disturbed until we get the photographer and the fingerprint expert. Just use your eyes and move carefully. Try out the back. One of you can open the back window as well as the door, let some air in."

There was nothing else he could do for the moment. He thought of the Buttermans. He would have Sidney Butterman telephoned at work and ask him to come home. He could identify the body before it was taken away then he could let his wife know. It would be too much for Mrs. Butterman on her own. Hart knew that Mrs. Butterman would not be able to cope with the loss of her only son.

Outside, Hart found the estate agent leaning on the

gate.

"Mr. Crimpton, you were going to tell me about this property when we went in. I think you said that it was rented."

"It wasn't occupied but it was reserved by a client, a client who wasn't ready to occupy it. He paid us to keep an eye on it until he was able to take up residence. I used to look in every three or four weeks."

"Who was this client?"

The estate agent hesitated.

"This is a murder, I'm afraid that I must press you for an answer."

"The name given to us was Steven Brown. He told us that he would be out of the country for six months or so and he paid us in advance."

Crimpton consulted a notebook.

"The address he gave us was Elvaston Terrace, N.W.3. I remember that he said he was a civil engineer and that he had a contract to fulfil abroad but he would be working in this area after that and he wanted somewhere ready for his family to move into. He said that if he liked the house and it suited him he would make an offer to purchase within three more months."

"What sort of person was this Mr. Steven Brown?"

"Fairly tall, dark hair, heavily built, forties...."

"You remember him well?"

"I have a good memory for faces. It always helps in our business."

"How did the victim inside gain entrance, do you think?"

"I have no idea. We have the only keys. Mr. Brown had the keys to inspect the property, but since he saw it and decided he wanted to rent it, nobody else has had the keys."

"Except you."

"Yes, I like to get out of the office now and again so

208

I have been the one who looked in to see if all was well."

"It's curious that all the services were still connected."

"All the meters were read after the last tenants left. Nothing was officially disconnected, if that's what you mean. Mr. Brown asked us to arrange that everything was available should he return suddenly."

"Then there should be some quarterly bills, shouldn't there?"

"I put all the mail I found on the front mantelpiece. We don't handle any other of our clients' business unless we are asked to."

Hart strode into the front room. There was a pile of envelopes, mostly circulars, lying on the mantelpiece. The estate agent gaped as Hart tore into them. There were bills from both gas and electricity boards.

"They'll only be estimates, of course." Climpton thought that it was a waste of time looking at them. Hart took the gas bill to the meter under the stairs and peered at the meter and the bill. He did the same for the electricity bill.

"Judging from the last official reading someone has been using quite a bit of gas and virtually no electricity. We had better try to trace your Mr. Brown."

Chapter Twenty-Nine

When the doctor and the photographer were finished and while the fingerprint man was busy, Hart decided to look out the back. By this time, Sergeant Bailey had joined him. The first thing to surprise him was the fact that the wall between the houses, on this side, was whitewashed, the second was that the yard was damp and grubby. It wasn't really dirty, it simply could not bear comparison with Edie Grant's next door. It had not been scrubbed for a long time and moss sprouted from cracks in the brickwork and the concrete.

Hart studied the wall then beckoned to Bailey.

"Do you see what I see?"

"Recent scratches and marks, skid marks."

Hart studied the ground and pointed to scuff marks by the wall and a little further away. Bailey opened the wash-house door and examined the floor. Next to the washhouse was a general store. There was a thin layer of earth over much of its surface. This store had housed tools and equipment used in the allotment. There were four large fertiliser bags full of manure or compost against the wall and one of his men was trying to move one of them and was scattering the contents in his struggle.

"Careful there, man! Get someone to help you, I don't want that muck getting in the way!"

The constable called for one of his friends to help him and, together, they moved the bags, searched where they had been and carefully replaced them. Hart waited until they had gone then crouched down and examined the floor near the door.

"Look here Sergeant! Use your nose as well as your eyes."

"There was something lying here, you mean? Yes, there are signs of dragging and, look sir, here's a piece of a button!"

"And there has been waste here, kitchen waste, before it was taken to the compost heap. That's what I smelt when I was examining the clothes."

"So Tommy Watson was killed here and his body stored in this shed before being taken to the park?"

"Precisely, my dear Sergeant! The white on the tips of his shoes was from the wall here."

"And the green stuff on his back came from this yard?"

"Yes, it's algae or something. There, at the bottom of the wall and along the ground, green slime."

"But why was it necessary to wait? It would have been quiet on the Sunday, wouldn't it, Sir? Whoever did it could have taken it on the Sunday night. I don't understand why he waited until the Monday night."

"Maybe he needed help and couldn't get it until the next day. It's a long way to carry a body and it wouldn't be easy along the side of the track."

Hart strode to the back door that led into the lane. It was secured by a yale lock, unusual for a back door.

"Get the finger print chap to see if he can get anything from this door. I doubt it, it's a bit too rough, but it's worth a try."

"Sir!" One of his men beckoned Hart indoors. "Mr. Butterman's here, Sir."

Sidney Butterman was standing in the doorway into the living room. He had arrived just too late to see the body in situ. He looked completely bewildered as he watched the finger print men at work.

"I got a message to come to No.20 immediately. I didn't understand it. What's going on? The message said something about my son, John."

He wanted to bluster about being called away from work and he had prepared a protest while he was driving, but the sight of the all the policemen searching the house filled him with a growing apprehension.

Hart took him gently by the elbow and led him out into the front room.

"I have very bad news for you, Mr. Butterman. A body has been found in this house and I'm very much afraid that it is your son's. We had to take it away. The gas fire had been burning for some time and there was a risk of further deterioration. When you feel ready, I'd like you to come down with me to the morgue and identify it."

There was a long pause. Butterman appeared to be transfixed.

"I thought it best for you to break the news to Mrs. Butterman, she knows nothing about what we've found. Do you think you could go to her and break it gently? It would be best coming from you. After that, when you are ready, I'll take you down. Mrs. Butterman too, if she would like to go."

There was no answer. Sidney Butterman turned and moved towards his own door like an automaton. Hart signalled a policewoman to follow him.

It was nearly two o'clock when Hart returned with the Buttermans from the morgue. Mrs. Butterman had fought against the idea that the body could possibly be her son. She held herself in check right up until the sheet was turned back from the face then she broke into a dreadful attack of hysterics. Her husband nodded his recognition, pale and silent, he was still in shock. He ignored his wife, it was the policewoman who was obliged to restrain and comfort her. Hart gently led them to the car. He found it very difficult to speak and, indeed, he didn't need to.

Once the Buttermans were safely inside their own home again, he decided that he must find something to eat. It was time to pay another visit to The Cavalier. He took Bailey by the arm and led him along the street.

"We might just be in time for a bite of lunch. This is a fine pub, here."

The barman looked at the clock, there were only five minutes to time.

"You'll have to be quick, gents, you know what the law is like!" He grinned.

They ate and drank as quickly as they could. When they finished, they were the only customers left. Hart approached the barman.

"There's one person I haven't asked you about. Did you ever know young Victor Grant, the son?"

"Young Victor? Yes, he used to come in quite a lot when I was first here."

"What was he like?"

"Well, I didn't take to him much. A bit of a fly boy. I never trusted him."

"In what way?"

"He was a bit dodgy, I can't say exactly. I used to count the change carefully, if you know what I mean. Something not quite honest about him."

"He had been spoilt, you think?"

"Well, he was nothing like his dad. Old Victor was as true as they come. Young Victor was always borrowing or on the make, he seemed to be always on about money. I suppose they didn't have much."

"Did he like the horses?"

"He had a flutter now and again but he wasn't a great gambler. He would grumble about losing, he never talked about winning."

"Was he a friendly sort of a bloke?"

"Well, he was alright, he didn't talk a lot. He didn't have many friends here."

"You mean in the pub?"

"Yes, he brought one or two friends in occasionally. I gather they were lads he worked with."

213

"He wasn't well liked?"

"Oh, I wouldn't say that, nobody took a lot of notice of him. You get fed up listening to the same chat all the time. It was always money."

"And then he went off to seek his fortune. He never told you who he was going to work for, did he?"

"No. He just stopped coming in. Victor told me that he had got a ship. That seemed a funny thing to me. He didn't seem to be the sort of fellow who would go to sea. Victor was proud of him but I couldn't see anything in that lad."

"You've never seen him since?"

"No, I don't think he has been back once. He's never been back to see his folks."

There had been continuous activity throughout the afternoon. Inspector Jordan had managed to contact the owners of most of the allotments near to Selborne Street and there had been a thorough search. Nothing significant was found there.

The men searching in Victor Grant's allotment found loose earth just next to the shed. When they dug deeper, they realised that the earth had only recently been disturbed and that the loose soil extended underneath the shed. More volunteers were sent for and, with great difficulty, the whole shed was lifted off its 'runners' and moved to one side. Clearly, someone had been digging underneath it. Hart was summoned and he brought Victor Grant to see what was happening.

"What used to be here before you built the shed?"

"That was the old rhubarb patch. There were five crowns of rhubarb. Edie didn't go much for rhubarb so I dug them out and built the shed where they had been."

"They were big crowns?"

"Yes, they were very healthy, a good crop we had

from them. They were very big. Surprisingly, they didn't take much digging out. I didn't miss them. You have to burn the leaves you know, they're no good for compost."

"How is it that the earth is so loose underneath the shed? It's taken six big men to move your shed. Who could get underneath it?"

Bailey took up the questioning.

"Mr. Grant, when your shed was vandalised, was it the floor that was damaged?"

"Yes, it was. It was because the floor was in such a state that I decided to rebuild the whole thing. The walls were almost untouched."

"Was there soil left behind on the floor?"

"Yes, now that you mention it, there was an awful mess, bits of soil and broken bits of floorboard all thrown together as though someone had been in a rage. Well, they must have been in a rage or they would never have strangled the poor rabbits. I had to take everything out and build it from scratch again."

Meanwhile the policemen dug on. They removed the loose soil and wheeled it into the middle of the allotment. Eventually they revealed a large hole, over two feet deep, four or five feet long and nearly two feet wide. Someone muttered that it resembled a grave. At the bottom of this hole they found a few scraps of string-like material and one or two small pieces of soggy cardboard.

"When did you first build a shed on this spot, Mr. Grant?"

"It was just after Tommy was born. I had intended to build a shed and I was in the way in the house on account of the new baby so I came down here and got on with it."

"You had to dig out the rhubarb first?"

"No, I made the base and the walls first, separately,

then I dug out the rhubarb, laid down the 'runners' and raised the side walls on the base..."

"You would have had to flatten the ground where the rhubarb was?"

"Yes, that didn't take much doing. The earth was very loose so I just banged it down with a spade. It wasn't rough, it was good soil."

"You said the rhubarb crowns came up easily."

"Yes, I remember thinking they would be the very devil, they had been in for about fifteen years, but, no, they came away very nicely."

"By then, your son, Victor had left home. He never saw the shed?"

"No, I could have done with his help at the time."

Dusk fell and the digging was called off and a constable posted. They left the allotment in a mess, all the more incongruous for having a shed leaning awkwardly in the middle of it. Hart considered the prospect of bringing lights and searching through the night but decided against it. As he explained to Superintendent Gresham, it was a general search and it could wait until daylight. The Superintendent was quick to point out that a second murder would certainly be bringing the big chiefs down on them never mind the reporters. He reminded Hart, rather tartly, that a promise had been given to the reporters implicating him. In reply, Hart claimed that events had overtaken him, he was sorry if the reporters had bothered the Superintendent but there were more important things to see to. He promised to let the Superintendent know as soon as there was any statement he could make.

He fell into a discussion with Bailey as soon as they got into his office.

"I've set Phillips to find out if anyone of the neighbours saw anyone enter 20, but I have little hopes.

216

It would be after dark. No one seems to see anything after dark in Selborne Street. The body must have lain in front of the fire for at least twenty four hours, maybe more, so we are thinking of Thursday as well as Friday. John Butterman didn't return home after leaving on Thursday morning and after putting his head into The Cavalier. My guess is that he was murdered on the Thursday."

"That would account for the build-up of heat in that room."

"Yes, now we have to see whether we can find the strange Mr. Brown. I rather expect that we will not. I believe that someone passing himself off to the estate agent as Brown used this house for some other purpose and that he met Butterman there, quarrelled with him and killed him."

"Hang on, Sir, that's a bit quick!"

"How do you suppose anyone could get into the house? By using a key, Sergeant, a duplicate key. And how did they obtain a duplicate key?"

"Someone in the office?"

"No, the mysterious Mr. Brown simply takes an impression while he has the key for the purpose of looking over the property."

"But why this particular property? What has Selborne Street got to do with two murders? What has Butterman got to do with Tommy Watson? What has...."

"Questions, questions, Sergeant Bailey, I believe that it is all coming together. Tommy Watson is looking for whoever killed his rabbits. He keeps an eye out from the embankment. What does he see from the embankment?"

"I've no idea, Sir."

"I checked from that position. He could see almost all the allotments from there but he could also see the back doors to all of Selborne Street. What if he sees someone enter the back of No. 20. He rushes back home, puts his bike away and scrambles over the wall. What he finds or sees there makes him try to climb back again but someone sees him and kills him. His body is dumped temporarily in the outhouse. The next night, they, because there had to be two of them, carry the body to the park via the railway. The boy was killed because he was a witness."

"The connection is the allotment?"

"Yes, it rather looks as though something was hidden in the allotment. Hidden fifteen years or more ago. It was hidden under the rhubarb crowns. A good place. Rhubarb leaves cover a big space. Nobody fusses rhubarb. They just let it grow until they cut it. Mostly people cut rhubarb in the spring when it is tender. They leave the big coarse stems and their leaves therefore there is plenty of cover. Years later someone wants to dig up whatever they have buried and what do they find? A shed! A great ugly shed. They break through the floor in the night and..."

"They find nothing! Someone had moved whatever was there, they are so wild with rage that they set about the rabbits!"

"Well done, Sergeant! That could be it. Now, while you were away investigating your fruit and vegetable merchant, Ridley turned up reports of a robbery, sixteen years ago, here, read for yourself. You will see that a driver of a getaway car escaped with £100,000. One of his partners is killed trying to escape, the other gets 20 years. He was released six months ago. The money has been waiting all this time. Where? The Grant's allotment!"

"Victor Grant!"

"Yes, Victor Grant the son! You remember that he left home after his apprenticeship. He didn't go to sea as he told his parents. There is no record of him using Pomfret's for a reference. He just disappears. He can drive. He talks of nothing but getting money from somewhere or other. He could have been the driver, it is possible. He buries the loot in a place agreed by them both. The law catches up with the hold-up man who gets a stiff sentence. There is an agreement, backed up by serious threats, to leave the loot until the hold-up man gets out..."

"Sixteen years! That's asking a helluva lot!"

"Fear! Fear and greed! You can wait a long time for £50,000 if you really think that by lying low you will get away with it. Victor Grant had no wish to be hasty, he had time on his side, he was young. I daresay he took some of it to get by on, but he was bright enough to realise that a sudden display of wealth would make people suspicious. He wouldn't dare to cross the hold-up man, whose name, by the way, was Morton..."

"Morton.... not a relation?"

"Yes, believe it or not, but not close enough to be involved. I've checked. Clifford Morton gets out and lies low, waiting his chance to make a move. Perhaps he has to make travel arrangements or something. Then he is killed in an accident. A total accident. Victor Grant is now free to pocket the whole of the loot."

Hart paused for breath. Bailey stared at him and slowly shook his head. Hart smiled.

"You don't look convinced, Sergeant, what are your objections?"

"The time, sixteen years is too long to wait. If you were someone who had always wanted money you wouldn't be able to keep your hands off it."

"Well, two things. One: fear of what your partner and his friends and relations might do to you, and don't think that Morton wasn't keeping an eye on his investment. I believe that he had a series of old lags checking. Two: if you want to hang on to your money, you lay plans so that you don't suddenly become wealthy and create suspicion. What plans? How about a little business? You can start a business and then expand it when the time is right. A perfect set-up."

"Do you think the young Victor Grant could be so cunning?"

"I'm not sure. It's all guess work at the moment."

"Where does John Butterman come in?"

"I'm still trying to figure that out. They weren't friends when they were young but, six months or so ago, the magic six months again, Butterman gives up his job and lazes about doing nothing with money in his pocket. He must have been let in on the secret or part of it at least. I can't think that he was a very reliable individual. Maybe he saw something and had to be bought off, anyway, he knows I am looking for him and he rushes off. Within twenty four hours he is killed."

"What about the house, No.20? Why was this house being used? Was it a look out post?"

"It must have been something like that. I wouldn't be surprised if Clifford Morton was behind that move. He would want a place to sort out and store the loot when the time came. It was very convenient for the allotment."

"It was also a risky place for Victor Grant to be, next door to the people most likely to recognise him, his parents."

"Yes, it must have been a danger for him, but he must have known that his parents never went out and that the street was very quiet, especially at nights. Anyway, he must have changed in, what was it, fifteen years since he left home. You see, it was the robbery that made him leave home. He needed to be free. There couldn't be any questions from his parents."

"So, all we have to do now is find Victor Grant

220

Junior."

"I think that Tommy Watson found him, by accident, when he went to buy his uncle a watch. You remember that pocket watch? That was meant for his uncle. He took it back to the shop when he had the money to pay for the engraving. While he was in the shop he changed his mind about what he wanted engraving on the watch. He also gave a false address. Why?"

Bailey shrugged.

"Because he saw someone in the shop, someone he knew only slightly from a photograph. He worshipped his uncle, he cannot have approved of young Victor Grant's desertion of his family. He must have been shocked and in haste he gave his own name to be engraved and a different address. When he went back to collect the watch, he took an old photograph to help him recognise the person he saw. He wouldn't have known anything about a robbery of course."

"Victor Grant can't have changed that much then."

"It will be very interesting to find out."

"What do you think has happened to the money, Sir?"

"I couldn't say. £100,000 is a bulky sum. It must take up at least 20 boxes, maybe more. It can't be in No.20, the men searched it today. It isn't in No. 22, or 24, they've been searched too. It is most likely where we will find Victor Grant. Let's move now!"

Suddenly Hart was all action. It was as though talking it over with Bailey had cleared his mind and strengthened his resolve. He didn't wait to inform Jordan or anyone else. He rushed out via the back, with Bailey in tow and drove off towards Grammond.

Chapter Thirty

The tedious business of waiting for the reports from all and sundry and the prospect of endless enquiries flooding in before there was sufficient information to base answers on gave added impetus to Hart's flight. As he explained to Bailey as they drove, he was also concerned to see whether Victor Grant would choose to make a sudden run for it. He hadn't enough to go on to involve a major operation and he didn't want to start a hare unnecessarily. He just had a strong urge to see for himself whether he was right or not.

It was an unpleasant night, cold and squally. The car was continually buffeted by side winds so that Hart had to hang on to the steering wheel. Nevertheless, Bailey needed to ask questions and this was as good a time as any.

"There are a lot of unanswered questions, Sir. What have the cigarette lighter and the cigarettes got to do with this, apart from Tommy Watson wanting to play detective?"

"He must have thought that he only had to present them to someone to make that person admit to being the vandal."

"Did he know who it was? Did he have any idea?"

"Somehow, I can't believe that he knew anything about the robbery. It could have been anyone as far as he was concerned. It could be that he saw Butterman enter the house next door and followed him in."

"You think Butterman killed him?"

"Butterman wouldn't have the nerve."

They travelled a while in silence.

"When was the money taken out of the ground, Sir? Would Grant have dared to move it without telling Morton?"

"I think it was dug up exactly as planned - after

Morton had been let out."

"But what about the rabbits, I thought that they must have been killed out of frustration."

"Frustration because Morton couldn't find his loot?"

"Yes Sir, it would have been a natural reaction."

"It was more likely to be a deliberate ploy to take attention away from the digging. It was the sort of thing that only vandals would have done."

"I wouldn't have trusted Butterman, Sir, if I had been the villain. Was he into a bit of blackmail, could that be why he was killed?"

"We don't know enough yet. He was so jumpy, thinking I was onto him, perhaps he had to be eliminated."

"This Victor Grant must be a tough character, then. It may not be too difficult to strangle a boy but someone of Butterman's size would be a different matter entirely."

"It takes a combination of strength and skill, I'm sure. This Victor Grant might have what it takes, I don't know."

There was another pause.

"I wonder what they used to move the money in, Sir?"

"Somebody I know says that there has been a blue van about recently, always at night. I wouldn't be surprised if that was the vehicle used."

"It's quite a walk to carry that amount of weight from the allotment to the road. They were taking risks about being seen."

"Yes, I suppose it helps that almost all the inhabitants of Selborne Street must be early-to-bed people. They probably chose a blustery night when no one would be about."

"Do you think that they kept the money at No.20?"

"Possibly, but there was always the chance that the

223

man from the estate agent's would find it."

"Wherever you keep that amount of money there is a chance that it will be found. I reckon that if it was stowed away in an old wardrobe in that house it would be safe. The agent's man would only look at the windows and doors and see that there was no rain coming in, that sort of thing. He wouldn't go through the furniture."

"Then it would have had to be removed on Thursday night, as soon as Butterman was killed. My source of information told me that the van was in the street on Thursday night."

They travelled on in silence until they were into the city.

"I've just remembered, Sir, you said that you were going to let me drive so that I would have the responsibility of parking in Grammond."

"There isn't going to be a problem where we are going at this time of night."

Hart found his way to the football ground and turned into Howland Road. As he had said, at that time of night, there wasn't much difficulty in parking but he drew in to the side before he had reached the shop.

"Which one is it, Sir?"

"Garrett and Morrison, just about fifty yards up on the right. Come on, we'll go for a stroll. Don't make it obvious, we'll go back, cross over and walk along the back street."

They moved casually, exactly as Hart had said. Having crossed the road, they turned down the next street and turned into the back lane. It was very dark but there were lights in a number of the windows above the shops. Most of them had flats above. Nearly all had garages and storerooms at the back. When Hart thought he had arrived behind the right shop, he gave it particular attention. To his disappointment, there were no lights and the garage and the side door were very secure. They would learn nothing from the back. They went on up the lane and turned back to the main road, keeping on the same side as the jeweller's.

They examined the front of Garrett and Morrison's. There was no sign of life. The shutters were strong and very secure. Hart looked at the front door to the flat above and briefly rapped with the knocker. He tried again, more loudly. There was no response. He took a step back and looked up. No light showed at any of the three windows.

"Damn! I hope we are not too late."

"Sir, are you sure he lives here?"

"Somebody from the shop lives here, I'm confident of that."

"But if Grant lives away from the shop, won't he keep the money where he lives?"

"You are right, but our enquiry could start here. His partner would confirm that he had joined the firm..."

"But you haven't an up-to-date photograph, Sir. He could deny knowing Victor Grant because, of course, he would have changed his name, then we would be back to square one and meanwhile he would be able to warn Grant that we were making enquiries."

Hart was shocked, shocked by the realisation that Bailey was right and shocked at his own impulsiveness. He hadn't thought it through. He had wanted to confront Grant as soon as possible. He had felt that time was of the essence. He had thought that the death of John Butterman would have precipitated a crisis and resulted in Victor Grant's panicking. He stood still, thinking. Had Victor already made a move? Why should he, he wouldn't know that the body had been discovered, with a bit of luck he wouldn't know that until Monday's morning paper. In any case, he had no reason to suppose that the police were on to him. If he was involved in this jewellery business and wanted to stay with it, he had only to lie low, running would only bring him trouble.

"Sir, it's the law!"

Hart was startled by Bailey's hoarse whisper. He looked back and saw two policemen approaching. It was clear that they were curious about the behaviour of two men peering up at the windows above a shop at this time of night.

"Let's slip away. I don't feel like explaining myself to members of another force at this particular moment, especially coppers on the beat."

The car was on the other side of the street. Hart felt sure that before they could reach it the approaching patrol men would have intercepted them. Suddenly a city bus turned into Howland Road and moved towards them. Hart was quick off the mark. He stepped off the pavement and waved his arm. The bus turned towards him and stopped. Hart and Bailey leaped aboard and the bus drove away smartly.

They had no idea where the bus was going. They were so relieved that they had escaped a sticky situation that they couldn't care. They bought tickets to the terminus but alighted only a few streets away. By the time they had walked back to Howland Road there was no sign of the constables on the beat, nevertheless, they wasted no time in starting the car and driving away.

Hart had gained nothing by his dash to Grammond apart from escaping from local headquarters. His frustration didn't help him to readjust on his return. Superintendent Gresham was awaiting him with the news that the Chief Superintendent was asking for a full report and that the Assistant Chief Constable had made a polite enquiry, hinting that he might fit in a visit. Worse, to Hart's ears, was the racket made by reporters and Gresham's wanting to know what he should tell them.

"The facts. Nothing but the facts. A dead body has been discovered, possibly a connection, not yet established. That's all we can tell them at the moment. Foul play, of course. There is simply nothing else. I am particularly anxious that the name be withheld for another 24 hours."

Hart telephoned Grammond Police and asked to speak to the same Inspector he had contacted earlier. Unfortunately there was no one above a detective sergeant available. Nevertheless, Hart needed co-operation and he needed it as soon as possible. He established his identity and said that the needed surveillance of a jeweller's shop in Grammond. If Grammond could not assist he was prepared to arrange it using his own men. He asked the D.S. to clear it with his superiors as soon as he could and to phone him back.

Then he asked for Inspector Jordan.

"Any reports in yet?"

"It'll be the morning before everything is typed up, Sir."

"Well, I'm stuck at the moment."

"The Chief Superintendent's report, Sir?"

"Oh, damn! Thanks for the reminder, Inspector."

Without the pathologist's full report Hart had to be brief, it suited him to be so. He had finished drafting it when the phone rang. It was the Grammond D.S. to say that he had been able to contact his superintendent who had said that Hart could go ahead on condition he kept him fully informed about it. There was no conflict of interest as far as he knew. Hart thanked him and made the necessary promise. He then called Sergeant Bailey and asked him to organise a discreet watch on Garrett and Morrison's premises. He needed to be informed of any activity, particularly involving transport.

Chapter Thirty-One

The reports were all waiting for Hart when he arrived the next morning. Sundays were slow to start in the station as elsewhere and he was grateful for it. He and Sheila had spoken on the phone to Louise last night. She was going to come home for a short break, bringing her boyfriend with her. He had lost none of his suspicions but he welcomed the opportunity of putting the young man to the test. Perhaps he had been wrong about him, yet, experience had told him that his first impressions were usually reliable. He would wait and see. He took up the first file from his tray, sat back in his chair and read steadily.

First, the pathologist's report: strangulation with a fine cord twisted from behind. Death had probably occurred over twenty four hours previous to the finding of the body, impossible to be precise because body's condition had deteriorated due to heat. Stomach contents: most recent: bread and meat, probably beef, together with evidence of food remains in mouth suggest that the last food ingested was in the nature of one or more sandwiches.

Victim: male, early thirties, 5' 11½", heavy build, light brown hair, brown eyes, wearing a light coloured raincoat, brown check jacket, grey flannel trousers, fawn pullover, cream shirt, white vest, white underpants, dark brown socks, brown suede shoes. Brown leather gloves in pockets of raincoat. Possessions included wristwatch, pocket comb, brown leather wallet containing driver's licence but no money, two handkerchiefs, bunch of keys and loose change.

Why was there no money in the wallet? John Butterman was known to be 'flush'. Had he run out of money and arranged to rendezvous with his paymaster to get some more or did whoever killed him take the money out of his wallet? If the killer was Grant, why should he take the money from Butterman, he had plenty of his own? To lay a false trail? What if the killer wasn't Grant, was he known to Butterman or did he surprise him, if so, what was he doing in that house? Hart considered the possibility of another person in the plot. He could think of no one who could have been involved from the beginning, but the more he thought, the more he realised how little he knew. It was quite possible that some other villain knew about the money and was trying to cash in, possibly someone who had been sent by Clifford Morton to check on the allotment while he was in prison.

He was suspicious about the room in which the body had been found. The mat on which the body lay was tidy and unwrinkled, everything seemed orderly and in place. Whoever killed John Butterman had taken care to leave the room as it had been before the killing. There was dust on the mantel piece and on most surfaces except the hearth, two of the chairs, the doors and the windowsill. His men had been thorough, there had been nothing underneath the mat, no dust or ash around the fireplace, no cigarette stubs anywhere, nor were there any fingerprints. The final act had been to wipe all doors and furniture. If mugs and plates had been used, they had been washed and replaced carefully. If the sandwiches had arrived in a wrapper, the wrapper and all debris had been taken away. There had been no rubbish in the dustbin outside. In the fibres of the carpet, there were recent breadcrumbs and tiny fragments of beef tissue and a variety of much older fragments.

It was almost as if the body had been planted, but Hart didn't think that likely. He was curious about the fire, had it been left on deliberately or by accident? If deliberately, why? To render the time of death immeasurable or to cause a fire? It had to be deliberate, there was no fingerprint on the gas tap.

In his tray were reports on the fingerprints on the watch and the cigarette packet found in Tommy Watson's pockets. They did not match with any on record. There was a suggestion that they were too small to be those of adults.

He had sent for the fragments of string found in the hole in Victor Grant's allotment. Taking a further look at them, it became clear that they were not string but pieces of fibrous tape that had once been coloured. It was almost certain, in his mind, that these would be unique to the company which used them. He telephoned Chester Securities. Being Sunday, there was no one at the office who could help him. It was too important a matter to leave until Monday. Hart decided that he would send someone, with the specimen fragments, to seek out someone on the managerial staff who might be in a position to identify them. Sergeant Bailey would be just the man to charm information from the skeleton staff and coax managers from their Sunday pursuits.

Also in his in-tray was a report that attempts to contact a Steven Brown had proved fruitless. The address he had given was false and there was no other lead. Hart decided to play a hunch and sent D.C. Phillips to find Mr. Crimpton and to show him two photographs, obtained with the aid of Inspector Jordan and a very up-to-date photocopier.

The last report was from Phillips on his enquiries in Selborne Street. No one had seen anything unusual in daylight hours and no one had been out after dark. Extraordinary! Didn't anybody look out of their windows? Didn't any of them have any sense of curiosity? Hart experienced a growing sense of outrage. Sheila would tell him that he was getting old. Thoughts of his wife prompted him to think of lunch. He would go early, but on the way he would call on Miss Jane Mason.

Not surprisingly, Jane Mason was not long out of bed when Hart called. She was very put out on account of being caught unprepared and on account of the police officer concerned not being Sergeant Bailey, the gorgeous looking hero of her interview at school. Her hair was not at its best and the bloom on her face suggested that morning ablutions had been postponed. The casual pullover she wore was elderly and spotted with food and her slacks were sadly grubby. Hart thought that she probably looked best in uniform. He recalled a party at a Nurses' Home he had attended in earlier days where he had had a similar reaction. The nurses he had admired in uniform had all been disappointing in their casual clothes.

Jane may have been casually dressed and not looking her best but she was alert and not averse to answering Hart's questions. She was not in a situation requiring her to show off in any way and Hart was pleased with her straightforward response. Her story remained exactly as she had told it to Bailey. She was sure that she had seen Tommy Watson. Hart had brought a copy of the photograph of John Butterman left by his father.

"Could this be the person you saw talking to Tommy Watson?"

"Yeh... yeh, it could be. He's about the right size but he isn't wearing a cap is he?"

Hart took out a pencil and scribbled for a few moments.

"Is that any better?"

"Mmm...It's a bit more like, yeh, it could be. I'm not absolutely certain. I wasn't taking much notice of this feller."

Hart thanked her, apologised for disturbing her on a Sunday and left.

After a good lunch, D.C.I. Hart was eager for action. He made diligent enquiries about the two early friends of Victor Grant junior. Gordon Bentley worked for his father at the 'Riteway Driving School' and wasn't too hard to find. He had not seen Victor Grant since he 'went off to sea'. In his opinion, Victor was good for a laugh but not much else. He remembered Victor taking driving lessons with his Dad. He had been keen and had passed his test easily. Bentley had thought that Victor might have taken to driving for a living or even taken to garage work, using some of his engineering skills. He was able to give Hart the address of Arthur Goodson who was married with a family and lived close to the Welbeck Road station.

Arthur Goodson, was immensely pleased to have a visitor that afternoon. His wife had demanded his commitment to painting the back bedroom, a task far from his liking and one he had postponed several times. He welcomed Hart in and responded happily to his questioning. He, too, had not seen Victor Grant since he had declared he was going off to join a ship. He had thought Victor a sly one. He thought that one of the reasons Victor had wanted to get away from home was his weird aunt. When pressed, he said that she was a bit silly, dressed herself like a teenager and set herself off to people.

"I thought that she very rarely left the house?"

"Victor's mam used to keep a strict eye on her but she often took a walk out."

"Did you know that she had had a baby?"

"Nothing would surprise me. Mind you, I didn't think she was all there. She was sexy enough. People that didn't know her and met her in the street wouldn't be able to tell, would they? That she was simple, I mean."

"She upset Victor, did she?"

"He said she was always making up to him. She was a lot younger than his mam."

"But she was a good deal older than Victor, surely?"

"I don't know how old she was, maybe ten years older, twelve at most."

"Before he left home did he do any driving for anyone?"

"Yes, he would do anything to drive. They didn't have a car you know."

"What sort of jobs did he do, driving?"

"He sometimes drove a van for one or two traders, just at weekends like."

"How did he get these jobs?"

"Oh, through the driving school. Sometimes traders would ask the Bentleys to recommend someone."

"Did he travel very far with these jobs?"

"No. I think they were all local jobs."

"So he made his fortune, did he?"

"Well, I thought those jobs were done on the cheap, for pocket money, like, but he was flush when he went off. He bought us all a drink and his wallet was full. He certainly didn't get that off his old man."

"He wouldn't make much as an apprentice either."

"No, but Pomfrets pay good wages once you are finished your apprenticeship. I stayed on after I finished mine and I've done all right, up to now."

"Did Victor Grant ever talk to you about going to sea?"

"Once or twice he did, but not round about the time he went. Funny that, wasn't it? He was very close about it. Never breathed a word. Just said he had the chance and had to take it. I kidded him that it was woman

234

trouble but he just grinned."

"Did you see a lot of him after work or did you only meet occasionally?"

"We usually met on Thursday nights the way we did when we were in the youth club. Now and again we would go somewhere at the weekends like to the football but he dropped out of the weekends. He kept saying he had something to do, some bird or other. I was more friendly with Gordon and two of the other lads so it didn't bother me that he wasn't about at the weekends. Anyway I started going out with Pat, the missus, soon after that."

It was well on into the afternoon when Hart returned to the station. He found Bailey waiting for him. He hadn't needed to go in search of high level management, the duty clerk had been working for Chester Securities for more than twenty years and he recognised the pieces of tape easily. His firm had used that kind of tape to secure boxes of banknotes for a very long time and still did. Only the colour had changed in all the time he had worked there. Better still, he said that the name might still be recognisable if more of the tape was available.

"We'll get on to that straight away, if there is the faintest hint of the name on any of the pieces, it will be the confirmation of my theories. I was beginning to think it was all too vague."

"Sixteen years is a very long time, Sir."

"So you keep saying, Sergeant!"

"So, what do we do now, Sir?"

"First, the tape to the experts, then we make a direct enquiry as to who is the partner who succeeded Mr. Garrett at Garrett and Morrison's. Check with whoever is watching the place that there is someone in, will you? If there is, tell them to get the name and address of this mysterious partner and we'll arrange to have him brought in."

D.C. Phillips returned from a rather boring afternoon. It had taken him longer than he had expected to find Mr. Crimpton, simply because the estate agent's was closed and when he had found the right Mr. Crimpton from the telephone book, he had a long journey to his home and a long wait for him to return from meeting someone. His wait was well rewarded though, he had recognised one of the photographs immediately. It was that of Clifford Morton. Hart was delighted.

"It's coming together!"

Unfortunately the guardian of Garrett and Morrison's reported that there was no sign of life in the flat above the shop and the shop remained unlit.

"Sir, are we likely to recover the money now? It rather looks as though Grant has disappeared."

"Don't be too despondent, Sergeant. We can't be certain of anything yet. We know that Clifford Morton took the house, we know he is tied into the robbery. We think Victor Grant is involved, we think that they hid the money in the allotment. We know that the money was taken from the allotment since it is no longer there. We are fairly sure that John Butterman was involved since his body was found in the house. What we have to consider is how could such a bulky load be removed and where could it be removed to."

"If Victor Grant is involved he could simply have taken it to the shop."

"Not unless he was prepared to let his partners in the shop know about it. I don't think he would dare to risk that."

"He could have taken it to his own house."

"Yes, wherever that is. He'll be sitting on it, waiting for the opportunity to bank it or invest it, a little at a time."

"But if they had moved the money to Grant's house, where ever that is, why did they keep returning to 20 Selborne Street? They could have abandoned the place and could have been safe, home and dry."

"Well now, Sergeant, either that is a mystery or....the money is still at No. 20."

"But, Sir, the place was searched after the body was found."

"I suppose it is just possible that the team missed it."

"Sir, there was an awful lot of it, it would be hard to miss."

"You're right, it seems we've got to wait until someone returns to the shop in Grammond."

"I could take a look at No.20 myself, Sir, if you like."

"I thought you just said that it would be hard to miss."

"It's better than sitting about waiting for word from Grammond, Sir."

"Sergeant Bailey, you argue one thing then do another! Where's your logic? Oh, alright, be off with you, there's no point in everyone sitting about here. But shouldn't you be at home?"

Bailey grinned at his chief over his shoulder as he left.

Chapter Thirty-Two

Bailey was happy to be off on his own again. Hart's last question had troubled his conscience more than a little. He had told his chief about the pregnancy, he and his wife were too excited by it to keep it to themselves and there was no reason why they should keep it a secret. However, the excitement had passed and the problems of looking after an unpredictable and demanding wife in the early stages of pregnancy had proved increasingly difficult and tedious. He was still something of a schoolboy at heart, he enjoyed his job and relished any freedom of action it might bring. He had been delighted to carry out the arrest of 'Chopper' Morton and he was eager to have another independent role to play.

He went down to the operations room and sought John Butterman's keys. It was already dark when he drove into Selborne Street and parked. The street was not well lit, most of the curtains were drawn and all the lights inside the houses seemed dim. An overcast sky increased the darkness. It was not cold, nor was there a wind. Bailey looked up and down the street and found it rather depressing. He never really liked terrace houses, there was no space to them. He preferred a garden or walkway of some kind to the side of a house. If he could afford it he would have a detached house where he could enjoy freedom from neighbours, but, even as he thought this, he remembered that neighbours could be useful. Not that the neighbours in Selborne Street had been very useful to each other.

He was standing fiddling with the keys for some time before he realised that none of Butterman's keys fitted the front door. He remembered the back door had a yale lock and, reluctantly, went round to the back lane. One of the keys fitted the back door and he duly let himself in. He wrinkled his nose against the musty smell in the back yard and recalled what he had seen yesterday. Carefully he opened the back door to the house and stepped inside.

He was not a queasy person but the smell of the body still lingered, together with the smell from the gas fire. It was difficult to see. He had brought a torch but he remembered that the electricity had not been disconnected so he put the light on. Something troubled him, he felt nervous. He was not normally nervous but this house had a depressing effect on him. He found that the light bulb was low powered and its poor light cast more shadows than he thought possible. No doubt, Butterman and Grant did not use electric light for fear of attracting attention. He imagined himself in their position, or at least Butterman's. Where had Butterman been standing when he was attacked? Where had his murderer been hiding? Perhaps they had spoken to each other? There had been no signs of a struggle. It could well be that he knew his murderer well.

Bailey went into the passage that led to the bottom of the stairs. He thought he sensed a draught. The sitting room on his left was decidedly chilly, in contrast to the living room where the heat had not yet been fully dissipated. He did not turn on the light but swept the beam from his torch round the room. There was a narrow three piece suite, not well upholstered, a couple of small side tables and an upright chair. It was just possible that the three piece suite might have something concealed in it. He took up the cushions and felt the base. There was only thin hessian with the usual wooden supports underneath. Nothing was hidden there, nevertheless he was careful to check all of the seats. He also squeezed every cushion but nothing could be hidden there. He turned and went upstairs. The stairs were thinly carpeted and creaked a little.

The bathroom was narrow and overlooked the back yard but its windows were patterned and it was not possible to see out even in daylight. A soap smell lingered and Bailey noticed that one of the taps at the washbasin dripped steadily. He hated dripping taps, even old ones were capable of having their washers replaced. The next room was the second or medium sized bedroom. It was barely furnished. There was a single bed, not made up, with pillows and folded blankets piled on the top. One single wardrobe stood at one side and a single upright chair stood at the other. Bailey opened the wardrobe and was greeted by a strong smell of mothballs. There were no shelves and no complications to the structure. Nothing could be hidden here. He swept his light round the walls and sighed.

Back in the corridor, he hesitated. The house was very still but he thought that he heard a noise. There was nothing. Even a cold house sometimes groaned or creaked. His own house was never quiet, due to the central heating. The small bedroom was comparatively crowded. A single bed, made up rather sparingly, lay alongside one wall, a small wardrobe and a chest of three drawers lay along the other. There was hardly room to move between them. An upright chair stood by the bed as if to serve the dual function of chair and bedside table. There was no possibility that any of these pieces of furniture could contain a secret horde. He glanced under the bed just in case.

Outside, on the landing, his torch beam located the hatch door to the roof space. It was just possible that the routine search had missed something and that the roof space harboured what they were looking for. He would check as soon as he could locate a stepladder.

The main bedroom possessed the most imposing furniture. The bed was high and had robust mahogany ends. It had been stripped, like that in the middle bedroom and bedclothes were folded on top of it. The wardrobe was quite handsome. It was of a lighter colour than the bed ends and was very substantial. It reached almost to the ceiling. Bailey pulled out the drawer below the wardrobe and found it full of bedding. He thought it overstuffed and pulled it further in order to search through the contents. The drawer stuck. He bent down to look and found that there were wooden stops at each end, preventing the drawer from being pulled out to the full extent. He would need to pull it up at the front and move it in a small semicircle in order to free it from these restraints. In fact, the load was too heavy. Even with both hands free it would be difficult. He set down the torch. The floor was covered with a shiny linoleum. The torch skittered briefly then rolled away under the bed and went out. Bailey cursed himself for not putting on the light when he had first entered. He rose and was about to go to the door when he froze.

There was just a tiny sound. A creak or the snapping sound a muscle sometimes makes when tensed. Several seconds went by. Nothing. In the distance he heard a tap dripping. He could not stay in this position. As he pressed the light switch down, he was prepared for an intruder. There was no one. Feeling rather foolish he shouted down the corridor.

"Anyone there?"

There was no reply. What would his chief say? He wouldn't dare tell him! With a smile he returned to his task. The drawer's load was very heavy but he managed to free it from its restraints and set it down on the floor. He rummaged through the contents and found nothing. He examined the space it had occupied. Nothing. It was clear that the drawer fitted too well for there to be space to hide anything in that cavity. There would be some difficulty in getting the drawer to go back in. Bailey decided to examine the rest of the wardrobe first. He pushed the drawer to one side and opened the wardrobe door. Again the smell of mothballs was almost overpowering yet there was nothing unusual there. He stretched an arm to both sides and felt the space. There was no room for false compartments or anything of that sort.

On the outside at the top there was a splendidly curving architrave of sorts. He recalled that these were usually detachable. This one was about three or four inches deep at its lowest point. He fetched an upright chair from beside the bed and stepped on it to reach a hand over the edge. Strange! His fingers only dipped by an inch or two. He reached further along, it was the same. He stood down and looked up. If there was a false layer, it could mean a total space of about two cubic feet. That would accommodate a lot of banknotes.

Bailey became quite excited. He realised that he could not move, never mind dismantle, the wardrobe by himself. It would have to be done in daylight by a team equipped with the necessary screwdrivers and chisels. He looked down at the drawer. Why did it need to be so big, it must be a full five feet by almost two and at least ten inches deep. It would have been easier if it had been two drawers. He groped under the bed for his torch. Suddenly the light went out.

Awkwardly positioned as he was, Bailey froze, yet again. There was silence for a moment then he heard a slow breathing. He looked towards the door and could just make out two feet as his eyes became used to the gloom. There was the same creak as weight shifted from one limb to another. Bailey silently drew his knees towards him, he thought it best that all of him was under the bed.

Chapter Thirty-Three

Hart never liked being inactive. If there was nothing purposeful to do at the station he fretted to be home. Just to await news from the look out at Grammond was far from sufficient to occupy him. He wished he had gone with Bailey. He turned over the pages of his notebook impatiently. His eye caught an item on Clifford Morton and he swung into action again.

"Inspector Jordan? Which hospital did Clifford Morgan die in?"

"Bardsley and Grange General, Sir."

"Can you get them for me? I want to know more about who was sitting with him. You remember that someone said he was from the police but it turned out that he wasn't. If we can find the staff who were on duty then, I'll go through and interview them."

It took a while for Jordan to establish that the Ward Sister who had reported the presence of the 'false' policeman was on duty that very day. Hart was delighted with this piece of luck and departed immediately, giving strict instructions that he should be told of any further developments at Grammond.

Bardsley and Grange General were further away than Hart could have wished. It was well beyond Bardsley itself and he hoped that there would not have been a change of shift while he was on his way. In fact, by the time he had found the correct ward, the shift was just changing. He was doubly lucky in that he found the sister before she left and that she was free to give him her full attention, having finished her duty.

Sister Meredith was four square and reliable. She met his eye and did not waver, nor was she excitable. She remembered that there had been two visitors. One came two or three times and the other, the one who claimed to be a policeman, came many times. She would not have remembered had it not been because of the fuss made by the police after the patient had died. Then all her faculties of recall had been brought to bear and now, she thought, she would never be able to forget. The one who came most often was fair and thin, tallish with a sharp nose and cold blue eyes. The other was also fairly tall, youngish looking, dark hair, pasty face, brown eyes.

Hart produced a photograph.

"Oh yes. That is the younger one, I'm sure of it!"

It was the photograph of John Butterman. Hart thought his journey had been well worthwhile.

Inspector Jordan met him in the lobby of the police station.

"Sir, there has been an extraordinary phone call for you. I could make neither head nor tail of it. The speaker was almost incoherent. Kept saying something about a van."

Hart's mind wasn't quite adjusted. He stood for a few seconds before he guessed who the caller had been. It had to be Eric Semper.

"I know who it must have been, Semper, a cobbler, Stoker Street I think. Can you get him back for me?"

Jordan could get no reply. Hart was troubled.

"How long ago did he phone?"

"About half an hour ago, Sir."

Hart bit his lip. Eric must have seen the van arrive. If this was Victor Grant he must have been on his way to the house. Bailey might still be there. Would Bailey be in a position to apprehend Grant? The D.C.I. had a sudden vision of John Butterman's body lying in front of that fire. Bailey could be expected to look after himself...up to a point. And why was there no reply from Eric Semper? Had something happened to him?

"Right, Inspector, get two cars out straight away to

244

20 Selborne Street! There may be trouble. I'll go with them. At the double!"

As they swerved and dodged their way through the evening traffic, Hart couldn't clear his mind of the body in front of the gas fire. It took the strength of a desperate man to strangle someone. Would Bailey be able to cope? As they raced up Stoker Street a vehicle approaching them switched on its lights, momentarily blinding them. Hart's driver swore and swerved instinctively but there had been no need, the other vehicle was soon out of sight behind them. Hart stared out at the corner. There was no sign of any van parked nearby. They rushed into Selborne Street and pulled up with a wrenching of tyres.

Eric Semper was huddled in the front doorway to No.20. He was sobbing with exhaustion. Hart indicated that he should be helped into one of the cars. There was no answer to their knocking so Hart was obliged to have the door broken down. They rushed into the dark corridor. From where he stood, Hart could see that the doors to the living room and the yard beyond were open.

"Check the yard! Be careful, our man's desperate! Now, every room!"

As though by instinct, he rushed ahead up the stairs into the large bedroom. He switched on the light and gasped at the chaos before him. Across his path in a monolithic diagonal lay a huge wardrobe. It was propped up by the end of a bed, which itself was turned onto its side. There had been an almighty struggle. Bedding was scattered everywhere. There were pieces of splintered wood among the bedding and one of the window curtains had been torn so that it hung like an abandoned flag on the scene of battle. Battle there had certainly been. Hart and one of his men applied all their strength to the wardrobe and levered it back to the wall. There was a moaning sound from beyond the bed. Hart heaved at the end of the bed and squeezed round. Bailey lay face down, one hand against his neck, blood oozing from his head.

"An ambulance, quick!"

Hart turned his sergeant over very gently. Bailey's face was severely battered but what concerned Hart most was the mark around his neck and wrist. Bailey had managed to raise his arm to his head to avoid the strangulation but the force on the wire had been such that his wrist had been deeply grooved.

"Get some help and clear the way ready for that ambulance."

By now it was established that whoever had attacked Bailey had escaped via the back lane. Most of the team were endeavouring to clear a space round the victim. Hart was trembling with rage. He could hardly attend to what his men were chattering about. He listened for Bailey's heartbeat and wrenched at his shirt collar to make sure that he had more air. The sergeant was breathing but very raggedly. One of the team managed, by brave persistence, to bring to his chief's attention that one of Bailey's legs was broken, probably as a result of the upset of the bed and the wardrobe. This enraged Hart further.

"Where the hell is that ambulance?!"

There was a small commotion in the doorway. Inspector Jordan had set off as soon as he had relayed the call for the ambulance. With astonishing foresight he had brought with him a doctor. There was a minimal introduction and Jordan drew the stunned Hart out of the room while the doctor made his examination.

"There's not much we can do for Sergeant Bailey until the ambulance arrives, Sir."

Hart went downstairs and out into the fresh air.

Across the street he saw a couple standing staring and recognised them as the Drysdales. Another couple arrived at his elbow and asked if they could help. They were the Fosters. No one else seemed to know or want to know what had been happening. Hart shook his head and thanked them politely. He stepped into the car where Eric Semper sat trembling. Hart spoke to him clearly and gently.

"Thank you for what you did tonight, Eric. I think you have helped to save someone's life. What exactly happened?"

The youth straightened up and took a deep breath.

"My parents had gone out. We had locked up. I went upstairs to get a book and saw the van parked below my window. I tried to tell them at the police station but I don't think they understood so I went down the street to see what was happening. There was a light moving in this house, the light went on in the bedroom then went off again. I saw movements. The curtain was pulled to one side. I knew there shouldn't be anyone in there so I knocked on the door as hard as I could. Then my strength gave out and you came."

"You did well, very well. Where was the van parked?"

"At the side of the shop."

"In Stoker Street?"

"Yes"

"It had gone by the time we arrived so that means your knocking scared the man off. Did you see him, Eric, when he got out of the car?"

"No, I didn't see the car arrive. I got the number though. PKJ 304 D."

"Excellent!"

Eric burst into racking coughs. Hart told his man to take Eric home and see that he was alright. He was to seek the parents and bring them back to their son. Soon after they had departed, the ambulance arrived and Bailey was taken away. Hart instructed Jordan that there should be a twenty-four hour watch on his sergeant just in case his attacker tried again. There was an immediate alert to trace the van.

Chapter Thirty-Three

Hart returned to the station deeply troubled, the memory of Bailey's battered appearance and the chaos of that bedroom were fiercely burned into his mind. He had not been so affected in all his years in the police force. He couldn't sit down. He strode backwards and forwards, picked up a file and put it down again, rested an arm on the filing cabinet and took it away again. A knock on the door finally made him pause. It was D.C. Phillips to report that No.20 had been locked up and a guard posted.

"Is there anything else we can do, Sir?"

"Yes, Phillips, I want a watch on the cobbler's at the beginning of Stoker Street. The boy there saw our villain. I don't want him harmed."

Inspector Jordan entered.

"You alright, Sir?"

"Yes, thank you, Inspector. I just need to calm down. You'll let me know as soon as we have news of Bailey, won't you?"

"Are we dealing with a maniac, Sir?"

"You might well say so. Somebody vicious and a very powerful, that's certain. Bailey must have put up a tremendous fight....which reminds me...if Bailey put up a good fight, our villain must be damaged too. Put out a call to all the local hospitals to check their casualty lists. At this time of night he won't go to a doctor, he'll go to casualty, but where? Grammond? Try them all within thirty miles."

"Right, Sir!"

At that moment, the phone rang. It was the Grammond watchdogs. Someone had returned to the flat above the shop. They had not seen whoever it was so they must have entered from the back.

"Inspector Jordan, another squad car, this time I'm off to Grammond, with a bit of luck we may have our man. Oh, and would you phone Grammond headquarters and tell them it's an emergency at the shop I asked to be put under surveillance. They'll know what I'm talking about."

The journey to Grammond was tense. Phillips and Ridley had come along too but they were unwilling to break the uneasy silence. They could see that their chief was in a murderous mood. Hart himself broke the silence just as they reached the outskirts of the city.

"I'm not sure what we will find. I believe that the man we are looking for has a connection with the jeweller's shop we are heading for. He may not be there, in which case we will get his address from whoever is there. When we do find him, he may prove violent. You saw the state Sergeant Bailey was in tonight? Right, be prepared! Keep your eyes open and your wits about you. It may be that this villain has gone to the local casualty department. If he has, and we need to find him there, we will have to proceed with great caution, we don't want the public to be involved and we don't want anybody to get hurt if we can help it. Keep your eye on me, I'll be giving the signals."

They arrived in Howland Road and pulled up directly in front of the shop. As they got out of the car they were joined by the two watchdogs, Fleming and Borthwick, who made a brief report to their chief. There had been no movement since the light had gone on upstairs, the light was still on.

Hart instructed two of the team to station themselves round the back in case someone made a run for it, then he knocked on the door. There was no immediate answer. His second knock was truly thunderous. Footsteps sounded inside, the door opened slightly and someone looked out angrily.

"What's all the noise about?"

Hart recognised the figure as the man who had been behind the counter when he had first visited the shop. He held up his warrant card and introduced himself. Very politely he asked if he may come in. Slowly, the man backed away and nodded. Four imposing policemen mounted the stairs. The flat was small and neat. In the living room were three people, a man and two women. Hart recognised one of them as the young woman who had remembered Tommy Watson's visit. They had been watching television but switched it off as soon as the visitors entered the room. The man who had admitted Hart and his team introduced one of the women as his wife and the other two as Miss Renton and Mr. Pearson.

There was an understandable atmosphere of bewilderment. The older of the two women looked shocked, the younger smiled with a detached amusement. The man who had been introduced as Pearson stared uncomprehendingly. He was not very tall and he was lightly built. His hair was dark and he sported a full but well-trimmed beard. His eyes were wary.

Hart turned to the host.

"Can I take it that you are Mr. Morrison?"

"Er...no, my name is Purbeck, there hasn't been a Morrison for many years."

"You have a partner?"

"Yes, Mr. Pearson here is my partner, what's this all about? Don't I know you...?"

"Yes sir, I called at the shop last week in connection with an enquiry we were making into the death of a young boy...."

"What has that to do with us...?"

"Do you have anyone else working for you?"

251

"No, there are just the three of us, Miss Renton and I work in the shop and Mr. Pearson does the engraving."

"Have you always been an engraver, Mr. Pearson?"

"Most of my life, what has that got to do with..."

"We are looking for a Victor Grant. You wouldn't know anyone of that name, would you, sir?"

Pearson paled visibly. He looked as though he were going to faint.

"You look ill, Tony, you'd better sit down. Why don't we all sit down."

Mrs. Purbeck waved a hand to them all and helped Pearson back into his seat. There were not enough chairs, only Hart among the newcomers could sit.

"What is all this about, officer? We've lived here for I don't know how long and we've known Tony for years..."

"Could you tell me where you were, sir, earlier this evening?"

Hart concentrated on Pearson. Mrs. Purbeck answered for him.

"We've all been out for the day. The weather was really fine and we all went to see my young daughter at Rockborough. It was Tony's idea, he stood us lunch on the way. We only got back about eight."

Hart was thoughtful.

"You aren't married, Mr. Pearson?"

Again someone answered for him, this time it was Miss Renton, the slim dark girl.

"Not yet, but not for much longer."

Hart turned his serious gaze on her. She smiled at him.

"We are engaged. Tony is coming into money very soon. I've agreed to marry him as soon as we have a house of our own."

"Could I ask when you are coming into this money, sir?"

252

Pearson sat silent, only his eyes moved.

"I'll ask you again, sir, do you happen to know a Victor Grant?"

There was a long silence. Mrs. Purbeck tried to interrupt again but Hart held up his large hand. At last, Pearson stirred. He sat up slowly and licked his lips.

"Could we continue this in private?"

There was a general outcry.

"Don't let them bully you, Tony, we'll get a solicitor, you don't have to answer any questions if you don't want to."

"They are right, of course, sir, but if you would speak to us now it will save a lot of time and trouble and would be better for you in the long run."

Hart stood up and Pearson followed him. They went down into the street and the cars bore them swiftly back to Clayton.

Chapter Thirty-Four

Hart wasn't sure what to expect as he faced Pearson across the table in the interview room. Pearson looked dazed and confused. He hardly heard Hart's first question. When Hart repeated it, Pearson shook his head as though to clear it and asked a question of his own.

"How did you find out? It was Butterman, wasn't it?"

"Let's start at the beginning, your name is really Victor Grant, isn't it?"

"Yes."

Hart was right in a number of things. Victor Grant had been the getaway driver in the Chester Securities robbery, he had buried the money in the allotment, he had needed to get away from home but needed to be within reach of the money. He had chosen Grammond as his base, had learned engraving and had worked for Garrett and Morrison, later, buying his way into a partnership. If things had worked out, he had planned to 'inherit' his share of the stolen money, marry, buy a big house, expand the business and live comfortably for the rest of his life. Quite evidently, he was proud of this scheme, telling it in his own way. Hart brought him down to earth with a thud.

"Why did you kill the boy?"

"The boy...the boy...we didn't kill him, we didn't, you've got to believe me! We found him in the shed that night. We didn't know who he was and how he got there, we had to get rid of him so we waited until midnight and took him through the allotments and along the railway line to the park. We thought that he probably came from the estate."

"How did John Butterman come to be involved in all this?"

"We needed to move the money ready for a getaway, Cliff helped to dig up the money and move it to the house but he was worried that we were both too far away to keep an eye on it. I didn't trust Johnny B. but there was no one else. He didn't know about the money, we only told him to keep an eye out. We paid him well and gave him a key and told him to check that the man from the estate agent should be the only visitor. Anyone else lurking about and he was to phone me. He was useful in other ways, he went to visit Cliff in hospital to check on how he was doing. I couldn't go, could I? I came through every Monday and met Johnny in the house for a check-up."

"Didn't he suspect something?"

"I told him that a friend was planning to lay low there and that he would arrive at any time. I said that he was wanted by the police. He didn't know anything about the money."

"He found out, though, didn't he? That's why he had to be killed."

"Killed! What are you talking about? He nearly died when we found the kid. I knew we were in trouble then. Sooner or later he was going to blab to somebody, he always had a big mouth. He'll bear me out about finding the kid."

"I hardly think he is in a position to do that..."

"If only there had been somebody else who lived near. There was only Johnny B. He knew the house and could come and go by the back door without attracting any suspicion. He was pretty sick about that body and blamed me for getting him into something bad. I had to give him a hundred to keep him steady. It wasn't enough to promise him more, I could see that he was going to ruin all my plans."

"So you did away with him?"

"I should have done shouldn't I? I would never have

been found."

"You realise what you are saying?"

"Well, it's too late now. All my plans are finished, thanks to him."

"Thanks to John Butterman?"

"Yes, it was him who blabbed, wasn't it?"

"Nobody blabbed, Mr. Grant."

"Then how did you know....and how did you know where I was? I only gave Johnny the telephone number."

"It was the boy who led us to you."

"The boy? The boy we found dead? How could he lead you to me?"

"He came to your shop and recognised you."

"Wait a minute! What are you talking about? The boy was dead wasn't he?. We found him last Monday. He couldn't have....he was dead, wasn't he?"

"That boy came to your shop three or four weeks ago to buy a watch. He wanted it to be engraved with his uncle's name. While he was in the shop, he saw someone he recognised and changed his mind. He put his own name on it instead. Now why should he have done that? Think about it, Mr. Grant."

"I don't know what you are talking about. How could that boy have recognised me?"

"Quite simply, he was a relation of yours."

Grant snorted with derision.

"You've got it all wrong. I have no relations, at least none of his age."

"That boy's name was Tommy Watson. Does the name not mean anything to you?"

"Oh yes, I remember, the television appeal called him that..."

"That was your mother's maiden name wasn't it?"

"Yes..."

"And your aunt's?"

There was a long silence. Grant's eyes bulged, he flushed then suddenly went very pale.

"Your aunt became pregnant not long before you left. The boy you claim to have found was her son."

"No! No! Impossible! It can't be! It just can't be!" His voice rose then failed. He held his head in both hands and sat as if frozen.

"You have never bothered to ask after your parents or your aunt, have you?"

"How could I? How could I?"

"They would have told you. They would also have told you that the birth caused your aunt to lose her mind."

Hart was relentless.

"You didn't know that John Butterman was dead?"

"Johnny dead? When? How?"

"He was killed in the same way as Tommy Watson. Strangled. His body was found in No. 20 Selborne Street. Tell me about it."

"Tell you, what can I tell you? It's the first I knew. He was alright the last time I saw him."

"Which was?"

"Monday, that was when we moved the body."

"Who would want to murder John Butterman? Did anyone else have a hand in looking after the money?"

"No! There was no one else who knew about it. Cliff died. I'm sure he didn't tell anyone. He didn't want anyone else to know about it. He said that at the time we took Johnny B. on."

"Where were you on Thursday last, Mr. Grant?"

"Thursday, I was out with Jenny, Jenny Renton. We went to the theatre, the Bondgate in Grammond. We went to see "Carousel", the amateur operatic society, she had friends in it."

"That would finish before 10.30. You would have had time to see Miss Renton home and still manage to

257

get to Clayton in time to murder John Butterman."

"Why should I do that?"

"Because he was cracking up and you didn't want him to blab, to use your word."

"No, I didn't, I sat up late with Jenny. We were hungry when we came out of the Bondgate so we went for a chinese meal. We took it home and watched television until the early hours."

"She will verify that, will she?"

"Yes, and so will my neighbour, Sam Foulds. He came in about midnight to ask me if I'd seen his cat. It goes missing every now and then."

"When you last saw John Butterman, you claim you gave him a hundred pounds to 'settle him'. What did you mean by that?"

"He was going to pieces after we got back from the park. I gave him a hundred to calm him down and keep him quiet. He liked money, who doesn't?"

"You have waited sixteen years for your share of the stolen money, do you expect me to believe that you thought that a hundred pounds would make you absolutely safe and that you weren't aware that your long wait was about to be jeopardised by an unreliable blabbermouth?"

"There was nothing else I could do, anyway he didn't know about the money and he didn't know where I lived."

"You could have arranged to meet him in the house and killed him there."

"I didn't! I didn't!"

"Whether he knew about the money or not is irrelevant. You would have had to face a serious charge in connection with the death of the boy. With the death of John Butterman you would have been a lot safer."

"You seem to have found me regardless of Johnny's death."

Hart had to concede this point. He took a rest and Inspector Jordan took over.

"What did you do with the money?"

"It should be still at the house. I decided not to move it until the business of the boy had blown over."

"Our men searched the house after the body was discovered, they didn't find anything."

Grant grinned but said nothing.

"It would be in your interest to tell us where it is."

"Perhaps...perhaps not."

"If someone else knew about the money they could have taken it, could they?"

"I suppose so, but who else knows about it?"

Hart recognised a sense of uplift in Grant's spirits. He was not prepared to pander to it. He beckoned Jordan to one side.

"We'll leave him for a while then start again when he's not feeling so cocky."

Chapter Thirty-Five

About midnight it was established that the blue van numbered PKJ 304 D was recorded as having been stolen in Manchester four months ago. Hart knew by then that Victor Grant had not been Bailey's assailant and he accepted that Grant had not killed Tommy Watson or John Butterman. He must now look for a third man.

He and Jordan laboured hard and long over Victor Grant but could not shake him from the testimony he had given. He had not told anyone about the robbery and he was sure that Clifford Morton had not done so either. John Butterman did not know about the money so could not have told anyone about it. He swore that he and Butterman had found the body of Tommy Watson and that he had not known about Butterman's death until the D.C.I. had told him that evening. Nor could they persuade him to reveal where the money was hidden.

They decided to charge him with involvement with the Chester Securities robbery for the moment. There was no question of allowing bail for the murders were not yet resolved and Hart thought that he may well need protection from the mysterious third man.

"Any word from our casualty departments, Inspector?"

"Not yet, Sir, I'm afraid. Are you sure he would be injured?

"Bailey was very fit, he would put up a fight. I'd like to bet he would give as good as he got. Check on the hospital, will you, they should have an idea by now how he is doing."

"Right, Sir."

Hart returned to his office. But for Bailey's dreadful experience he would have enjoyed the satisfaction of knowing that most of his ideas had been proved right. He was niggled about the money and furious that Grant was playing games by not revealing where it was hidden. Did the stupid idiot think that he still had a chance to take it and enjoy it? He would only add to his sentence. Anyhow, he would get a team round to have another search. Momentarily, the thought occurred to him that Bailey's assailant may have taken it but he rejected this idea. If he had been hunting for it when Bailey came on the scene he had not had time to carry it off after the struggle.

Where would he himself hide it? First, he would have to get it from the allotment to the house. There must have been at least twenty boxes or bags, maybe eight or ten cubic feet in all and quite heavy. How could he have done it? He had to be inconspicuous, even if it was in the late evening. It couldn't have been very late because the police watching Morton would have been curious about his late return. Two men carrying bundles, probably two or more journeys, they must have been conspicuous. It would have taken Hart, himself, at least four trips. Suddenly, it dawned. He pictured the allotment. It was right in front of him, of course, the wheelbarrow! Immediately, he realised where the money was.

"Sir, I've spoken to the doctor who examined Bailey. He says that had Bailey not managed to raise his wrist to his head he would most certainly have died. The force on the wire or whatever was used was terrific. One side of his neck was deeply scored and there was damage to the ligaments...."

"But he is going to pull through?"

"Yes. It will take time but he should make a full recovery."

"Thank God! They took him to the Cottage Hospital

didn't they? I hope they have all the facilities, it isn't very big you know."

"The doctor talked of transferring him once he had regained consciousness."

"I trust they will let us know immediately they do. There must be a police guard the whole time, or at least until we have caught our villain."

When Hart returned home in the early hours, Sheila was fast asleep and did not stir. He got into bed as carefully and silently as possible and had just drifted off to sleep when the telephone rang. It was insistent, its sound volleyed and faded as it fought for his attention. That first deep sleep took some shaking off.

It was the duty sergeant at the police station, he was most apologetic but he had taken a telephone message from Bardsley and Grange General Hospital, a Sister Meredith. She insisted that the Chief Inspector should be told. She had seen the man that he had been enquiring about.

"You did right, Sergeant, I'll contact her straight away. Will you get the number back for me? Thank you."

Hart leapt out of bed and went over to a table by the window. It took a while for someone to answer his call. He asked for Sister Meredith and a dull nasal voice at the other end asked which ward she was in. Patiently, Hart explained who he was and said that the matter was urgent, he did not know which ward she was in. The voice at the other end was not much moved and again asked which ward she was in. Hart's voice became icy.

"This is a very urgent police matter, please find out which ward she is on and connect me as soon as possible."

After a long delay he found himself connected to the Nurses' Home and as there was no explanation of this there was a most confused conversation with a charming but sleepy young woman. Eventually she understood what he was asking and, after a conversation with someone else, she referred him to Ward 10 as Sister Meredith had agreed to swap duties with one of her friends. It took another interminable delay before he was through to Ward 10.

"Oh, it's you, Chief Inspector! I'm sorry I couldn't ring you earlier but we've been terribly busy. I couldn't get to the phone for ever so long. It's just that I saw the very man you were asking about, tonight at about 11 o'clock. I came through casualty to check on something and I saw him quite clearly. He'd been in a fight or something."

"You couldn't tell me if he was detained or if he went away again?"

"No, I'm afraid not, but they would tell you on casualty."

"He didn't see you, did he?"

"No, he was talking at the window as I passed by. I'm sure he didn't see me."

"Good. I'm very grateful to you for going to the trouble to let us know."

It was on Hart's lips to warn her that the man was dangerous but he hesitated to alarm her. With luck, she would not see him again.

He phoned again and asked the nasal voice to put him through to Casualty. This time there was no delay. Hart explained who he was and asked about a man who had attended about 11 o'clock that evening.

"There were four men in about that time, Chief Inspector, which one do you mean?"

Hart was perplexed. He wasn't in a position to describe the man. Somehow, he hadn't expected this problem on a Sunday evening.

"I was hoping you would be able to help me there.

We are simply looking for a man who was involved in a fight earlier this evening...."

"Well, Sir, these men were involved in a car crash. Three were in cars and the other was a pedestrian...."

"I'll bet the man we're looking for is that pedestrian. Was he the last man to register with you?"

"Yes, he came in a little after the others."

"Could you tell me the nature of his injuries?"

"Well..."

"This is a very urgent matter."

"I was going to say that I don't know the full extent of the injuries, there were superficial facial injuries and he had a damaged left arm, possibly broken. He was examined and went through to the X-Ray Department."

"Could you tell me if he was detained in hospital?"

"I could find out for you, but it's unlikely unless he was suffering from concussion or something like that."

"If he had a broken arm he would have to have it plastered then make an appointment to come back to have the plaster removed, wouldn't he?"

"Yes, that would be the usual thing but if he wasn't from this area he would be referred to his own doctor and his local hospital. If you would wait a few minutes, I'll check if he is still in the hospital."

There was another delay and Hart thought of his bed.

"The last of those men, the pedestrian, gave his name as Robert Burns, his address, 2 Bright Street, Glasgow 14. He wasn't detained and he did not come back here to make an appointment. Shall I ask the duty doctor what happened to him?"

"Yes please."

There was another long delay before the admissions clerk reported that she couldn't get the doctor, he was very busy. The accident had created something of an emergency. Hart thanked her and said that as the person he was enquiring about had left, there was no immediate hurry, he would send someone to get the particulars tomorrow, or later today, he looked at his watch.

Sheila was fully awake by this time and called him back to bed. He needed no urging.

"Robert Burns! A pedestrian from Glasgow in Bardsley!"

"What on earth are you muttering about, dear?"

Chapter Thirty-Six

D.C.I. Hart had very little sleep before he set off for the station that morning, but once he had eaten his breakfast he felt a great sense of urgency and when he arrived at his desk he was bursting with energy. Jordan followed him in with two reports in his hand. One was from the Cottage hospital to say that Bailey had had a comfortable night, the other was in answer to a request for information about John Thresher.

"This last one has just come in. You remember you asked me to check on John Peter Thresher the Chester Securities robber who was killed by a bus trying to escape. He had form, two convictions, one for armed robbery. He came from Bardsley. Mother, a widow still living, a brother, Phillip James, born 1930, has form, assault. He was in prison at the time of the Chester Securities robbery, Sir."

"Was he now? That's interesting. I wonder if he was to be the original driver? He might be our man. If the brothers were close, he could be after his share. If he was in prison there should be a photo on the files. Can you get one, Inspector, as quick as you can?"

"Right, Sir, but it could be a while."

"That can't be helped, we need it badly. Meantime, we have the mother's address. Somebody will have to go to check if he's at home or get his present address from his mother. Send Phillips and Ridley to me, we'll go together and I'll show them something on the way."

The two D.C.s were astonished when Hart drew up outside No. 20 Selborne Street. He greeted the constable on duty and led the two detectives through to the back yard. The musty smell still pervaded the store shed next to the wash-house. He hauled at one of the bags of manure that stood along by the wall.

"They were moved and the whole place searched on Saturday, Sir."

"Yes, I saw them being moved, Ridley, but no one thought to look inside, did they?"

Hart proceeded to dig his hands into the smelly material and to pull it out. After only a few handfuls he beamed at the others and drew out a plastic bag.

"No one dreamed of getting their hands dirty with this lot, did they? Somebody was very cunning. He used his eyes. In the allotment was the means of transporting the money, a wheelbarrow and next to it was the manure heap and a box with empty fertiliser bags. Even at night, no one would have suspected much if they had seen fertiliser bags being wheeled from an allotment."

Hart continued to bring out plastic bags full of money.

"Right, Ridley, fetch that constable in and collect this lot together. I'll phone for a car to take it back to the station. Phillips and I have to make that call in Bardsley."

Hart watched Ridley's expression from the kitchen window as he washed his hands. He had to admit that Ridley was completely natural, if he found something distasteful it registered unmistakably on his face. Ridley may well have had a career on the stage as a stand-up comedian, so flexible were his features. There was no time for further amusement, the car was soon on its way to Bardsley.

Dimchurch Row was a terrace of very old stone dwellings straggling up a steep hill on the northern outskirts of the town. In the clear morning sunlight they looked quite picturesque.

As they drove up the hill they could see vehicles and people milling about towards the far end of the row.

267

"I wonder what all that is about?"

"That's a hearse, Sir. It's somebody's funeral."

To Hart's astonishment and discomfort, the hearse was drawn up in front of No.18, the very house they had come to visit. They parked further along and walked back. Neighbours stood at their front gates watching and talking softly. Others stood on the opposite side of the road, a respectful send-off committee. One of the drivers stood by the hearse, drawing on a cigarette, his eye on the front door, Hart lowered his voice and gently asked whose funeral it was.

"It's old Mrs. Thresher. Died on Thursday. Well liked she was. Hasn't had an easy life. You knew her did you?"

"No, I knew her son."

"Here they come..."

Hart backed away as the coffin emerged from the front door supported by the official bearers. It was followed by a very small group of mourners. They were all female except for one elderly figure bent over a stick. There was no sign of a son. Hart studied the faces of all the neighbours around him, no one registered surprise. Everything appeared as it should be.

"Quick, back to the car. We'll follow them to the cemetery."

He and Phillips sauntered back to the car as circumspectly as possible and started the engine. They fell in behind the cortege and proceeded as far as the cemetery gates. They parked just outside and hurried up the path on foot. Suddenly, they were aware of how large this cemetery was, for another cortege of vehicles swept silently down towards them on its way out. They were obliged to step clear onto the grass and to stand still until it had passed. When they looked up the path again, they were not sure whether the mourners at a graveside on a low knoll ahead of them were those they had followed or not. There were many more mourners now than had left the house. A quick glance round established that no other funeral was taking place though some mourners from the previous funeral were still making their way out.

"Sir....."

"Patience, Phillips, we mustn't rush. Just keep your eyes open. The service won't be long."

The press of figures so near the grave prevented either of the detectives from seeing the chief mourners. Phillips slowly climbed the slope to the right in order to have a clearer view. Hart realised that the son must have been among those who had met at the graveside prior to the arrival of the coffin but whether that was a matter of extreme caution or simple convenience he could not have known.

The service ended. Slowly the black clad figures broke away, singly then in twos and threes. The son had to be there, Hart told himself. He moved quietly towards the centre of the group. Briefly, a young woman, head bowed, got in his way. She looked up as he muttered an apology and fixed him with a glare of deep mistrust. She lingered in front of him as though summing him up then hissed,

"Should you be here?"

"I don't think I know you? Do I?"

Hart's voice was low, scrupulously polite and sufficiently weighty to offer no possible offence. The malice in the woman's eyes indicated that she was deeply offended, nevertheless. Hart moved to one side. For a moment, he thought she was about to make a scene, but someone, unaware of any exchange, took her arm and moved on down the slope. The woman walked away but her head turned to watch Hart for some time as she did so.

The small diversion was sufficient to allow some members of the mourning group to move away in other directions unobserved. When Hart reached the graveside there were only the parson and the gravediggers left on the spot. Paths led in two different directions down the other side of the slope. Two or three mourners walked slowly away down each. Hart turned to look at Phillips. Phillips was waving his arms energetically and pointing. The D.C.I. tried to see where he was pointing but a group of very substantial gravestones obstructed his view. Phillips ran down to him.

"Sorry, Sir, I didn't think it right to shout. Someone ran off over there and swung himself over the wall, it must have been our man."

"Is there a road on the other side of the wall?"

"Yes, I think so, Sir."

"Then we've lost him, dammit!"

Hart turned and called after the parson.

"Excuse me, vicar, could you tell me if Mrs. Thresher's son was at the graveside?"

"Son? I wasn't introduced to a son. I'm new here. I didn't know the family. I was only introduced to the members of the family gathered in the house this morning. I'm sure that there was no mention of a son."

"Oh, there was a son. I think he has been away, I was hoping to meet him today, although it wasn't the happiest of times to do so."

"No, indeed...Mr. er....?"

Hart saw no need to prolong the conversation or to reveal the purpose of his visit. He thanked the new incumbent and hurried back to the car. Phillips was most troubled that they had failed to find Thresher, blaming himself entirely. Hart put him at ease.

"Don't blame yourself, Phillips. You were quite right, it was a funeral, we couldn't shout and scream just as it ended. We haven't much to go on. It might have been different if we had had a warrant for his arrest."

Had records made a mistake? Did the son know about his mother's death? Had he not been in touch with her? Was the mother the sort who cast off her erring sons? He thought it most unlikely. Two villains in the family, both unmarried, rather suggested a close knit family unit. He was certain that the figure Phillips had seen climbing over the wall in a hurry was Phillip Thresher.

"While we are in the area, let's pay a visit to the Bardsley and Grange General Hospital. I'd like to do some checking."

Chapter Thirty-Six

The casualty doctor's report on the injuries sustained by 'Robert Burns' made interesting reading. There were cuts and bruises to the head and forearms, a cracked bone in the forearm and bruised and split knuckles. One eye was badly bruised but the vision was not damaged. The doctor had the perspicacity to put a question mark after the stated cause. He had doubted the claimed involvement in the car crash.

"The wrist was plastered, I presume?"

"Yes, I suppose so."

The nurse who was attending to Hart studied the card with the details and deciphered the scribble.

"If he was a visitor, he would be referred back to his doctor. Yes, he's given his doctor's name and address back in Glasgow."

"Was the injury to the wrist severe?"

"I'll fetch the X-Ray."

The obliging nurse swept off down the shining corridor. A doctor emerged from a side room and Hart was obliged to explain his mission once again. In answer to Hart's question he said that there would be pain and the hand would not be moved easily but the arm would be relatively free. Of course, the arm would be kept immobile by means of a sling. Hart persisted, could the arm be carried without a sling? The doctor looked at him quizzically. It was possible, but there was always the risk of further damage as well as pain should there be a knock or unnecessary movement.

The nurse returned with the X-Ray and the doctor took it upon himself to interpret it. There was a hairline crack but no displacement. He had not examined the patient himself, of course, he couldn't say how extensive was the bruising but there was visible evidence of swelling that suggested a sharp blow.

Undoubtedly it would be painful. He turned and smiled condescendingly at the nurse.

"There wouldn't be a full plaster on it, would there, nurse?"

"No, doctor, it would have to be a half plaster until the swelling had died down."

"None of the night staff would be about now, I suppose?"

"No, I'm afraid that they would have gone off duty early this morning."

"What I really want to know is, could this man walk about without making himself recognisable, without his arm bringing attention to himself?"

"Yes, it is possible. He could have walked out without it being plastered at all, come to that. If they were busy last night they might not have noticed. But why should he want to do that?"

"If he knew he was wanted in this area, he wouldn't want to be recognised. He would try not to have further treatment until he was a good way away."

"You think he only wanted to be assured by the X-Ray that he wasn't too badly hurt?"

"Exactly. Thanks for your time and trouble, Doctor."

Phillips was curious and as they drove back to the station he couldn't refrain from breaking his chief's silence.

"Why shouldn't he just lie low, Sir, he doesn't know we are on to him, does he?"

"He'll have a pretty shrewd idea of procedures. He would guess we would enquire about injured men needing treatment. That car crash must have been a godsend to him. He was able to check in at casualty without too much suspicion."

"So the casualty people didn't report him. Then how

did we know that he had been there, Sir?"

"It was one of the sisters. She remembered him as the man who had sat at Clifford Morton's bedside when he was in a coma, three or four months back."

"That was a lucky break!"

"Yes, but he's still on the loose and that worries me."

"Why, Sir, we've got the money and we'll have him sooner or later."

"It's the motive, Phillips. I don't think the money is the motive. Why should he set about Sergeant Bailey so deliberately? I think that he intended to murder him."

"But why should he want to murder Sergeant Bailey, to stop him finding the money?"

"No, I think that he thought that Bailey was one of the thieves."

As they were about to pull in at the station, Hart caught a glimpse of a gathering of pressmen at the entrance.

"Quick, you slip out and don't let on. I'm off to lunch. I'll be in directly."

Hart was as good as his word. He returned within the hour and submitted himself to being interviewed. He withstood the onslaught of the press well, his gastric juices having been fully engaged. He was pleasant and altogether unruffled even when mentioning Bailey's condition. However, there was sufficient determination in his manner to impress the most critical among them. He declined to have his photograph taken but made the suggestion that Sergeant Bailey's might be featured instead. He made no mention of the Threshers but simply said that there was a lead and it was being followed.

After this he had to submit to the questioning of the County Detective Superintendent. This was a more

274

detailed affair and it helped to clarify his mind. The Superintendent was a cautious man who liked things to go 'by the book'. He was appalled at what had happened to Bailey but was delighted that the money had been recovered and that Victor Grant had been apprehended. He wanted to flood the area with extra police immediately. Hart resisted because he felt that that would alarm Thresher and would send him underground and until there was a photograph available there was too little to go on. He pointed out that only Bailey had seen his assailant and then only in the dark. Not enough was known. When he asked what was to be Hart's next move, Hart could only answer that he had to wait until they had a photograph. The van registration number was the best chance of tracking Thresher.

After the Superintendent had gone there were two other visitors. The first was Sidney Butterman who had had got over the initial shock of his son's death and had become even more aggressive than before. His wife had taken to her bed and he was in total ignorance as to the arrangements that could be made for his son's funeral. He needed information and he was also spoiling for a fight. Hart told him that the body of his son could not yet be released and that he would be informed as soon as it was possible to remove it. Butterman asserted, again and again, that had Hart gone in search of his son when he had first reported him missing he might still be alive today. Hart suggested that when Mr. Butterman had attended the coroner's court he would know all about the circumstances of his son's death and he could ask questions then, but he pointed out that at the time Mr. Butterman had first enquired about his son, his son was probably already dead. He was stung into adding that if Butterman's son had been available for questioning at the time that he had called at their home he might still be alive today. They were deadlocked for a while then Hart stood up and escorted Butterman firmly to the door. On the phone, he gave the desk sergeant strict instructions that he was not to allow Butterman in again until the case was over.

The second visitor came as a great surprise to Hart. It was Victor Grant Senior. He was as diffident as ever, dressed in what must have been his best suit though it hung rather loosely on his stooped shoulders. He accepted a chair with a gentle smile and apologised for disturbing the D.C.I.

"No problem, Mr. Grant, anything I can do to help?"

"Well, it's just that so much seems to have happened but we don't know what it is."

"A lot has happened, you are quite right."

"I suppose I shouldn't ask, when you are so busy, but....but....will we be told?"

"You mean, will we tell you when we find who murdered Tommy?"

"I don't think Edie wants to know. She's been through a lot and now she's reconciled to looking after Jane. She wants it over and done with."

"I think I understand."

There was a long pause.

"But I want to know. I want to know all about it."

Hart saw a steely glint in Victor's eye, a hint of what Victor had been as a young man, but something more.

"I've had a long time to think about it. Tommy was a good boy. The best. He never did anything to hurt anyone. I want to know what happened to him and why. I miss him, I'll miss him growing up..... I need to know."

The thought that the truth about young Victor might prove destructive to his parents had already occurred to Hart. It was very much in his mind at this moment.

"Was it really John Butterman's body that was found next door? Had he anything to do with Tommy's death?"

"Mr.Grant, I can tell you that it was John Butterman's body. I can also tell you that he was killed in the same way as Tommy. We don't know yet, for sure, who killed them, but it was almost certainly the same man."

"What has next door got to do with it?"

"That's a long story and I don't think I can tell you yet. I can only say that Tommy thought that something was wrong next door, climbed over the wall to see and was killed there. Later his body was taken to the park."

"Butterman had nothing to do with Tommy's death?"

"No, I'm fairly sure about that."

"To be killed so near home!"

"I appreciate that it must be a terrible thought....you never heard any noises through the wall?"

"No, we never did. We had no idea....was someone living there?"

"No, we don't think they did more than visit the house."

There was a long pause.

"You will tell me when you know more?"

"I'll let you know as soon as I can, Mr. Grant. Try not to worry about it."

"But I do. I haven't much else to occupy myself with now."

Immediately Victor had left, Inspector Jordan entered. Hart was overjoyed at what he brought. The enterprising inspector had not waited for records to despatch the photograph but had sent a man to obtain a copy and to return post haste. Together they studied the likeness. It meant nothing to them. It was of a fair haired man with a narrow nose, pronounced cheekbones and thin lips pressed tightly together. The chin was square and strong but the most notable feature was the eyes. Even allowing for the photographer's flash, they were hard and staring, the pupils tiny and the colour of the irises very pale.

"I'm sure that psychologists would have a field day with this photograph. Let's get it printed straight away. If John Bailey is conscious and able, I want him to see this immediately."

A short time later, Hart and Phillips were on their way to the Cottage Hospital. There was little light left in the sky and a heavy build-up of clouds threatened to blacken out what little there was. Rain soon battered at the windscreen and Hart was obliged to use his headlights. The weather had been so good for such a long period, he found himself surprised and put out by the storm.

Hart swung into the drive and was about to drive up to the main entrance when he remembered the contretemps of his last visit. He swerved to the side and drove round to the car park at the back. It was surprisingly empty.

"It mustn't be visiting time yet, Sir, it can get full quickly."

Hart grunted and made to get out of the car, regretting that he had not brought a coat or an umbrella. He turned back to switch off the headlights and accidentally turned them to full beam.

"Look, Phillips, that's the van!"

On its own, almost directly under a large tree, stood a dark coloured van and picked out in the beam from Hart's car was the registration number PJK 304.

"You are right, Sir, what is it doing here?"

"Quick, phone the station, I want as many men as they can muster! He must be inside. I've got to get to Bailey!"

Hart ran round to the main entrance as fast as he could. As he careered through the door he almost knocked over a figure in uniform. The indignant squawk was familiar to Hart but he had no time to look back. He demanded to know which ward housed Sergeant Bailey and raced for the lift.

On the third floor he emerged from the lift to find a bed being wheeled into the ward ahead of him. It was Robert Shaw, he was sitting up looking quite happy. When he saw Hart, his eyes lit up in recognition.

"They're shifting me over here 'cos I'm nearly better."

"I'll see you later, Robert. We're in a bit of a hurry just now."

"Come for an operation, have yer?"

"Something like that!"

He squeezed past and ran ahead. The ward he had entered was a general ward. It opened out from a narrow corridor exactly as the ward Hart had visited last. There were only a few beds and the space beyond them was partly occupied by ladders and dismantled decorator's staging. Evidently this ward had just been decorated and patients were being returned or transferred a few at a time. He looked round but saw no sign of Bailey. Suddenly a door in the corridor opened and a sharp voice called after him.

"Who are you looking for?"

"I'm are looking for Sergeant Bailey. I was told he was in this ward."

"In here!"

The ward sister had a commanding voice and it vibrated with disapproval. Hart hastened to identify himself and went through the door she had indicated. It was a small side ward, well lit and comfortable. The constable on duty stood up, he had been sitting just inside the door. By the bed sat Diana Bailey, John's wife.

"How is he?"

Hart approached the bed and saw his sergeant swathed in bandages. His neck had a very broad thick layer of wrapping. His face was more lightly dressed, but one eye was completely covered. His left forearm was very thickly bandaged and one leg, heavily plastered, was resting on some kind of metal frame. Bailey was awake and smiling, propped up by several pillows. Hart's question was answered by the ward sister.

"He'll live, if he is left undisturbed!"

"I have a very important question to put to him. I promise you that I'll only ask the one."

"Right, but he is not to move! He must lie still. There is to be no excitement!"

The sister stood by, quite without trust in these newcomers.

Hart took out one of the printed photographs and held it in front of Bailey's face.

"Don't try to move. If you think this is the man, just say yes."

This was almost too much for Bailey who wanted to move his head, to gesture and to speak all at once. The sister glared. Diana Bailey laid a restraining hand on his shoulder and he let out a sigh.

"Yes."

"That's all we want to know. Just relax, we are on his tail. Just concentrate on getting better. We'll let you know what happens."

They were shepherded out by the sister.

"You see! The least excitement is bad for him. Necks are tricky! I hope that he can be left alone now."

"I'm grateful to you sister..."

"Careful with that bed down there! We've just been painted!"

"Sister, I don't want to alarm you but there is a possibility that your patient there may be attacked again."

"In here, nonsense!"

"We've just seen the van the assailant drove parked outside as we came in. There is a good chance that he is in the hospital now."

"What is all this nonsense? We've got work to do in here. Hospitals aren't for cops and robbers. Are you suggesting that a stranger is going to come in here and try to attack one of my patients?"

"It is a distinct possibility."

"Really!"

"I have asked for reinforcements. If necessary we will have to search the whole hospital."

"I suppose it isn't sufficient to train in nursing, midwifery, ophthalmology and all that lot, now we have to learn ju-jitsu! Put that back!!"

The sister had eyes in the back of her head. Her last remark was made to a young nurse who was just bringing a bottle from the sluice.

"There's a time and a place for everything on my ward. He'll have to wait or go himself! Do what you have to do, Chief Inspector!"

Chapter Thirty-Seven

Very soon there were four squad cars a van and a dog team outside the hospital. Jordan had come with them and he despatched a number of men to various strategic points round the outside of the building before the rest of them entered. Hart met him on the ground floor. He had asked for a senior member of staff to be present and from him he got a thorough picture of the layout of the hospital. Hart thought it best that the search should be made simultaneously on all the wards but first the basement and the ground floor including all the administration areas would be covered by the whole team.

There was no operating theatre, only a suite of treatment rooms and a small X-Ray department. There was a great deal of trouble unlocking storerooms and offices but eventually the laundry and all store rooms in the basement and every room and cupboard on the ground floor was searched and relocked as appropriate. The kitchens were a big problem as there were many places where someone could hide and work was still going on. There were stretches of wet floor and footprints everywhere. A door to the yard outside was constantly opening and closing as rubbish was taken out and trays of meat and vegetables brought in from the cold store outside. It would be easy for someone to enter by this door, but hardly unnoticed. No one claimed to have noticed any strangers pass through.

Hart was particular in posting men at strategic points so that any attempt to skip back would be foiled. Of course, the work of the hospital had to proceed and nurses and orderlies frequently crossed and recrossed the searchers' paths. It was a tedious job to make sure that all the people in uniform were whom their labels claimed them to be. Fortunately this was quite a small hospital.

As they proceeded to the next floor, Hart left copies of the photograph of the wanted man with whoever was in charge of each ward or department. At one end of the short corridor which connected the lifts and the stairs at right angles to the wards, one of his men alerted Hart to the presence of wet footsteps on the floor. This was at a window that gave onto a fire escape. The footprints led onto the stairs. They faded quickly on the next floor because, for some unknown reason, the same corridor on the next floor was carpeted.

Hart was aware that time was against him. Soon visitors would arrive and they would certainly offer an opportunity for Thresher to escape undetected. He made up his mind, it would be his responsibility, visitors would have to be kept out until either Thresher was apprehended or it was established that he wasn't in the building. The only reason for the presence of the van in the car park had to be the presence of Phillip Thresher inside the hospital. The only reason for the presence of Phillip Thresher inside the hospital had to be his intention to kill John Bailey whom he thought was the driver of the getaway van who had, albeit unknowingly and indirectly, been the cause of his brother's death. It seemed inconceivable to Hart that the van had simply been abandoned there.

He posted men inside the main entrance with strict instructions to allow no one to enter. Visiting time would commence just as soon as the search was over. This did not suit the hospital staff but they were assured of the serious nature of the search and they were reconciled to a shorter period for visitors - if the search was over within a reasonable time.

The remainder of his forces he divided and sent one half upstairs to the next floor. The wards themselves were open and did not conceal anyone easily. The rooms at the entrance to each ward presented most opportunities for concealment. There were toilets and bathrooms, sluices and large linen cupboards, a small kitchenette, an office and a side ward.

On the top floor, one of the searchers noticed that rain had been let in at the window giving onto the fire escape. Someone had opened the window but there were no wet footprints coming from it. Had that person gone out by the window? A signal was sent to the watchers outside. Meanwhile, on the ward where Bailey lay, someone else noticed a disarray in the linen cupboard. Sheets had been disturbed and there were drips on the floor and wet patches on two of the shelves.

"Someone 's been in here. My cupboards are never left like this I can assure you!"

The sister was adamant. To Hart, the signs were that someone had stood in the linen cupboard for quite a while. He realised that Thresher had been very close to Bailey. Perhaps he had been frightened off by the presence of so many policemen. There were two men guarding Bailey's side ward now. He had to respect Thresher's daring and his cunning. Suddenly it occurred to Hart that the opening of the window might have been a ploy to draw the searchers outside. He redoubled his efforts.

Jordan joined him in the corridor. His men had inspected all the fire escapes and were keeping an eye out but they were hampered by the rain and the bushes. There were many places to hide and to cover movement.

"Movement, that is it, I think this man knows his way around and is keeping on the move. The staff must try to stay in their places until we've finished."

That last was more of a wish than a possible command.

"Is this what you are looking for?"

The ward sister held out a soggy raincoat bundled up.

"It was thrown to the back of the top shelf in my linen cupboard. And there is a white coat missing! There should have been six in there, now there are only five."

Hart blessed her efficiency and passed on the word that a white coat was what they must look out for, but he was not optimistic, he felt that they were on a circus roundabout with Thresher constantly changing horses and staying out of reach.

A moment later the calm was broken by a dreadful clangour. Fire alarms sounded in all the corridors. Hart rushed downstairs to reception. The duty engineer appeared from the boiler house and studied a chart studded with tiny light bulbs inside a cupboard. The alarm had been set off on the second floor but there was no indication that anything was amiss. An internal emergency team of firemen gathered while the engineer was in his cupboard, they set off for the area designated. The receptionist phoned the fire brigade. There were sounds of movement from all parts of the hospital. Hart looked at Jordan in despair.

"He is going to make his move now. Upstairs, quick!"

They raced up the stairs, trying to avoid groups of people coming down in an orderly fashion as they had been instructed. Patients in beds were being lined up outside the lifts on each floor and, over the murmurs of alarm, stentorian voices were calling for silence and no panic. Hart and Jordan had difficulty in squeezing past into the entrance to Ward 5.

Sister Docherty was in firm control, she had experienced fire drills many times. Her beds were lined up neatly, waiting their turn. At the rear, Robert Shaw bounced with excitement. The two officers had opened the door to the side ward and had wheeled Bailey's bed into position ready to leave. Hart and Jordan were at a loss as to what they could do but they stood at the entrance to the side ward darting glances in every direction.

Suddenly the alarms stopped ringing. The engineer had found the button that had set off the alarm. The glass had been broken by someone, whether by accident or not he couldn't say but there was no sign of any fire in that area so he had switched the alarms off. All the patients and their minders were instructed to return to their wards. No sooner than they had returned when the fire brigade arrived and a further search was made. Hart was horrified at the arrival of more strangers and the further confusion that they brought. How easy it would be for Thresher to leave as a fireman. He rushed down to the entrance to be ready for any sudden drama.

There was a very excited and noisy throng jammed between the main door and the glass doors which gave onto the entrance hall. The policemen on guard were hard pressed to prevent them bursting in. The downpour outside had obliged the visitors to seek shelter in this confined space. Fortunately, Jordan had had the presence of mind to have further visitors stopped at the gate to the grounds but his action had been too late for the thirty or so already gathered at the door. The firemen had squeezed a way through them and had rolled out hoses on the floor ready for action and were now endeavouring to disengage their unnecessary hoses from the feet of the visitors who were becoming more angry by the minute.

Hart called out in his strongest voice for the crowd to move back.

"This is an emergency, ladies and gentlemen, please

be patient...."

"An emergency? A bloody pantomime, more like!"

The voice at his elbow was familiar. It was Mrs. Shaw waiting to see Robert.

"Have you not got him yet? It's taking you a time! What do we pay good money for? You're worse than teachers, you lot!"

"Mrs. Shaw. Good to see you. You must thank Robert for me, he has been most helpful."

As before, Mrs. Shaw's jaw dropped. As he turned away, Hart thought he saw another female face he recognised. He turned back but the face had gone or he had been mistaken. He hurried away before Mrs. Shaw could renew her harangue. Nevertheless, he remained not far from the entrance until the fire service had extricated themselves and had departed. His spirits sank as he contemplated the opportunities that had presented themselves for a successful escape.

Chapter Thirty-Eight

Robert Shaw had been so entertained that, before he could return to the ward, he was obliged to visit the toilets. His recovery was such that he was no longer strictly confined to bed. He enjoyed such freedoms and vowed to explore the hospital before he was discharged. He found the toilets of Ward 5 much brighter than those of Ward 6, they had just been painted. He gazed round him as he stood at the urinal. There had been a broken soap dispenser in the Ward 6 toilets and he had enjoyed playing with the slow trickle of liquid soap that leaked from it. He had drawn a number of things on the mirror with this lurid green liquid. It was great fun. The fuss made by the sister had been even greater fun. The soap dispenser here was new. Everything looked new and temptingly clean. He stepped away from the urinal and moved over to the washbasins. He flipped the soap container, it emitted a mean drop of liquid, hardly enough to coat the end of his finger. He sighed. Suddenly his eye caught something in the mirror. A figure in a white overall was standing inside one of the toilet cubicles. Quickly he hid his soapy finger behind his back.

"Just testing!" He called cheerily, "You never know do yer?"

The white clad figure moved towards him. Robert thought he ought to go, but the figure anticipated his move and got between him and the door.

"Kid, is there a laundry basket in the main ward?"

"A big straw thing on wheels?"

"That's right."

"Yeh, there's one just inside the door."

"My mate left it behind. I don't want him to get into trouble. It should have gone down an hour ago. Do you think you could bring it along for me while I clear up in here?"

Robert couldn't see anything to clear up but he felt a bit guilty about his own intentions.

"Yeh. Why not? I'll fetch it."

"Don't let sister see you!"

"Watch me!"

Robert loved a challenge, especially a challenge to authority. It took him only a couple of minutes to move the laundry basket. Sister and her attendant junior nurse was busy rearranging beds at the bottom of the ward where the painters' scaffolding planks had caused problems.

He pushed the toilet door open slightly and spoke through it.

"Here y'are."

To his astonishment, his new acquaintance showed no gratitude but seized his arm in a painful grip.

"Now, kid, come with me and act natural. You are helping me move this to the lift.....wait!"

He drew Robert back through the door and held him still.

"Here....!"

A rough hand grasped Robert's mouth, stifling all protest. Footsteps in the corridor receded.

"Right, move and take care, not a sound out of you. Just push alongside me."

The two walked to the end of the ward corridor pushing the basket before them. A uniformed policeman hastened past them with only a glance. By now, Robert realised that he was in trouble. There had been a fuss going on in the hospital but no one had explained what it was about, then the excitement of the fire alarm had taken over. Now there was a new excitement, a dangerous and painful one of which he was the centre. What was it all about? Clearly, this was a criminal of some kind, like in the pictures, and he himself was a hostage.

They stopped in front of the lift. The man held Robert's arm fiercely and nodded. Robert understood and pressed the button. The lift arrived swiftly and silently. It was empty. As the man leaned on the basket to move it forward, Robert sprang to his right. He had judged his moment cleverly. The grasp on his arm had slackened just a little and the man was looking to the other side, wary of interruption and thinking of how to get the basket into the lift. Robert's movement was directly contrary to that of his captor who was handicapped by having the use of only one arm. Robert was able to wrench free and stagger to the floor. The man was wild with fury but caught in a dilemma. He hadn't time to do anything about the boy, he had to go down. There was someone coming up the stairs.

From where he was lying, free but far from safe, Robert saw the doors close and the man disappear. Never had he felt so relieved.

"What are you doing down there?"

An elderly orderly turned from the top of the stairs and stared at Robert in disapproval.

The peevish nature of this question, so totally out of context, stung the boy, he was caught between laughter and tears.

"I'm havin' a rest, aren't I!"

"Cheeky young sod! Where should you be?"

Chapter Thirty-Nine

Hart, in the main hall, saw the lights indicating the descent of the lift. By this time the firemen had departed and the D.C.I. was pondering his next move. Jordan had checked that the fire engine had departed with the right number of men but that hadn't been sufficient reassurance for his chief. He was about to return to the top floor when the lift descended. He turned to Jordan, standing beside him.

"Now, what have we here?"

Jordan gave him a sharp glance. He thought that the strain was beginning to tell. The lift went on into the basement.

"Curiouser and curiouser! Who's in the basement, Inspector?"

"Forbes. He's watching the lift down there, Sir."

"There's only one way out of the basement, isn't there?"

"There's an exit with a ramp coming up just beside the kitchens and there are men posted outside there."

"Get the dogs round that side just in case he gives us the slip."

Jordan summoned his patrols on his radio telephone.

"They're in position if he tries to get out that way, Sir."

"Good, then that should be alright. Let's take a look, all the same."

The two men raced down the stairs, signalling to two others as they went. There was a double door at the bottom of the stairs and darkness beyond. They heard banging in the distance and a sudden crash.

"Where's the light?"

"And where's Forbes?"

There was a dull light spilling out from the lift on their left but they had to scrabble for the corridor light

291

switch before they found it. When the light came on they saw P.C. Forbes lying a few feet away, unconscious and bleeding from a head wound. There was another crash somewhere ahead.

"He's got to the door. We'll have him now!"

They rushed towards the turning to the exit ramp. There was no one to be seen but a cold blast of air at their backs made them turn quickly. Behind them was a short corridor. In the poor light from the main corridor they could see several laundry baskets parked almost at random. Above them, rain gusted through a large gap. The double doors of an ancient trapdoor hung vertically. Above the noise of the wind and the rain, they heard, all too clearly, the sound of a car being driven away.

Chapter Forty

A hasty reformation of the patrols had established that no one lingered in the grounds. No visitors had been allowed in or out of the gate since the departure of the fire brigade, however, a policeman at the gate reported that a nurse, or someone claiming to be a nurse, had driven away at about that time. She had appeared to be alone but, of course, the boot had not been searched. Hart felt sure that this had been the getaway car and the fleeting glimpse of a woman's face in the crowd near Mrs. Shaw nagged at his memory. That must have been the woman driver.

There was no consolation for him. The search had been bungled. Thresher had been always one step ahead and luck seemed to have been entirely on his side. He seemed to have known the hospital well. Could he have had an accomplice who was employed there? It seemed too much of a coincidence.

A conference had been called the next morning in the operations room. Hart arrived seemingly unruffled and, if anything, more vigorous than ever. Only the few who knew him well could tell from his voice how badly he felt about the failure of the search. He wasted no time in outlining the reasons for that failure and emphasised how important it was for his men to be able to cope with the unexpected. He allowed just a hint of humour to slip into the account of the arrival and departure of the fire brigade but he was scathing about the man on duty at the gate who had allowed the car through without checking with his superiors. He demanded that the whole team should be aware of the seriousness of the case and told them in a few words that he expected a higher level of initiative and alertness from them. He admitted that there were no leads on Thresher at that moment. A check would be made on the staff of the hospital, both present and past, to find out if Thresher had a contact, since he had known his way about so well and had been aware of the almost forgotten trapdoor into the basement.

"Sir, why was there a trapdoor there?"

"I have now been told that, a long time back, coal was delivered there. A new boiler house was built onto the other side of the building, at ground level, before the war. It used anthracite which was stored alongside. The inside of the basement was kept clean after that and the trapdoor never used. No one remembered it last night."

"Sir, Thresher couldn't have been sure that he would not be arrested in the grounds."

"You might think that, but he had worked out that the trapdoor could be approached by a car or van. The woman accomplice was waiting for him to break. He must have reckoned on making his move while the fire brigade were getting in our way. Somehow he wasn't able to go while the firemen were there, perhaps one of you was in the way. The boy, Robert Shaw, gave him a totally unexpected opportunity to make his way to the lift. After that, it was his luck that we did not know about the trapdoor and concentrated our outside team on the normal exit to the basement."

Someone suggested that as it was a one to one situation, Forbes watching the lift ought to have been able to tackle Thresher.

"I agree, but Thresher was cunning, he expected to use Robert Shaw as a hostage to get him past anyone down there. When the boy escaped his grasp, he had to think of something else. According to Forbes, last night after he came round, Thresher hid in the laundry basket. Forbes assumed that it had been sent down on its own and pulled it out into the corridor. He was completely taken unawares when Thresher sprang out and attacked him. We have to acknowledge that Thresher thinks on his feet and thinks quickly. He has also been very lucky. That sort of luck cannot hold. Next time the luck will be with us."

The next time was the problem. Thresher had disappeared. Hart had had a plainclothes man keeping an eye on the family home at Dimchurch Row. He reported that since the departure of the mourners after the funeral feast, no one had been near. The house was locked up and deserted.

There were few relations but there had been sufficient mourners at the funeral to suggest a wide circle of friends. Hart detailed a squad to make urgent enquiries of the neighbours and all friends known to them. It was unlikely that Thresher would make an obvious move but he must shelter with someone. He was still suffering from a broken forearm. That would need attention and rest. Another squad was detailed to enquire of all doctors and clinics within the area. Details of Thresher were already being circulated to all other forces with a general call for him to be apprehended. There was little else that Hart could do for the present other than fall in with Inspector Jordan's suggestion of a television and radio appeal. He set the rest of his men to find out Thresher's movements or whereabouts since leaving Langbridge prison. Until sightings or information from neighbours or friends came in, everyone must wait as patiently as possible.

Chapter Forty-One

"Hullo, Victor. It's a while since you've been in. Come inside and have a cup of tea. Eric will look after the shop, won't you lad?"

Fred Semper and his wife were genuinely pleased to see their visitor and settled him down in an armchair with a cup of tea in his hand.

Victor had been leaving the house more often since his sister-in-law had returned. It was largely because he felt he must get out from under Edie's feet and give her a little less to attend to, but partly because he had become very restless since Tommy's death. He had a feeling deep within him that he was partly responsible for the boy's death. This feeling had grown since he learned that Tommy had been killed just next door. He felt he should have been more in touch with the boy, he had not spoken to him enough. Conversation between them had almost dried up. He attached no blame to the boy for this, the blame was entirely his and Edie's. They had been so concerned with their own troubles they had not thought sufficiently about the boy. For the first time he realised how lonely Tommy must have been.

Today he had found an excuse to call at the cobbler's shop, a pair of slippers needed stitching. He had always enjoyed a chat with Fred Semper and now he rather needed it. He was pleased to be invited into the back.

"Eeh, I'm sorry about all the trouble you've been through, Mr. Grant, How's Edie taking it?" Mrs. Semper was genuinely solicitous.

"Well, you know our Edie, says little, just gets on with things. We've got our Jane back now so she's got her hands full."

"That'll be her sister, she's been away a rare long

time, hasn't she?"

"Aye, best part of fifteen years."

Fred Semper interrupted, anxious that they didn't appear to be prying.

"Did you see the news on telly last night?"

"Nay, we've never had telly."

"There was a photo of the man they're looking for to do with the murders."

"They've found someone then?"

"Well they just said that they were looking for this man in connection with their enquiries. They asked for him or anyone who knows him to come forward."

"No one we know?"

"They said he was from Bardsley, that's all."

"Fred, don't go on about it, you'll upset Mr. Grant."

"Nay, I want to know. I want to know who he is and why he did it!"

Victor's vehemence took them aback. He had always been such a quiet man.

"Well, perhaps they'll repeat it. They sometimes do on the one o'clock. Why not stay and watch it with us?"

It was too early, Victor was not attuned to long visits and Edie expected him home for lunch, but he went back after lunch and studied the picture of the wanted man very carefully.

Later, as he was returning home, he met Sidney Butterman. They had not met face to face for many months. Sidney Butterman had not yet returned to work and he was looking a little down at heel. He was harassed and felt far from well. His wife had shown no inclination to leave her bed and because of this his world had changed totally unexpectedly. He was obliged to do all the chores and the shopping and, without fully understanding why, he felt diminished and unhappy. He was still bewildered and shocked by the death of his son. He thought he had known him through and through yet what had happened had gone against all his understanding. What had John been doing in No. 20?

He hardly recognised Victor Grant even when he stood directly in front of him.

"Well, Sidney, it has been a sad time for both of us."

"Oh....er..."

"How is Julia taking it?"

"Mrs. Butterman is not well, not well at all."

"I'm sorry to hear that. Is there anything we can do?"

"Er....no, I don't think so....thank you."

The stiffness was natural to Sidney Butterman but it was compounded by a real awkwardness at being at a disadvantage for the first time in his life.

Victor wanted to ask him about his son's presence in No. 20 but realised that the man was much too distracted, this was not the time. He passed on, his eyes turning to No.20 as he walked towards it.

The front door had been repaired and there was no longer a policeman on duty at it. The buzz of reporters and television crew had departed. What had been white hot news only a day or so ago was virtually forgotten. He and Edie had been troubled, yet again, by newsmen at their door but they had managed to ignore them. As before, the reporters seemed to sense that nothing would be forthcoming. Perhaps their editors preferred a mystery angle after all. They did not hang about quite so long this time.

Victor was filled with a great curiosity. What could have been the secret of this ordinary house? Why had both Tommy and that flabby neighbour of theirs been doing there? What was the connection? The house didn't look particularly sinister yet there had been a great fight and a policeman had been taken away injured. He and Edie had been asked about it but they had been at the other side of the house and had heard nothing. Whenever they heard any noise they always believed that it came from the street and didn't concern them. The Nesbits at No. 18 would not have heard anything, they were very deaf and had great difficulty hearing their own doorbell.

Victor paused to look through the front window. There was nothing to see. The same furniture that had been visible in passing for months past was exactly in the same place. There were no changes, there was nothing unusual. Victor recalled the features of the man he had seen on the television news bulletin. What had that man to do with No. 20? He shivered, the face had been cold and brutal. The thought of Tommy encountering such a man was deeply upsetting. Victor stood back and looked up at the windows of the bedrooms. He tried to visualise them in terms of his own house. The rooms would be reversed, of course, but they would be the same size. He thought it was strange that he had never been inside although he had known Joe Skinner well for a number of years. Then it dawned on him that he had never been inside any of the other houses in the street. For years he and Edie had lived out their own limited lives close to yet distant from all of their neighbours.

He noticed that the curtains of the small bedroom were heavy and hung in large folds. The material was of a dark blue colour. There were no curtains up at the big bedroom window, it looked exceedingly bare. This was where the fight had taken place. One of the constables had told them about it. The curtain pole had been torn down in the struggle. Presumably the Estate Agents were unwilling to go to the trouble of replacing it. Well, they would have to, sooner or later if they were to rent it out as furnished. He turned in at his own door.

Though Edie Grant's day was full, now that her sister was in need of her care and attention, Victor's was more free. He could not have anticipated this, he had spent years sharing the household chores and the worry about housekeeping, trying to keep in touch with Edie and her fussing, trying to be the understanding buffer between her and the world and Tommy. Now there was a vacuum. There was not the same tension. There was still the fuss, indeed there was more bustle now, but it was all a little outside him. It revolved about him rather than included him and he was grateful for that, he could not have helped with Jane except, perhaps, to lift her occasionally and Edie preferred to manage that herself. In his restlessness, he took to walking into the yard to look at Tommy's bike, to stare at the wall to imagine where Tommy had climbed it. He often went quietly into Tommy's bedroom to sense the boy's presence and to gaze into the next door yard.

He began to stir himself. It had been a week since he was down in the allotment, there would be much to do there. The police had kindly replaced the shed where it had stood before the investigation but there would be a lot of mess to clear up. The Chief Inspector had not explained to him what the search had been about, he had merely said he would tell him when it was all over. As Victor strode down the path he speculated about the hole that the policemen had revealed with their digging. It had looked very like a shallow grave at first. Clearly, something had been buried there, but whatever it was, why had it been hidden in his allotment? He regretted not asking more questions at the time, but he had always been a patient man, he had learned not to be curious and to wait for explanations.

He spent a happy two hours or more tidying up and seeing to one or two little jobs that had been neglected.

He had been so preoccupied that he had become almost cheerful. There was a spring in his step as he locked up and turned for home. As he set off down the path a voice hailed him. It was George Hepworth.

"Hello, George, it's a while since we had a chat."

"It is, I wouldn't have stopped you now except I wanted to tell you how sorry we both were about your boy."

Victor felt a twinge of guilt. He had been happy for a few moments having forgotten Tommy and everyone else while he was busy.

"Ah, yes, it has been a very sad time..."

"The officer in charge came to see me, you know. He wanted to speak to anyone who had seen the boy on that Sunday and I had seen him up on the railway embankment that afternoon."

"Back there? What was he doing there?"

"He was sitting staring back at the allotments as if he was keeping watch."

"Was he now? He had an idea that he was going to catch the people who wrecked the shed and destroyed his rabbits. Did I tell you about that?"

"Yes, I think you did. It was about autumn time wasn't it?"

"Aye, about then..." Victor's mind began to whirr.

"Well, I'll not stop you. Take care, my regards to your missus!"

So, Tommy had seen someone or something, it must have been something to do with next door. He had come home and climbed the wall and was killed. Surely he wasn't killed on account of a few rabbits! No one could have carried out such a killing just for that. He remembered the sight of Tommy's face down at the morgue and his head spun. As he turned into the back lane he was obliged to clear tears away from his eyes.

As he did so, he was aware of a figure hurrying away ahead of him. It was a tall, thin stranger. The figure turned out of sight at the end of the lane. Victor paused at the back door to No. 20. He could not have been sure but he had a distinct feeling that the figure had moved away from this door. But that was impossible. There had been a police guard over the property for two or three days afterwards. His mind must be playing him tricks, it was all this pondering about young Tommy. He entered his own back door and set about preparing supper.

Supper was a silent affair, as usual. Edie was keeping one ear alert to any noise from upstairs from her sister, her talk was only of the food they would need to shop for the next day. Victor looked carefully at his wife, earlier she would have enquired sharply about such a stare, now she hardly noticed. He realised that she was content, content if not happy. She had her sister to nurse, her own sister. Could it be that here was a link with the past? Did she imagine she was back in her family home looking after her young sister? He shook his head sadly. Later he went up with her to see if he could make himself useful. He was sent down with the tray. He busied himself with the washing up.

Left to his own thoughts he rejoiced that the nights were getting lighter. He would spend more time in the allotment now. He had not yet set any seeds this year, he would have to hurry if he wanted to avoid buying plants, time was getting on. His recent troubles had made him forget the calendar. He looked out above the back wall to the sky. Yes, there was hope there. Perhaps the allotment would help him to come to terms with everything. There was a brief flash of light from the upstairs window then it was dark again. Eight o'clock, he would listen to the radio for a while. Since Tommy had died they had got into the habit of going to bed very early. Now, he thought, things would change. He might even go out to stretch his legs, to the Sempers or to The Cavalier. It seemed that Edie would welcome being left to herself imposed routine.

The next morning, Victor rose in a more cheerful mood. The time spent in the allotment had been refreshing. He had noticed that his injured arm was responding to exercise, at long last. The doctor had said that it would probably take a long time and he had been right. He didn't mention it to Edie, he would wait until he was sure then surprise her. He set off to do the shopping with a lively step. It was a bright, sunny morning with just a slight hint of chill. He looked up at the sky and smiled.

At that moment, a cheery voice broke into his thoughts.

"Mr. Grant, you do look well. Remember me, Mrs. Drysdale. You called when you were asking about Tommy."

"Oh yes, Mrs. Drysdale, I remember now, you were very kind to the boy."

"I only wish we could have done more. I only stopped you to ask if there is anything we could do for you or Mrs. Grant."

"That's very kind of you.... I'm afraid that my wife is...well, very independent...."

"Oh, I understand. Don't think for a minute that we would want to intrude but if you want to get out of the house for a few minutes, please call. We would be very pleased to see you. I know that these have been trying times for you and you may want to be left alone, but please remember that it's an open invitation."

There was something completely sincere and natural about the woman's invitation that moved Victor Grant deeply. He knew that Edie would never bring herself to accept but he also knew that no one had ever made such an open gesture of friendship since they had come to live here. He hastened to thank Mrs. Drysdale and hurried on.

It was on the way back, he looked up at the windows of No. 20, it seemed that was what he always did. A strange feeling gripped him. He paused but felt a little foolish so he went on to his own door. Inside the house he emptied the shopping basket rather distractedly.

"Something wrong?" Edie had been watching him.

"I'm not sure. I must be wool-gathering."

"Well, let's get these put away. I'll have to do a washing today. Are you going down to the allotment?"

It was as if she were wishing him away from under her feet. He rather welcomed the suggestion.

"Yes, the weather looks right. I think I will go down this afternoon."

Chapter Forty-Two

The next few days were not too happy for D.C.I. Hart. He came in for a great deal of criticism from his superiors and the press. There was little he could say to anyone and he was in trouble partly because he said so little. He did not know what his next move would be, he had to wait for news of Thresher.

The enquiries of the Thresher neighbours had come to nothing. There was respect for the dead Mrs. Thresher and a general ignorance about her relations. Some of the friends were identified by the neighbours and they were carefully interviewed. Such interviews revealed nothing except that Phillip Thresher was a loner, without a particular home base. Some of the family friends hated him, some admired him. Those who admired him said little. Those who hated him made much of what they took to be his neglect of his mother, since he had rarely visited her in her last illness. His short temper was legendary, as was his grudge-bearing. He was generally considered cold and selfish. He had had a number of girlfriends and had cast them off lightly when he had lost interest in them. No one seemed to know who his current girlfriend was.

Hart wondered what it was about the man that inspired admiration. It could only be his contempt for the police and law in general. There was little humanity in him. The current girlfriend had been his saviour at the hospital but how long she would retain his affection remained an open question. She might prove to be the best lead, unfortunately no one could or would help to identify her.

Two things cheered D.C.I. Hart during this difficult period. First, Louise had arrived for her 'short break' bringing with her not the dubious Francis but someone else. This had astonished her parents, who were agog to hear how and why Francis had departed but they were kept guessing. Francis had been replaced, very firmly, by down-to-earth Geoffrey, and Louise appeared to display complete calm and determination in this. Her father was much happier with Geoffrey and was delighted that Louise had proved so independent and spirited. He was almost ashamed of his former doubts.

Second was the rapid recovery of John Bailey. He had been released from hospital and was convalescing at home. Hart was one of the first to visit him. He found his sergeant remarkably cheerful and eager to return to duty. The damage to his neck was clearly visible and made Hart wince every time his eyes caught it. The bruised and battered face was much less in evidence. The plastered leg looked awkward but Bailey assured him that it gave little trouble. In spite of a hoarseness of voice, which his wife cautioned him about, he was anxious to be brought up to date. If that meant speaking, he would just have to speak.

"There's not a lot I can tell you, except that I've had a very useful substitute in D.C. Phillips!"

"A good man Phillips, but not the best, of course!"

"Well... someone will have to persuade me, in due course."

"Perhaps promotion would be a good idea, Sir."

"Sergeant Bailey! You never give up, do you?"

"Will Thresher know that I'm not the 'third man' now, Sir, with all the publicity?"

"Well, he could think you were the driver before you became a copper, but you are a bit too young. Even a stubborn villain like Thresher should have worked that out by now."

"Who will he be looking for now?"

"I can't guess. I think that he will lie low for a while, at least until his arm has healed, then he might skip off abroad."

"Does he know that the money has been recovered, Sir?"

"Probably not, I haven't let the press know anything about the robbery. They are still concerned with the murders but they don't know anything about the motivation. They are guessing wildly and I'm happy to let them. The sad thing is that Victor Grant will have to know about his son, sooner than later, and that is going to devastate him."

"So Thresher might be still looking for the money?"

"It's just possible."

"Surely it is quite likely, Sir? He would need it to make a clean getaway. You said that John Butterman had an empty wallet when you found him. Doesn't that suggest that Thresher was short of money?"

"You are right. Thresher doesn't seem to have any obvious source of income. I shall be taking note of any robberies in this area. Meantime we must just wait."

"What if Thresher simply gives up, goes to ground or clears off. The case may never be solved."

"That would be too easy. We've circulated his description and had his picture on television. There's bound to be a lead sooner or later."

"Time is going by, Sir, it's a few days now...."

"Patience, patience! We're not sleeping on it, you know! By the way, Jordan found out from various records that Mrs. Amelia Margaret Thresher had worked in the laundry of the Cottage Hospital since before the war. Altogether she worked there for thirty years. Thresher's knowledge of the hospital goes back to his childhood. He must have played round there and was familiar with the old coal hole."

"What about the woman accomplice. Did she work there too?"

"No, that's where we are stuck. She knew the place

but there is no one on the staff who could be her. We've checked it thoroughly. She's someone local, I'm fairly sure, but we have no leads."

When Hart returned to the station the desk sergeant beckoned him over.

"Two young girls waiting for you, Sir. I've put them in Interview One. They wouldn't say what it was about. One of them is in floods of tears."

"Oh dear! What now? I suppose I'd better find out. Fetch a policewoman along will you?"

Together, the D.C.I. and the policewoman went to see what their visitors wanted. Hart recognised Jane Mason immediately. The other girl was plump, bespectacled and very fair, this would be Angela Thurrock, he remembered Bailey's report. Angela was weeping almost uncontrollably.

"Don't worry about Angela, she'll get over it. She's frightened of police stations but it was her idea to come here."

"Why did she want to come here, Jane?"

"She wanted me to come, she's only here to keep me company."

"You'd better start at the beginning."

"It was that bloke on telly, the one you said you wanted to interview. He's the one. At least I think he is. Anyway, whether he was or not, I've seen him. He was walking along Headlaw Road last night. This time I'm certain. I didn't know what to do...."

"Steady on, slow down. Now, you saw this man we are looking for in Headlaw Road last night. Did anyone else see him?"

"I don't know. I was on my own. I was on my way to the chippie on the corner of Simpson Street. He must have been in there because he had a packet in his hand. He was in the full light from the shop window. He had

308

a cap on so that's why I know he was the same man. I didn't know what to do, I thought he might catch me staring so I hurried in. I was that frightened I could hardly say what I wanted...."

"You didn't tell anyone in the shop?"

"There was just me at the time and I was frightened he might come back."

"But you could have told the people behind the counter."

"Nah, Billy Moore is nearly deaf, you always have to shout at him. I didn't want that bloke to hear me, did I? I just got the order and ran home."

"What about when you got home, did you tell your parents?"

"They thought I was making it all up. They said that nobody would believe me. They never believe me anyway...."

"You are sure it was this man?"

"I got a good look at him on telly. I'm sure he was the same man."

"But you said he was wearing a cap, you can't have seen his face properly if he was wearing a cap."

"It was his eyes and his nose. You can't make a mistake about them, ooh, horrible they were. I saw them clearly. He was tall and thin like it said."

"A pity you didn't come and tell us straight away..."

"I wouldn't have come at all but for Angela. I told her about seeing this man and she said I must report it. I thought it was too late, but she said...."

Hart thought Jane was a little too excited, it all smacked of vivid schoolgirl imagination. If she had told her parents, why hadn't they believed her, why hadn't they been the ones to persuade her to report? They knew her only too well. He let her ramble on. Suddenly she changed tack.

"You remember when you came to our house? You

showed me a photo and drew a hat on it. Well that wasn't the bloke. When I saw this fella with his cap on I knew who it was, it was him."

"Who, who are you talking about?"

"The one who was talking to Tommy outside the Roxy."

Chapter Forty-Three

Victor Grant worked in his allotment for most of the afternoon. He found his arm was more useful than he could have expected but he was careful not to strain it. The sun came out about three and lent him some encouragement. Needing some string he went into the shed and immediately found himself thinking of Tommy again. He saw that the rabbits were neglected and decided that he must get rid of them. He would give them away to the Hibbert boy or any of Tommy's friends who would take them. He couldn't look after them himself, it would be like keeping himself anchored to the past. He would go round to the Hibbert's that evening.

The sun made him look about before he left the allotment, it had turned into a glorious afternoon. He had a sudden urge to see for himself what Tommy had been watching from the embankment. Slowly and deliberately he made his way to the slope and struggled up it. He squatted down at the top and took in the whole view. There was something fascinating about a big open space with a host of details inviting to the eye, he mused. He had never been up there before and the experience was exhilarating, It was a remarkable vantage point. He let his gaze wander from allotment to allotment. .He knew many of the gardeners and could see a few of them at work. They were the older men with plenty of time on their hands Beyond the allotments he could see the back of Selborne Street and picked out his own house and back door, or at least part of it.

He stood up quickly. Yes, he was not mistaken, someone had emerged from the back door of No.20. It was a woman, judging from the shape of head, even from that distance he felt sure. What could she have been doing in there? He was suddenly very angry. What had been his usual anxious bewilderment gave way to a cold determined reasoning. Nobody should have anything to do with that house other than the estate agent's representative, who always used the front door. There was mischief afoot. He was going to look into it, after all he was acting on Tommy's behalf.

Victor climbed down and made his way along the path between the allotments. His stride was firm and unhurried. When he reached the back lane he tried the back door to No.20 and found it unlocked. He did not go in but went to the end and turned the corner. This was the direction in which both the figures he had seen coming out of 20 had taken. In their case, he was sure, they had used the side lane down to the 'Causeway'. They would have taken a bus into the centre of the town and away from curious eyes. He himself walked slowly back along the front of Selborne Street. He looked up at the bedroom windows of 20. The light was beginning to fade but he remembered his sudden sense of unease that morning and wondered about it. He turned and entered his own front door.

Edie Grant was bustling up the stairs as Victor closed the front door behind him.

"Our Jane's not well. Her breathing is bad and she has a temperature." She called down to him.

"We'll have to get the doctor. You'll have to go down to the surgery. I hope he's not started yet. You'll have to bring him back with you. Be quick, won't you?"

Victor was immediately diverted. He hurried up the street and was lucky enough to encounter Jim Foster just getting out of his car. Victor was quick to explain his emergency and Jim Foster immediately took him down to the nearest surgery. He also brought the doctor and Victor back again and stressed that he would be available if Victor wanted any further help.

It did not take the doctor long to diagnose pneumonia together with all the signs of a slight stroke. Jane Watson was seriously ill and, given her normally poor mental and physical condition, she was not likely to linger long. This came as a great shock to both Edie and Victor. Edie was particularly distressed as she naturally assumed that the care Jane was receiving at home was better than that she had been receiving at the nursing home.

The doctor tried to comfort her.

"I am sure you have done everything you could for her, Mrs. Grant. It seems to me that your sister's condition has been the culmination of a long weakness. In her condition, you could not have known and she could not have told you. I'll make arrangements for her to go into the Cottage Hospital as soon as possible. They'll send an ambulance for her as soon as they have a bed ready. She'll have the best of attention there."

Edie was about to protest but the doctor forestalled her.

"She is in too dangerous a condition for you to try to deal with her at home. She must get to hospital as soon as possible. I've given her an injection. If she struggles for breath, give her a whiff of oxygen from this bottle. There's nothing else you can do except keep her comfortable."

After the doctor had left there was a long silence. Both Victor and Edie were numb. Of the two, Edie was the most upset. She sat in the fireside chair utterly exhausted. The events of the previous two weeks and now this had knocked her out. She could neither move nor speak. After a while Victor spoke softly,

"One of us must stay by her bed."

He got up slowly. Edie made no move. He sat at the side of the bed for over an hour. Jane lay still, heavily sedated, her breathing was frighteningly noisy and irregular. Suddenly there was the sound of a siren and the ambulance drew up outside. Loud knocking alerted Victor to the fact that Edie had not answered the door. He raced down to let the ambulance men in and helped them up to the bedroom. Together they eased the patient onto a stretcher and manipulated it into the ambulance.

"Are you coming along, sir?"

Victor was unsure.

"Please wait just a moment."

Edie was still sitting in the armchair staring straight ahead of her.

"Will you go with the ambulance, Edie?"

She did not answer.

"I won't be long, then."

It was two hours before Victor returned home. Edie was still sitting in the same position. He was hungry and prepared something to eat but she would not share it. He cleared it away, went upstairs and tidied Jane's bedroom. The house was still and empty. He shivered and went downstairs again. He sat and gazed into his wife's face but she looked through him.

He moved to take her hand but she snatched it away and rose in a sharp movement. At first it seemed that she was not sure where she wanted to go. She walked towards the door to the kitchen then changed her mind and turned towards the other door. Victor sat still, listening to her climbing the stairs. He sat for a long time and eventually dozed off in the chair. He awoke to knocking at the front door. It was a policeman to say that the hospital had asked someone to inform Mr. and Mrs. Grant that their sister had passed away not long after Mr. Grant had left the hospital. Victor was not surprised, he had been warned and he thought it for the best, Jane had been mercifully released.

The next morning, Victor was very worried about Edie. She got up as usual and prepared the breakfast but when he came down he found her distant and seemingly unresponsive. He had told her about Jane when he went to bed. Edie had been awake but had not answered him. Now it was as if she didn't want to listen to him. He tried to tell her that they must go together to the hospital and make arrangements for the funeral but she ignored him. He thought that she needed time to get over the shock and decided not to push her. He went, himself, and completed the arrangements at the hospital.

On the bus on the way back he reflected that no such arrangements had yet been made for Tommy. His thoughts returned to the house next door. Perhaps he had imagined it all. He couldn't be sure about the people he had seen. They might have just been walking up the back lane. Then he remembered the short gleam of light as he stood at the kitchen sink the night before. It could not have been Edie, she had been in the bedroom at the front. It had to have come from upstairs next door. Someone had used the bathroom and had inadvertently switched the light on and off again, that had to be it. This time he made a very careful study of the bedroom curtains of No. 20 as he walked up the street. He had a welder's sense of line and interval and made a note of the distance between the edge of the curtains and the vertical window bar. Even as he did so he realised that anyone hiding there would not close the curtains fully, such movement as he believed had been made must have been from someone touching the curtains only. He sighed and found himself unusually tired.

Inside his own house there was no rest. He found Edie sitting exactly as he had left her. Her body was cold and she was no longer breathing. He couldn't believe it. He worked away to try and get some colour into her hands. Her eyes were still open and somehow he thought life must remain. He tried to raise her, to no avail. He massaged her thin cheeks and held them in his hands to warm them. It was totally unacceptable that this energetic and unflagging woman should so simply slip away. She had never been ill. He couldn't remember a day that she had not organised and led. He thought that the only time she had taken to her bed had been when she was due to give birth to their son. She had been the strong member of the family round whom everything and everyone revolved.

Victor had no tears. It was much later that he realised that he had not wept. The three blows had come in quick succession. He was shocked and dismayed but he was not ready for grief. His practical sense was still strong enough to sustain him. He left his wife where she was and went to find help. Again it was the Fosters who came to his aid. It was the same doctor who returned with them. He examined Edie carefully and shook his head.

"Your wife has had some sort of heart attack. How old was she, Mr. Grant?"

"Sixty next month. It's no age at all."

"It isn't really, but she was clearly exhausted looking after her sister."

"Yes, she has been with her almost night and day, but she has always been strong. She has had a lot to put up with, what with the death of Tommy and then her sister. She was probably more shocked than I realised."

"A combination of exhaustion and shock. Did she have any problems with blood pressure?"

"I couldn't say. She hasn't seen a doctor since our son was born more than thirty years ago. She always seemed to be healthy."

The doctor made a face.

"Well, there aren't any signs of complications. I think that the end would have been peaceful. However, since she hasn't been examined in such a long time, I'm afraid there will have to be an autopsy and it will be a matter for the coroner. I'm sorry about all this you have had to go through, but there is no alternative."

Victor had a number of visitors during the rest of the day and he was grateful. Fred Semper and his wife, the Drysdales and the Fosters, all helped to keep him focussed. By tea time, Edie's body had been removed. Victor had been perplexed by the difference in procedure. Jane's death had been certified almost immediately, Edie's was to be a matter for the coroner. Jim Foster explained that the difference lay in the fact that Jane had been examined regularly at the nursing home and her condition was a matter of record. Edie didn't have an up-to-date medical record. An autopsy was necessary to establish that the death was from natural causes. The thought that there could have been any other cause did not trouble Victor. He had no doubt in his own mind that his wife had been worn out.

Suddenly he was alone. He could hardly remember being alone. Not only that, because Edie had governed all the times and seasons in the house, he suddenly felt at a loss. The routine was missing, the little automatic things established by habit. He had become accustomed to looking towards her for approval or disapproval, he had reacted to her expression. He sat down but felt that it would be wrong, he felt that he couldn't sit doing nothing when Edie wasn't there. He needed to be busy. If he couldn't be busy he must have someone to talk to. He would deliver the rabbits to the Hibberts.

He left the house intent on calling at the Sempers on his way back from the Hibberts, the Sempers had encouraged him to do so. As he passed No.20, his eyes moved to the windows. The curtains upstairs hadn't moved, perhaps they never had. Downstairs was different, in the gloom of the sitting room he became aware of the open door. He could tell that the door was open because, beyond it, for an instant, a light moved. It must have been a torch. He was certain this time. He would not call on the Sempers, he would call at the police station.

Chapter Forty-Four

Much of the early excitement that was natural to a murder case had evaporated from the Welbeck Road station by this time. This was a time of checking and cross checking information. Sporadic calls claiming the sighting of Phillip Thresher were coming in and were being logged and checked. There was still an air of business but some of the electricity had gone. No one was hurrying.

Victor Grant had called once before so now he confidently asked for D.C.I. Hart by name. The desk sergeant asked him what he wanted to see Hart about. Victor was quite unwilling to tell anyone other than Hart but he said it was to do with the wanted man. The sergeant buzzed the D.C.I. but got no answer.

"He's in the building somewhere, I know because he was through here just a minute ago. You go along there to Interview Room Two and I'll ask him to come to you when he's free. I'm sure it won't be long."

That was a mistake for which the sergeant had to answer over a long period. Victor wandered unaccompanied down the corridor and found himself at the open door of the operations room. There were two or three people talking together over a desk to one side and another with his back to him at a typewriter. Ahead was a large blackboard with an outsize map with lines and symbols drawn on it in red ink. Victor was fascinated and found himself drawn into the room. For a minute or so, no one noticed him. He had time to let his eye wander around the walls. There were lists and notices in abundance and here and there a photograph. The wanted man was there quite clearly and near him there was another photo-portrait of the same size. Victor stiffened. The face was bearded but there was something about the eyes and the nose and the cheekbones that was familiar.

"I'm sorry but you can't come in here. Was there someone in particular you wanted to see?"

A pleasant policewoman had come in behind him. Before he could answer, Hart stood in the doorway.

"Mr. Grant..."

Hart saw at once the direction of Victor's gaze.

"Come into my room. What can I do for you?"

He drew Victor outside and along the corridor towards his own room. He pointed to a chair and sat down opposite. Victor had been invigorated by his walk down to the station, now he was drained. He sat down, white and trembling.

"You look ill, can I get you anything? Look, I've a little whisky here."

Hart reached into a drawer in his desk and produced a flat bottle and a small metal cup. He poured whisky into it and held it out to Victor. Victor took it gratefully and swallowed it in one gulp. Again Hart filled it. This time Victor sipped gently at it. Hart took advantage of the interval to try to divert his visitor.

"Now what did you want to see me about?"

Victor did not know where to start.

"Is all well at home?"

"No." Victor shook his head. "Nothing is well at home."

"Something has happened?"

"Mrs. Grant died today, about twelve o'clock. Her sister, Jane, died last night."

Hart was shocked, not only was the news totally unexpected, there was something deliberate and mechanical about Victor Grant's voice that disturbed him. He knew that Victor had recognised his son's photograph, this, together with three deaths in the family, could well unhinge him.

"That's dreadful! I'm ever so sorry. Can you tell me

about it?"

"Jane developed pneumonia. Edie simply died while I was at the hospital."

"You shouldn't be here, you should be staying with someone you know."

"I'll be alright."

"You haven't any other relations you could stay with?"

Victor shook his head, he wasn't really listening. He was trying to frame the questions he needed to ask.

"Our son had something to do with Tommy's murder?"

"No, I can promise you that."

"Why have you got a photo of him in that room?"

"He had something the murderer wanted, that's all. It was pure chance that young Tommy stumbled..."

"Pure chance. Murdered by pure chance!"

Victor spoke quietly. There was a pause.

"Our son did go to sea. I didn't tell Edie, but his deferment papers came and I sent them to the Merchant Marine office in London. There was no other word so they must have traced him."

"I can tell you, now, that he has been living in Grammond for some time..."

"Wherever he is, you can tell him that his mother and his aunt are dead."

There was no life in his voice, he spoke quietly and mechanically as though he were an automaton.

"You would like to see your son?"

"No! No!" His voice grew, "No, I don't want to see him. I don't want to see him again. He can see his aunt at the Hillcrest Chapel of Rest if he wants to. He won't be able to see his mother yet."

He rose and turned towards the door.

"You didn't say what brought you here?"

"It doesn't matter now."

"I think you had better have someone to go with you."

Victor didn't object so Hart asked one of the policewomen to see him home in one of the cars.

Victor thanked the policewoman. She had stayed long enough to brew him some tea and he appreciated her quiet sympathy. As soon as he had closed the door behind her, he set about his task deliberately. Upstairs on the landing there was just room for the extending ladder to the loft. He took a torch and carefully rummaged in a far corner. He climbed down bringing with him a small, flattish toolbox wrapped in sacking. He didn't worry about the dust he was scattering, Edie wasn't there with her eagle eye and it was too late anyway.

Downstairs, he fetched a small oil can and a clean cloth, spread a newspaper on the table and set the toolbox on it. He heard Edie's intake of breath in his mind and a wry smile flickered on his lips. Carefully he unwrapped the box and took out a revolver. He weighed it in his hand and thought that it was heavier than he remembered, but then he had been a lot younger. It would have been nearly eighteen years since he had shot with it. He hadn't handed it in. That was because it had not been officially issued. There had been keen competition between units at the time and he had been encouraged to practise once the C.O. had learned of his skill. Where the revolver had come from he couldn't say, but it had been passed to him in its holster and he had not been asked to sign for it. Someone had slipped up, perhaps they had thought that it would have been returned very soon afterwards. He had been proud of it, Edie had hated it. When the rest of his kit had to be handed in, he had left it at home, well away from Edie's sight.

Methodically, he took it to pieces and oiled it thoroughly. There didn't appear to be anything wrong with it. Once reassembled, it worked smoothly. Carefully, he fed bullets into the chamber and whirled it, again, every movement was smooth and trouble-free. He laid it to one side and set about clearing everything else away.

For a long time he sat at Tommy's bedroom window in the dark. He wanted to establish the pattern of movement next door. Whoever it was needed to lie low during the day but they also needed to eat. The man, at least, would not want to expose himself needlessly. Victor thought that the woman must be acting as the messenger. She had left the back door unlocked yesterday, which suggested that she intended to return in a short while. She would not wish to be found fumbling with the lock in daylight.

As he sat patiently, Victor wondered if Tommy had done the same. Had he spent hours watching for movements next door? What had he seen, who had attracted his attention? Had it been his son, Victor? What had he to do with it? Surely Tommy would not have known Victor? Yet he had had an old photograph of him. Perhaps he had seen him and recognised him. Old Victor tried hard to imagine what would have gone through Tommy's mind, if that were so. The boy had given no indication. Why hadn't he confided in his uncle? He shook his head, he must concentrate on his present task. He must not let his mind stray. Above all, he must not drift off to sleep.

He had been sitting for a long time when he heard his door knocker sounding. He couldn't be sure who it could be. Perhaps it was one of his neighbours coming to enquire about him and to cheer him up. A second knock caused him to rise half automatically but he shook his head and sat down again. His mind was made up, he was going to carry out his plan and nothing must get in the way. Fortunately, the knocking was not repeated and he was able to concentrate on his vigil again.

Even so, his thoughts tended to wander. He had reacted badly to the sight of that photograph in the operations room. He had been deeply angry and hurt. He had long ago reconciled himself to never seeing his son again. The damage he had done to his mother by leaving without so much as a backward glance had been inexcusable. He hadn't minded so much himself, for Tommy had slowly but surely taken the place of his son. Victor had been more his mother's son, he had never felt very close to him. Nevertheless, his reappearance, even if only on the wall of the operations room, had been an intrusion. Never to have made contact when he had been so near was unforgivable. The thought that he had any connection at all with the hunt for the murderer was monstrous. To make this discovery within hours of the deaths of Jane and Edie was grotesque if not obscene.

He forced himself to concentrate on his self-appointed task. Sure enough, at about 10 o'clock, there was a movement in the yard below. The night was not particularly dark, whoever was moving did not need a torch. Victor's eyes were equally accustomed to the dark. As the figure drew back the yard door he could tell that it was the woman. Either she was leaving for the night or she was going to fetch something to eat. It was not too late for fish and chips. Whatever the reason, it suited Victor. He rose quietly and found his way downstairs and into the lane.

First, he tried the backdoor to No. 20. This time it was locked. If the woman returned during the night she did not have to worry about lingering over the key in the lock. There was no alternative, Victor had to climb the wall. He had a ladder, the only problem was to proceed silently. To his immense satisfaction, his injured arm proved to have recovered most of its powers. The ladder was placed against the dividing wall and Victor climbed it quickly. He paused on the top of the wall then crouched and lifted the ladder carefully over. He was not so much worried about the noise he would have made, it was the possibility of turning an ankle or some such injury that decided him not to jump.

Victor was relieved to find that the back door to the house was not locked. He turned the handle very slowly indeed. There was no sound. He eased it forward. Still no sound. He stepped inside quickly, shut the door behind him and stood stock still. He began to wonder if anyone was there when he heard the unmistakable sound of a toilet flushing. Now he needed all his wits to move about this unfamiliar territory in the dark. His eyesight was good and he gave himself a long time to accustom his eyes to the room, nevertheless he moved very slowly and carefully. It took him a good ten minutes to reach the door into the inner corridor. There were no creaking floorboards or squeaky doors, so far. The worst would be the stairs. He edged along to where the stairs began, the inner door to the front porch was immediately in front of him, the stairs were on his left, the reverse to his own house. He didn't have the opportunity to test the stairs. There was a crash from the yard behind him. Someone had stumbled into the ladder.

He leaped into the front porch and flattened himself against the wall. The door from the kitchen was flung open and a hoarse voice whispered as loud as it could:

"Phil! Phil! Come down! There's somebody here!"

A voice answered from the top of the stairs.

"What's up? Keep your voice down."

"I told you not to come back here! There's a ladder in the yard. Someone's been in. I locked the back door, somebody's climbed in."

"You mean somebody's inside the house? Right, come up here and fetch the torch. It's by the bed. We'll soon see. Maybe it's somebody I've been waiting for."

The woman made plenty of noise as she hurried up the stairs. The man made none and Victor could not be sure whether he had moved or not. He waited, very tense. The glass door was ajar, it shielded him but prevented him from seeing what was happening. His chance came when the woman returned from the bedroom with the wobbly light of the torch. From the shadow it cast on the glass, he could see that the man was already on or about the bottom step. He had moved like a panther. Victor had to move now.

Thresher hesitated at the bottom of the stairs then turned towards the kitchen, his back to Victor. Victor sprang forward to thrust his revolver into the back of Thresher's neck. At this moment the hall light went on. D.C.I. Hart stood in the kitchen doorway. Both Victor and Thresher were taken aback but Thresher was the quicker to recover. He leaped towards the sitting room doorway. He was not quite quick enough for Victor, whose finger was on the trigger. The shot was deafening in such a confined space. Thresher collapsed in a bloody heap.

"I'll take that, Mr. Grant!"

"Not yet, Chief Inspector!"

There was another ferocious report and Victor Grant fell at the D.C.I.'s feet.

Chapter Forty-Five

Inspector Jordan had found the events of that evening almost as exciting as those of his last visit to Selborne Street. Not that he was the sort of man to admit to excitement. He had responded to his chief's call in the same way as last time. This time there were two bodies and an arrest. The length of time it took for all the formalities, photographs, examinations and searches seemed endless. When it was all over and he and D.C.I. Hart gathered themselves together at the station, he was anxious to ask a question or two before they dragged themselves home.

"How did you come to be in the area in the first place, sir?"

"I wasn't happy about old Victor. I thought I would look in on him on my way home. When I got to his door, there were no lights on, I knocked twice and got no answer so I assumed he had either gone to stay with someone or he was fast asleep. If he was asleep, I didn't want to disturb him. Instead, I popped into the Cavalier for a nightcap. Who should suddenly arrive but the woman I had recognised at the hospital. I remembered, then, where I had first seen her, she had been at the funeral. She was the one who asked me what I was doing there. She had only gone to the Cavalier to buy cigarettes. Two packets and some matches. That told me enough. I followed her and saw her slip into the back of No. 20. I had a bit of trouble, she had locked the door after her, but for that, I might have been able to prevent the deaths."

"So Grant Senior set out to kill Thresher. How did he know that Thresher was next door? Would he have heard him?"

"Neither he nor his missus heard the fight with Bailey, or so they said, so I don't suppose he heard him.

Perhaps he saw something. He came down to the station earlier last night but never said what he had come for. He was so upset at seeing that photograph of his son that he went off without saying. I reckon he came to tell me that he had seen something or someone next door."

"If he did that, sir, it suggests that he hadn't the intention to kill Thresher at that stage."

"You're right. Perhaps his mind turned over when he realised that his son had some sort of link with the death of Tommy Watson."

"Not a happy ending."

Hart raised his eyebrows.

"I mean, it's not a conclusive end to the case, Sir."

"Ah. You are telling me that we had no firm evidence that Thresher killed Tommy Watson."

"Nor John Butterman, sir. We only know for sure that Thresher attacked Sergeant Bailey and attempted to kill him with a wire noose."

"That will be sufficient to satisfy the coroner. Anyway, we still have Victor Grant Junior. His side of the story will certainly involve Thresher. At the very least, there's no one to get hurt now, the tale can be fully told to all and sundry."

"Well it will be a full day tomorrow, the press will want the full story and not only the press....."

"The full story, we may never know the full story. Did you know that Jane Mason claimed that Tommy Watson met Phillip Thresher outside the Roxy on the Saturday night before he was killed?"

"How could that be? Sir, if that were true it would mean that the boy had recognised Thresher from somewhere."

"Perhaps he had seen him hanging about the house or perhaps the allotment."

"But why should Thresher hang about the

allotment? He didn't know that the money had been hidden there, did he?"

"We simply don't know. But if Jane Mason is right, it must be more than a coincidence."

"Sir, what can possibly link the two together? The girl must be mistaken."

"That was my first reaction, I'm not so sure now, but we may never know. Just as we may never know whose lighter it was that Tommy Watson carried about with him, the 'clue', he thought, to the identity of the person who destroyed his rabbits."

"Won't the woman be able to fill in some of the gaps?"

"Well, as you saw, she was hysterical and had to be sedated. I'm going to start on her first thing in the morning. She may know nothing. I don't know how much Thresher would confide in her, we'll just have to wait and see."

Margaret Ann Fordyce was not only Phillip Thresher's girlfriend, she was distantly related to his mother. She was the daughter of one of Mrs. Thresher's cousins. She was close to the Thresher family as a child but her parents had moved some distance away when she was ten or eleven. Although she had met Thresher again and had become attached to him four months before, none of the remaining relatives knew this nor could any of the neighbours have been able to guess at such a thing. Like Thresher, she was secretive and antisocial. She had earned a living as a shop assistant in a number of places, leaving home at eighteen when she felt she could comfortably survive without her parents. She was not a missing person but to all intents and purposes she may well have been. It suited them both to be footloose and anonymous.

It took a very long time to persuade Meg Fordyce to

say anything. She was shocked by what had happened and she still felt deeply loyal to her boyfriend. Hart sensed that she was both shallow and vain and played upon her weaknesses. He exhibited every sympathy for her and in that he was not entirely hypocritical. Slowly he made her believe that, now Phillip Thresher was dead, she was what mattered, she had to look out for herself. He did this without maligning Thresher and this helped to overcome the hurdle of loyalty. She was not well-disposed towards the police and it took Hart a good deal longer to gain sufficient confidence from her for her to speak out. His gentle attitude when they had met at the funeral certainly helped. She had been furious at the time, believing his presence insulting to the dead Mrs. Thresher as well as dangerous to Phillip. Now she began to see the reasonable side of this particular policeman.

It was encouragement and sympathy that eventually brought out her story. She had known of Phillip Thresher's bitterness about his brother's death from first meeting him. He had talked to her about the planned robbery. He had been chosen as the van driver but, as luck would have it, he was arrested and sentenced for a different crime before the planned robbery was due to be carried out. He never knew who the substitute driver was. He visited Clifford Morton once during his long sentence but Morton warned him that the police were watching him and would tell him nothing. He suspected that all his conversations with visitors were bugged. All Morton would say was that he, Phillip Thresher, would not be forgotten. When Morton went into hospital after he was run down, Thresher kept an eye out and visited him regularly, treading warily in case the police were also keeping watch. Morton was in a coma and never recovered, he learned nothing from him. There was another visitor, however, someone who came occasionally. Phillip Thresher followed him on at least three occasions. He was led to Selborne Street and came to know it well. The tall, flabby individual, didn't seem to have anything to do with the robbery, he didn't seem to be the type, but he didn't have a job and he did seem to have money to spare. Thresher watched him carefully.

He discovered that he sometimes gained entry to No. 20 and was met there by another man from time to time. He made it his business to get into No. 20 and to look around. He had thought all was well, the street was quiet, no one was about but as he left by the back door he had bumped into a boy on his bicycle. He told the boy he was looking for someone and invented a story about a gardener, to fit in with the presence of all the allotments. The boy had asked him if he had been there before and Thresher had said yes, he'd been to the allotment but wasn't sure which was its owner's house. He stopped to light a cigarette and the boy asked him what brand it was. This was too much for Thresher, who thought the less he talked to the boy the better. He told him to piss off and walked away.

The next night, he had arranged to take Meg to the pictures and they had agreed to meet at the Roxy. While he was waiting outside, the boy he had spoken to the previous evening cycled up to him and asked him if he had lost a cigarette lighter. He had been angry at the time but played it cool and sent the boy off.

There had been nothing unusual about No.20 but it seemed a useful place for a hideaway. Thresher couldn't see what the man was using the house for but wondered if it was a meeting place for someone concerned with the robbery. The only other use the house could have had which concerned his brother's visitor was as the hiding place for the stolen money. He decided to investigate and he had gone in on the Sunday just as light was fading. He chose this time as it enabled him to look round without the use of lights. He had not been there for long before the same boy climbed over the wall between the two houses and came to the back door. Thresher had let him in so as not to attract attention. The boy showed him a lighter and asked him if it was his. Instantly, Thresher recognised his brother's initials J.P.T. engraved on it. He was filled with rage and demanded to know how the boy got it. The boy said something about killing rabbits, he wasn't listening to what Thresher was asking, he was actually threatening Thresher. Thresher made a grab for him and the boy ran into the yard. He tried to climb back over the wall but Thresher was too quick for him, he got a noose round his neck and tightened it.

Meg Fordyce didn't believe that Phillip Thresher meant to kill the boy. Hart had other ideas about that, remembering Thresher's temper. Anyhow, Thresher had to hide the body until he worked out what to do. He dragged it into one of the sheds in the back yard and substituted a lighter of his own for the one the boy had brought with him. Hart pressed her as to why Thresher should trouble about the lighter. Fordyce could only think that Thresher wanted everything to be as normal as possible, the lighter with the initials on would have been incriminating.

Thresher then lay low until after the body had been discovered. When he read in the newspapers that a boy's body had been found in Chevely Park, he knew that someone had been into the house and that person wanted his business kept secret, otherwise he would have revealed the finding of the body to the police. The business had to do with the robbery. He went back in on the Thursday night and kept vigil. Sure enough, the tall, flabby individual he had followed from the hospital came in via the back door. He greeted Thresher as though he was expecting him. Thresher was most suspicious of him but later took him for a fool, he had jabbered about being 'a driver' but 'at a price'. This had infuriated Thresher who had already decided he would have to kill him. He strangled him then and there and tidied the place up. Hart asked about the gas fire. Fordyce smiled at this and said that Thresher was pleased with that particular touch, it was simply to make difficulties, nothing more.

After the second murder, Thresher wasn't sure of himself but he felt he had to pursue the hunt for the driver. It was unlikely that Butterman, his second victim, was the driver and he was curious to find out who Butterman was intending to meet in the house. He decided to make the house his base. The single bedroom overlooked the front door, he decided to sleep there from time to time, once the police had finished with it. The bed was already made up, he would make use of it. He was not already in the house when he encountered Bailey. He simply followed him in. He did not know that Bailey was a policeman, then. When he saw him searching for something, he naturally supposed he was someone connected with the robbery. He had seen Bailey in The Three Bells and Bailey had denied that his friend at the bar was a policeman. Bailey could well have been 'the driver'. Thresher was determined to kill the man who had betrayed his brother by driving off in a panic. Bailey had fought well but Thresher would have succeeded in killing him if the wardrobe had not fallen, striking his arm a glancing blow. At that point he was aware of someone knocking at the front door. This decided Thresher to turn and run.

From then on, the arm was a major problem. It wasn't just that it was painful, that could be born, it was out of action. He had to find out how serious was the injury. He avoided the Cottage Hospital and went out to the Bardsley and Grange General. He knew that there would be a police check on casualty wards so he was delighted that within seconds of his arrival, there was a minor emergency. A car accident produced casualties needing immediate treatment. He followed them in, claiming to have been a pedestrian hurt in the same accident. No one disputed or argued, he was given an X-ray, told that he had a hair-line fracture and that the arm would be plastered and that he should report to his own doctor. He dodged out of the queue for the plaster room and left, confident that the arm would heal itself in due course if he didn't strain it.

The next day he saw, in the local newspaper, a report on the injured man in No. 20 Selborne Street. Although the report claimed that the man was a police sergeant, Thresher was convinced that he was 'the driver', policeman or not. The memory of Bailey and what he had said that night at the Three Bells was strong. The report said that Bailey had been taken to the Cottage Hospital.

That suited Thresher very well. He was very familiar with the layout of the Cottage Hospital, having played there as a child. Meg Fordyce, too, was familiar with it. Together they made a plan of escape. Thresher was not sure what he was going to do or how he was going to do it, he was simply going to reconnoitre, if he saw an opportunity he would kill Bailey. He would leave during visiting time if all went well, no one would notice him. If there was trouble, he would leave by the basement trapdoor. Meg Fordyce was on hand with a car ready to drive off.

That, essentially, was the story up to the previous evening. At this point, Meg Fordyce wanted to ask questions. Hart was quite happy to answer a few of them. He told her that Victor Grant was the next door

334

neighbour, uncle of the boy Thresher had killed. He told her that John Butterman had not been 'the driver'. He told her that 'the driver' was already in custody. He would say no more. He deliberately left her with moral consequences to ponder but after so long a day spent in getting her to tell her story and after listening to that story told in her personal way, he doubted whether she could or would be willing to ponder the morals of such a desperate tale.

He despised Thresher for being such an eager killer, for being so unfeeling and so thoughtless. Had Thresher waited to ask his victims enough questions he would have had little need to kill them. The boy had been no real threat and Thresher hadn't wanted to believe the newspaper reports about Bailey. The urge to kill had driven him on far beyond the requirements of revenge. In any case, revenge itself was unreasonable, given the lapse of time in the case. There was an uncomfortable idea in Hart's mind that Thresher had used the idea of revenge as an excuse for some sport. Killing was the exercise, the rest was excuse, even the money had not been of primary interest.

Chapter Forty-Six

Inspector Jordan's prediction had been accurate. That day was exceedingly hectic. The sequence of murders was front page news in all of the dailies. Photographers and pressmen crowded the foyer and forecourt to the police station. Adding to the general noise and confusion, a television crew had turned up with an ungainly van full of equipment. Great lamps and reflectors were wound out, their cables threatening to trip everyone up.

Hart's superiors were also present long before a further statement was given. The Detective Chief Superintendent was relieved that it was all over but hardly satisfied with the outcome. In that, Hart agreed with him. The ending had been melodramatic and messy. What had happened to Victor Grant disturbed the D.C.I. though he realised that Victor had only further distress to face when his son came to trial. It had all happened so quickly. It was certainly an unexpected ending. He was relieved and pleased that his Super was willing to talk to the television crew, he never liked publicity and this case had involved him more than some of his others, he felt he could not have given a simple statement at that time, had he been asked.

His main task that day had been the questioning of Meg Fordyce. It was almost five in the afternoon before she had signed her statement. She seemed to have been exhilarated by the experience. As she read the statement through, she smiled at what she thought was her own cleverness. The writing was a testament to her being, 'their being' except that it was her writing, she was now the important one. The man of whom she had been in awe, the man who had controlled her every thought and move, was receding in importance. He was the villain but wasn't it herself that was telling his story? Didn't he now entirely depend on her for his fame? She glowed at the idea of her superiority over him now that he was dead. Hart's persuasiveness had been very successful.

Inspector Jordan glided into Hart's office soon after Hart had finished, with copies of the statement.

"That ties everything up, don't you think, sir?"

"Yes, it took all day but she was more than willing at the end. So much for bonds of affection and loyalty!"

"But she had nothing to gain by hanging back?"

"Not from our point of view. She would have the respect of all villains for not speaking to the police."

"She still has the chance to make a lot of money by selling her story to the press."

"Yes, I think that she will be happy to do that. She will have a nest egg for when she comes out of prison."

"She won't get a long sentence...aiding and abetting?"

"It depends on the trial judge. Do you know, Jordan, I don't really care. I don't approve of what Victor Grant tried to do but I'm so sickened by that pair, petty criminals with murderous intentions...to think of the life the Grants led and compare it with theirs...it doesn't bear thinking about."

"The Threshers were both violent. Was it a matter of chance that Victor Grant was taken on as driver?"

"Yes. Unbelievable, really! Why they took him on I don't know."

"It destroyed his family."

"But not him!" Hart scowled. "I liked old Victor, a very interesting character, there was an underlying strength in the man, but it was the boy I was most sorry for....."

"You told me long ago, sir, not to get involved. I hope that you haven't weakened now?"

337

Hart saw a faint glimmer of a smile on Jordan's face.

"Come along, Jordan, I'll buy you a drink at my favourite pub. I want to talk to you about some possible promotions."

Three boys leaned up against their bikes outside the newsagent's.

"They aren't at their best yet. They've been badly neglected."

"Where are you going to keep them?"

"In the back yard. We haven't got an allotment."

"You're going to breed them, are yer?"

"Why not? I don't know much about them really, but I don't see why I shouldn't breed them."

"If they live!"

"I thought Tommy had a lot of them?"

"He did at one time, but somebody got in and killed them. These are another lot."

"Was it a fox, then?"

"Nah, it were vandals. I remember he told me."

"What were vandals doing down at the allotment?"

"Knockin' his rabbits about."

"They never went down there just to knock his rabbits about?"

"There's nowt else down there, is there?"

"Anyway, his uncle said I could have them."

"I thought his uncle killed himself?"

"That was late on that night. He came round to ours and brought them earlier on. He said Tommy would want me to have them."

"Why did he say that? You weren't that close were yer?"

"He should have gave them to Stewey Potts! 'E was 'is best mate."

"Well, he didn't did he?"

"Hey up! It's Robert! How are yer lad?"

Robert Shaw sauntered up rather self-consciously and greeted the three paper boys. He had just been released from hospital and had sneaked out of the house while his mother was out. He felt that he had done plenty of lying about, he wanted some fresh air and a friend to talk to. He knew that he would find someone here, whatever the time of day.

"What's new then, since I've been away? It seems like ages."

They fell to chattering about the deaths at 20 Selborne Street. Robert, for his part, was eager to pass on his adventures in hospital. Inevitably, the talk got round to Tommy Watson. They didn't know all the connections in the case but they were shrewd enough to put a few things together. Robert made the most of the police visit to him in hospital and the adventure with the man called Thresher. Jim recalled his interview at school. They felt that they were party to the investigation. The other two had gone to a different school, they had missed that excitement, they were mere bystanders. They had absorbed most from the local newspapers. There was much embroidering of the facts. All four imagined what had happened in different ways.

Suddenly, Robert let slip that Tommy had told him that he knew who the vandals were. There was a sharp silence.

"How could he have known?"

"It were the bloke shot in 20, weren't it?"

"Why should that bloke want to vandalise the Grant's shed?"

"Aye, why should a stranger want to knock rabbits about?"

"It'll come out in trial won't it?"

"He showed me a lighter he had found. It had

initials on it. J.T.P. like intertwined."

Terry Phipps went pale and stepped back a pace.

"You're not going already, Terry? It's only...."

"I've just remembered, I promised to do a message for me Mam. I'll get in real trouble if I don't get back before she goes out."

"You'll have to get the skids on, then!"

"I'll come with you, Terry. See yer, lads!"

Jim and Robert waved them off and returned to more serious matters. After a while, they decided to wander up to Stewey's house. They felt instinctively that they had to stick together, the friends of Tommy. They owed it to him, somehow. They hadn't met together since his death. They had a lot to remember and they wanted to talk about all the excitement, to put it together, to try to understand it. Somehow it seemed so remote from the Tommy they had known. Tommy, his bike, the pictures, the football, the laughs in class, what had they to do with murder and the police? They would discuss it as long as they remained together.

"My mam said I shouldn't play football in the park."

"Where else can you play it?"

"Not since what we saw."

"Oh, that's long ago. Come on, Hen! She'll not know anyway!"

"She said not to play here anymore."

"You can't stay out of the park for ever!"

"Well, that's what she said."

"Come on, Hen. You can be Finney this time."

"Well..."

"Come on, Hen. You can't not play football!"

"What if....?"

"What if what? It's all over, Hen. It can't happen twice, can it?"

"Well....."

340

"This is Bobby Charlton...."

"Who?"

"Bobby Charlton, plays for Man. United. He's their wing..."

"No he's not, then...."

"Yes he is, don't you read the papers?"

"No, me Mam won't let me since..."

"Here it comes, the ball comes through from the right back, the centre half takes it cleanly, punts it up, Charlton takes it on the run...."

"Pete!"

"What?"

"Pete! Look!"

"What?"

"Look! Look over there, Pete!"

"........Hen, I'll dot you one! You did that on purpose!"

www.ingramcontent.com/pod-product-compliance
Lightning Source LLC
Chambersburg PA
CBHW030920050726
47498CB00003BA/835